HURST

THE POST-APOCALYPTIC THRILLER

ROBIN CRUMBY

The Hurst Chronicles Reader Newsletter

Sign up for the Hurst Chronicles newsletter and be the first to hear about the next books in the series as well as reader offers, short stories and exclusive content, all for free.

Sign up now at Hurstchronicles.com

Website: HurstChronicles.com

Twitter: @HurstChronicles

Facebook: Facebook.com/robincrumbyauthor

Disclaimer

Hurst is a work of fiction. Names, characters, businesses, places, events and incidents are either the products of the author's imagination or used in a fictitious manner. Any resemblance to actual persons, living or dead, or actual events is purely coincidental.

© Robin Crumby 2016

❀ Created with Vellum

"Therefore wait for me," declares the Lord, "for the day when I rise up as a witness. Indeed, my decision is to gather nations, to assemble kingdoms, to pour out on them my indignation, all my burning anger; for all the earth will be devoured by the fire of my zeal."

Zephaniah 3:8

Chapter 1

This was an ancient place, remote and desolate. Peaceful, yet witness to centuries of warmongering, standing ready to do its duty. A never-ending vigil set to the rhythmic rise and fall of the ocean.

It was only a matter of time before all this would be swept away. The castle's resolute defences were imperceptibly weakened by every breaking wave, sweeping in from the Channel, sent crashing against the groynes and stones.

A pale sun rose silently and unnoticed over Hurst Castle. Shadows stretching over the rippled tidal waters that all but surrounded it, bar a narrow finger of shingle linking the fortifications to the mainland.

Hurst's seventy-four occupants were slumbering in their quarters. The more recent arrivals were camped out in the east wing. Tents pitched where grass and space allowed. In the dorm room in the main building, a shaft of sunlight pierced the makeshift curtains. Two grey blankets strung across the large stone window aperture prolonged the darkness. The shaft of light fell across the pillow of one of the iron-framed beds, bathing the unshaven face of a man in white light as he began to wake.

Zed stretched and yawned, looking around at his companions. Packed tightly together, a sleeping mass of washed-up humanity snored gently. There was a low snuffle of someone stirring in the corner, heavy breathing and the universal stench of unwashed bodies and morning breath. From outside came the low sound of waves breaking gently over the rocks and shingle spit, seagulls soaring above the castle that spoke of a new morning, bringing with it new hope. For many, the sounds reminded them of former lives, holidays by the seaside, long-forgotten memories.

A base need to breathe fresh air and enjoy the peace of the castle in the early dawn compelled Zed to take his morning constitutional walk. He was fond of rising before anyone else was up and having the place to himself.

Stepping outside, he squinted, shading his eyes, taking a moment to bathe his face in the sunshine, inhaling deeply the sea air. His hair was unkempt and unwashed, long sideburns grew down his cheeks and a tuft of hair stuck upright. He wore a grubby T-shirt with chest-high salt stains from unloading stores from a visiting fishing boat the previous day. He had the air of someone who looked after himself, a loner, a survivor with the scars to prove it. It wasn't that he didn't enjoy the company of others; he did. But when push came to shove, he had no time for the weak. Survive or die. Get in his way and face the consequences.

Leaving the castle keep and its cold grey stone walls, he meandered sleepily, still yawning, through the Tudor archway. Beyond the gate was a narrow strip of grass that stretched for one hundred metres or so to the western walls of the fort, extended in Victorian times. A large marquee dominated the interior. Half a dozen smaller tents were pitched haphazardly around it. Passing the canteen he took the stairs two at a time. Up on to the raised walkway and ramparts, he looked south-west across the narrow channel towards the Isle of Wight and the Needles rocks. There was still a faint haze that shrouded the island in a light mist, slowly evaporating as the shadows shortened on the water.

Scanning the horizon across the salt marshes towards Keyhaven, a pair of swans glided gracefully against the incoming tide within the sheltered estuary that lay behind a narrow shingle spit. As he turned to look back along the raised roadway that ran on top of the shingle, the movement of a dark shape in the distance interrupted his gaze.

The figure was limping awkwardly. A long heavy coat several sizes too big was draped around its shoulders. On the castle walls Zed reached for the pair of binoculars that lived in a large blue plastic IKEA storage box under the bench seat. He took a couple of seconds to find and focus on the man in the distance. There was no question. What had first appeared as a limp was more severe in focus, the left leg dragging heavily on the shingle, scraping at each step. His progress was laboured, but he showed no sign of discomfort or pain as he approached.

Zed lowered the binoculars and squinted with his bare eyes. The hint of a smile appeared on Zed's lips. He reached back into the blue container and brought up a hunting rifle. Loading a single bullet into the breach, he took careful aim at the man in the distance. Adjusting his position a couple of times, he relaxed into a wide stance, the rifle resting on the edge of the brick wall. The cross hairs of the telescopic sight danced around the head of the approaching figure. He was still perhaps two hundred metres away now, making steady progress. Zed regulated his breathing before exhaling deeply.

The rifle shot rang out across Christchurch Bay, echoing

around the battlements, shattering the silence of the early morning.

A flock of birds rose startled from the salt marshes. In the fenced-off field next to the lighthouse, a herd of dairy cows flinched, wild-eyed and bumping into each other. The two horses bolted. One jumped over the low wire fence and charged away from the noise, its hooves clattering on the pebbles as it galloped along the beach.

Chapter 2

From the castle entrances, startled figures emerged from their slumber, still rubbing their eyes, alarmed by the single shot. There had been no bell to warn the inhabitants of an imminent threat. Two men raced towards the stairs to the western ramparts, clutching their boots and clothes.

Zed ignored the commotion behind him, cursing his luck as the figure continued its slow methodical lurch towards the castle, unharmed and undeterred. Its pace seemed to quicken. The first shot had gone high and right, splintering a rock over the man's shoulder. Zed hurriedly reloaded the rifle. He adjusted his aim slightly to the left to account for the light breeze coming across the bay from the island. Wrapping the rifle strap tightly around his left arm, he steadied the barrel against the raised concrete and fired again. This time the figure's head rocked back violently, before collapsing onto the shingle, twitching.

Those who had ignored the first shot and passed it off as something else now sat bolt upright. Muffled cries of alarm could be heard throughout the castle. Raised voices joined together as people emerged from every door and tent to congregate in the courtyard pointing towards the suspected source. Zed's back was turned, silhouetted on the ramparts, the rifle hitched on his hip like a triumphant hunter.

Still buttoning his shirt and rubbing the sleep from his eyes, Jack hurried towards the base of the wooden staircase, breathing heavily from his race across the courtyard. A Royal Navy issue blue sweater with elbow patches had ridden up exposing a neat potbelly. His thinning hair was wild, his brow furrowed with concern.

"What the hell's going on?" shouted Jack from below, squinting up at Zed.

Zed didn't respond, but muttered something under his breath that Jack didn't catch. The older man took the stairs two at a time, his limbs stiff and sore from yesterday's exertions.

The others stepped aside to let their leader pass. Jack stood panting, fighting to catch his breath. He snatched the binoculars from Zed and slowly scanned the shingle spit, trying to locate the body. Shaking his head, he grabbed the rifle from Zed's grasp and put it back in the storage box.

"He was unarmed. Why did you have to shoot him?" asked Jack.

Zed stared back at him, defiantly. "He was infected."

Jack was aware of a gathering crowd watching their exchange. He felt compelled to act, shaking his head. "Every living soul for miles around will have heard that shot."

"Shame there's no one left alive to hear it then," said Zed with a wry smile, unrepentant.

Jack laughed, but there was no hint of humour in his demeanour. Inside he was seething, but trying to keep a cool head. "We don't know that. Next time, why don't you hand out invitations, put up signs..." Jack turned to address the others. "How many times? How many times have we talked about this? We agreed no guns for a reason. We don't want to attract attention. Warning shot only if they don't get the message. If it's only one of them, don't waste the bullet."

"Just keeping my eye in." Zed smirked, refusing to back down or admit he was in the wrong. "I haven't fired a shot for days."

"And there's a damn good reason for that. We don't have ammo to waste. You know that. There are precious few bullets left for that rifle, then what? Congratulations, Zed, you just volunteered yourself to lead today's scavenging party."

"Anything to get out of here for a few hours." Zed eyeballed the older man before wandering off to find something to eat. The first smoke from the canteen drifted towards them.

A red-haired woman appeared below, her head part-covered with a bandana, her face pale, drawn and anxious, still buttoning up a man's shirt several sizes too big for her. She raced up the stairs to join Jack and the group on the raised walkway. Passing Zed halfway up the stairs she paused to stare at him as he brushed past her. She waited for an explanation, but he ignored her puzzled look of reproach.

"What was it?" asked Terra, catching her breath, watching Jack peering through his binoculars.

"Hard to tell from here," said Jack, squinting, "but looks like he was infected. Been a while since one made it all the way out here along the shingle. We saw a few in town yesterday, so maybe he followed our trail."

"Why did Zed have to shoot him, for God's sake? Couldn't he have just warned him off? Told him to go away?" said Terra naively.

"You really think harsh language would have made him turn

around? They don't take no for an answer. Either way, they're dead now."

"Not before that shot will have drawn every living soul for miles around."

"Or unliving, you mean..." said Tommy, a gangly adolescent standing nearby.

"Ah, Tommy, our resident comedian. Perhaps you'd be so kind as to roll the cart out and dispose of that body before we sit down for breakfast. Take young Samuel to help."

"Sure, no problem, Skip," said Tommy with a hint of mockery, punching Sam on the shoulder.

"Nice one, dickhead," mumbled Sam under his breath.

As the others drifted off to find breakfast, Terra remained behind with Jack, looking back over the camp towards the lighthouse and beyond towards Southampton. In the distance, Fawley Oil Refinery belched smoke hundreds of feet into the air leaving a grey smear across the morning skyline. A burst pipeline or perhaps a storage container left to burn. There was no one left to put it out. It would burn until the oil ran out.

"What we wouldn't give for a few hundred gallons of diesel for the generator," said Terra quietly.

"We've drained every garage and farm for miles around, but we'll find more. Don't you worry," reassured Jack.

His elbows touched Terra's as they both leaned over the railing. A comfortable silence passed between them. They watched the camp below as it came to life. Hurst's inhabitants busied themselves with washing, preparing food, stitching and sewing, feeding the animals and generally cleaning up the night before. It was a hive of organised activity. Everyone played their part.

Terra turned her head towards Jack and smiled. "You need to get a handle on that Zed. He sets a bad example."

"I know, Terra. I'll talk to him, okay? He's never going to change though, you know that. His heart's in the right place, but he does things his own way. I don't want to drive him away. He's one of the best scavengers we've got. We need him."

"He fights for himself, Jack. He'd turn on you in a moment if you got between him and his prize."

"You're wrong, Terra. His loyalties are very much with us. He's just got a case of cabin fever, cooped up here for too long. That's all. Will do him good to get out and about." Jack wrinkled his nose, sniffing at the wind. There was something foul in the air, downwind of the latrines. "He thinks we should be doing more to form alliances with the other survivor groups inland from here, that we have our heads in the sand." He shook his head. "I've said it's too dangerous. We don't want to go stirring up a hornet's nest and draw attention to ourselves. He doesn't agree."

"You need to keep an eye on him. That's all I'm saying," she said, stroking Jack's arm affectionately. "Same goes for Riley. I don't trust either of them."

Jack cleared his throat, intrigued by Terra's views on two of his most trusted lieutenants. "Don't you worry about Zed. He's just a big kid. His bark's worse than his bite. Reminds me of my lad Jason. Bless him." There was a distant look in Jack's eye as he was reminded of his son. He hadn't thought of him in months now. It was just too painful. "Just needs a firm hand and a kick in the backside from time to time."

Jack beamed a broad smile and playfully nudged Terra in the ribs. He wandered off to eat, leaving her alone to digest his response.

Chapter 3

Out on the shingle, Tommy and Sam pushed the low-slung cart towards the crumpled heap in the distance. The tyres needed some air. Tommy was trying to make light of their task, but Sam was having none of it.

"What did you have to go and say that for? Now I'm stuck here with you when I could be having breakfast," grumbled Sam.

"Oh, quit your whining, will you? It's not like you haven't got me into trouble before."

"You're joking, aren't you? I'm always covering for you," continued Sam. "Anyway, what did Zed have to go and shoot the guy for? What was he going to do, start climbing the walls? This place is a fortress."

"The state he was probably in, he was on his last legs, anyway. If you ask me, Zed did him a favour. Put him out of his misery. Saved him a long walk back to whichever hellhole he came from."

Sam shook his head. He didn't agree with violence, unless there was no other way.

It took both of them to push the cart up the small slope and along the raised roadway that joined Hurst Castle to the main-land. Roadway was perhaps too grand for what it really was. In truth, it was no more than a man-made shingle bank, reinforced with concrete and strengthened periodically to keep out the worst of the weather. South-westerly storms had a habit of battering this stretch of coastline, washing away whole sections. But that hadn't happened for years now.

The shingle was just wide enough for a Land Rover or four-wheel drive vehicle. In the early days, they had shuttled stores to the castle from local shops but now it was too dangerous, for fear of ambush by rival groups. Supplies came by boat from the island or trade with the network of Solent forts which formed part of the wider coastal defences built almost five hundred years ago by King Henry VIII to defend the south coast against invasion by the French. Today those same forts, or at least those modernised and fit for habitation, had formed a loose alliance to work together where possible. They exchanged goods and skills, occasionally joining forces to form raiding parties when making scavenging runs into local towns. It was safer that way.

Once at the top of the slope, Tommy jumped into the cart, laughing as they bounced along. He had known Sam since school. Sam had never truly forgiven Tommy for stealing the love of his life, Sarah, who worked at the local dairy. But "mates is mates" and their friendship was strong enough to get over that little wrinkle.

Tommy's old man had run the local butcher on the high street for eleven years until he got sick with throat cancer and died the following year. While his mother mourned, Tommy had grown up fast and volunteered to take over the family busi-ness, setting aside his aspirations for apprenticeships and further education. It was his way of treasuring the memory of his father. When he closed his eyes, he could still picture him standing behind the counter in his striped apron, smiling at customers. He remembered the old-fashioned bell that rung when the door was pushed open, the tiled floor covered in sawdust.

There were two other young lads who helped out in busy periods and at the weekends. It had been an uneasy working relationship. Tommy was only nineteen, no more than a year or two older, yet Tommy was a fair boss. He was firm when he needed to be, like when they turned up late or when one wasn't pulling his weight. He always made a point of buying his workers drinks at the end of the week on a Friday night in their local pub. It's what his father would have wanted.

Sam had been a pillar of support when Tommy's dad was enduring the daily torment of chemotherapy, growing weaker by the day. He used to come round with a four-pack, a party bag of Doritos, and play FIFA Football on the PlayStation to cheer up his friend. Sam was the strong silent type, with an intelligent thoughtful look about him. He was a good and loyal mate.

Back then, Tommy still lived at home with his mum. Just the two of them once they'd buried his father. She had become withdrawn after his father's death, as if her pilot light had been dimmed by the months of caring, knowing that nothing could save her childhood sweetheart. Her days were lost in reverie, an air of melancholy settled on her every thought and deed. Tommy was the only one who could still make her smile and restore something of her former cheery self.

When the Millennial Virus had first struck, his mum was among the first to fall. He suspected her job at the chemist was to blame, through regular contact with the sick. But in reality, the virus had struck seemingly at random and with the speed of wildfire. It was all over mercifully quickly for his mum. He had taken her to A&E but the place was like a refugee camp. After a cursory look from a distracted nurse, they had sent her home with painkillers to get some sleep. By morning, she was dead.

Sam's quick thinking had saved both of their lives. That fateful morning Tommy had been woken by the blare of a car horn. Staggering downstairs in his dressing gown after a sleepless night, he unlocked the front door, eyes bloodshot, nose red from blowing, to find his best friend gesticulating wildly and shouting out the half-lowered window for him to get dressed and get out.

Sam had seen the morning news and driven straight round. Panic had started. The emergency services were being overrun. Cities were emptying as the sickness spread. Lines of cars blocked exits. A tide of humanity staggered under the weight of its worldly possessions. People carried what they could. Impractical valuables soon to be discarded. Irrelevant and redundant in a world turned on its head. A litter of suitcases abandoned on the side of the road.

Tommy had packed a rucksack in two minutes flat with some clothes, a torch, food and water. They had driven to the seafront, running through their options. Where could they go? Where was safe? In the end, they drove back to the house, locked the door and perched nervously on the edge of the sofa watching BBC News 24. Clutching a can of lager at ten in the morning, Tommy kept repeating himself in disbelief every two minutes, to the annoyance of his friend. The pair had watched with increasing alarm, batting theories around about Ebola or bird flu. Whatever it was, it looked really bad. The authorities were doing their best to contain the outbreak, telling people to stay indoors and avoid contact with others. A succession of health experts argued about cause and origin. Some said it was a strain of avian flu. Others said it was like nothing they'd ever seen before. A designer virus or even a new kind of terrorist attack? In truth, no one knew. There was no vaccine, no cure. Things happened so fast.

Sam and Tommy reached the body on the shingle beach.

The man was probably in his thirties, lying awkwardly, his leg at an unnatural angle. But what was most disturbing was his face. His lower jaw hung loose, one side blown away. The back of his head was a mess where the bullet had exited. The whites of his eyes were yellow and flecked with blood, like someone who hadn't slept for days, staring lifelessly skywards. The sickness was etched into his face. The typical grey pallor, sunken eye sockets, and evidence of dried blood in his nose and ears. Considering the trauma to the head, there was surprisingly little blood.

"You get the head end," said Tommy, barging his friend out the way. "Ready on three."

Sam wore garden gloves, avoiding direct contact. The body was skeletal thin yet surprisingly heavy. As the trolley bumped and bounced along the roadway, the man's leg slid over the side. The material rode up, exposing two inches of skin, blotched and covered in sores.

They dumped the body next to a pit some thirty feet across and ten deep. They rolled the man over the edge, sliding down to join the other human shapes at the bottom. Tommy grabbed a jerrycan and poured kerosene, dowsing the bodies, splashing indiscriminately. He struck a small flare and threw it down on to the funeral pyre. They both stood there impassively watching the blaze, enjoying the warmth on their legs and bare arms.

Chapter 4

Jack strode back through the main castle gate next to the guardhouse. He stepped over the narrow-gauge rail tracks and crossed a weathered patch of grass. The tracks had been laid in Napoleonic times to deliver stores to the castle from a military dock and landing area, long since dismantled. He continued to the old white lighthouse, set apart from the eastern end of the castle fortifications.

The lighthouse was modest but comfortable. There he lived a simple, almost monastic existence that imitated his former life aboard merchant ships. After the hustle and bustle of the castle camp, the silence and solitude were a welcome relief. Many of the rooms were unfurnished, filled with salvaged equipment and gardening tools. The views across the Solent stretched uninterrupted in multiple directions.

Jack paused at the doorway, a puzzled expression etched on his face. He noticed the tide slowly rising to cover the salt marshes and sheltered estuary towards Keyhaven and Lymington beyond. Something about the smell of the place reminded him of a former life. He had served in the Royal Fleet

Auxiliary for twenty-five years, before using his pension to buy his very own fishing boat, the *Nipper*.

The modest vessel had become his pride and joy, not to mention his livelihood. He had skippered the boat for the last few years, sometimes on his own, but mostly with a deckhand. He knew these waters well. Every rock, every tidal eddy. The narrow western entrance to the Solent was notorious for its strong tides. The Needles rocks at the tip of the Isle of Wight were a graveyard to dozens of sailing ships and steamers in days gone by. Some of those ships had paid the ultimate price.

As the skipper of a small fishing boat, Jack had a profound respect for the sea. A capricious playground for yachtsmen but a series of calculated risks for fishermen like him who plied their trade hauling lobster pots in all weathers, day and night. There had been a small but established community of fisherman in Keyhaven, and Lymington five miles beyond. Jack was well liked and respected and knew most of the others. They were territorial, drank in different pubs, fished their own particular sites. Each meticulously mapped by GPS above water and by depth sounder below.

The unexpected sight of a sail rounding the headland to the east interrupted Jack's reminiscences. It was a small sailing boat. He estimated it was no more than thirty feet in length. He slid his wire-framed glasses up on to his forehead and peered through the binoculars. On board and hailing him with a slow wave was a man he didn't recognise. There was a small child beside him, wearing a yellow oilskin jacket.

Jack made a mental note to reprimand whoever was on lookout this morning. There had been no warning of the stranger's approach.

The man on the boat looked back at Jack through his own binoculars and raised his hand again to wave. He cupped his hands, shouting as loud as he could. Jack wasn't sure he heard what was said but waved back, more through habit than genuine welcome. He did not approach the quay to help, keeping a safe distance.

When the sailor had finished mooring up, attaching lines fore and aft, he cupped his hands again and called out in an educated voice, enunciating clearly as if Jack might not speak English: "May we come ashore?"

"Stay where you are," cautioned Jack, gesturing him to stop.

"Please. We're not sick. Can you at least spare us some food and water? We're willing to trade."

"You can moor up and shelter for the night and then be on your way. We might be able to spare you some water and bread, but we've precious little else."

"We don't have much food, but we have some flares and a first aid kit. Look, we're both healthy. We've not been in contact with anyone for days. In fact, it's nice to have a conversation with someone for a change. Please, I'm begging you."

"I'm sorry. It's too risky to let you in."

There was an uneasy silence as the man on the boat stroked his son's hair and whispered something in his ear.

"What are your names?" offered Jack.

"I'm Simon, and this is Toby."

"Where have you sailed from?"

"Weymouth. We left yesterday, borrowed this boat, grabbed what we could. I'm no great sailor, but we got this far."

Jack stood impassively still, his arms crossed. Simon shifted uneasily, wracking his brains for another way to convince Jack to take them in.

"Please, just give us a chance. We're hard workers. We'll do whatever it takes."

Jack looked him up and down and tried to guess what Simon had been before the outbreak. He wore an open-necked striped shirt frayed at the collar and red trousers that bulged slightly at the waist. His Nike running shoes were heavily worn. Jack's guess was a City worker, maybe an accountant or solicitor. Someone who had never done a real day's work in his life. Never felt the sun on his back as he toiled. He embodied everything that Jack despised: blood, privilege and money.

"We don't have much use for lawyers and accountants round here," he taunted playfully. "This is a working community. What skills do you have? Any trades?"

Simon blushed, pushing his glasses up his nose, alert to the edge in Jack's questions. "Funnily enough, I was a solicitor. I ran my own practice." He smiled defensively. "But...but..." He looked like he was searching for something, then erupted enthusiastically, "I know first aid. I used to grow my own vegetables..." His voice tailed off, trying hard to think of something else he could claim to be good at.

"We've got a doctor already. Can you cook?"

"Yeah, not bad. My mother was Italian," he said, nodding confidently. "I make a mean spaghetti bolognese, if you can find me the ingredients, that is. Fresh herbs, tomatoes, oregano, mother's secret recipe. I could tell you but I'd have to kill you," he snorted. "I see you have a greenhouse back there, so you must have quite the set-up here. Surely you have room for a couple more?"

"Simon, I'll level with you. We've got a lot of mouths to feed already, and we're just barely getting by as it is. But if you're not afraid of hard work, can pull your own weight around the place, and do your bit, then maybe?"

There was a look of desperation about the pair of them that Jack had seen so many times before. The boy looked close to tears.

"Look, please," continued Simon. "We'll do anything. Just give us a chance. It's hard out there, just the two of us. The boy needs a proper home, kids his own age. You have other children, right?"

"We have children, yes. Lots of children," said Jack with a sigh, remembering why he enjoyed the solitude of the light-house. "How were things in Weymouth? Are there many survivors?"

Simon stared at the ground, lost in thought for a second, his voice softer: "Not many. We got hit bad, no warning. I lost my wife and daughter early in the outbreak. Me and Toby didn't get sick. We moved around a fair bit, from house to house, living off whatever we could find. It was hard, but we survived. We had some close shaves. Things got crazy. Gangs rampaging, looking for food. We hid during the day and moved around at night. We got caught a couple of times, had all our food stolen. One time, they left us for dead—" He broke off, remembering the horror. "I don't want to live out there, not any more. I'm begging you... please. Just give us a chance."

"Listen, I'll speak to the others, okay? That's the best I can do. No promises. Stay here. Consider yourself in quarantine. If you're both fit and healthy with no sign of infection in forty-eight hours, then we'll talk. In the meantime, keep yourselves to yourselves. Don't go wandering around. If you approach the main gate, you will be shot. Am I clear? If you need anything, shout. My name's Jack, everyone knows me."

"Nice to meet you, Jack. And thank you!"

Jack turned on his heels, shaking his head. He was getting soft in his old age. Just what they needed. More mouths to feed. More blooming kids. He smiled to himself and walked back to the lighthouse.

Chapter 5

J ack finished getting dressed and grabbed a rucksack from behind the front door. He wandered back the short distance that separated the lighthouse from the castle walls through the main gate to the canteen to join Terra and a small group of others who were still finishing their breakfast. The smell of coffee and fresh bread lingered.

Terra poured him some coffee from a large catering kettle, burning her hand on the metal handle. She sucked at her fingers, wincing as the pain subsided. Jack studied her with a glint in his eye. There was something different about her today, though he couldn't put his finger on it.

She was an attractive woman, almost two decades his junior, but old beyond her years. This morning she had made little effort with her appearance. She wore loose-fitting clothes fit for a day's work. Her shoulder-length auburn hair was tied back under a headscarf. Jack lifted the cup to his lips and blew away the steam, still too hot to drink.

"Who's meant to be on lookout duty this morning? A yacht's just arrived. No warning. They just crept in without anyone noticing," said Jack flatly.

The others stopped what they were doing and leaned in excitedly.

"Really? How many are they? Where did they come from? What did they say?" asked Terra, curious to hear about the world outside and whether Jack would let them stay. At times it felt so claustrophobic here. So little was known about what was going on beyond the castle walls. When the broadcasts had ceased all those months ago, the world got smaller quickly. They relied on word of mouth, rumours, and stories from other survivor groups.

Jack told them what little he knew and cautioned them against approaching the boat until the new arrivals had passed quarantine. They would need to decide whether to accept Simon and Toby, but in the circumstances, he could hardly turn them away.

They had already taken in five more the previous week, swelling their numbers to breaking point. But with two team members gone this last month, one from a suspected tumour, the other missing, captured or killed by a rival group, they needed to maintain their strength. They needed a full complement of working men and women.

According to Jack's roster, all told, there were sixty-two ablebodied adults living at Hurst Castle, himself included; thirty-seven men and twenty-five women. Then there were three unable to work through injury or old age, and twelve children, the youngest being five years old.

Jack considered himself a good judge of character. He believed everyone deserved a chance. In his experience, giving people a little responsibility at an early age transformed them. Tommy was something of a protégé to him. He had the making of a leader, a good heart, knew what made people tick. Two ears, one mouth, and he used them in the right proportions. With the right direction, he showed promise. Tommy was from the school of hard knocks. Had grown up quickly when his dad died. Jack had a long history of similar nurturing projects during his time in the service. He believed even the bad apples, the most delinquent and wayward individuals, could be brought back to the straight and narrow. There was good in everyone, you just had to find it and cultivate it.

His military background, management skills and grey hairs had made Jack an obvious candidate for leader. Sure, there had been others, wannabes making a grab for power and position. They had spoken with passion and conviction about their plans, their hopes for the future. But in the end, Jack's pragmatism and composure, not to mention his strong belief in pastoral care, won the vote. He had been one of the first to arrive at Hurst and the group had never forgotten the warmth of his welcome. He had provided sanctuary for them in their hour of need.

When the sickness had first appeared, Jack calmly packed his old grey Land Rover with tools, food, a shotgun and his fishing gear as if he was going to sea on the *Nipper*, but this time headed straight to Hurst.

After years of cruising past the castle on his way out to sea to pick up his lobster pots, he had always admired the impressive fortifications. He made a mental note that should the world end any time soon, there were worse places to hole up and wait things out.

Hurst had much to recommend it. It had its own generator, was only reachable by boat or by four-wheel drive vehicles along a mile and a half of shingle spit. It could sustain a large group of people in relative comfort. The thirty-feet-high walls would keep out any undesirables and with a bit of luck, they could rebuild again from here.

In the first few weeks, Jack had welcomed successive survivor groups from the local area. He had established a quarantine zone in the inner courtyard where new arrivals could wait the forty-eight hours to show they were clear of infection. He provided them with shelter, warmth and what little food they had in the early days. Hurst Castle had quickly become a sanctuary from the chaos outside.

Jack wasn't everybody's first choice for leader. He was fond of rules, which others disagreed with or saw as petty and unnecessary. He insisted that all weapons be surrendered at the gate and put in the castle armoury for safe storage. All food was placed in the dry storerooms beneath the castle walls, where shells and ammunition had once been housed. Food was rationed out equally. Everybody worked their fair share. Everyone had a role to play, including all but the youngest children. No freeloaders, no passengers. It wasn't much, but people respected Jack and rewarded his trust with their loyalty and hard work. As a result, the community had grown, swelling to a size where their resources were stretched.

He had made Terra his second in command. Together with an inner circle of advisers and lieutenants, subdividing responsibility for food, accommodation, and animal welfare for their small herd of cows, pigs and sheep. If Jack was the patriarch, then Terra was Hurst's unofficial matriarch. She was a capable woman. She had been reticent about sharing too much about her story when she first arrived. Everyone assumed it was too difficult for her to talk about, some personal tragedy. They had all suffered in some way.

Terra had confided in Jack that she revelled in her anonymity here. A clean break from the mistakes of her past. Her slate wiped clean. She could be anyone she wanted to be. The new Terra she chose for herself was authoritative yet likeable, confident and sassy, accessible yet complex. For the first time in a long while, she looked in the mirror and said she liked who she saw. She had adopted the name Terra. She said it sounded earthy and fearful.

The whole place ran like clockwork, thanks to Terra. She cared for the sick, helped run the kitchen canteen, looked after the kids and kept things organised. She had hit it off early with Jack and they had a close friendship.

In the goldfish bowl that was life at Hurst, people whispered. The pair's mannerisms and body language were scrutinised intensely. When they exchanged stolen glances, or sat together, talking conspiratorially in hushed tones, most likely about planning and operations, people noticed and winked.

Jack chose Zed to be in charge of defence. What Zed lacked in discipline, he made up for in survival skills and what Jack called "bush craft". Though he had never admitted as much, Jack suspected Zed had spent time in the military.

Hurst Castle had provided a rich cache of weaponry from its museum displays covering five hundred years of history. From ornate swords, axes, and maces through to whole suits of armour dating back to Tudor times when Henry VIII had the castle built. The museum also had an impressive collection of World War II weaponry, including Sten guns, Bren guns, rifles and pistols. Most of them were useless without their firing mechanisms.

The scavenging parties that Zed led in search of food and supplies made a curious spectacle. A motley crew standing ready for inspection before they headed out, carried a smorgasbord of knuckledusters, helmets, firearms and swords. Zed had kept the best for himself: a double-headed axe, sharpened daily, that split logs with a single blow. On trips to the forest tracking deer and rabbits, gathering mushrooms and berries, he liked to keep the axe strapped between his shoulder blades, like a hunter.

Zed and Jack had fallen out publicly over the smallest of things, from castle rules to food rationing. Zed held that the guys who took the risks deserved the lion's share of the rewards.

Terra had never trusted Zed. She made sure that one of her own people kept an eye on him and reported back. Zed was the source of many of their discussions. In the end Jack argued that Zed's good deeds outweighed the bad. They both knew that a time would come when Zed's loyalty would be tested, and she knew he would put his own interests before those of the community.

Chapter 6

Zed loaded the last of the gear into the Land Rover and wandered back to join his group of seven. Lucky seven, Zed thought to himself. Two teams, two cars, the way they had done things for weeks. He unfolded the ordinance survey map and rechecked today's search area marked with large red and black felt-tip crosses and blocks, showing where teams had already searched. Red circles highlighted supermarkets, hardware stores, pharmacies or other areas of potential interest. Most of the obvious places had been looted some time ago. Black circles with skull and crossbones were areas to be avoided, where rival groups had set up camp or where pockets of infection remained.

There was a relaxed air of normality about their conversation this morning, as they huddled together, smoking and laughing. Bob, Riley and Joe had made these trips dozens of times. To them it was routine, but it remained Zed's job to prepare them properly for each and every trip and remind them of the very real dangers ahead.

Each three-man team carried water, food, torches, rope, and a handheld radio with a range of about two kilometres. The seventh team member stayed with the vehicles while the two teams conducted house-to-house searches or systemically swept larger stores. If one of the teams got into trouble they could radio the others for support. Every team member carried a weapon. Several of them had both blade and firearm, chosen from the armoury.

Zed had trained them well. Riley, in particular, knew how to handle herself. He watched her tie back her long brown hair in a ponytail, sharing a joke with Bob. She wore a grey Puffa jacket, jeans and ankle-high walking boots. Once she'd rechecked her rucksack, she inserted a long-handled machete in the sheath attached to the front of her webbing and jumped up and down a couple of times to check for any rattles.

The rest of today's team was made up of three recent arrivals, whose turn it was on the camp rota system. Will was a jovial thirty-something builder, originally from South Africa. He was a bear of a man with a luxurious beard. He looked in good shape, despite months of living out there, before coming to Hurst. The other two were younger, probably in their late teens. Mila and Sean had arrived together. They were bold as brass, cocksure in their youthful arrogance, but underneath the bravado, Zed could tell they were bricking it. Everyone did on their first trip.

Zed did his best to settle their nerves, brief them and assign them roles, teaming them up with the more experienced guys. Zed would drive Mila and Sean in the Land Rover. Will would stick with Bob and Riley in the Mitsubishi Land Cruiser with Joe as their driver and seventh man.

As the two-car convoy rounded the wall and headed out west, a silhouetted figure on the battlements waved them off with a mock salute and a smile to Zed, which he acknowledged with minimal effort by raising a single index finger off the steering wheel.

After bumping along the spit at a steady crawl they joined

the coastal road that ran along the seafront at Milford. They turned on to the main road out towards Lymington, passing dozens of abandoned cars. Many had their doors open, some burned-out, others with bodies still visible inside. They had cleared the road some time ago and pushed the cars on to the grass verges and pavements. In places, the convoy had to slow to walking pace to navigate the resulting obstacles and rusting metal chicanes.

Today their search area was a row of houses on Lymington high street, some five or six kilometres away. They would be outside of radio contact with home base. That meant that they were on their own if things went "turbo", as Joe was fond of saying. That didn't worry Zed. They had made these trips dozens of times, in and out, with few complications.

Coming along the main road through a fire-damaged Pennington and into Lymington town centre, they passed a supermarket, swept clean in the first few days of the outbreak. Nothing now remained, except shopping trolleys, smashed together at one end of the car park by the recent storms.

"People would have paid good money for that back in the day," joked Joe, pointing at the twisted pile of rusting metal.

"Yeah. Deserves to be in the Tate Modern. 'Shopping trolley sculpture' by Damien Hirst. Price tag two million pounds," added Sean, with no small degree of sarcasm.

They all laughed, despite their nerves.

"Never again. Those times are gone," said Zed. "Good riddance."

"The only thing money is good for is burning," said Sean, laconically.

"Right on, brother. Citizen Sean here has spoken," mocked Joe.

Along the high street they inched forward, watching for

movement on either side. The car in front pulled up in a side street so they could start their search on foot.

There was an eerie quiet at street level. A lone seagull soared on the breeze, scanning for scraps. A cardboard box skated along the pavement. Newspaper rustled, caught on the railings of the local bank, its ATM screen dark and lifeless.

There was widespread evidence of a rapid exodus. Unchecked looting, storefronts smashed in, doors kicked down. Loss of power had silenced the alarms and blinded CCTV systems. Some storekeepers and homeowners had stayed behind to protect their property, shouting impotently at the looters to keep back. The police never came. Those that stayed behind in the towns had most likely died. Only those that got out survived.

Zed's team operated in silence. Hand signals were passed between the team members as they crept along separate sides of the street. They stopped several times to listen and observe. There was no one around. Halfway along, they reached a large town house with a front window smashed in, its front door intact. They crowbarred the top and bottom hinges. After some brute force and grunting they levered open the lock. Zed gestured to Sean to take the left and Mila the right as they stepped inside.

The hall and staircase were deserted, untouched by the chaos outside. The living room to the left was filled with book-shelves, two large brown leather sofas and an armchair. Family photos of holidays and Christmases spoke of happier times. Sean picked up a framed photo and smiled at the laughing faces of children playing on a beach. The shelf had a heavy layer of dust. He replaced the silver frame carefully, opening drawers one by one, looking for anything usable.

Mila ran a finger along the spines of several of the books. The castle library was well stocked, but they were always on the lookout to add to the collection. She grabbed a couple of novels that looked unfamiliar and a large visual encyclopaedia the children would like, together with a French dictionary. She stuffed them into the large rucksack.

In the kitchen, the cupboards were mostly bare, aside from tinned tuna and vegetables. They grabbed some spices and wrapped the sharp knives from the drawer in a tea towel to keep them safe as they continued their search. Under the stairs they found tools, oil, glue, cleaning products and other household items that were always in demand.

A noise from the floor above made all of them look round. Sean and Mila stared anxiously at Zed, who gestured for them both to stay calm and follow him. He normally stuck to the ground floor, but something told Zed that it was worth the risk to continue the search upstairs. They crept silently, planting one foot in front of the other, carefully, step by step. They kept their eyes focused on the landing above through the banisters. Zed's revolver was drawn, though he only had two bullets loaded. A large creak betrayed them and they froze for a few seconds to listen.

At the top of the stairs, outside the first door, Zed signalled to the others, counting down to zero from three. They barged through, splintering the lock and swept the room, pointing their weapons into each corner. There was nothing. Just a large bed and two wardrobes.

They tried the next bedroom. A child's room with movie posters of *Transformers* and *James Bond*. There was a PC monitor, keyboard and desk, a Manchester United duvet cover and matching pillowcase.

They readied themselves outside the last bedroom, nodding to each other, weapons ready. Zed kicked open the door and charged inside, closely followed by the others.

The stench was overpowering. Mila recoiled, covering her

nose and mouth with her sleeve. Lying on the bed was a family of three, the mother and child locked in a final embrace. Their skin pale and drawn tight across their faces, mouths open in a silent cry of anguish, their eyes blank, staring at each other.

Sean approached the bed and peered over them.

"Poor bastards," he whispered.

At the sound of his voice, the father's mouth opened and let out a pained groan. Sean jumped back startled, his knife drawn. "Holy crap! That scared the bejesus out of me."

Zed barged Sean out the way, covering the bed with his weapon, keeping his distance.

"He won't hurt you. He's barely alive. The other two are long gone," said Zed, dispassionately.

"Shouldn't we put him out of his misery," suggested Sean, recovering his sangfroid, but still visibly trembling.

"No point," countered Zed. "Leave him be. Check the bathroom and study and then let's get out of here."

They regrouped downstairs, their rucksacks half-filled with an eclectic selection of batteries, books, food and tools. They moved on to the next house, this time empty. The occupants had left a chaotic trail of clothes and personal items discarded on the stairs and in the hall in their hurry to get out.

Above the mantelpiece Sean spotted a ceremonial sword, perhaps an antique relic of a military career. He turned it over in his hands, testing the weight. It might make a useful weapon if sharpened up a little, its edges dull, never before used in anger. He grabbed a stack of CDs for their sound system back at the camp. On special occasions, Jack would let them power up the generator, drink some of Liz's home brew and toast departed friends. Then there was the thorny issue of Jack's limited CD collection, consisting mostly of Led Zeppelin and Pink Floyd. Anything new or modern would be cheered by one and all.

Their rucksacks virtually full, they were just sweeping the

third house when Zed's radio crackled into life. A loud beep signalled that one of the other team was trying to contact him.

"Zed, it's Joe."

"Go ahead, Joe."

"Four cars, repeat four, just drove into town and are heading straight towards you."

"Thanks, Joe. We'll sit tight and wait this one out," replied Zed. "Bob? You there?"

"Yes, mate. We're nearly done. Riley is upstairs, Will is keeping watch by the doorway."

"Okay, Bob, let's keep our heads down and wait for this lot to pass through."

"Roger that."

Zed and his team had learned the hard way that tangling with rival groups was best avoided. Live and let live. Fighting was a last resort. You tended to live longer that way. The team would lay low until the threat had passed.

Chapter 7

In the row of shops and flats across the street, the other team was finishing their sweep. They had a decent haul of tinned food, pasta, some clothes, several bottles of spirits and cans of fizzy drinks.

Will stood outside the house scanning the high street in both directions, humming a nursery rhyme about a "springbok jumping over the moon" that had just popped into his head. Where had that come from? He took a long draw from a cigarette and exhaled noisily. A thin plume of smoke funnelled upwards into the grey overcast sky, as his mind wandered to happier times growing up. He felt a long way from his family home just outside Johannesburg.

Bob joined him on the top step and shared his cigarette.

"Tell me again where you were before Hurst," asked Bob, clearing his throat.

"Not far from here actually. I was holed up in a new-build town house for a while with a couple of lads I worked with on construction projects. When things started breaking down, we got out of town and drove straight to this old farmhouse we knew. The property had been empty, mid-renovation. The owners had moved out to escape the dust and disruption. They were living abroad in Portugal or Spain, I can't remember which."

Bob nodded, keeping watch up and down the street, waiting for Will to continue.

"We got by, picking fruit and vegetables from the garden, helping ourselves to whatever we could find. They had this walk-in larder there with dry stores. When one of the others got sick, I panicked and bolted. Never went back. I wasn't taking any chances. I'd seen how quickly the sickness spread. I just left everything behind. My clothes, my mates, everything and just drove until I hit the coastal road. I sat in the car for an hour with the engine running, staring out to sea. For the first time since I immigrated to England, I felt completely isolated, divorced from everything I had known. I realised that it was up to me to make a new life somewhere safe, to find other survivors and rebuild."

Bob took another drag from the cigarette, flicking the ash and wheezing again. "You were like me. You got lucky, eh? How did you find Hurst?"

"I spotted Jack's headlights bumping along the shingle roadway and followed him out to the castle after dark."

Will remembered his first impressions of the place. The precautions they had taken with him. Held at gunpoint, quarantined until proven fit and healthy, treated with suspicion, questioned.

"You guys were different from the other groups I'd encountered. You took no chances. I was a potential threat to your way of life. I respected that. Like the old days back home in South Africa. Living in fear of carjacking and armed robbery, HIV and infection, snakes and spiders, crocs and hippos. Being surrounded by danger keeps your senses alert. I never allowed myself to drop my guard. That's what kept me alive. Survival meant finding a community, sharing resources, having others watch your back, pulling together. I didn't want to live alone, not any more."

"You're lucky though," repeated Bob. "You've got skills, something Hurst needed."

"What's that then? My rugged good looks?"

Bob laughed, shaking his head. "No, I meant your builder skills. The fact that you can fix stuff. Repair walls, plumbing, that kind of thing. Those are in demand now. So much to do all the time. You take all that for granted, but the rest of us have had to learn most of that for the first time. How to fight, look after animals, grow food, store rainwater. You learned all that growing up."

Will squinted at Bob, sizing him up. He was an office worker, ill-suited to this new world. Bob was right; he took his upbringing for granted, but it had trained him to survive, to stay alive. He took another draw on the cigarette and turned his head towards the squeak of brakes and a low rumble in the distance from a diesel engine. There was an urgent tap on the window from the upstairs room.

Riley was gesturing for them both to get inside. The approaching convoy navigated around the debris in the street. In the distance a delivery lorry was parked perpendicular to the road, backed up to a shop. Its doors were still open. Its driver slumped over the wheel, the windscreen shattered by a bullet.

Will ducked, wondering if they had seen him. He flicked his cigarette into the gutter from the top step and went back inside, closing the door quietly behind him. Bob beckoned him over, put his finger to his lips and they both crouched under the windowsill as the convoy came into view. They could hear Riley's footsteps on the floor above as she took up position watching the road from the upstairs bedroom.

The convoy slowed and stopped not twenty metres from where they were hiding. The lead vehicle was a top-of-the-line

Range Rover, an Overfinch with four male occupants. Just behind were a red Transit van, a people carrier and a beaten-up Peugeot estate car, panting noisily at the rear.

Will peeked again but ducked quickly as the car doors opened and he saw about a dozen men begin unloading their gear. They were well organised, heavily armed with automatic weapons. Several of them were dressed in dark combat fatigues and camouflage jackets. Shielded from view behind a white net curtain, the pair watched the group. The leader, a clean-shaven man with slick brown hair, black combat trousers and a dark Barbour jacket stood talking to two others. He was giving instructions and pointing towards the shops and houses down the road.

One of the men with an automatic rifle slung under his arm looked over towards the house where they were hiding. He was studying the door with crowbar marks near the lock. His eyes flicked down and locked on to the still-lit cigarette smouldering in the gutter. He whistled through his teeth to get the rest of the group's attention and wandered over, scanning the first-floor windows. He picked up the cigarette butt, put it to his lips and inhaled deeply before stubbing it out under a heavy boot. Pressing his face to the glass, he cupped his hands to the ground-floor window, shielding the reflection and peered in. One of the other men joined him outside the house and with a silent nod from his partner he raised his rifle butt and smashed in the window.

Glass showered down onto Will and Bob. They didn't have time to get away, falling backwards, hands protecting their faces from the glass and glare of the outside light. A rifle was now pointed at their heads by the silhouetted figure.

"Keep your hands up where I can see them. Stand up. Slowly, slowly."

Bob and Will did exactly as they were told.

"Who are you? And what are you doing here?" demanded the man with the rifle.

He moved further towards them, no longer haloed by the bright sunlight, so Will could get a proper look at him without squinting. He looked paramilitary, wearing the same improvised uniform as the others they had observed, probably stolen en masse from a department store or outfitters. He was heavily bearded with steely eyes set slightly too close together. Will determined to appeal to his better nature.

"We're just looking for food, that's all." Will kept his hands behind his head, trying to remain calm and not provoke the man, feeling the blade of the knife pressed against his thigh in its leather scabbard. He wondered whether Bob could distract him while he made a lunge for his throat.

"Where's the rest of your group?" said the man towering over Will, pointing the rifle from one to the other. He was on edge. Try to keep him calm, thought Will, keep him talking.

"There's just the two of us," Will lied. "This is Bob and I'm Will."

The man looked past them into the room, unconvinced. He waved to the other men to take a look inside. Just then, the radio in Bob's pocket crackled with static.

"Give me that," scowled the man with the rifle.

He was local, Will was sure of that. He looked half-familiar. Bob reluctantly passed him the radio. He turned it over in his free hand, stepping aside as he was joined by his leader, the man from the Overfinch, shaking his head at Bob and Will. The black Barbour jacket he wore looked brand new, with a crisp black shirt and tie, cargo trousers and polished shoes. He looked a little like a bailiff to Will, with the same air of menace and efficiency about him.

"Just the two of you, eh? So who's that on the radio then?"

His voice was distinctive, educated. He was never very good

with regional accents. Somewhere up north? Manchester was his best guess. Bob stared back, trying to think of a convincing response. "It's not our radio. We just found it."

The man in black stared back at him, his head tilted to one side. "Don't try my patience." He raised the radio to his mouth and pressed the button to talk. "This is a message for the friends of Bob and Will. If you want to see them again alive, come out now and show your faces. You will not be harmed."

There was nothing but static.

"Last chance. I'll count to five and then one of them dies." He counted slowly, staring blankly at the pair of them. Will glowered back defiantly as the count reached its conclusion.

The man raised his gun and pointed directly at Bob's head. "Time's up. Come out, come out, wherever you are, this is your last chance before one of them dies. Eenie, meenie, miney, mo..."

Will interrupted him. "Look, we're just looking for food. Please, check the rucksacks, take what you want, just let us go."

The man with the rifle rummaged through their packs and confirmed their contents.

"How many of you are there? Where's your base? Tell me, now," the man in black shouted, frustrated with their refusal to cooperate. He looked like the sort of person who was used to getting his own way.

Bob shifted uncomfortably. He seemed on the verge of caving in. With a fierce stare, Will cautioned him to keep quiet. The exchange of glances was not lost on the man in black. He pointed to Bob and slid his finger across his throat.

Chapter 8

The single shot was muffled but unmistakeable from across the street. Zed paced the room, staying hidden from sight. He threw his head back in frustration, before getting a grip on his emotions.

"We can't risk going over there," he whispered, peering through the shaft of light between the curtains. "There are too many of them."

"We can't just sit here and do nothing," challenged Mila angrily, encouraging Sean to support her. They were both terrified. They were just kids after all.

"Both of you, listen to me. We're not going to do anything. Think about it. We're outnumbered and outgunned. Best-case scenario? They're bluffing and trying to lure us out. Worst-case, we come out guns blazing and take a few of them with us, then we all get captured or we all die. It's lose-lose. This way, we manage our losses and live to fight another day. So all three of us are going to sit tight and wait this out. Got it?"

Mila scowled at him. She didn't like it, but she didn't have a better plan. She knew he was right. Maybe, just maybe, it had been a warning shot designed to draw them out of their hiding places. Zed was sure they would take the others back to their camp alive.

Across the street, the door opened and Will was marched out towards the people carrier, his hands tied behind his back. There was no sign of Riley. The men loaded up their gear again together with the two rucksacks, taking a final look around before climbing back into the vehicles, and the convoy pulled slowly away.

Zed waited five minutes to make sure no one had stayed behind and then stole across the street. Inside, he met Riley coming down the stairs.

"Where's Bob?" she said, concern manifest in her body language, both of them fearing the worst.

On the living room floor, Bob's body lay prone. There was a perfectly round dark hole in the middle of his forehead. A circle of blood spread slowly outwards on the carpet. Zed scratched his fingernails across his face, put his head in his hands and let out a primeval cry. Riley came up behind him and put a hand on his shoulder.

"There was nothing we could do," she conceded.

"What about Will? Where's Will?" said Mila anxiously, the colour draining from her face.

"They took him," said Zed, coming to his senses. He leaned out of the smashed window, looking back down the street after the convoy. "But I've a good idea where they're going."

Chapter 9

J ack grabbed the last of the sacks, heavier than the previous
dozen. With Sam's help, they cradled the load between
them, walking sideways, cheeks puffed out, towards the
pontoon and the *Nipper*. Its engines were throbbing rhythmically, ready to leave, water spurting from the engine outlet every
few seconds. They stowed the last sack with the others, brim-full
of potatoes and carrots, neatly tucked in rows, made fast with a
frayed rope under the bulwark at the stern. They hauled a large
blue tarpaulin tight to keep their cargo dry and stop it from
sliding with each roll of the waves, not to mention the wind and
weather on this morning's voyage.

Jack looked up at the grey skies, his eyebrows furrowed at
the sight of dark clouds threatening in the south-east, bringing
squalls and rain. Nothing to get excited about, mind you but he
was experienced enough as a skipper to never underestimate a
storm and its ability to create havoc even in the sheltered waters
of the Solent.

The *Nipper* cast off and angled away from the jetty, heading
out under full engine into the deeper waters of the shipping
channel. They made towards their first port of call just a few

miles away east towards Cowes. Looking south towards the Isle of Wight, they passed Fort Albert, converted into luxury apartments several decades ago but unsuitable to host a group of any reasonable size. Despite its Napoleonic grandeur and imposing position, facing Hurst on the opposite side of the western entrance to the Solent, it looked deserted.

Passing Yarmouth, Sam pointed to the harbour entrance where The George hotel had once stood, next to the ferry port. Little now remained. It was a burned-out wreck. Its ancient timbers lay blackened and broken where it had collapsed in a fire. Jack shook his head, remembering the many nights out he had enjoyed in Yarmouth pubs with friends and acquaintances.

In the distance loomed the enormous hulk of the *Maersk Charlotte*, its decks stacked seven or eight stories high with containers of all different colours. Jack thought from a distance it looked like a giant Lego ship, but as they got closer its true scale was breathtaking. Nearly one thousand feet of Sovereign class shipping vessel. Its hull was painted a pale blue, with a rectory-red waterline just visible, fully laden as she was. On board, its modest crew of fifteen had been swollen by dozens of others taking refuge. Without unloading the containers on shore, their cargo was mostly useless or inaccessible. However, many of those opened onboard yielded unusual and unexpected treasures. Four hundred thousand litres of bottled water, three thousand kilos of white rice, a dozen Yamaha pianos, four Kawasaki motorbikes, cut timber, plastic sheeting and tents. Humanitarian aid no doubt heading for Somalia, Ethiopia or Sierra Leone. The list of containerised goods went on and on. A veritable treasure trove, a modern-day Aladdin's cave. The ship had set up shop as a floating trading post, open for business day and night, ready to trade with whoever and whatever came their way.

The *Charlotte*'s captain, Anders Bjørklund, was an amiable

Norwegian. Like Jack, he had served in his country's navy for many years before retiring and taking command of a container ship. He had travelled the world and had the T-shirts to prove it, literally. He had more tall tales of nautical adventures, of wives and beautiful ladies, to entertain the small company who gathered to drink Ukrainian vodka and eat meatballs in their comfortable ship's canteen. Somali pirates had boarded no less than three times, or so he said.

Rounding the stern and entering the wind shadow created by the ship's enormous hull, Jack shifted the throttle into neutral. Using the tide to take way off and come slowly alongside, he waited patiently for the stairway to be lowered.

The *Charlotte*, like so many of her sister ships, had been heavily fortified to counter the threat of pirates in the Gulf of Aden on its route through the Suez Canal past Somalia. Its walkways were caged, with gates compartmentalising access to parts of the ship. Fire hoses were mounted on the guardrail to ward off any skiffs or high-speed launches that got too close. These defences had provided welcome protection against unwanted visitors in the Solent. Her hull was roughly painted with warning messages to deter the curious and inquisitive. The most prominent of them read "Boarders will be shot: do not approach within 50 metres".

One of the crew appeared at the rail and waved to them, cigarette hanging from his lips. He grabbed the bowline from Sam and fended off the fishing boat as it came alongside. Once they were secure fore and aft, Jack and Sam climbed the stairs and came aboard the *Charlotte*.

Chapter 10

After a cursory pat-down and bag search for concealed weapons, the Filipino deckhand led them in silence along the *Maersk Charlotte*'s walkway through a series of locked gates and stairways up towards the bridge and the main entrance to the crew quarters. Sam looked nervous as the gate was padlocked again behind them, locking them in, but Jack's silent nod reassured him. The deckhand heaved open a large watertight door and they stepped over the raised edge.

Inside, the air was warm and stale. It stank of unwashed bodies, mildew and boiled cabbages. Their rubber boots squeaked noisily on linoleum tiles that stretched out in front of them to the left and right. They headed up another flight of stairs and through an interior doorway into a brightly lit soft-seating area. Bookcases and posters of swimwear models decorated the walls, together with table tennis and football apparatus. They found Anders talking animatedly with his second in command, a younger man with designer stubble and an angular face. Anders rose and greeted them warmly, throwing both arms wide to embrace them.

"My good friend, Jack. Welcome, welcome. How are you?

And here we have Sam, I think. You are well too, I hope? What have you brought me today? Come, sit, have some coffee, relax."

Jack took a seat opposite Anders and helped himself to freshly brewed coffee from a large metal pot. Proper coffee, thought Jack to himself. Anders always had the best of everything,

Anders' second in command sat arms crossed, watching Jack as he inhaled the delicious aroma of freshly roasted coffee with his eyes closed, savouring every second. When Jack looked up from his moment of indulgence, the man opposite held his gaze and nodded slightly, acknowledging Jack's gratitude for the simple pleasure of a good cup of coffee. Standing over by the bookshelves, Sam held back from the others and perched nervously on the side of a trestle table erected next to the wall, watching the three men carefully, listening intently to their conversation from a respectful distance.

"I think you remember Victor, my first officer," said Anders. "He just came back from Portsmouth. You made many new friends, I think, yes?" he said, nudging his first officer.

Victor nodded and smiled, revealing a gold tooth. He leaned forward and grabbed a shortbread biscuit, snapping one ostentatiously between his teeth. "Perhaps," he replied enigmatically, raising his eyebrows and waving the remaining half of the biscuit in small circles, his mouth still full.

Jack thought Victor looked rather pleased with himself.

"We have, how do you say...?" Victor paused, considering for a second, "established lines of communication."

He was most likely Polish or Latvian, Jack wasn't sure, he couldn't place the heavily accented English, other than somewhere in Eastern Europe.

Anders took over the story, his patience with Victor's amateur dramatics exhausted.

"We are talking with the Royal Navy in Portsmouth. Or

rather, what's left of them. Out of seventeen thousand personnel, there are less than four hundred still there, holed up like rats in the old naval dockyard. It would seem that all their weapons and fences and ships couldn't keep the virus out. Victor here met with their leader, Captain Armstrong. He is someone we can do business with, I think."

"And what news from anywhere else? Are they in contact with other groups?" asked Jack hopefully.

"He did not say," said Victor curtly with a dismissive wave. "I did not ask. We were too busy talking about other things." Victor leaned back in his seat, looking relaxed and smug, like the cat that got the cream.

Anders took over again. "You tease them too much, Victor. Look, we have something, maybe, you might be interested in, Jack. Something good. You want a look?"

Jack looked intrigued and nodded. They rose as a group and Jack and Sam followed the other two men down a narrow corridor, under strip lighting that flickered from time to time. They entered a larger hold below the main deck. In boxed wooden crates, their lids already crowbarred open, lay what looked like rifles secured in grey cut-out foam to protect them in transit.

Anders reached in and lifted one out. Turning it over to inspect the sights and stock, he pulled back the firing pin and inspected the empty chamber. Jack recognised them instantly from his time in the service. They were standard-issue SA80s used throughout the British military. What he wouldn't give for a few of those for the guys back at the castle, rather than farmers' shotguns and barely functioning museum pieces.

"We also have ammunition, 9mm pistols, grenades and this beauty." He reached down and patted a larger tripod mounted machine gun, with boxes of ammunition stacked next to it. "Quite a haul, yes?" Anders looked incredibly pleased with himself.

"Impressive, Anders. How much did that little lot cost you?" asked Jack.

"A pretty penny. But worth it. Your Royal Navy was very willing to trade. It took a bit of persuasion of course, but they have hundreds and hundreds of weapons and no one left to fire them. They are as useless as ice cream to an Eskimo. Is that the expression? Or coals to Newcastle, I like better. Meanwhile they have no, shall we say, creature comforts. Food, yes, but hardly any cigarettes, drink, and certainly no recreational drugs. What can I say? The captain likes his Russian vodka. We let him have half a dozen cases, for now. And enough pills to make them forget all about the virus."

Jack eyed the merchandise greedily, stroking his chin thoughtfully. "But, Anders, we both know he doesn't have what I have. Fresh vegetables, bread baked this morning, home-grown apples picked yesterday from our orchard. Very hard to come by. I have your usual delivery if your men can give me a hand. In exchange for, shall we say, five of those rifles and a couple of pistols? We'll take as much ammunition as you can spare."

Anders wagged his finger. "Well, it is true, we are very fond of Hurst potatoes and cabbage. Not so much the carrots, too sweet. Makes a change from tinned vegetables. Keeps us healthy, no?" He laughed, stroking his paunch. "We grow fat and lazy here. Not like you, Jack. While you work, we have little to do here but eat and drink all day long. It is very tiresome." He chortled at his own joke and considered Jack's proposal, moving his head from side to side. "But as you and me we are old friends, why don't we say three rifles, two pistols and bullets for both? When you bring me more, we can trade again. There are plenty more where these came from. And our new friends at the Royal Navy have unlimited stores to equip a whole army. I'm sure if we asked nicely we could get you a helicopter, perhaps. He has a whole store of engine parts and electrical spares. You name it.

Victor has seen it. They have a set-up to die for. They have a hospital, accommodation for hundreds, fences and soldiers to keep them safe, cooks and kitchens. It is sanctuary, my friend. They could take all of us."

"So why are you still here, Anders? Why did Victor come back? Sounds like you found something better. A way out of all this. A return to normality. A new start."

"Because..." Anders paused, wagging his finger at Jack. "I do not trust him. And besides," he went on, stretching both arms wide, looking around him, "how could I leave the *Charlotte*? This is my home."

Jack drained his cup and nodded. He knew exactly what Anders meant. He felt the same way about Hurst. It would take something special to make him leave his adopted home.

Chapter 11

J ack and Sam unloaded the share of their cargo that
belonged to Anders in return for the rifles, boxes of ammunition and a few other assorted items, including personal gifts from Anders.

It was Anders' "thing", an indulgent and entirely sentimental
act he always undertook when he knew Jack was coming. He
took great care in selecting some toys for the Hurst children,
whom he knew by name. Boxed *Transformers* for the boys, *Toy
Story* figurines for the girls. He normally added a couple of
bottles of vodka and cigarettes for the grown-ups.

Jack shook hands with Anders, the two of them standing on
the bottom step of the stairway exchanging warm farewells. Sam
uncleated the bowline and left it on a slip, ready to cast off as
soon as Jack was back on board. There was a strong swell
running that made the *Nipper*'s gunwale rise and fall two metres as each wave surged past. The small fishing boat yawed
from side to side, making the jump treacherous.

Jack stood poised on the narrow platform, waiting for the
optimum moment to step aboard. When the *Nipper* rose on an
approaching wave, he balanced gracefully on the raised gunwale

and jumped the last few feet to the deck next to some fishing nets. Sam cast off the stern and raced the length of the boat to do the same at the bow. They drifted back along the towering hull of the *Charlotte,* angling away and heading west, onwards on the last leg of their journey.

Their final destination on this morning's excursion was Spitbank and No Man's Land forts. The two forts, passive sentinels for some one hundred and fifty years, stood guard over the shipping lanes at the eastern end of the Solent. They were both accessible by boat from the mainland via Gosport and Portsmouth, or from the island via Ryde. Together with Hurst and the other Solent forts, they made up a formidable chain of castles, forts and shore batteries constructed during Napoleonic times to defend Portsmouth against the threat of invasion by the French. The fortifications had made this stretch of English coastline one of the most heavily defended in the world. In the end, the forts had fallen victim not to attack but to the advance of naval weaponry. Modern, longer-range cannon, not to mention the advent of peace, had combined to ensure the forts' obsolescence, soon after completion.

Today, the forts stood isolated and windswept. Yet they had lost nothing of their imposing grandeur.

Like Hurst, the inaccessibility of Spitbank and No Man's Land was both a tonic and a boon to the survivor groups that occupied them. On one hand, the forts provided a sanctuary from the chaos and disorder that had befallen towns and villages on the mainland. On the other, their inaccessibility was a curse.

It was said that the occupants of the forts had watched the events on the mainland unfold with a strange detachment. Huddled round their single working radio set, they listened to the news reports of spreading sickness and widespread rioting from the relative safety of the forts. It reminded the older members of the group of the Blitz, so many years before. They shook their heads with growing concern until, several days later, all live broadcasts ceased transmission. Looped public safety announcements were all that remained, telling people to stay indoors. When the power grid failed, all they heard was white noise.

Fuel for the forts' generators ran dangerously low, and was held in reserve for winter. When the oil ran out, they became wholly dependent on scavenging trips for fuel and food. Their first choice was to head to the island where the lower population density made things a little safer. Scavenging trips to Portsmouth and Gosport were more lucrative but considered too dangerous. The forts' occupancy numbers had dwindled as supplies grew increasingly scarce, driving many away. Today, only a small group could be sustained at both sites, of some twenty or thirty souls each.

Jack stopped first at No Man's Land and stood on the *Nipper's* foredeck exchanging pleasantries with Shannon, a fisherman's widow and formerly a café owner from Cowes before the breakdown.

Sam secured the large lifting hook from the pulley to hoist the last of the sacks while a young man above directed proceedings. Sam held the sack steady on the first part of its ascent as it swung out over the water in the light breeze.

A grey foam clung to the lower rungs of the ladder. Waves lapped rhythmically against the base of the fort, alternately exposing and covering the green and brown seaweed that clung to the stone. When the last of the sacks was lifted off the deck, they lowered two large fuel drums full of diesel and a small Kawasaki portable generator being offered in exchange before casting off. Jack steered the *Nipper* the short distance to Spitbank, as a strengthening wind drove them onwards.

They had made this trip a dozen times. The *Nipper* came

surging up to the rusted iron and steel stairwell that stretched from the very top of the wall and plunged fifteen feet into the murky depths below the waterline. The waves here rolled in from the Channel, smashing against the stone and sloshing between the supporting columns. At the last minute, Jack jammed the engine astern and the *Nipper* slowed abruptly to a complete stop, two or three feet from the platform. Sam looped a line round an iron ring as the boat began drifting back in the current.

Spitbank fort was circular in shape. Its thick stone walls were reinforced with iron, built to withstand cannon fire from the marauding French. Its own gun ports now stood vacant and bricked up, where cannon would have faced seawards.

Jack reached up at head height and heaved himself off the *Nipper*, climbing the stairwell towards the main entrance set thirty feet clear of the waves. He stopped midway up to look back and admire the *Nipper* from above. The reinforced glass in her small wheelhouse reflected the morning sun as she wallowed in the light swell. Sam was busy tidying ropes and putting out extra fenders to protect the bow from scraping against the jetty.

At the top of the stairwell, Jack found the place deserted, its heavy doors closed to visitors. He had grown used to a welcome party, half a dozen smiling faces, waving as they approached the fort. There were around thirty residents at the last count, four of five families, a few children he had grown fond of. Nice bunch, Jack thought to himself. This morning there were no children's faces pressed to the glass, no lookout in the main building, nothing. Perhaps they were all inside having a late breakfast. He shrugged.

He tried the door handle but found it locked. Where was everyone? He cupped his hands to the glass trying to peer inside, scanning for movement. He tried to wipe away the salt and spray from the glass but realised it was condensation on the inside. He rattled the door and knocked to get their attention, listening at the glass for the sound of footsteps. The dark shape of a woman near the door startled him as she rose slowly from the shadows, adjusting her hair and wiping tears from her eyes.

Jack recognised the face instantly. Susan, or Susie, as he liked to call her. Her appearance was altered. She looked pale and drawn, dried-up tears had left dirty tracks. Her eyes were dull and lifeless. She was no more than thirty, but looked older, her face weathered, pressed up close against the glass.

The reinforced window was built to withstand the worst of the winter storms, thick enough to muffle her voice. He cupped his ear to the crack, trying to make out what she was saying against the waves and wind swirling around him.

"I can't let you in, Jack."

Her words sent an icy chill down his spine. She repeated them, shaking her head until he understood. Jack gulped and took an involuntary step back.

"When did this happen?"

"Last week. One of the children got it first, we're not sure how. Little Grace coughed all night and the following morning, two more had come down with it. We were too slow, Jack, we didn't isolate them fast enough." She shook her head and the tears started again. "In three days, half of us had it, and by then it was too late. It spread so fast."

"I'm so sorry, Susie. Is there anything we can do for you? We have food and supplies."

"Save it," she said bitterly, forcing a smile. "Don't waste it on us."

She pressed her moist palm to the glass and looked mournfully into Jack's eyes. He put his own hand up to mirror hers. The glass was cold, but he thought he could feel the faint warmth of her skin.

"Pray for us. But don't come back," she called out, her voice breaking with emotion.

Jack managed a weak smile. "We will," he mouthed, nodding his head gently. He turned, closing his eyes for a moment and then hurried away.

At the top level of the stairwell, he scratched a large skull and crossbones into the stone with his knife, warning others never to approach this cursed place again.

Chapter 12

Picking their way along the main road at walking pace, the Hurst convoy rounded abandoned cars and other detritus that littered their path. The lead vehicle, a bulky Mitsubishi Land Cruiser, carrying Mila and Riley, bumped heavily over some loose rubble. With a loud hiss, their back right tyre deflated. The Mitsubishi rumbled over to the side of the street and stopped, scraping on its rims.

Zed pulled in behind them and switched off the Land Rover's ignition. He leaned forward over the steering wheel and peered at the buildings to the left of them, scanning for movement. A row of suburban houses on the outskirts of town overlooked what would once have been tidy flowerbeds full of roses and hydrangea bushes and manicured lawns. Today, those same gardens were an impassable tangle of weeds and bushes, grass growing lush and long. He shook his head, muttering to himself.

"So what?" said Sean, sat in the passenger seat. He shrugged his shoulders, oblivious to the danger. "We got a spare, yeah? We fix it and be on our way. It'll take ten minutes. Tops."

Zed shook his head. "Not here. Not now. In broad daylight? If that convoy comes through here we'll be sitting ducks."

He jumped out of the car and closed the driver's door quietly, not wanting to attract any unwanted attention. They were vulnerable here and needed to get moving fast. Riley was already out, inspecting the damage, hands on hips, shaking her head.

Zed got down on his hands and knees and felt around the circumference of the tyre, feeling for a hole. He found it quickly. There was a large gash made by a fallen piece of sharp masonry and glass. He picked out a couple of smaller shards and dropped them, clinking on the tarmac. He sat back on his haunches, scratching the back of his head.

Sean stood behind him. "What do you want to do, boss? Fix it or come back later when it's dark?"

"We hide it someplace safe and come back. There's a lock-up round the corner we can use. Transfer all the gear to the Land Rover and get out of here."

"You sure about this?" asked Riley. "What with Bob and Will, and now this? It's not our lucky day. I say we cut our losses and come back tomorrow and start again."

"I'm not leaving Will out here. We find out where they took him and then we make the call."

He unholstered his revolver and put another couple of rounds from his breast pocket into the empty chambers. He spun the wheel and snapped it shut with a tilt of his wrist. A boyish grin illuminated his face. Life felt better with a loaded gun.

"Boys and their toys," mocked Riley.

Zed looked back at her, his head cocked to one side. "We owe it to Will to at least try, don't we? You'd do it for me, right, Riley?" He smirked.

Riley shook her head and walked away. They both knew the answer.

Mila and Sean helped transfer their gear to the other vehicle. Cardboard boxes and rucksacks were packed full of the stuff they had scavenged from this morning's house searches. It was food mostly, plus a few other assorted items, CDs, books and tools. The back of the Land Rover was packed to bursting. They had stacked a couple of boxes on the back seat, making things a little cramped when they all climbed back in, shoulders touching. Zed was suddenly aware of the warmth of Mila's wrist resting on his shoulder. Her hand was trembling ever so slightly. He grabbed her hand and held it tightly. She squeezed back and whispered, "I'm scared, Zed."

He forced a smile. "We've been in worse scrapes than this. We'll be fine."

Zed had driven the Mitsubishi around the corner, its back tyre deflated, bumping along on the rubber and rim. He was gone for a couple of minutes, long enough for Riley to worry, watching the street the way he'd gone. She was just about to follow when he jogged back into view. He'd parked in a small residential cul-de-sac that ran parallel to the main road. It was well hidden in a carport attached to a semi-detached retirement bungalow. It would be safe there. At least for a while.

Zed climbed back into the driver seat and slowly pulled away. If his hunch was right they were no more than a mile from where they were heading, following the most likely trail the other group would have taken. Before the outbreak and on any normal day, the one-mile journey would have taken them a few minutes. But things had been far from "normal" for some time, thought Zed.

Road surfaces had degenerated quickly without anyone to repair them. From smaller potholes, vegetation spreading out from verges and walkways, weeds and tree roots pushing through the tarmac and whole sections collapsing, it was treacherous to the unwary, to say the least. Another few years and some of these roads through the forest that had existed in some form since Roman times would be reclaimed by nature.

They were heading for the hospital on the other side of Lymington. Zed had heard talk of another group holed up there and thought he recognised one of the men who'd taken Will. He knew him by reputation only. A former policeman, given the imaginative nickname "Copper" by those who knew him locally. Supposedly one of the good guys. Or at least he used to be. Who knew what he had become.

Chapter 13

Will woke up and blinked rapidly, rubbing his eyes. His sleepy gaze fixed on a poster promoting safe sex with a picture of two teenagers holding hands. Above the young couple was a list of clinical conditions and names for sexually transmitted diseases, superimposed on a fluffy cloud. Will recognised some of them but puzzled over others. Chlamydia? What the hell was that? His head was still pounding and the words danced a little, making his vision swim. He shook his head to try to clear his thoughts. A sharp pain made him reach up and touch the back of his scalp. His fingers came away damp with blood that was leaking from the crude gauze and tape, surrounded by matted hair crusted with dried blood. He tried to raise his other hand but it jerked back, handcuffed to the bedpost.

Memories of earlier events came flooding back into focus. The scavenging trip. Being discovered by the other group. How had they found them hiding? Of course, Will, you idiot. The cigarette butt. Stupid schoolboy error, he thought to himself. He remembered the hood over his head. A short drive in a large diesel vehicle. Yes, he was sure it was diesel from the sound of the engine and the distinctive smell. They had taken him to a large building, which he assumed was a hospital from the overpowering stink of disinfectant that masked something else he couldn't place. His hunch was quickly confirmed by the sound of boots on linoleum tiles and what little décor he could see through the hood.

He closed his eyes and tried to remember. It was all a jumble. The interrogation. The man they called "Copper" slapping him hard whenever he failed to answer their incessant questions, one after the other in quick succession. They had asked him about Hurst, how many people were there, how they were armed. So many questions. They had injected him with something. That explained why he was still a little light-headed. His thoughts remained muddled.

He sat bolt upright as one painful memory broke through the fog. They had killed Bob. Shot him in the head. The neat circle in his forehead, the blood on the carpet. Why? They didn't need to kill him. His anger boiled over and he slammed his fist down against his knee. The self-induced pain helped clear his head and brought his situation in to sharper focus.

The hospital room was virtually bare, a private overnight room for one person. Other than a tired-looking hospital bed, there was a cheap pine wardrobe and a side table with flowers in a vase that had long since wilted and died, the water green and stagnant. In the corner was a plastic-looking chair with brown vinyl upholstery with ridges running vertically. A grey metal wall bracket for a TV screen, and an aerial socket were the only evidence that remained of creature comforts.

He checked the drawers of the bedside cabinet. There wasn't even a Bible. But wait, was he getting confused? Maybe only hotels had Bibles next to the bed? He couldn't remember, it was all such a long time ago since he'd stayed in a hotel on holiday. The clean sheets, the buffet breakfasts.

A thin layer of dust covered the whole place. The broken blinds allowed through a few shafts of sunlight that struck the whitewashed walls next to the door. Dust hung heavy in the stale air. Other than the pervasive smell of disinfectant, there was something else that lingered. He couldn't quite place it.

His mind wandered as he thought back to his first job helping out in a meat processing plant in Sandton, back in South Africa, working with chicken carcasses. It was the smell of death and it made his mouth suddenly dry and devoid of saliva.

The window rattled a little on its hinges, not quite closed, cool air seeping in. He got to his feet and, leaning as far as the cuffs would allow him, he managed to flick the corner of the white aluminium blinds, allowing a fleeting glimpse of the outside world. He was on the second floor, and down below he could make out a series of heaps on the tarmac. The blinds fell back into position again and he stretched and flicked them again. The hairs on the back of his neck stood up as he realised that one of the heaps was piled with shoes. There were hundreds of shoes, of all shapes and sizes and colours. Children's shoes, high heels, brogues, slippers. So many shoes.

He flicked the blinds again, leaning as far as he could. The next heap was even larger, towering precariously with what looked like clothes of every description. There were trousers, shirts, dresses, coats, hospital dressing gowns, and socks. It reminded him of a scene from a war movie he had seen. What was it called? Allied soldiers liberating prisoner camps in 1945, finding piles of clothes and shoes, gold teeth, reclaimed from the bodies, surplus to requirements. It made Will shudder remembering. He looked again beyond the heaps where smoke was billowing from a fire pit.

He turned away as the blinds fell back into place. He realised with horror that the discernible shapes he could make out in the smouldering remains were human.

Will closed his eyes and wept at what the world had become. A haphazard descent into savagery. The remaining vestiges of civilisation falling away like leaves from a tree. What remained was barren and brittle.

Chapter 14

W ill wasn't sure how long he had slept. He had only closed his eyes for a second. His head had stopped throbbing so much. There was a light tap on the door and the sound of keys rattling in the lock. The heavy fire door with a small viewing window swung open and the large frame of a bearded man filled the doorway. He had a rifle with a wooden stock slung just visible behind his back. He stepped inside and glanced around the room, checking that Will was still cuffed to the bed. He moved aside for a young man wearing a white coat, glasses, thin stubble on his chin. He was moderately tall with black hair, Indian or Pakistani. Will studied him closely as he whispered with the guard, their exchanges awkward, as if the doctor was somehow uncomfortable in his own skin.

The guard swung the heavy metal door closed behind him, sealing them off from the bustle of the hospital beyond. Will heard the key turn and heavy footsteps walk away down the corridor.

"How are you feeling?" asked the doctor, his hands thrust deep in his coat pockets.

Will sized him up before answering. "You don't look old

enough to be a doctor," he barked as he swung his legs back up on to the bed, putting his hands behind his head, ignoring the doctor.

"Hey, listen, if you don't want me to take a look at that cut on your head, fine by me. I'm just doing my job." He made to leave, turning his back on Will.

"Don't kid yourself, yah. You're as bad as the rest of them. First you beat the crap out of me, and now you want to fix me up? What kind of hospital is this? Don't tell me, you were just 'following orders'," he mocked.

"Whoa there, mister. I'm one of the good guys. Don't lump me in with that other lot. Those new guys are off their rockers. Nut jobs. I've been here since the beginning, before those guys took over. We could have got out, they gave us that chance, but we chose to stay. They made this place secure and for that they get my gratitude. For the record, that doesn't mean I like what they do or how they do it."

Will shrugged his shoulders and looked back, unrepentant. The young man dumped his bag on the floor, strode over to the chair and unrolled the tools of his trade on the bedside cabinet. The surgical kit contained scalpels, scissors, and what looked like a sewing kit with syringes all neatly secured in their Velcro holders and fabric loops. Will eyed the scalpel and imagined the damage he would do to his torturers if he got the chance.

Will inclined his head submissively towards the doctor. He ripped off the gauze and tape without warning, ignoring the patient's howls of protest. He leaned in close to get a proper look, peering through the glasses at the nasty-looking cut behind Will's left ear. Some heavy bruising surrounded the wound. He donned a pair of disposable surgical gloves and gently pressed either side of the long gash.

"Yes, you'll definitely need stitches. How did you get this, dare I ask?"

"One of your boys hit me from behind. Won't forget him in a hurry. The others called him 'Copper'."

"Okay. I know who you're talking about. Friendly chap. Like I said, I don't condone violence. I just get to patch people up. More work for me, you might say."

Will winced as the doctor worked, gasping a couple of times when gloved fingers pressed too hard. For a big hardy builder, who had been a labourer all his life, he hated needles and blood. At school, he was forever the boy who fainted in the playground after slicing his shin open on a rusted nail. He'd been balancing on a wooden plank when he slipped and fell. His classmates knew better than to make fun of him. Will had always been just a little taller and heavier-set growing up which made others fear him. His physique and imposing presence had made him a promising rugby player until he clean broke his wrist when he was barely twelve and never played again.

Looking down at his feet, Will mumbled into his chest, his voice sounding awkward and strained. "You're Indian, right? Never been treated by an Indian doctor before."

"Well, you clearly haven't lived long in this country then. My father was a dentist, my brother a surgeon, my sister a paediatrician. You could say it runs in the family. Anyway, I'm British, born and bred."

"Fair enough. I don't have a problem with it. I was just making conversation. So what do you know about this virus?"

"You're asking the wrong person, I'm afraid. I mostly get to look after old people here. Routine stuff really. Dementia, Alzheimer's, Parkinson's, palliative care. Don't get to see many killer viruses or tropical diseases on the south coast. Big city hospitals get the high-profile cases. Ebola, malaria. Shame really. Might spice things up."

"Be careful what you wish for."

"My knowledge of viruses is really dated, goes back to

medical school and stuff I picked up from the press and journals they had in the staffroom. I know bits and pieces, but nothing of any use."

"But as a doctor, you must have some idea what we're dealing with. What if you had to make an educated guess?"

He pondered the question thoughtfully and then launched in to his answer with growing confidence. "Well, it sounds a lot like the Spanish flu pandemic. The outbreak after the First World War killed millions, more than the war itself. But the Millennial Virus is more deadly and spreads quicker. Of course, cheap airline travel and tourism probably accelerated all that. Based on the patients we saw and treated, I'd say around one in ten people have some degree of immunity. Some were worse affected than others, but most died within three to five days, and very few got better. We threw everything we had at it. We did little more than prolong their agony for a few hours or days. The outcome was almost always the same. It's a very effective killer."

"It sounds like you admire the virus?"

"Don't you? Mother Nature has been perfecting the flu virus over millions of years and it looks like she's cracked the code this time. Of course, if the CDC, you know, the Centre for Disease Control in the States, or the World Health Organization are still functional, then they may have developed a vaccine. By now you might expect them to have inoculated health workers and the military. Right now they may well be mounting a rescue mission to save us 'Brits'. Who knows?"

"But could it be done if they have the right resources?"

"Sure. We already have a lab here with all the kit. If you got hold of samples of the virus, an electron-microscope, biohazard suits, air purifiers, then no question, we could keep trying till we found something that worked. Might take decades though. All we'd need would be an army of scientists, unlimited money and resources. Hey, throw in someone with immunity, patient zero...

while you're at it, perhaps find me Elvis and Lord Lucan. But take a look around you. We're mostly working in the dark ages here. We barely have enough power from the emergency generator to keep the lights on, let alone anything discretionary. We have a skeletal team, and the man in charge is a psychopath, but apart from that, we have everything we need."

The young doctor finished up the stitches behind Will's ear and patted him on the head like a dog. "There you go. Good as new."

"Thank you. I owe you one. What's your name?" asked Will.

The doctor smiled. "Doctor Ganesh, but you can call me Raj."

"Well, Raj, if I figure out how to get out of this hellhole, I'll come and find you."

The doctor packed up the plastic case with the syringe, scissors, bandages and other assorted items, paused at the door to say something and thought better of it. He knocked twice and heard the guard jangle his keys. The rotund guard opened the door just wide enough to let him pass. Will sat on the side of the bed smiling, opening and closing his fingers in a childlike goodbye. The guard curled his lip and slammed the door shut.

Will puffed out his cheeks and slumped back against the wall, exhausted.

Chapter 15

"Quiet, please. This meeting of the Hurst council is called to order. Nathan, can you bring us up to speed on today's business," said Terra, leaning back in the ornate oak chair, positioned at the head of the table. Its knotted wood was richly stained, a beautiful Victorian antique from Lyndhurst in the New Forest. The back and headrest were ornately carved with stags and holly.

Nathan's body visibly stiffened with the responsibility conferred on him. He began to reel off the agenda items carefully noted on a pad of yellow lined paper. Terra yawned and looked out the small window of the upstairs room across the inner courtyard. Rain squalls were sheeting intermittently against the glass, her thoughts elsewhere. Nathan's monotone droned on in the background. He worked through various day-to-day household matters ranging from how few eggs had been laid this past week to the perilously low stores of fuel for the generator. Even with the recent wet weather, the butts collecting rain water from every rooftop around the camp were close to empty. Nathan walked everyone through the rotas for night watches and scavenging duties for the following week.

The other heads of department took it in turns to give their own quick updates, going round the table, sharing their questions and concerns before Nathan handed things back to Terra.

She leaned forward, blinking rapidly as she tried to organise her thoughts. Each of the council members were loyal and true, hand-chosen by her or Jack, selected as much for their competence as for their alternative viewpoints, unafraid to challenge when opinions differed.

"There is one other matter I need to raise," she began. "Last night, the door to the food store was forced and a number of items taken." There was a small gasp from the two women at the far end. "The inventory we took last week confirms that we are missing the following..." Nathan passed her the yellow pad and she fumbled with the spectacles that hung around her neck. She peered down past her nose, running her finger along the listed items: "two packets of biscuits, one bar of chocolate, three bags of crisps and one tin each of pineapple and tuna."

The two women at the far end exchanged glances and one of them, Liz, mumbled something Terra didn't catch. It was Liz who ran the kitchen and was more than a little protective of the meagre stores and ingredients her team had at their disposal. Perhaps she had her suspicions already. There were several likely suspects; new arrivals who had not yet earned Terra's trust.

Liz leaned forward and whispered conspiratorially with the woman to her left with flowing blonde hair that reached down to her shoulders, which she wore in plaits. Terra guessed Greta was around thirty. She spoke with only a hint of a Swedish accent in otherwise flawless English. Her short unsuccessful stint as a trainee detective in Gothenburg had earned her the position as keeper of keys at Hurst. That made investigating the theft her responsibility, but she looked affronted that Terra had not spoken to her first before speaking to the council. Let them sweat for a while, Terra thought, smiling to herself. She ignored their private discussion and continued undeterred.

"As you all know, theft is a very serious offence and one that must carry the most severe penalty. I want the whole place searched. Leave no stone unturned until these items are found and the culprit apprehended."

"Can I ask why I was not consulted first, Terra?" asked Liz indignantly. "Last time I checked, the kitchen and stores were my responsibility."

"This isn't the first time food has gone missing, is it?"

Liz blushed, her eyes narrowed at this veiled slur, but she knew better than to push Terra too far, taking a moment to compose herself. "And what do you intend to do with them when you find them?" she asked instead.

Terra deflected the question to Nathan. "The rules are clear. Punishment for theft is banishment."

Liz stared back at Greta and then Nathan. "I agree, but, Terra, banishment means almost certain death for the perpetrator. Should the council not be granted the opportunity to vote once the party responsible is discovered?"

Liz's tilted head reminded Terra momentarily of Bella, her old Labrador. How she missed the dog she had raised from a puppy. Bella had been at the vet for an overnight stay when Terra got caught up in the evacuation. She spent three hours stuck in a line of traffic that crawled to a halt and then never moved again. She wondered whether someone had let Bella out of that kennel. Best not to think about it. Lock it away with all the other unpleasant memories from that time.

Liz went on, undeterred by Terra's vacant expression. "There is a precedent after all. Remember that guy from Bournemouth? Robbie. The one who hit Tommy with the piece of driftwood. Needed nine stitches. Jack didn't banish him, he just locked him up for three days, taught him a lesson. It was all handled with a handshake and an apology. So why do you think theft warrants banishment?"

Nathan cleared his throat. "It's the code, that's why. The code exists for this very purpose. It is written. It is known and public. All those who choose to stay within these walls and accept the sanctuary and security this community offers, agree to abide by the code. There can be no order without the code. Surely, as council members, we all understand this?"

All heads turned towards Cedric, or Scottie as he was affectionately known, as he roared with laughter, banging his coffee mug on the table with some theatricality. He had been silent to this point, listening absent-mindedly with a smile spreading across his face. He shook his head. "Your petty bureaucracy is laughable. People out there are dying by the thousands. Law and order have failed. Gangs roam the towns raping and murdering while we sit here arguing about stolen biscuits."

Terra gripped her armrest a little tighter. This wasn't the first time Scottie had undermined her authority. After a life on the stage, he was a consummate performer, intent on grabbing the limelight. It was said he had cut his teeth in Scotland's smallest and pokiest theatres, treading the boards to a handful of spectators before getting his big break. Signed to play Macduff in a Royal Shakespeare Company production of *Macbeth* in a nation-wide tour that finished in Southampton, he had fallen madly in love with a local girl who worked in the foyer at the Mayflower Theatre and never left.

"Scottie," interrupted Terra, "we have survived this far because of the code. Without law, there is chaos. The code is what binds us together. Without it there is anarchy. Is that what you prefer?"

"Of course not, but we are a civilised society, are we not? Context must be considered before sentence is passed. When all the facts are known should the matter not come before the council again? Whoever said that the code was absolute? It should be a guide, to be interpreted, with flexibility if needed. If extenuating circumstances exist, then some degree of leniency is called for."

"We must make an example of whoever did this. The council demands it. Punishment is due."

Nathan's intransigence provoked another melodramatic outburst from Scottie, throwing his hands up in despair. He pushed back his chair and stood up, pacing the room in frustration. "I'm warning you. This will not play well with the people. Justice must be seen to be done. I put it to the vote that once the culprit is discovered, we assemble a court and a fair verdict reached by a jury of peers and equals."

Terra considered the request and glanced at Nathan and the others sitting around the table.

"Very well. Those in favour of holding a trial raise your hands." Terra counted the hands just to be one hundred per cent certain. "Motioned carried." She shrugged. "So be it. Greta, I'll leave it to you to find the individual or individuals responsible."

Chapter 16

Tommy helped Simon grab the last of the cardboard boxes stacked on the roof of the boat's small cabin. Keeping one foot planted on the wide wooden slats of the pontoon, Simon raised his leg awkwardly as if he were practising t'ai chi, but without the grace or balance, tottering ungainly as the boat lurched towards him. He straddled the guardrail and reached for the box.

Toby stood silently with his back to his father, hands thrust deep in the pockets of his blue shorts. He was watching red mullet swim lazily around the polystyrene float of the jetty. The mullet sucked greedily at the seaweed that clung to the boat's rudder. The brass propeller glinted invitingly, reflecting the beams of sunlight that danced in the flowing tide, a few feet below the surface. *Lady Lucy III* was stencilled in large green letters on the stern of the thirty-two-foot Contessa yacht, her home port of "Falmouth" written underneath in italics. Chipped and weather-worn, there was an incongruous graphic of a bathtime duck, faded as it was by sun and seawater, smiling bashfully, waddling through a cartoon puddle.

The main halyard that stretched from the top of the mast

tapped out a light rhythm in the morning breeze. Small waves lapped against *Lady Lucy*'s hull, sending ripples radiating outwards. Toby watched as a long tail of seaweed tethered to the jetty float swam back and forth in the tidal flow. From the engine outlet, a thin slick of oil spawned multicoloured shapes and patterns on the surface of the water. A large bubble span, skating against the tide in the breeze.

Simon passed Tommy the box containing the last of their tinned food, rice and pasta over the guardrail. Stepping back down on to the jetty, *Lady Lucy* rolled back into equilibrium, its fenders and warps groaning their farewell.

"Come on, Toby," Simon called over his shoulder.

Toby lifted his head, looked out across the salt marshes towards Keyhaven, kicked a small pebble into the water and ran after his dad. He fell into step, part supporting the weight of the box. Toby looked up wide-eyed, searching out his father's smile.

They walked over a small wooden slatted bridge that spanned what would have been the original moat of the castle, now bone dry and no more than a grassy ditch. Above the rounded arch gateway was a large royal crest painted red with the monarch's coat of arms and "V.R. 1873" in gold letters underneath. Toby paused to wonder what the initials stood for before skipping after Tommy and his father. An old-fashioned lantern in black gunmetal swung over the entrance. Toby tiptoed precariously along the narrow-gauge railway tracks that ran straight through the tunnel and into the courtyard beyond. They passed the guardhouse on the right-hand side, formerly a gift shop where visitors to the castle bought their entrance tickets.

Liz was waiting for them in the storeroom. She examined each item, calling out its contents to be noted in their inventory, sorting the tins and pasta onto one of the long trestle tables stacked high with supplies.

"Horse chestnuts?" said Tommy, picking up one of the more exotic-looking tins and reading the English translation on what looked like a Thai label. "Been a while since we had foreign food eh? Can't say I'm a fan, always gives me the runs."

"Don't listen to him," said Liz, snatching the tin from Tommy and nudging him out of the way with her shoulder. "What would you know? No taste, you lot. You wouldn't know haute cuisine if it bit you on the nose."

"A whole ocean of fish right on our doorstep. But we eat what we're given, ain't that right, Liz? Give me a nice piece of haddock any day of the week."

"Just you remember it," she responded defiantly, turning over the next tin in her short stubby fingers. "Baby carrots," she called out to Connie, one of the teenagers who helped her in the kitchen.

Simon and Toby watched their exchanges in mild amusement, looking around the canteen. It was basic but functional. Liz knelt down so her face was level with Toby's.

"I bet you didn't know that a small garrison of soldiers lived here during the war. They were responsible for guarding the Solent against attacks by German U-boats or motor torpedo boats."

Toby listened, enthralled as Liz told him more about the history of the castle.

"Come on, I'll show you the old theatre," said Tommy.

Liz called out after them: "Thanks for the Thai goodies. I'll have a think what I can make with chestnuts. Perhaps we'll have a curry then tonight, Connie."

Tommy gave them a walking tour of the castle, pointing out the dining hall, library, and the small shared dormitory where they could sleep tonight. He introduced them to various people as they went.

They stopped at the theatre and Tommy explained all about

their busy schedule of upcoming shows. Scottie's performances ranged from recitals of Shakespearean soliloquies, sonnets and longer passages he performed from memory. He was somewhat of a Hurst treasure, greeted with a mixture of mild amusement from the young, and muted rapture from the more senior members of the group.

Standing next to the stage, Tommy passed Toby an inflatable parrot they were using as a prop. "They're just auditioning for parts in *Treasure Island*, if you're interested in having a go. You'd make a great Jim Hawkins. I wanted to be a pirate but they won't let me have a speaking part."

Simon ruffled Toby's hair. The boy looked suitably embarrassed at the unwanted attention.

"Scottie adapted the script from the original book. Riley found him a copy. You should have seen the look in his eyes when he was presented with this dusty old copy. Clutched it to his chest like it was treasure itself. To think a book could have that kind of effect on a grown man," mocked Tommy, shaking his head. "He's something of an acquired taste, I suppose. He never fails to draw a crowd."

In truth, Scottie revelled in his role as Hurst's resident entertainer. Most evenings he organised public readings from well-known works. A genius with voices, accents and bringing the words on the page to life in a way that captivated young and old. *Charlie and the Chocolate Factory* for the youngest children before bedtime, *Harry Potter* for the teens, and even the adults would sit enthralled by readings from Dickens, Hardy or Hemmingway. He was forever nagging the scavenging parties to find them more books. Books, books, books, as if that was more important than food. Riley dutifully obliged and usually brought home a paperback or two. Occasionally she found a first edition or rare tome that had Scottie stroking its cover, enthralled by dedications or author signatures. He was something of a collector.

Everything just sounded a little bit better when Scottie read it. He added a vocal range and dramatic delivery to even the most boring of roll calls and memos. He had a knack of making anything sound more interesting. It reminded Tommy of how TV commercials used to get well-known Hollywood actors like Michael Douglas or Harvey Keitel to do voice-overs.

Tommy walked them back outside to the courtyard, pointing to a large whitewashed section of the castle wall where he told them they projected feature films for "Movie Night" every third Friday in the month. It made for one of the more popular and social evenings at Hurst. He remembered one of the scavenging teams bringing back an old-fashioned reel projector and two boxes of 8mm films they'd found while searching the attic of a house owned by a movie fanatic or someone working in the business. They told how the house had been cluttered with film props and memorabilia, photos of movie stars, past and present.

It was the same with the Hurst museum. Scottie made a habit of collecting similar trophies recovered from the local area. From paintings and books to statues and even larger antiques, he considered it their duty to salvage art and preserve it for future generations. The walls of the museum were now adorned with old masters, a Constable together with several impressionist works from Cezanne, Monet and a Pissarro. They even had a piece by Damien Hirst, which divided opinion, but Scottie loved it all the same.

The movies they showed on those special evenings were mostly classic war films and Westerns. There was nothing more modern in the collection, but it didn't seem to matter. They would sit outside on milder spring or summer evenings under the stars. Lying on picnic blankets or deckchairs late into the night, Scottie would operate the projector, changing reels to the groans of audiences. The changes always seemed to come at a particularly gripping cliffhanger moment, scrambling around to locate and mount the next reel. His regulars would never tire of the *Magnificent Seven* or *The Guns of Navarone*. Tommy knew every scene, every line, every word. He annoyed the hell out of whoever he sat next to by mouthing the words and telling people his favourite bit was just coming up.

"Right here we are." Tommy gestured towards two mattresses that lay in the corner on the floor. The beds looked a bit tired, the covers moth-eaten and torn, but they would be dry and safe. They would sleep well tonight, Tommy was sure of it, patting Toby on the shoulder. He clapped his hands and made to leave before remembering something.

"Jack asked me to ask you if you wouldn't mind putting *Lady Lucy* on the river mooring for tonight. Looks like there's a storm coming in." He grimaced, peering out of the window at dark clouds heading their way.

"Thanks, Tommy. Really appreciate it. We're going to be very happy here, aren't we, Toby?"

Toby smiled weakly at Tommy, but didn't look too convinced.

Chapter 17

Terra rested her hand on Nathan's shoulder, standing behind him as he finished up the notes from the meeting. When the last of the other council members had left she sat down opposite, with a sigh loud enough that he looked up, eyebrows raised.

The room was silent other than the sound of the ink pen scratching on the yellow pad and Nathan's shallow, efficient breaths. Terra noticed his tongue peeping out furtively between his lips as he concentrated on the task at hand. She was still troubled by the question of the missing food and curious about the council's response. She didn't trust Liz, but it seemed unlikely that she was implicated in any way. Sloppy and careless perhaps, but she wasn't dishonest. It took a liar to spot another. Liz didn't have the brains or the imagination for it. Certainly no match for Terra. Riley on the other hand... She didn't trust her or Zed as far as she could throw them, which was why she had one of her people watching them and reporting back.

Outside, the early evening rain had eased and grey clouds were being chased away, replaced by clearer skies and the faint streak of a rainbow in the dying light of the setting sun.

Nathan collected the papers, pulling the heavy oak door closed behind them with a metallic clank as the locking mechanism engaged. They slowly descended the uneven stone steps, treading carefully to avoid grooves dug over hundreds of years, where heavy crates had been dragged to the courtyard below.

Two children raced up the stairs past them. The first nearly barged into Nathan. The second one feinted left then right before squirming past, head down. Nathan grabbed the lopsided pile of papers before they could slip from his grasp. Terra stopped and watched the children go with a wry smile, shaking her head.

She froze mid-step, and they both looked up at the sky. Echoing off the walls came a familiar rhythmic hum that made them stare at each other. It was a sound they had not heard for many months. A helicopter. But that seemed totally incongruous, implausible even after all this time.

They hurried down to the courtyard, looking in every direction, trying to place the sound that echoed off the old brick and stone. The metallic throbbing grew louder and louder as the black shape of a helicopter hove into view. Terra got a fleeting glimpse only as it swept over the castle and banked round, making several passes, perhaps scanning for movement and a place to land below.

Dozens of people dropped whatever they were doing and headed out of the main gate, some still holding tools. In a few short seconds, the whole of Hurst had emptied out on to the flat grassy area outside the main walls and stood staring up into the dying light. A young girl was pointing up to the evening sky, following the movement of the helicopter with her finger. Its red navigation lights started blinking on and off as it circled the castle.

Terra didn't recognise the make of helicopter at first. It was long and angular, stealthy and graceful at the same time. Bit like a Lynx. But definitely not like the more portly Sea Kings she had grown used to seeing on rare occasions shuttling in and out of the Royal Navy base at Portsmouth. It was shark-like, powerful and menacing. She had never seen one like this in real life, but had watched enough war movies and the like to know that this must be a Blackhawk or something very similar, which meant only one thing: it had to be American.

Nathan shouted something she didn't catch. He paced over and shouted again, directly into her ear: "We shouldn't take any chances. We should break out the weapons, just in case."

Terra nodded and Nathan ran off to tell the guards to be ready for anything.

Chapter 18

The Seahawk, the navy variant of the Blackhawk, banked over Hurst one more time, its engines flaring as the pitch and direction of the sound changed again, noise funnelling through the gate and reverberating off the walls of the passageway. The helicopter's searchlight slung under the nose powered up, illuminating the landing zone behind the gathering horde. It came into a hover over the flat grassy area, sending dust and loose debris swirling in all directions.

The crowd that had assembled, tightly packed together, retreated a few yards, shielding their eyes from the glare and dust storm that swept over them. A young girl pointed in disbelief. She wore a loose hand-me-down dress embroidered with faded violets. Turning her back to the helicopter, she held the hem of her skirt as it fluttered against her skinny legs.

The Seahawk landed, its twin engines powering down. Its rotor blades began to slow, and the high pitch whine abated rapidly. There was a pause before the cabin door slid open and two soldiers in battle gear jumped down, boots landing heavily on the shingle, automatic weapons held tightly at the ready.

Their faces were obscured by what looked like gasmasks. They were clearly taking no chances with infection.

A well-groomed officer in military fatigues appeared behind them. He strode confidently towards the group, pulling up around ten metres short, keeping his distance. He cupped one hand to the side of his mouth and shouted over the dying engine noise to make himself heard. "Who's in charge here?"

His voice was a little muffled by the surgical mask covering his nose and mouth. There was a slight pause as eyes turned towards Nathan and Terra. The crowd parted to reveal its leaders.

Terra stepped forward, holding one arm half-raised in acknowledgement.

"Ma'am. My name is Lieutenant Peterson from the warship *USS Chester*. Is there somewhere we can speak in private?"

Terra gestured towards the lighthouse. "Yes, of course. Follow me." Nathan put a hand on her shoulder and motioned as if to go with her, but Terra shook her head.

The American turned his back on the crowd, relaying commands to the two soldiers through the microphone in his sleeve. He pressed the earpiece more tightly into his ear, listening for their response. They took up position by the helicopter, alert to any danger.

Nathan and the rest of the Hurst group watched Terra and the officer leave in silence. Once they reached the lighthouse door and went inside whispers from the crowd erupted into a full-scale hubbub.

Toby held his father's hand tightly, trying to read his expression. It was a mixture of hope and excitement. His father reassuringly squeezed his hand, but his palms were hot and clammy.

Chapter 19

The two-hour trip back to Hurst from No Man's Land Fort felt longer that afternoon. Sam and Jack did not speak much. They were both lost in thought, standing side by side in the cramped wheelhouse. A fine drizzle formed specks on the windscreen that joined together in the buffeting wind to make tiny rivulets. A sudden rainsquall lashed against the glass, as the single wiper struggled to clear, half of its rubber blade missing. It did little better than smear the glass every few seconds in jerky motions.

Sam made some tea for them and put some music on to lighten the mood. "More than a woman", one of Sam's favourites by the Bee Gees, strained to be heard over the engine noise and sheeting rain as they belted out in their distinctive falsetto.

The smell of diesel fumes permeated everything. It never failed to make Sam feel a little queasy. The dog-eared charts, the worn cushions, the small cabin with two bunks down below. Everything smelled damp and faintly flammable. Jack drained the last of the tea from his stained coffee cup. Its outside was decorated with a faded photo of his six-year-old godson in his pyjamas. The tea was warm and wet, but tasted of nothing much as the bags had been used multiple times. The powdered milk was borderline revolting. Jack sighed and wondered what had happened to his godson and his sister Pauline. Whether there was any chance they had got out of Winchester in time. He doubted it. There was little enough reason to hope.

The *Best of the Bee Gees* compilation moved on to "Staying Alive". On a better day with a good catch and homeward bound, this song never failed to result in a full-scale disco inferno on the *Nipper*. It was not uncommon to find both men gyrating and wildly bumping hips in the cramped wheelhouse, in a full-on karaoke duet. Today they both listened in silence.

Jack was deep in thought, shaken by what he'd seen at Spitbank. He refused to allow himself to pity, to mourn. To indulge the suffocating sense of sorrow and despair that lurked like a shadow just out of sight. It was up to him to set an example, wasn't it? He couldn't afford to show weakness or self-pity. He was their rock. They looked up to him. He wasn't a religious man, but it made him angry to think that God had allowed this to happen. That good people were made to suffer. That wasn't right. Where was the justice in that?

His private anger was interrupted by a question from Sam. He shook his head as if he could physically dispel these dark thoughts and turned to face Sam, his eyes vacant for a second. "What was that you said, Sam? I was miles away."

Sam had to shout louder to be heard over the noise of the music and the rain, now hammering against the glass and wheelhouse. "Do you think we'll make it, Jack? I mean, do you think what happened at Spitbank could happen to us?"

Jack glanced at Sam and noticed tears welling in his eyes. He looked out over the sea towards Cowes, and Yarmouth beyond, taking a deep breath before answering. "That's up to us, Sam. That's why we take precautions, right? We can't let it happen. The quarantine zone, the code, the rules we live by? We've fought too hard to make it this far. We owe it to ourselves and to each other to survive."

"But we can't live like this forever, can we? How long before they come? Before someone comes to rescue us?"

"What makes you think anyone's coming?" Jack replied indignantly.

"But it stands to reason that others must have survived. Did as we did. Not just here, but everywhere. Maybe other countries weren't affected."

"We've talked about this a hundred times though, haven't we? If they were coming, they'd have come already. Why wait till now? We've watched every day for ships, listened to the radio. We shouldn't give up hope, but chances are no one's coming to rescue us."

He regretted that last sentence, noticing Sam's lip quiver as he fought back tears. Who knew? After all, maybe Sam was right?

"I refuse to believe that," said Sam, shaking his head. "They can't all be dead. What about people in Africa or Australia? Maybe there are whole countries that survived. I reckon someone somewhere has figured this all out. Found the cure maybe?"

Jack nodded and smiled weakly. "That I don't know, Sam. But we can't afford to sit around and wait for help to arrive. It's up to us to make a new life for ourselves, on our own. Maybe one day, they'll come. But until then..." His voice trailed off.

"But, it could be years, right? Or maybe they never come, what then?" His voice sounded brittle again. It had been a long day.

Jack put an arm around his shoulder, looking him steadfastly in the eye, with a smile forming on his lips. "Until then, we've all got to believe they will, eh? Don't we, lad?"

Just then, the radio crackled to life.

"Jack, it's Terra. Come in, over."

He snatched the handset from its cradle, bolted to the wall at head height. He depressed the receiver to speak: "Jack here. Go ahead, Terra."

"How far out are you, Jack?"

"What's up? Why the urgency?"

"There's someone here to see you." Her voice sounded clipped, hard to read.

Jack looked back at Sam puzzled. He wasn't expecting any visitors today. "Who is it, Terra?"

There was a pause, and then they heard Terra's voice barely above a whisper as if she'd moved to somewhere more private, not wanting to be overheard.

"You're not going to believe this." There was a moment of silence and Jack looked back at the radio to check it was still receiving.

"Spit it out, Terra. Who is it?"

"It's the weirdest thing, Jack. But there's an American here to see you. Arrived in a helicopter. Says his name is Lieutenant Peterson. Will only talk to you personally. Says he'll wait. But you better hurry."

"Roger that. On our way."

Jack put his hand on the throttle and nudged the levers forward to make sure they were at full ahead. He was trying to coax every last ounce of power from the two ageing diesel Volvo engines. An American, eh? thought Jack to himself. Well, that's a turn-up for the books. Wonder where he's come from. And what he wants with us.

With the extra encouragement, the *Nipper* surged powerfully through the waves with the tide now behind them, sweeping them back towards Hurst.

Chapter 20

The helicopter sat squat on its haunches beside the lighthouse, its rotor blades drooping slightly towards the ground. A couple of the bolder kids crept closer. They circled the aircraft, pointing and laughing, trying to peer through the window into the cockpit. Inside, the pilot was talking animatedly into his headset, the top half of his face obscured by a grey visor. One of the soldiers whistled through his teeth and gestured for the boys to keep their distance. They got the message and backed away.

Tommy strode over to one of the soldiers, chin up, hands thrust into his pockets. His patience exhausted, he wanted answers and he was fed up of waiting for someone to tell him what the hell was going on. His bravado was paper-thin though and his confidence stuttered, unsure of whether to go through with his plan.

The soldier held up the palm of his gloved hand cautioning Tommy to stop as if to say: "*That's close enough.*"

Tommy's confidence evaporated when he saw the gun close-up. It was a black Colt M4 Carbine, a weapon he had used many times, though never in real life. Playing *Call of Duty* and other computer games, he had a good knowledge of military hardware, enough to know that this M4 was not fitted with the grenade launcher the Navy Seals used. Awkwardly, he extended a hand of friendship, waiting for the soldier to acknowledge him. The soldier remained motionless and left Tommy's hand hanging there. He dropped his hand back to his side, feeling a little foolish. The soldier looked straight through him as if he wasn't there.

Tommy had had enough of this. He sneered back, sizing up the soldier. The American wore dark blue camouflaged combat gear, overlaid with webbing and pouches. Underneath was what looked like body armour, metal plates protecting his chest and abdomen. He reminded Tommy of an American footballer in all that gear, accentuating his size. The soldier was enormous, several inches taller than Tommy, who himself was no midget. He gulped as he noticed the sleeves of his shirt bulging with what Tommy imagined must be heavily tattooed biceps like Arnold Schwarzenegger. A proper corn-fed American redneck, he thought. He laughed nervously, looking down at the soldier's boots and back up at his face, taking in his size again.

There was something about the soldier's attitude and unfriendliness that got right up his nose. Weren't they meant to be on the same side? He felt emboldened, staring in to the mask, trying to eyeball the guy.

The soldier remained static, motionless, like one of the Queen's guards at Buckingham Palace facing a tourist. He repositioned the semi-automatic weapon a little on his shoulder, glanced at his partner and made sure Tommy saw him check the safety was on. He flexed his trigger finger before straightening it again and resting it back on the outside of the trigger guard. Tommy got the message and stepped back, his arms raised, head down submissively.

Behind him there was a palpable sense of excitement, mixed

with anxiety. There were so many questions they each wanted answered.

Scottie was the first to break the silence. "So where have you come from?"

Before the soldiers had time to answer, Scottie's question was quickly followed by a flurry of others as they each gave voice to their hopes and fears.

"How did you get here?"

"Are there more of you?"

"Where's your ship?"

"Are you here to save us?"

"How many survived?"

The soldiers ignored their questions, but Scottie answered on their behalf. "He cannae say. They've been told not to speak to us. Isn't it obvious?"

"I thought we were all on the same side," said Tommy hopefully.

"Clearly not," shouted one of the others, frustrated at the soldiers' refusal to cooperate.

"They're just taking precautions. They dinnae know we're not sick," conceded Scottie.

"Maybe the States didn't get the sickness like we did," said another.

Scottie shouted back. "Naw, Sarah, I wish that were true. Don't you remember? It was everywhere. You must remember. Every major city experienced outbreaks. New York, Washington, Chicago, Los Angeles. Everyone and everywhere. There was nowhere to hide."

"So why would they come if they're not here to save us? Perhaps we've got this all the wrong way round. Maybe it's them that need our help?" Tommy laughed and those around him joined in.

"That's a very good question," repeated Scottie. "Why are they here?"

In the distance, they could hear the low chugging of the *Nipper's* engine just before she rounded the headland and hove into view. Tommy ran down to the jetty and waited patiently to catch the bowline from Sam. Jack turned off the ignition, grabbed his bag and stepped ashore. Tommy fell into step beside him. As they walked towards the lighthouse, he brought Jack up to speed on the events thus far and led him to where Terra and the American were waiting inside the lighthouse.

Tommy knocked lightly on the sun-blistered wooden door, its off-white paint peeling and flaking. They heard footsteps inside and the door opened wide. Lieutenant Peterson was sitting upright and alert at the kitchen table, his face dimly lit by a single kerosene lamp. He held a steaming cup of black tea in what looked like one of Jack's camping mugs he used for fishing trips. The American made to stand and his chair scraped back on the slate floor. He strode over to greet Jack, brushing past Terra who stood warming her back on the stove. The door swung closed behind him, leaving Tommy out in the cool damp evening air of the approaching nightfall.

Chapter 21

On the crest of a man-made bank overlooking the hospital, Zed and Riley were lying flat on their fronts on the grass. Zed scanned the outside of the buildings through some pocket-sized Zeiss binoculars. They were both watching carefully for any movement, hidden from view beside a small coniferous tree, a scattering of daffodils at its base.

They had parked the Land Rover a discrete distance away in a quiet back street and walked the remaining quarter mile. Keeping to the shadows, stealing from cover, they had raced across open ground one person at a time.

Zed passed the binoculars to Riley and whispered, "What do you think?"

Riley took them, put the strap round her neck and slowly brushed aside the daffodils with her free arm to clear her field of view. She did a slow sweep of the hospital buildings, lingering a couple of times before continuing her scan. "You already know what I think." There was an edge to her voice. "I told you. This is a suicide mission."

"We're not leaving Will here," responded Zed tersely, tired of Riley second-guessing him.

She shot him a look loaded with thinly disguised scorn. "You're putting the entire group at risk, and for what? We don't even know for sure he's in there. You want to know what I'm thinking? Is this a rescue mission or some weird macho bullshit? Because that's what it feels like. Take a look around you. Your little 'band of brothers' doesn't stand a chance against these guys. They're better armed and there's probably a whole army of them down there. We go in, there's a strong chance we don't come out."

Zed swallowed hard, trying to master his emotions. He let out a deep sigh, shaking his head. "Riley, you're not listening to me. We're not going in guns blazing, okay? We wait till it's nice and dark and creep in ninja-like around the back where no one's watching. We'll be in and out again before anyone even realises we were there."

Riley laughed sarcastically, but the look in her eyes was deadly serious. "Zed, it's your call. I'm not going to argue with you in front of the others. But I'm just telling you, I don't like this. It's risky. And it's not too late to change your mind and turn back. No one will think less of you. For all we know, Will could already be dead or moved someplace else. It's a big call. What if more of us get captured, or one of those psychos decides to start shooting? What then?"

Zed looked down for a second, clenching his fist, bristling at Riley's condescension. He tore out a handful of grass and held the blades up to his nostrils, inhaling deeply. It was intoxicating, like pure bottled summer. It reminded him of happier times. Mowing the lawn on a hot mid-August day, collecting the clippings, sitting in a deckchair reading the paper, T-shirt off, enjoying the sunshine. He closed his eyes, savouring the memory. He looked down for a second, weighing Riley's words, letting the grass fall slowly from his fingers. He couldn't risk losing another team member, could he? There was no way he could guarantee their safety. He nodded, his mind made up. With a raised eyebrow he answered in barely above a whisper. "We just have to make sure we don't get caught. When have I ever let you down?"

He winked playfully and instantly regretted it. Riley wasn't in the mood. She muttered something under her breath and handed the binoculars back to Zed, sliding down the bank to join the others who were relaxing against a crumbling old brick wall.

Zed looked over his shoulder and watched her go before continuing his surveillance. He swept the maintenance area of the hospital once more. Industrial bins overflowed with hospital waste. A ten-feet-high fence was flecked with bits of newspaper caught in the mesh like a fishing net.

A gust of wind toyed with sheets of newspaper, dancing in the air, sending a cardboard box scraping across the tarmac. Litter carpeted the whole area. In one corner, several vehicles had been abandoned, windows smashed in. An ambulance sat with its contents disgorged around it, tyres deflated, its bay doors swinging open in the breeze. He moved twenty metres to his right so he could get a better look round the corner into the staff parking area. The chimney for the incinerator towered over the main building, a wisp of grey smoke escaping from the rim. There were about twenty vehicles, a few of them abandoned wrecks, harvested for parts or fire damaged. Parked in a line closer to the main entrance, he saw several serviceable cars, trucks and a Tesco lorry backed up for unloading. Further away, he could make out a pair of Range Rovers like the ones he had seen on the high street, parked up under an awning. His hunch had been right all along.

Zed shook his head. The fence was the problem. It protected the whole of the back of the hospital. He had to assume this whole area was regularly patrolled with a lookout on the roof.

This crew was well organised and not to be underestimated. They worked with an almost military efficiency. On his own he backed himself to infiltrate the facility, but with a couple of inexperienced teenagers in tow, he was less sure. Perhaps Riley was right after all. Was he putting the whole team in danger to save one man? It was a big call.

Their best chance of entry was via a tree whose branches overhung part of the fence. If they could climb the tree and shuffle along a sturdy-looking branch then he was confident they could make it over. Their next challenge was going to be getting in unseen and finding where they were holding Will. They needed to find a door or window, somewhere quiet and unseen.

He found what he was looking for on his final sweep: a fire door behind one of the industrial waste bins. He doubted it was still alarmed. It would be protected by a simple metal rod that locked in place top and bottom. The doorway was almost completely hidden from view by the waste bin and a burned-out estate car. They could work on the lock without fear of interruption.

After one hour of observation, he was satisfied that there were no patrols. If they could get over the fence, they had a good chance of getting in without being discovered. He crept back down on his hands and knees to find the others talking quietly, hidden from sight.

They would need to sit tight for another hour waiting for dusk, though not too dark that they couldn't see what they were doing. Torches were a bad idea as they could be seen from miles away and would attract unwanted attention.

The hospital was a prime site and could comfortably host several hundred people, a much bigger group than Hurst. Its location in the town made access to food and stores relatively simple. Zed didn't fancy his chances in a fire fight. Stealth was their best option.

Once inside, Sean said he'd been to this hospital before so knew the approximate layout. The maintenance area was unlikely to be occupied, and from what they'd observed, the overnight patient wards on the first or second floor of the east wing were the most likely places they'd be holding Will. And if not, that was a good place to start their search.

They each checked their equipment. As well as the revolver and the shotgun, they had an eclectic assortment of weapons laid out on the grass from a machete and an ivory-handled dagger to the double-headed mace which Zed still had strapped between his shoulder blades. Riley uncocked the sawn-off shotgun she carried, peered down the barrels to make sure they were clear, loaded two shells and snapped the barrels closed with a satisfying click. In the side-pocket of her rucksack she placed a further box of shells and made sure she had a couple of spares in her hip pocket for easy access. Sean was lying on his back against the rucksack, meticulously sharpening the blade on the ceremonial sword he'd found earlier with a small metal file. He tested the edge with his finger every few minutes to check its sharpness before continuing.

Mila sat cross-legged, watching the others, her back to a tree. Her khaki shorts had ridden up, exposing a three-inch scar on her right thigh. She tied her hair back and picked a blade of grass out of her mouth, wiping it on her knee. Joe sat opposite her and took a long swig from his canteen before offering it to the others. Despite their meagre diet, Joe's early middle-aged spread had proven hard to shift. Everyone else seemed to be losing weight but him. He was fed up of being the butt of their jokes. Lard-ass, fat-boy, tubby. He had heard them all. Tommy told him he was thick-skinned. Deep down, Joe was hurting but too proud to let them know they had landed a punch.

Joe had been watching Mila all day; he couldn't take his eyes
off her. Ever since she'd arrived at Hurst, he'd been mesmerised.
She was at least fifteen years his junior, but she had so much
vitality. She was athletic and slim-hipped and knew the effect
she had on men. Zed hadn't figured out whether Mila and Sean
were just friends or something more. It had been bugging him
for days. She caught Joe staring absent-mindedly and he looked
away embarrassed.

"What you looking at, Joe? Seen anything you like?"

Joe mumbled something back, struggling to hide his
blushes. Sean grinned at the pair of them and mischievously
threw a small stone at Mila, hitting her on her ankle. She looked
up angrily.

"Hey!"

He ignored her protest and whispered, "Don't waste your
time. She ain't worth it."

"Just because I don't fancy you, Sean, don't mean nothing.
Perhaps you're just not my type," said Mila coquettishly.

Zed shushed them and they fell silent. "Let's cut the chat and
switch on. Do you want me to run through the plan one more
time?"

They all shook their heads.

"No, Zed, we get it," sighed Riley.

"And we'll keep going over it until it's locked and loaded."
Zed looked around each of the group, lingering on the two
teenagers, Sean and Mila. "Planning is what keeps us safe."

Zed unfolded the piece of paper with Sean's crude sketch of
the hospital and its layout. "So, let's go over this one more time.
I'm on point. Riley is bringing up the rear. The rest of you stay
alert and focused. Two teams sweeping the first and second
floors, here, here and here," he said, pointing to the overnight
wards on the map. "Hand signals only. We can't afford to make
any noise. If we see anyone, we hide. Don't take any chances.

Okay? Now everyone get some rest. We move out in thirty minutes."

They all nodded. Mila closed her eyes and started humming an old Aretha Franklin tune, "Respect". She finished tying back her long dark hair in a ponytail that reached down past her shoulders and part way down her back. When she was done, she put on a grey baseball cap from her rucksack that cast a shadow over her petite nose and narrow lips. She wore no make-up and had a smear of mud or grease across her left cheek. It didn't matter much. She still looked beautiful. Joe followed her lead and put his cap over his face, resting his eyes for a few minutes.

Zed sat back against a telegraph post and tried to relax. Inside, his heart was beating unusually fast. This was a big call taking an inexperienced team into a well-defended and densely populated environment that he knew virtually nothing about. They would need luck on their side. He looked around the group, weighing up their strengths and weaknesses. From what he'd seen of the new arrivals, they were both fit and able. If they had to get out of there quickly, Joe was the weak link, heavy and slow. He had taught them all what little he remembered about self-defence and hand-to-hand combat. Joe was powerful, threw a good punch. Riley and Sean showed some skill with a knife. As for the rest, he had no idea. Did they even know what they were letting themselves in for? Riley did, Mila looked terrified but was hiding it well from the others. The others were hard to read, but chances were they were all terrified. If they could find out where they were holding Will, then maybe, just maybe they could get him out from right under their noses without anyone noticing. They owed it to Will to at least try.

Zed closed his eyes and ran through the plan once more in his head. It was up to him to get them in and out safely, without casualties. There was no margin for error tonight.

Chapter 22

R iley was the last over the fence. The sleeve of her jacket caught on some barbed wire and ripped. Off balance, she landed heavily on the grass verge below, twisting her ankle a little. The fence rattled behind her. "Nice one, Riley. Get it together," she muttered to herself.

The rest of the group was already at the fire door. Zed started loosening up the frame with a crowbar, splintering the wood around the locking mechanism. It took around ten minutes for the reinforced surround to cave in, and with a loud creak Zed levered open the door a crack. He got his fingers inside and wrenched open the door wider, its rotten base scraping against the concrete floor. Inside, it took a moment for their eyes to adjust to the gloom. They picked their way carefully around some machinery and shelving units. The room was completely dark, other than a rectangle of light from the doorway and from two narrow skylights that cast fading shadows across the machinery.

Double doors led through to one of the main corridors running north to south as far as the eye could see. From Sean's crude drawing of the hospital layout, Zed figured this would take them to the stairwell that led to the upper floors. The corridor was eerily quiet. There was not a soul about.

They regrouped in a consultation room off to their left, huddling together around Zed. He crouched down, one knee on the linoleum floor.

"Where the hell is everyone?" asked Riley.

Zed shrugged his shoulders. "Looks like no one's home. So let's make the most of it. According to Sean's map there's a stairwell just up here, right?"

Sean leaned in, angling the piece of paper towards him to check and nodded.

"Okay. So let's head up to the next floor. Mila, you stay with me. The rest of you go with Riley. Stay together. Let's get this done quickly and get out."

Zed led the way back into the corridor, keeping to the left side and pausing at each doorway to listen. Where the walkway opened out into a lobby area, there was a lone flickering candle in a saucer, but still no sign of anyone.

Riley pointed to a blue sign directing them to the stairwell. She put her hands to the heavy door and put her weight against it, easing it open silently. At the foot of the stairs, she craned her neck to peer between the railings, making sure there was no one coming. Zed was already suspicious. It was all going a little too well. Were they walking into a trap?

At the top of the stairs, Riley cracked open the door to the first floor, listening carefully. She crouched down, her fingers pressed to her lips. They could all hear voices. She opened the door wider and stuck her head around the corner. About thirty metres away she could see half a dozen people, with their backs to them.

They stole across the corridor and waited out of sight. Zed waved Riley forward, encouraging her group to start their search, while he and Mila stood guard and spied on the hospital group. They had no trouble keeping to the shadows. The first floor was poorly lit with candles and kerosene lamps. Skirting around the back of the group, they followed the U-shape until it opened out into a large atrium that overlooked a lobby area. Below them they could hear voices and the unmistakeable sounds of a large gathering, bodies pressed tightly together, feet shuffling and a man coughing.

Zed took up position next to a large pot plant, his senses alert. To their right, around a dozen doctors and medical staff were leaning over the railing listening. A few of the doctors had their arms crossed. Their body language seemed hostile as if they were removed from whatever was being discussed below. Two men in white lab coats whispered conspiratorially, but he couldn't catch what they were saying from this distance.

Zed crept forward, Mila beside him, and peered between the railings at the sea of faces gathered on the ground floor. A couple of hundred heads were facing away from him, craning necks and squinting into the relative gloom to see what was going on at the far end of the lobby. He crouched low but still couldn't see what they were looking at.

The crowd fell silent as a man's voice carried across the room. It was a voice Zed recognised from earlier in the day. Clipped, Mancunian, slightly nasal with a hard edge. The hairs at the back of his neck prickled as he remembered the man in black's face across the street from earlier, his fists clenching tight, remembering what they had done to Bob.

"You all know how hard we've fought to get this far. It hasn't been easy. We've all lost someone or something. But together we're getting stronger by the day. Look around you. We have food, a roof over our heads, weapons, and security. We even have our own doctors to treat us when we get sick. But if we are going to do more than just survive, we need to expand our operation."

There were murmurs of approval and nods from a few of the heads.

"Every day our patrols bring back men, women and children from places around here. Every day we learn about other survivor camps throughout this area. Dozens of them, big and small. Beyond the New Forest, there may be hundreds more groups like us, surviving, holding on, waiting. We have a good set-up here. We have everything we need. So why do we need to change?"

He paused, letting the question resonate with his audience. "Let me tell you why. We have a chance to become something more. To take a lead. To build a new world order based on our rules. No one can tell us what to do any more or how to think or how to act. We don't have to go back to the way things were. We can build something new, something better."

Zed found himself nodding. He sounded a lot like the man he wished Jack would be. He was right. Survival was not enough, but Jack didn't think like that. The man in black's speech crystallised some of Zed's unspoken thoughts and hopes for Hurst.

The whispers below grew to a louder discussion, and another man's voice, deeper and menacing, appealed for quiet in vain. He put his fingers to his lips and whistled sharply until the room fell silent.

"Even now, our doctors are working hard to understand more about the virus, to find a cure. In time, we hope to synthesise a vaccine, however long that takes."

There were louder murmurs of approval as if, for a delicious moment, several amongst them dared to hope that such a vaccine was within reach. He waited for the crowd to fall silent.

"We don't yet know why but certain individuals have natural immunity to the virus. We're getting closer to finding out every day. With the right resources and support, there's no reason we can't find the answer and mass-produce a vaccine. We can start inoculating hundreds, maybe thousands, of survivors. Spreading the word, spreading the cure, not just to the New Forest but also to the whole region. Perhaps even the whole country. Imagine for a second the power and influence that discovery would deliver. Starting tomorrow, we begin reaching out to other groups. We invite them to join forces with us."

A dissenting voice from the back shouted out, "What if they don't want to? You can't make them."

The man in black laughed dismissively, pointing in his direction. "You're right. No one can force them to join us. But..." He paused for a moment. "They would be foolish to stand against us."

There were hoots of derision from those members of the audience who distrusted the man in black and his thinly disguised ambition. He was forced to wait until the raucous noise from the increasingly partisan crowd abated before he could continue.

"There will be those that disagree with our methods. Let them. When they see what we are building, when they hear that we have the cure, when they see what the future holds, then they will understand. Our way of life means growth and prosperity. Security for all. If they join us, then we all stand together, united. They are either with us, or against us."

It was clear to Zed that the assembled crowd was deeply divided. The whole room seemed to erupt, catalysed by the emotive discussion. It seemed like all of their anger, their hopes and fears boiled over with factions shouting at each other. There was some pushing and shoving. Men squared up to each other, fingers jabbed in faces. A couple of punches were thrown, as order rapidly degenerated.

Zed had heard and seen enough. It reminded him of the early days at Hurst before the community coalesced around a common vision for the future. He slipped away from the railing, beckoning Mila to follow him. Together they joined the others, searching the rest of the first floor.

Most of the rooms were either locked or empty. Double doors to a larger overnight ward were barred from the outside with a piece of wood padlocked in place. There was a good chance that this was where they were holding Will. Two small square observation windows were papered over with dried tissue. Riley scratched some off with her fingernail. She heard a chair scrape from the other side and muffled voices.

She peeled off more paper, trying to see inside. Riley jumped back startled as a bearded face filled the square window. He looked dishevelled, his hair grey and unkempt. He started banging his fists on the door weakly. She gestured for him to stop, afraid that the noise would attract attention.

The old man put his face to the crack and whispered, "Please help us." He rattled the handle on the double doors, but they were securely fastened.

Riley looked around the door frame for a key but saw nothing.

Zed joined her at the double doors, thinking Will might be inside. He could make out about a dozen beds with every inch of floor space occupied by men and women. Who knew how long they had been kept there? Judging by the filth and foul stench it had been some time. They looked malnourished. Some could barely stand. They huddled close to the door, appealing weakly to Riley and Zed to get them out.

"We're looking for Will. South African guy?" whispered Zed as loud as he dared.

The old man shook his head. "There's no one of that name or nationality here."

Zed turned to go, but the old man called him back. "Please. Don't leave. You've got to help us. You need to understand what's really going on here."

"What are you talking about?" He frowned at Riley. "Look, we'd like to help you but without the key..."

"Wait, please. You need to get word to the others. They're experimenting on us. Sometimes we can hear their screams. No one ever comes back. Every day, they take one more of us away..."

Zed looked at Riley, struggling to understand. What kind of hospital locked people up and treated them like lab rats? He rattled the padlock and heavy chain securing the makeshift bar, blocking the doors from being opened. "Believe me, we want to help you, but there's nothing we can do. The door is padlocked. I'm sorry. Unless you know where they keep the key?"

"The fat man always has the key on a chain around his neck. He always keeps it locked." He slammed the door again in frustration.

"Look, we'll come back if we can and try and get you out."

They backed away from the door. Zed felt bad leaving them here like this. He knew they were leaving them here to die, to face torture, experiments, heaven knows what. He hurried down the corridor to rejoin Riley and the others who were checking the rest of the rooms on this floor. He couldn't shake the feeling that they had stumbled upon something significant, but the truth was eluding him. What were they doing to them? What did the old man mean when he said they were experimenting on them?

"Come on, let's find Will and get out of this place," said Riley, pulling at Zed's sleeve, eager to leave.

Chapter 23

On the next floor, the two teams split up and set off in opposite directions, sweeping silently from room to room. There was still no sign of Will, and Riley was beginning to lose hope. She had made the grim discovery of a waiting room being used as a mortuary.

Five bodies were laid out in an orderly row with a sheet over each of them. Riley pulled her sweater up over her mouth and tried to avoid breathing in the stench. She lifted up the corner of a sheet covering the body closest to her and recoiled at the sight of a body ravaged by sickness. A young woman's blue eyes stared blankly up at the ceiling. The victim could have been no more than eighteen. Her face was gaunt, her skin drawn tight. Dried blood crusted around her nose and ears. She wore a pale yellow dress with a plunging neckline, her bra strap exposed. Along her alabaster-white left arm was a crop of needle marks, many in small red circles. Riley had seen her fair share of death, but seeing one so young, in the prime of her life, chilled her to the very bone. Judging by the girl's face, she had died only very recently, probably in the last twenty-four hours. She was surprised they hadn't moved the bodies already. Back at

Hurst, they burned the dead to reduce the risk of contamination.

She moved to the next section through a heavy security door with a keypad entry system whose screen was inactive. The sign above the doorway was marked "Restricted Access – No Admittance". To her surprise she found the door unlocked. She pushed on, her senses alert, checking behind her, making sure no one was following.

Riley whipped her head around at the sound of a light tapping from one of the rooms at the end of the corridor. Treading lightly, controlling her breaths as best she could, she leaned against the painted wooden door, listening carefully.

"Hello, is there somebody there?" came a child's voice from inside.

The girl sounded very young and frightened. Zed had been very clear. They were here for Will. They couldn't save everyone. The girl's voice interrupted her moment of indecision.

"I can hear you breathing. Please, can you get me out?"

Riley tried the handle but the door was locked. She got down on one knee and looked through the keyhole. A green eye with long lashes close to the hole blinked back at her. The top lock was basic, the kind Riley knew how to open with a credit card, providing the lower mortise lock wasn't engaged. She checked her pockets but found nothing. There wasn't much call for credit cards any more. She looked around her and noticed a door open to what looked like a staffroom. A nurse's uniform hung next to a cheap white desk with a grey computer monitor, its screen lifeless. She checked the pockets before finding a set of keys with a "lucky eight ball" attached.

On the third attempt, the key turned. Before she knew it, a little girl wrenched the door open from her grasp and brushed past her. She was no more than ten or eleven, with long dark hair, dressed in clothes that looked a size too small for her. She hugged Riley and stepped back to get a proper look. Riley checked to make sure there was no one else hiding inside.

The girl said her name was Adele. She had been brought here a few days ago with her older brother Jamie. They had been separated and she hadn't heard or seen him since. She rolled up her sleeve and showed Riley a series of pinprick-marks on her skin where they had injected her and taken her blood. For the last two weeks she had been held in isolation. She wasn't sure why, but it meant better food and daily injections.

Riley studied the marks on her arm, too many to count. Who would do this to a child? she asked herself. She had worked in the health system long enough to recognise what looked like the arm of a junkie, but why would they repeatedly inject a child? Adele didn't look ill. Why keep her in isolation? Why would they do that? There was no way she was leaving a child to die in this place.

"You're coming with us," said Riley, with a smile. The little girl grinned, revealing a couple of missing teeth. Riley dropped down on to her knees so their faces were level. "First, I have something very important to ask you. We're looking for a friend. His name is Will. He's South African. Do you know where we might find him?"

The girl shook her head and balanced on tiptoes to make herself taller, taking Riley's hand to steady herself.

Sean reappeared from his sweep of the other corridor. He looked Adele up and down, shaking his head. "Who the hell's this? We can't take a kid, Riley. She'll only slow us down."

"I don't want to hear about it, Sean. She's coming with us. We're not leaving her, okay? End of story."

"Fine. She's your baggage." He tutted to himself and wandered off to check the last of the rooms.

"He's okay when you get to know him," said Riley, reas-suringly.

They made to leave but the little girl pulled her back. "Wait. There's someone else. She's like me, Riley, but older. Her name's Stella."

She dragged Riley along. Her delicate soft fingers laced through Riley's, and they stood outside the last door. They tried all the keys, but none of them worked. Riley shrugged her shoulders.

"Sorry, kiddo. We could go back to the nurse's station and try the drawers."

Adele stared down at the floor. Her whole body seemed to sag. She straightened suddenly as if electrified by a thought. She tried the handle and to both of their surprise the door swung open.

There was the sound of coughing, and a young woman sat up in bed, clutching a brown hospital blanket to her bare chest. She glowered at Riley, clearly annoyed at the intrusion. Her eyes darted furtively across to Adele. There was a flicker of recognition, but her expression remained the same: a curious blend of defiance and vulnerability. She looked back at Adele, confused.

"Who is she, Adele?" she said, before addressing Riley directly. "What do you want?"

"She's here to rescue us," said the girl brightly.

"Not exactly," corrected Riley. "We're looking for our friend Will and found you two instead." There was something about the girl that Riley didn't trust. Riley pointed to the door. "All the other rooms were locked. How come yours isn't?"

The young woman yawned and swung her legs off the bed. She reached over and grabbed a top that lay crumpled on a blue plastic chair by the wall. Facing the wall, she dropped the blanket. She was underdeveloped for her age with slim hips and a narrow waist. Her pale shoulders and back were covered in small red marks and dark bruises. Her spine and rib cage were clearly visible as she hunched over. Riley noticed her wrists.

They looked raw and swollen where she must have been tied up previously. The girl threaded her arms through the sleeves of a grey-white sweatshirt with a faded Mickey Mouse on the front.

She glanced back at them, her face half-hidden again by reddish-blonde hair. She looked like a frightened animal, wild and untamed. "They leave mine unlocked because they know I won't leave."

"Are you a prisoner here?"

"You wouldn't understand. It's not as simple as that."

"Try me," said Riley.

"They...they keep me here," continued the girl. "I can't leave."

Riley looked puzzled. "In what way? Are you a patient or a prisoner?" she said scornfully and regretted it. The words just slipped out.

"It's not like that." Her cheeks flushed red. "Look, if I do what they say then everything's fine. They bring me food, treat me nice. But if I don't then they beat me. At first I fought back, but now I've learned to just shut up and let them..." Her voice trailed off.

The girl looked down at her bare feet, wiggling her toes childishly. She was about Mila's age, but pale and thin. Riley walked over and put an arm around her waist. "Come on. Let's get you out of here. You're coming with us."

Stella seemed uncertain. "Please, just leave me here. If they find me out of my room, they'll only beat me again..."

Riley insisted. "We're getting you out of here. Someplace safe. Where you don't have to live like this any more. How did you end up here anyway?"

Stella told them her story in barely above a whisper, stopping several times to compose herself. They'd captured her and two of her friends a few miles from here almost a month back. Her friends had refused to cooperate and were badly beaten. They took them away; she didn't know where. One of the men was kind to her and protected her from the others. She ended up here in this room, sleeping for most of the day, reading books, waiting for the man to visit her. She started to cry, beginning to remember the pain and horror she had been subjected to. Riley had seen this defence mechanism before in victims of abuse. The mind just disconnected. Adele started shivering as suppressed memories came flooding back. Adele walked up to her and hugged her tightly. Nevertheless, Stella seemed uncertain about leaving. They each grabbed a hand and half supported her as her legs grew weak again.

Sean was speechless when they found him. He shook his head at the latest addition to Riley's entourage and walked away. There was still no sign of Will and they were out of time.

Stella pleaded with them to finish up and get out of there. She stood nervously gnawing her fingernails. The "monsters" would be back soon and she didn't want to be around when they came back. Just then a piercing alarm made them all flinch, splitting the air close to their heads. They looked at each other, confused.

There were footsteps coming towards them along the corridor. Riley ushered the group into the nurse's station to the right and took a deep breath. She unhooked the strap securing the shotgun to her backpack and readied herself. She braced the stock against her shoulder like Zed had shown her and waited, half-hidden behind the doorway. As the footsteps grew louder she released the safety catch and put her finger lightly on the trigger.

To her relief, Zed and Mila appeared around the corner. They stood staring at Riley wide-eyed, trying to catch their breath. Mila leaned against the wall, fighting for air. "They're coming," she said.

Zed was cradling his left wrist, grimacing with pain. "We need to leave now."

Stella tugged at Riley's sleeve. "There's another way out. Follow me."

Zed exchanged glances with Sean. "Who are these two?"

Sean shrugged his shoulders. "Don't ask. Riley's waifs and strays," he responded sarcastically and followed the girl.

Chapter 24

Stella led the way as the group threw caution to the wind and hurried down the stairs to ground level. She was light on her feet and seemed to know her way around the maze of passages and waiting rooms. Riley had to shout louder than she dared to get Stella to slow down. Zed and Sean were bringing up the rear and in danger of losing contact with the lead group. Behind them they could hear raised voices. They didn't have time to lose.

Zed's arm was in a bad way. It had all happened so quickly. Mila had been grabbed from behind and in the scuffle to free her, Zed had fallen. In the resulting wrestle with one of the guards, his hand and wrist were badly cut by shards of glass from a glazed partition wall. Mila had undertaken some running repairs. She had torn off a strip of her shirt and bandaged the injured arm as best she could. As they ran, blood soaked through the cotton material and dripped on to the grey linoleum tiles, leaving a clear path for their pursuers to follow.

At the bottom of the last flight of stairs, they regrouped. Riley counted heads. She noticed Zed cradling his left arm and wincing in pain. He nodded. "Don't slow down on my account."

At the doorway to the main corridor, she nudged open the heavy fire door and checked the path ahead. There were voices off to the left and torchlight dancing along the walls. To their right there was silence. In all the commotion, Riley couldn't be sure whether it was left or right. Which way led back to their point of entry?

Joe caught up with her and pointed right and they wasted no time in making it back to the way out through the maintenance area. They passed the machinery and out through the fire door, which hung broken on its top hinge. Stepping outside into the cool night air, it was pitch black. A light mist hung in the trees. An evening dew had transformed the grassy slope ahead of them into a sparkling carpet of water droplets hanging from every blade. Out here, the alarm sounded distant and strangely muted. Their eyes adjusted quickly to the darkness. They couldn't risk using one of the torches they carried as it would only reveal their position.

Riley pointed towards the large oak tree overhanging the fence. Sean reached it first but found the lowest branch was out of reach, almost ten feet from the ground. He got down on his hands and knees and waited for Riley. She straddled his shoulders and with a grunt he lifted up. Once she'd manoeuvred herself into a secure position, gripping the branch with her thighs, she reached down with her right hand and, with Sean's help, she levered Adele and then Stella to join her. Joe was next. It took a couple of attempts before Sean took a deep breath, changed position and tried something different. Offering his cupped hands instead, Sean braced with one knee and manhandled Joe high enough for the others to pull him up, puffing and soaked in sweat.

While the others shuffled along the branch and over the fence to safety, Riley kept watch on the fire door. They were out of time. In the distance, near the front entrance, she could already see a small crowd gathering, squinting in to the darkness, their lanterns held high. Mila went next, which just left Zed and Sean.

The fire door to the hospital burst open and three men emerged into the night. Beams of light from their powerful torches arced round in opposite directions trying to locate the Hurst group.

Turning to Zed, Sean insisted, "You're first, big man. With that busted arm, there's no way you can pull yourself up on your own. We don't have time to argue."

"I'm not leaving you behind, Sean."

"I'm lighter and I can jump higher. Come on, quickly." He stooped down and cupped his hands together. Zed didn't like it but Sean was right. He planted his right boot, and with one hand, he reached up as high as he could manage. Between Joe and Riley they heaved Zed's large frame up and onto the branch, which creaked loudly under their combined weight. Zed gasped in pain as his body weight rested briefly on his busted arm.

The torches flashed up to their position, homing in on the noises, and two of the men hurtled across the parking area towards them. A wild shot rang out, going high and wide. It was enough to get the rest of the group scurrying with more urgency along the branch and jumping down the other side of the fence.

Sean stood underneath the branch swinging his arms, looking up hopefully, readying himself to jump. Riley and Joe reached down as far as they could, their fingers splayed wide. Sean looked back over his shoulder at their pursuers. It was now or never.

He leapt as high as he could but only managed to touch fingers with Joe, who couldn't grab hold. He landed heavily and readied himself for another go. The armed men were close now and a volley of automatic fire peppered the tree. Riley and Joe lay flat against the branch and were unharmed. Adrenaline pumping through his veins, Sean leapt as high as his tired legs would allow. Riley managed to grab hold of his wrist as Joe reached down and held the sleeve of his jacket. They hoisted him up slowly, straining, every sinew bursting. Sean reached up and got a hand on Joe's back, a smile forming on his face. He relaxed just a fraction, sensing safety within his grasp.

Riley felt Sean's whole body tense as a shot found its mark in his lower back. His grip weakened and his arm went limp as his life force drained rapidly. As best they tried, they couldn't pull him up. He became a dead weight in their hands. They tried one last time, but his eyes were closing and with a shriek of despair from Riley, Sean's clammy fingers slipped from her grasp as he fell on to the grass below. His limbs crumpled awkwardly underneath him, lifeless. Riley stared after him, shaking her head in disbelief.

"He's gone, Riley. Come on," shouted Joe.

She was sobbing lightly and he had to drag her away. Gunshots splintered the wood over their heads but they were well hidden in the foliage. Zed stood next to the fence, his revolver raised, taking careful aim at the approaching group. He fired a single shot but didn't stay to see if he'd hit his target. The others followed Zed up the bank and away to their rendezvous point in the dip by the wall.

Zed paused on the crest of the bank and counted the others in. As they passed him, he put his hand on each shoulder, a weak smile on his face as he welcomed the new arrivals, Stella and Adele. Riley was the last to arrive.

He reached out to pull her up the bank, but she ignored his help.

"Don't touch me."

He shrugged and took one last look at the hospital before turning away. Their pursuers hadn't tried to follow them over the fence, but he could be sure they would assemble a search party to hunt them down at first light. There was no time to waste.

Chapter 25

Will's eyes flickered open and he sat bolt upright, gathering his senses. The fire alarm was real, not part of his restless dream. It must be running off a back-up system. There was a commotion outside his room. He was still handcuffed to the bedpost, but stood up as best he could, straining to hear the raised voices outside. If it was a fire, someone would come and let him out. They wouldn't just leave him in here, would they? Unless someone had deliberately activated the alarm.

He tried to ease the handcuffs over his balled fist, but it was no good. He had tried a hundred times already. How did they manage it in the movies? Was there a trick to it? He spent a couple of minutes hawking up some spit from an otherwise parched mouth and throat. He spat on his wrists for lubrication, but however he contorted his thumb and fingers, the result was the same. His thumbs were red raw from his repeated efforts.

Footsteps in the corridor were followed by the familiar jangle of keys. The handle turned slowly and the door was flung open. The shrill wail of the alarm alternated pitch every second. He shielded one side of his head with his free hand. Three men surged into the room. The first had a swagger about him, an automatic rifle held at the stock, pointing towards the ceiling. Behind him stood the man in black. He pushed the door closed, his head cocked to the side.

"Looks like your friends from Hurst have come to rescue you. Shame they won't find you," he mocked.

The two henchmen laughed sycophantically. The thug at the rear of the group looked on menacingly, chewing gum, with a fixed snarl on his face. He looked like a down-on-his-luck bouncer from an after-hours club. He was dressed head to toe in paramilitary black. They all were. Perhaps it was the fashion round these parts. Paramilitary black was the "new black".

The thuggish man's cold impassive eyes stared straight through Will as if he wasn't there. On his shoulder was a discoloured patch where an epaulette or rank insignia would have normally been. This had to be the man they called "Copper", though he'd never seen his face until now. He was barrel-chested, with a thick neck, the hint of a colourful tattoo just visible above the collar and heavy stubble on his chin that had been shaped into a goatee. He shaved his scalp to within a millimetre. Will could smell the man from where he sat. There was a heady blend of sweat, alcohol and unbridled aggression. He was a powder keg of testosterone with a short fuse, just ready to go off. The back of Will's neck throbbed as a timely reminder of why not to provoke a psychopath without good reason.

"Well, your friends have made a wasted journey. They won't find you up here. They're looking in the wrong place, for starters. Don't worry, Will. We'll catch them, that's what these guys do, catch people. Isn't that right, Copper? They'll hunt them down wherever they're hiding. And when we do, we'll send them back to Hurst in pieces."

It struck Will that the man in black was trying just a little too hard. Trying to appear tough and ruthless. Playing a part and

living up to the expectations of those around him, but not altogether convincingly. He tried to imagine what this man might
have been before the breakdown, before the world had
collapsed in short order, like a house of cards. He imagined a
downtrodden middle manager in a regional sales office. Years of
frustration heaped upon him, of being talked down to. A broken
family. Absent parents. A messy divorce. Children taken away
from him by court order. A lifetime of bitterness and disappoint-
ments that had led to this point: the birth of a sociopath. Will
pitied and despised him in equal measure. Wasn't he just the
product of a dysfunctional society, one that had deserved to
collapse? Or maybe he was just born an evil bastard. Nature or
nurture, he wasn't sure which.

The man in black half turned towards Copper, but didn't
look directly at him.

"Take your squad and go set up a little surprise party for
them. A roadblock on the main road. Don't bother bringing me
prisoners. I want them all dead."

"You got it." Copper turned and left with a final dead-eyed
glance at Will.

"Oh, he really likes you," said the man in black. "I think he's
dreaming up a fitting demise. Something truly monstrous for
you when your time comes."

"And I'm saving something special for him too." Will blew
him a kiss, but it was too late. Copper didn't look round and kept
walking out the door and down the corridor, his rifle slung over
the shoulder at his side.

"You're not learning, are you? Didn't we teach you some
manners last time? I can forgive rudeness once, but if it's
repeated, well, then..." He wandered closer and caressed the
back of Will's head, lingering around the fresh dressing which
was already stained a light brown. He pressed his fingers into

the wound, enjoying Will's discomfort. "We wouldn't want those stitches opening up again, would we?"

He grabbed a fistful of Will's hair and jerked his head backwards. Will looked up undaunted as the man in black sneered. "You people are pathetic, holed up in that big castle, cowering behind your high walls. You really think they're going to stop my men from barging in there and taking it for ourselves? I've always fancied myself living in a castle. Perhaps I'll choose a wife from your group, eh? Or maybe I'll just slaughter the whole lot of them." He pointed to the handcuffs and gestured to the other man. "Unlock him from the bed but keep the cuffs on. We're going for a little drive."

"If you're going to try and make me talk about Hurst again, forget it."

"No need. You told us everything we need to know, not that you'd remember. One of the doctors here injected you with a potent cocktail of drugs that would have made a condemned man sing like a canary. Let's just say you were more than helpful. I'll be sure to tell all your friends before I kill them that you were the one who gave up all of Hurst's secrets."

Will looked confused. He had absolutely no memory of what he'd said, but at the back of his mind, he was beginning to think he'd told them exactly what they'd wanted to know. He knew Hurst's defences like the back of his hand, having repaired walls, fixed drains and leaking roofs, even fortified doorways over the last few weeks. There were a couple of places where, with a grappling hook and some climbing skills, you could get over the castle walls unseen. Once inside the main wall, a single person could get in and open the main gate to a larger force. There were only ever a couple of guards at night, a single patrol every hour. The castle would fall. There was no question. Unless. Unless he could get a message to them first and make sure they were ready to repel the attack.

"Whatever you think you found out, whatever you think I told you, you don't stand a chance. Your plan will never work. Hurst has never fallen in more than five hundred years. It's a fortress. Don't go thinking you can just waltz in there and everyone will lay down their arms and surrender. They'll fight to the death to protect what's theirs. I can assure you, they're heavily armed and the castle is well defended. Your men will die and you will lose. My life is unimportant."

The man in black was puzzled by Will's bravado. He studied the side of Will's head, leaning closer. There was almost a tenderness to his voice. "I admire your spirit, Will, really I do. In fact, that's exactly why you'll be my personal guide. I want you to see the whole thing."

They heard footsteps in the hall. A man in a white coat was running down the long hallway towards them. It was the same Indian doctor who had treated Will earlier. The guard stepped into his path, blocking the doorway and motioned for him to slow down. Raj skidded to a halt, bent over, hands on knees, just outside the door, trying to get his breath. Just then the alarm fell silent and a sense of normality returned. The guard glanced at the man in black, who nodded, and he stepped aside to allow the doctor to pass.

"The girls are gone," said Raj, his voice trembling.

"What girls?" asked the man in black.

"The test subjects for the clinical trials. Adele and Stella."

"Why weren't they locked up like the rest of them?"

Raj looked uneasy, unsure how to respond. "Perhaps the guards were listening to your address, like the rest of us."

"Amateurs," he spat in disgust. "How many times have I told them?" He ran his fingers threw his hair, and scratched the back of his neck, lost in thought for a few seconds.

Will seized on this setback. "What's so special about those

girls? You have hundreds of prisoners here. Why them?" he asked provocatively.

The man whipped around in a flash. He drew a knife and held it to Will's throat. The blade nicked the skin so that a tiny pinprick of blood trickled down his neck.

"Did you have something to do with this? We thought they were here for you, but perhaps you were the diversion all along."

Will shook his head, breathing heavily, leaning his head away from the point of the blade. "I assure you, I had nothing to do with this," he whispered.

The man in black slapped Will hard across the face with the back of his hand, knocking him backwards on to the bed. Turning back to face the guard and doctor, his face was red, his throat and chest blotchy with rage.

"Those girls are critical to our research. We've got to find them. Do whatever it takes!"

"Don't worry, sir, we'll get them back. We know where they're heading at least," said the henchmen, attempting to calm him.

"They can't have any idea how important those girls are to our research," added the doctor.

"Hurst will pay for this," swore the man in black.

Chapter 26

I t was Stella's idea to head to New Milton. They couldn't risk going back to Hurst that night. Chances were their pursuers would try to follow them, or worse, set an ambush. Now they all knew full well what "being a prisoner" really meant at the hospital, none of them wanted to see the place again. New Milton was as good a route as any. It was a longer way round, but the road through the forest would be deserted and safe.

Stella sat in the back seat of the Land Rover Defender with Mila's head cradled in her lap. Mila was inconsolable at having left Sean behind. Every few minutes she repeated, "I can't believe he's gone."

Stella's own relief at escaping the clutches of her captors had given way to what Riley said was post-traumatic shock. As a precautionary measure, Stella's mind seemed to have disconnected itself from the vivid memories of her ordeal. In a semi-catatonic state she mechanically stroked Mila's hair, staring unblinking out of the passenger window. She gave no indication that she was listening as they replayed every moment of their escape and debated their options for the night. Staying out in the open was high-risk. They could break into a farmhouse off the main road and hope it was unoccupied, or drive through the night on unfamiliar roads to make it back for dawn.

"Chewton Glen." Stella's voice startled them and they all looked round.

"Do you mean *the* Chewton Glen?" asked Riley. "It's a big country hotel not far from here. Is that the one you were staying at before you were caught?"

Stella nodded, avoiding eye contact, preferring to look out the window into the forest. "They're good people. They know me. We'll be safe there. They'll take us all."

Zed looked at Riley and Joe who both nodded. No one had a better plan.

"Works for me," said Joe.

Zed drove in silence, hunched over the wheel trying to see where he was going in near darkness. He couldn't risk headlights, but a crescent moon cast a pale light where it pierced the tree canopy. The Land Rover bumped along at a slow crawl, heading away from Lymington. He found his eyes adjusted quickly and if he took it really slow then driving in the dark was just about manageable. In a couple of places the road surface had been washed away or badly broken up by tree roots. Several fallen trees blocked their route, but they were able to go round them where the forest floor was dry and firm. In a few more years, this whole heavily wooded section might be completely impassable. Littered with fallen branches and storm debris, it already looked more like a farm track than a major highway.

It was past midnight and while the rest of them dozed in the back, Zed and Riley took it in turns to drive. Travelling at walking pace, it took them more than an hour to reach the outskirts of New Milton. They skirted the main town centre, sticking to smaller country lanes, completely deserted as they had hoped. Approaching New Milton from the west, Zed stopped the car in the middle of the road by a small bridge over a brook and switched off the engine. In the silence, they could hear the sounds of the stream and a light breeze that made the tall trees to their right sway gently. They were not far from the entrance to the hotel, and Zed put his hand on Stella's shoulder to wake her. She startled, crying out in alarm before remembering where she was.

"Are we there already?" Stella looked around her in the darkness, but didn't see anything she recognised.

"The Christchurch Road entrance is just up here on the left," he said, pointing up the roadway.

"How do you want to play this, Stella? We don't want to go surprising anyone."

"Just turn your lights on and approach the gate so they know you're coming," said Stella naively as if it was the most normal thing in the world.

"Sure, that might work," said Riley sarcastically.

Stella stared back at her, puzzled. "Why wouldn't it? Isn't that what normal people do?"

Riley shrugged and nodded at Zed.

"Okay, you know these people. Let's do it your way and see what happens." Zed sounded exhausted. He'd lost a lot of blood and was struggling to stay awake. The thought of a good meal and a bed for the night sounded worth the risk. "But if this doesn't work, let's make sure we're ready to return fire and hightail it out of here, yeah?"

"These are my friends," reassured Stella, who seemed to have perked up a bit, so close to home.

Zed powered up the spotlights mounted on the roof of the Land Rover to ensure even a half-blind person would see them coming. He revved the engine a couple of times, its diesel notes straining and insistent, just to make sure they could hear them too. Stella leaned forward in her seat, recognising the high brick wall that surrounded the stately grounds to her former home.

A large grey delivery truck was parked in front of the main gates, completely blocking the way in. Zed left the engine running and half opened his door peering out to see if there was anyone around. The entrance looked disused and he was about to suggest they try the other entrance when he got the distinct impression they were being watched. A powerful searchlight clicked on, nearly blinding everyone in the Land Rover. The passengers sat shielding their eyes with their hands.

A female voice on a megaphone cleared her throat and instructed them to get out of the car. The four doors opened wide, and very slowly Zed and Riley stepped away from the protection offered by the door. They squinted into the light, hands above their heads, trying to make out the silhouette of a person on top of the truck.

The rear passenger door opened and Stella jumped out with a big smile spreading across her face.

"Is that you, Stella? You have got to be kidding," said the surprised voice on the megaphone.

Stella could barely contain her excitement, hopping from foot to foot.

"You made it back. I don't believe it. We thought you were dead. Wait, where are the others? Are Tabs and Martha with you too?"

Stella shook her head. "They're still at the hospital. They captured us a couple of weeks back. Four guys jumped us. These guys got me out and we came straight here."

The searchlight powered down and for a moment the entrance plunged into semi-darkness again before some lower level sodium flood lights flickered on, bathing the group in a soft orange glow. The woman disappeared from view as she climbed down the back of the truck, squeezed through a small gap between the wall and the bumper and strode over to Stella. Standing a few feet apart she looked her up and down before throwing her arms round her. "It's so good to see you. Welcome back, girl." She slapped her a few times on the back for good measure. They did a little dance together, jumping up and down, clutching each other.

"Thanks, Mary. These are my friends. Joe, Zed, Riley, Mila and the little one there is Adele. They rescued me. I promised them shelter for the night."

Mary strode over to the rest of the group and shook each of their hands. The warmth of her welcome cooled somewhat when it came to Zed and Joe. She looked them up and down and shook her head. "The boss ain't gonna like you being here. Let's leave that till the morning. Any friend of Stella's is a friend of mine."

She fished the keys to the truck out of her breast pocket and climbed into the cab to move it out of the way. Winding down the window, she shouted over the noise of the engine starting up. "I'll meet you by the main entrance."

The truck rolled a few yards back, just wide enough to allow the Land Rover through. Mary leaned out of the window and waved them through. Zed headed up the long gravel drive towards the main hotel building in front of them.

Two figures stood warming their hands in the cold night air, rifles slung over their shoulders. One wore a long winter coat and a beanie hat, with leggings and trainers. The other had a Russian-style fur hat with flaps covering her ears. It was nearing the end of their shift and they both looked chilled to the bone. It was still very early. They paced around, stamping their feet, waiting for the Hurst group to unload their rucksacks.

"Let's get you inside before we all freeze to death," said the girl in the fur hat. "Emily will find you a place to sleep for tonight." She looked back at Zed with mild surprise, like she hadn't seen a man in a long time. "You'll need to surrender those weapons."

Inside they stood next to the reception desk lit by a large kerosene lamp, waiting to be patted down. When it was Riley's turn, the sheer volume of knives secreted about her person raised eyebrows. For the first time in as long as she could remember she felt naked without a weapon, other than a small blade hidden behind her belt buckle.

Stella led the group through the hotel, holding high a Tilley lantern to light their way to an extravagantly furnished drawing room hung with gilded framed paintings showing Victorian watercolour scenes. Zed collapsed on the nearest leather sofa and swung his legs up, not even bothering to unlace his boots. He was dead on his feet.

Stella handed Riley the lantern together with a pile of folded grey blankets. "I'll see you all in the morning for breakfast."

"Are you not staying with us?" asked Adele.

"Not tonight. I've got a lot of catching up to do. You'll be fine here. Sleep well," said Stella, before turning to leave, locking the door behind her.

Riley shrugged. Perhaps it was just a precaution to stop them roaming the hotel in the night. She draped a blanket over Zed who was already snoring, his mouth open, and bedded down for the night in an armchair. She pulled the blanket up around her chin and was asleep within seconds.

Chapter 27

Riley was the first awake. She watched the others sleeping, enjoying the silence and the sunshine streaming through the window. Mila looked so peaceful, curled up in a ball in the corner. Riley's attention flicked back to Zed, his forehead damp with perspiration. With a sharp intake of breath, Adele sat up, her eyes wild.

"Bad dream?" asked Riley.

"Every night, I have the same dream," replied Adele, blushing as if this was an admission of weakness. "I always wake up just as I'm about to find out what happens."

"How frustrating. What's the dream about?"

"In my dream I can fly, soaring above a city, reaching out to touch the clouds. I swoop down just above the rooftops, skimming the grass, dancing in the air. Then all these people start coming out of the houses. Families and children pointing up at me, laughing. It's like all their prayers have been answered. But then this fire starts burning me up from inside and I'm being pulled towards a black hole in the sky. I have no way of stopping it." There was a pained look on Adele's face as if she was still troubled by the vivid images intruding into her waking thoughts. "What do you think it means?"

"Dreams are funny things." Riley shrugged. "They're your subconscious mind making sense of what's been going on, replaying images, sounds, things that troubled you. Remember, you've seen a lot of weird stuff for someone so young. Your time in the hospital, the drugs they were giving you, maybe even what happened to your family during the outbreak. Heck, I wouldn't worry too much about it. We all have bad dreams from time to time."

There was a momentary look of alarm as Adele hunted for something that was no longer in her pocket. Searching around her in the folds of the blanket, she found a treasured memento of home and family. She clutched the key ring in the shape of a rabbit's foot to her breast, closing her eyes and mouthing a few words in gratitude, before inserting it deep into a jean pocket for safe keeping. Riley looked over at Zed who was still dead to the world, but the others were stirring, yawning and stretching, taking in their unfamiliar surroundings.

Looking outside, a flower bed ran directly beneath the window. Pink roses brushed against the lower half of the glass. There was a red dawn, scattered clouds hurrying across the horizon. Was red sky a good or bad omen? Riley could never remember.

There was a quick-fire rap at the door. Adele was there first. She rattled the round brass handle but found it locked. Stella's voice from the outside sounded flustered and told them to stay put while she ran back to grab the key from reception. The white panelled door swung inwards to reveal Stella standing there, smiling. She picked Adele up off the floor and hugged her tightly while apologising to the group for locking them in overnight. The sisters who ran the place were very particular about their rules, she explained.

Stella showed them to a large bathroom on the ground floor where there was a chemical toilet, buckets of fresh water from the stream and towels that were clean if not exactly fluffy by hotel standards. The Hurst group took it in turns to wash, relaxed in each other's company. Joe averted his gaze as Mila stripped to her underwear. Riley unwrapped a bar of lavender soap, releasing the sweet smell from its waxy cover, stopping to inhale the fragrance. It had been some time since she'd smelled anything so delicious.

When they all had finished scrubbing their hands and faces, Riley dressed in the same clothes, stiff and scratchy against her skin. They trooped back out into the hallway where Stella was waiting to take them to the main dining room. There, they found almost a hundred people eating their breakfast, tightly packed together at tables set for four or eight diners. Something seemed odd to Riley as they squeezed between chairs. All the eyes in the room followed their progress.

The room fell quickly silent. One person dropped a knife clattering onto the floor, but didn't reach to pick it up, a look of surprise frozen on her face. They seemed to be staring at Zed and Joe in particular. Riley was puzzled. Had they not seen strangers before?

Stella knocked at a door with a frosted glass panel that led into a private dining room. Warm sunlight bathed this end of the hall which looked out over orderly, well-maintained flower beds bordering freshly mowed lawns.

On the opposite side of the table facing the door they found the Mother Superior Stella had warned them about. The description was spot on. She was a formidable woman with a handsome face, that some might say was a little too masculine, long and angular. The sister reminded Riley of Princess Anne. At either side sat two nuns, studying each of them carefully. Sister Theodora was conservatively dressed in a spotless black habit and white wimple. She held her head high, peering through glasses perched on the end of her nose. Her thin, almost colourless, lips were expressionless as she waited for the group to settle. Riley noticed clear intelligent blue eyes that would once have been striking. She found herself staring at a wart on the Mother Superior's forehead.

"Thank you, Stella. That will be all."

Stella paused as if she had expected to stay with her new friends. She smiled weakly at the group, did an odd sort of curtsy and left.

"Please have a seat." She gestured to the six seats facing her. "Do help yourself to coffee." She slowly stretched out her hand to extend their hospitality to the new arrivals. "There is milk, flatbread, apples and pears too."

She waited for them to take their seats before continuing. "Stella tells me we owe you a debt of gratitude for returning her to us. For that we thank you. As I'm sure you can imagine, we are not accustomed to receiving strangers in the dead of night."

She watched in silence as the group gave in to their hunger. They devoured the flat bread and fruit, their first meal in nearly twenty-four hours. When there was nothing left, they slumped back in their chairs, satiated. Joe wiped his face with a frayed sleeve where juice and milk had dribbled down his chin into the folds of his neck.

Sister Theodora leaned forward, demanding their full attention. "Now I want to be perfectly clear. In these unusual circumstances, we have bent our rules to give you food and accommodation before you head back to Hurst Castle. Stella of course stays with us."

Zed frowned at Riley, puzzled by her choice of words. "That's up to Stella, don't you think?"

The sister ignored Zed and continued to address Riley. "The rest of you ladies are most welcome to stay. You will find that we are mostly self-sufficient." She smiled her best, most welcoming smile. "The local stream provides us with unlimited drinking water. We have a small generator for electric lights in the winter. As for food, we grow our own vegetables and have cows, chicken and sheep. We even have a swimming pool we fill in the summer. Here at the Chewton Glen, our residents are free from the worst excesses of man and the evil he has brought upon us."

Riley blinked, her eyes narrowing, not entirely sure she had heard the sister correctly. "Wait, you said only the women were welcome to stay. What about these two? Are they not welcome?"

The sister cleared her throat, her eyes remained fixed on Riley, piercing and cold. "Oh dear. Perhaps Stella did not explain. This is a sanctuary for women. We do not usually allow men here at all."

"Since when did men become the root of all evil?" asked Zed accusingly.

The sister laughed, seemingly amused by the naivety of the question. "Since men began subjugating women to their will. Since the dawn of time. Since Adam corrupted Eve. We have chosen a life free from violence, brutality, rape and murder. Men have no place in our lives here."

The two nuns on either side nodded their approval, but remained silent.

"So while men, women and children are dying in their millions outside these walls, you dare pass judgement on half the population?" continued Zed incredulously. He rose unsteadily, gripping the table for support, his chair scraping on the flagstone floor.

"If we are to survive and rebuild, we all must make sacrifices."

"It's hardly a balanced community, is it? How do you expect to rebuild?"

"I assure you, we're more than self-sufficient. Our residents have learned the skills they need from books. We no longer have need for the brute strength of men."

"It's not very sustainable though, is it? What about the next generation? How do you expect to have children?" asked Riley.

"Men still have one small role to play in our future. And for that we keep several for breeding purposes."

"Breeding?" snorted Zed. "We're not animals, you know? You can't just lock people up like that, like you would a bull or a stallion and let them out when you're ready for them to breed."

She ignored his attempts to provoke her. "I assure you that is precisely what we have chosen to do." She smiled, revealing even, white teeth, unblemished by the vices of nicotine, sugar or alcohol. There was something about her that struck Riley as vaguely sinister, like something out of an Alfred Hitchcock movie.

"You're off your rocker, you are. Stark raving bonkers." Zed wagged his finger at the sister, but his eyes had started to glaze over. He seemed to sway a little on his feet and slumped back into his chair. He winced with pain, cradling his wrist. The colour had drained from his cheeks.

Unmoved by Zed's weakened state, the sister's thin lips relaxed a little in triumph. "You should get that arm looked at immediately. You are clearly not a well man. In the circumstances, we shall forgive your lack of manners and ingratitude. Tell Stella to take him straight to the infirmary."

Riley was shaking with rage, incensed by the sister's condescension and intolerance. "You really are a piece of work."

"My child, please don't take this personally. The world has changed."

"Since when did the principles of kindness, charity, forgiveness, generosity and all those other things they teach you in Sunday school cease to apply?"

"We all must adapt to survive. We are in unchartered waters.

God created this virus to punish mankind for centuries of wickedness. Rather like Noah and the Ark, the sickness is simply God's way of purging the world of its vices: wealth, power and violence. We will all be washed clean, so we can start again. Here at Chewton Glen we are doing God's work, building a new Ark, if you will."

"Those are just Bible stories," interrupted Adele, her child-like voice defiant. "There's no such thing as God."

"Silence, you impudent child." The sister stiffened, ready to strike the girl before she noticed Riley primed, on the edge of her seat. She softened her tone. "Children should be seen and not heard."

"Don't you see? The virus doesn't discriminate between good and evil, between black and white, between men and women. The virus doesn't judge. It kills everyone. The few that survive run and hide, like you, here."

"God watches over us and protects us. We're not hiding from anything or anyone. We're simply waiting until the purge is complete and we can start again. Stella is very much a part of that regeneration."

"I don't know who you think Stella is. But I can assure you she's not the person you're making her out to be. She's seen things no girl her age should see. They had her locked up at the hospital, at the mercy of her captors. She was abused, mistreated, God knows what."

Riley pulled up Adele's sleeve, revealing the collection of red marks that covered her arm. "They experimented on them, took their blood, injected them. They had hundreds of prisoners there. These two are the lucky ones."

"What they do in the name of science is their business. There's nothing I can do about that," replied the sister, adjusting the folds of her dress. "Now she's back with us, Stella's safety and wellbeing is my responsibility. Stella means a lot to us here. She is one of the chosen few, and we are very relieved to have her back with us. It's out of the question that she should leave again."

Riley leaned over the table and glowered at the sister. "Stella is free to do whatever she wants. No one is going to stop her coming back to the castle with us," insisted Riley, helping Zed to his feet.

"Are you threatening me?" challenged the sister, seemingly amused by the suggestion. "It would be highly inadvisable for a girl in her condition to over-exert herself."

"Wait. Are you saying...?" Riley paused, turning the idea over in her mind. "You mean to say, Stella is pregnant?"

"Precisely. She's part of our regeneration programme. She was impregnated before she left and we are most pleased to get her back."

Chapter 28

Riley and Stella waited outside the infirmary for the nurse to assess Zed's injuries. She asked about the circumstances of his injuries and whether there was any chance of blood poisoning, perhaps from a rusty blade or metal. Riley wasn't sure how it had happened, but agreed that was possible.

"We've put him on a drip to replace lost fluids, but I'm afraid he's much too weak to move today. He'll need bed rest for several days to get his full strength back," explained the nurse.

The strain of the last twenty-four hours had crept up on Riley. She suddenly felt overwhelmed and exhausted. Stella reached out and took Riley's hand in hers, leaning her head on Riley's shoulder. "I'm sure he'll be fine. He's a fighter."

"I've never seen him like this before," said Riley in just above a whisper. Inside she was shaken up.

"He should really be in a hospital, where they can care for him properly," continued the nurse.

Riley and Stella looked at each other and laughed. "We're not taking him back to that hospital, don't worry about that. He'll just have to stay here and get better. We appreciate everything you're doing for him. Is there anything we can do?"

"He's dehydrated but the drip should replace some of those lost fluids and deal with any infection. I'm doing the best I can with what I've got here," she said, shaking her head, her eyebrows raised, as if she disapproved of the violence that had caused these injuries. "We should see an improvement in the morning."

Riley grimaced and put her hand on the nurse's shoulder. "You've been very good to us. Thank you."

The nurse smiled. "I'll keep an eye on him, don't you worry. You'll be the first to hear when he comes round. I'll try and let him sleep as long as possible. It's nice and quiet up here, so he shouldn't be disturbed."

The main staircase and ornately carved wooden banister curved round as it descended into the lobby area. Standing on the bottom step was one of the sisters, her arms crossed, as if she'd been waiting for some time. Riley was still angry from their earlier encounter and in no mood for another confrontation. This sister seemed different; she had a warmer disposition than the authoritarian Sister Theodora. She looked a few years younger than Riley. It was hard to tell, she could only see her face, but Riley guessed mid-twenties. She had well-proportioned features, a dark complexion and round gentle eyes. Stella introduced her as Sister Imelda.

"Please, call me Sister Mel, everyone else does. I understand that the man you came here with is not well enough to travel."

"You could say that. He is on a drip with a nasty fever. Needs to rest up before we move on."

"That's most regrettable. Bearing in mind he was injured saving Stella, Mother Superior has agreed that you can all stay until his strength recovers."

"That's good of you. Thank you," said Riley, genuinely grateful but mindful there would be conditions attached. "What about Joe?"

The sister cleared her throat. "Sister Theodora has insisted that..." Her voice trailed off as if she didn't know quite how to say what had to be said. "Look, we are all grateful for everything you've done, but...the Mother Superior is adamant that Joe be confined to quarters, in the stables at the far end of the complex. Sister Theodora's decision is final. Our terms are non-negotiable, I'm afraid." Sister Mel's bottom lip quivered ever so slightly, revealing her discomfort at the awkward position she found herself in.

"Doesn't look like we have a choice, right? It's the sisters' way, or the highway?" mocked Riley, infuriated by their intransigence.

"Please don't shoot the messenger, Riley. I don't make the rules. Sister Theodora does. I just get the unpopular job of enforcing them." She shrugged.

"I still don't understand why you all put up with her. You could leave, go someplace else. Why do you stay here? You don't have to live like this."

"Isn't it obvious? Because followers need someone to follow. Sister Theodora does what she believes is right. She is doing God's work. And the women here respect her."

"But the whole 'no men' thing is medieval. A breeding programme for goodness' sake? It's inhuman to keep men, or anyone for that matter, locked up like that. How do you square that with your values as a Catholic and a Christian?"

"None of us like it, Riley, but we're doing this for the greater good. And Stella here is part of that. She's been chosen to become a mother, to give birth to the next generation. To be part of our future."

Stella looked awkward as they talked about her, avoiding eye contact.

"And did anyone stop to ask Stella and the other girls whether they wanted to be part of this? She's just so young, for goodness' sake. Being forced to have babies at her age. They're still kids."

Stella looked up, her eyes heavy with tears. "I was chosen, Riley. But it was also my choice. You don't understand. I want to help, to be part of this, to make a difference. Don't you see? I volunteered for this."

"I guess not. I think you're all certifiable."

Just then, there was a small commotion as Joe emerged from a corridor with his hands tied in front of him. The guard was a squat buxom woman in a blue polo shirt and khaki shorts, with a ruddy complexion. She pushed him forcefully from behind. Joe lingered for a second beside them. "This is ridiculous. Apparently, I'm a danger to the community and can't be trusted to keep my hands to myself. I need to be locked up, Riley, in the stable, like an animal. These people are doing my head in."

"I'm so sorry, Joe. Listen, it's just for a day or two until Zed's better. Do it for Zed, yeah? We don't have a choice. I'll come see you later on. Try and stay out of trouble."

Joe was led away still grumbling, prompting another poke in the back from the stocky woman. He glanced over his shoulder and raised an eyebrow, breaking into a low whistle mimicking the theme tune from *The Great Escape*, which drew a snigger from Stella and Riley. The guard was not amused and hurried after him, tutting.

They followed Sister Mel outside to a large vegetable patch where three women, with large wide-brimmed straw hats and white smocks, were planting potatoes and carrots in neat rows that stretched ahead of them in newly turned earth. A rusting metal wheelbarrow stood next to them, spilling over with cabbages and potatoes, still covered in earth.

It was still early morning, but a spring sun was already beating down. Riley rolled up her sleeves and started rubbing her hands together. She tapped the nearest worker on the shoulder, who finished her planting before removing her gloves and giving Riley her full attention. She had a kind, gentle face, her eyes glinting with the exertion of her activities.

"Sorry to disturb you. We were wondering if we can maybe help you." She turned to Stella to explain. "Listen, if we're going to stay here for a couple of days, they may as well give us something to do."

"We wouldn't say no. There are some Wellington boots and gardening gloves in that shed over there. You might want to get changed first," said the woman, sitting back on her haunches.

"Good idea. Why don't we go and grab the others?"

Riley and Stella hurried off to the orchard to find Mila and Adele, where they were talking with two teenage girls in the shade of a large apple tree. Mila was asking them a flurry of questions about life at Chewton Glen. The older of the pair called herself Gina, introducing her friend as Lexie. They were both local, from just up the road in Christchurch, and had known the sisters from their church group.

"Not like we're particularly religious or anything, it was just something our mums made us do on Sundays. Course they're not around to tell us anything these days." Gina nudged Lexie in the ribs and they both giggled girlishly.

"So, come on," said Mila. "Dish the dirt on the whole 'no boys' thing. Two young girls like you? Pull the other one."

Gina and Lexie exchanged furtive looks. Lexie shook her head at Gina, imploring her to keep quiet, but Gina couldn't help herself. There was something about Mila, a sense of mischief that made it all right to tell these strangers everything, even if it meant getting into trouble. Gina looked like she was dying to tell someone and why not these two outsiders?

"Right, we'll tell you okay, but this goes no further." She leaned in close. "These boys we know, right," she gave a little laugh, "they live just round the back over there, in that big house. Sister would go mental if she found out. One day, we saw them through the fence and had a little chat with them, we did, didn't we, Lexie?" Lexie nodded coyly, her fingers fiddling nervously with the acne on her chin. "And, we've met them for a drink a couple of times. They bring the booze and we let them have certain favours in return. Ain't that right, Lex?" Lexie shook her head, but Gina was emboldened and wasn't stopping now. Her eyes blazed with brazenness.

"What sort of favours?" asked Adele from a distance, hanging on their every word. They'd forgotten she was there.

"Never you mind, little one, this is grown-up talk. Lex gave both of them a little kiss last time, didn't you, Lex, you little minx."

Lexie was mortified, her face flushed with shame, but there was a defiance about her, as if she was relieved someone else knew what they'd been up to. The secret had clearly been burning inside her.

"But aren't you worried about infection?" asked Mila in a moment of seriousness. "How do you know these boys haven't got the sickness? Aren't you putting your whole community at risk?"

"I ain't thought of it like that. Suppose you're right. Still, if we were going to get sick, we'd have got sick by now, wouldn't we?"

"Back at Hurst we have to follow quarantine procedures," added Mila. "It's dull but necessary. All new arrivals have to be kept apart for forty-eight hours before they're allowed in to the camp."

"We'd be in so much trouble if the sisters found out," said Gina, clearly worried.

"Found out about what, Gina?" said a disapproving voice. No one had noticed the silent approach of the Mother Superior, her hands thrust behind her back.

"Nothing, sister. We was only talking," said Gina, blushing scarlet.

"I doubt that very much. You will both come and see me in my office after lunch. And you," she said, pointing at Mila reproachfully, "may I remind you that you are a guest here. I would ask that you not lead our girls astray."

Mila started to defend herself but the sister cut her short. "Stella, take our guests back to the house and give them something useful to do. The Devil makes work for idle hands."

"We were just offering to help with the planting," suggested Riley, by way of support.

"Indeed. Or you could try the kitchen. Anna could use your help peeling potatoes. Now off you go," encouraged the sister.

"Thanks for nothing. Getting me into trouble like that." Gina tutted, leaving Mila open-mouthed, protesting her innocence.

Chapter 29

Four vehicles parked up outside the Ship Inn on the quayside in Lymington. Around a dozen men dismounted, unpacked their gear and headed inside. The mood was relaxed, but they moved with quiet efficiency and purpose.

Will was hauled out of the back seat, his hands still tied, and made to wait by the VW van while the guard finished his cigarette. He watched the man in black as he shooed at a nearby seagull. The seagull glided a few yards away and voiced its displeasure, its mocking call echoed back from the row of buildings that lined the quayside. Several other gulls swooped down and joined the first in a shrieking chorus. He kicked wildly at the nearest one almost losing his balance.

"Bloody seagulls. Go on, get lost."

The quayside was much changed since the last time Will was there. He remembered visiting yachts moored three-deep at the jetty, fishing boats unloading their catch to waiting lorries, children's faces daubed with ice cream and old ladies sitting on park benches, feeding scraps to pigeons. Gone were the days of easy meals for scavenging seagulls. Like many creatures grown dependent on humans, centuries of learned behaviours were hard to shift. Yet, old habits die hard and the seagulls blindly followed the men around, opportunistically waiting for something dropped, hoping for a scrap thrown their way.

The guard stubbed out his cigarette and pushed Will through the doorway into the semi-darkness of the pub. The windows were boarded up at the lower level, reinforced with wooden batons nailed in place. Behind the bar counter, the former landlord, an elderly man and his thirty-something daughter, handed out snacks and drinks to the group from the hospital.

Copper's squad set up camp in the family restaurant area towards the back. They were already discussing this evening's sortie, disassembling and cleaning their weapons, loading bullets into magazines, unpacking and repacking pouches in their webbing to ensure there was nothing loose that might rattle. Stealth and surprise were critical to their success. One man unpacked an ordnance survey map, marking up positions and approaches with a red marker pen.

The man in black joined them, greeting members of Copper's group, slapping one on the back. The man twisted round, perhaps resenting the unwanted contact, before recognising who it was, and feigning a smile. Copper was over in the corner, smoking a Cuban cigar, a gift the publican had welcomed him with. It struck Will as a small token but an important mark of respect for his position as de facto leader of the group. Copper spun the empty cigar tube between his stubby fingers on the darkly stained varnished surface and laughed at one of the men's bawdy jokes. He never took his eyes off his leader, studying his movement and easy mannerisms like a vulture watching its prey, biding his time.

"Any sign of the Hurst team?" asked the man in black. He stood in front of Copper, legs wide apart, like a cowboy. Attached to his belt was a large bowie knife in a sheath with a black leather strap secured to his thigh. The strap looked uncomfortable to Will, poorly fitted and pulled too tight.

"No, nothing. Complete waste of time. We waited all night and came here at first light."

"Where are they?"

"Perhaps they went via New Milton. Or we got there too late, who knows?"

"It doesn't matter now. We'll find them sooner or later. We know where they're heading. Are the boats ready?"

"Yeah. We're good. We're set to leave at dusk." He snatched the map from the other table and laid it out in front of them, smoothing out the creases. "Our pilot, Trevor, says it's no more than half an hour from here." He pointed to the fisherman's quay on the chart. "Tide's with us. We'll head round in three groups. First group's with me in the R.I.B. We'll take a wide sweep past the salt marshes and out into the main channel before swinging up here and attacking from the south at what should be slack water. We've got all the gear you wanted, and Griff here has done some rock climbing in the past. He says that the castle wall shouldn't be a problem. Then your group stays inshore and brings the main group via the sheltered Keyhaven side and wait for our signal by the main gate. According to our friend here," he pointed at Will, "resistance should be minimal. Couple of guards at the main gate, two-man patrol on the wall. Once they're taken care of, the castle is ours."

"Good, good. Well done, Copper. I can't wait to see the look on their faces. Remember, we need the two girls alive. As for the rest of them, well, I'll let you and the boys have some fun. Let off some steam. Save their leaders for me. They know what's coming to them after their little jaunt last night."

At the other end of the bar, next to a smashed-up cigarette machine, there was a dusty old piano. One of the men from the hospital wandered over and lifted the lid. He tried a couple of keys and found the piano was in relatively good working order. Flexing his fingers, he took a moment to get his bearings and launched into the introduction to *Skyfall* to the muted cheers of the rest of the assembled company. They stopped what they were doing to listen in awe. Music was such a rarity these days.

Copper took a long draw on his cigar and blew a perfect smoke ring that glided across the table towards the man in black. A broad grin stretched across Copper's face. He must be relishing the thought of flexing his muscles and getting some action, thought Will.

Will made himself comfortable on the bench seat under the window, wondering how on earth he could get a message to Hurst to warn them before it was too late.

Chapter 30

Tommy left the lighthouse and hurried after Jack. Terra and Sam were already on board the *Nipper*, stowing their luggage and topping off the fuel tanks from a five-gallon yellow jerrycan.

Since emerging from their meeting with Lieutenant Peterson, Jack and Terra had both been monosyllabic. Tommy watched them whispering. What were they keeping from him? He already had a hundred unanswered questions buzzing around his head.

"But I still don't understand. Why is Peterson gathering together all the leaders from each camp? To discuss what exactly? Are they here to rescue us? Are they part of a relief mission? Please, Jack," implored Tommy.

"The American told us it's all classified, for our ears only," said Jack. "He said it's a matter of national importance. We're not meant to talk about it, even to you. All you need to know is that we'll be gone for a night. That there's a 'Summit' being held on the Isle of Wight and that Terra and I are invited."

Terra put a hand on Tommy's shoulder. He was almost beside himself with curiosity. "Listen, I know this is killing you not knowing, but it's for the best. There are people who don't want this meet to happen. People who would do anything to stop this alliance. Trust no one, that's what he said. There are other forces at work here that should not be underestimated."

"What other forces?" asked Tommy. "Do you mean like the French? Or are we talking the Russians, or maybe the Chinese?"

"He didn't say, Tommy. But it stands to reason that the Americans' presence here will attract others, both good and bad. Anyway, listen, we've already told you too much. You're to tell no one about any of this. If people ask, say that we've gone to see Anders on the *Charlotte*. There could be spies, even here at Hurst. People who would kill for that information."

"Okay, okay. But, Jack, you know we can be trusted. How long have we all known each other? Two years, give or take?"

Jack smiled in sympathy but turned on his heels and started walking again. There was nothing more to say. Jack climbed the small steps covered with old carpet and half hurdled the *Nipper's* gunwale, athletically for a man of his advancing years.

"Trust me, Tommy. This is good for Hurst. You know we've been trying to broker an alliance with the other survivor groups for months. This is our chance. If the Americans can pull it off, it will ensure peace, trade and co-operation for months, maybe years. Even if there's the smallest chance of that, we need to be there, at the negotiating table when that deal is brokered."

"And if it's not, what then?" cautioned Tommy.

"We've got to try, Tommy, you must see that. Hurst is isolated and weak on its own. Joining together would secure our future."

Tommy nodded but he didn't look too convinced. Terra came up behind him and put her arms around his shoulders. "Listen, we promise to tell you everything we can when we get back. Until then, you and Nathan are in charge. Try and keep a lid on the rumour mill, won't you? We'll get word to you when we're on our way back tomorrow morning. But remember, the transmitter range isn't great so you'll probably see us before you hear us."

Tommy's body language spoke volumes. He hated being left in the dark like this. He stood shoulders slumped, forlornly watching their final preparations, like a scolded child.

Sam cast off the bow as Jack unlooped the mooring line at the stern and handed it to Tommy. The *Nipper's* bow drifted out in the tide as Jack hurried back into the wheelhouse and put the engine lever ahead slow. The *Nipper* responded with a churning of water astern, propelling her slowly out into the main channel, heading east towards Cowes and Osborne Bay beyond. Tommy raised his hand in farewell and watched them disappear from view behind the lighthouse.

Jack knew the way with his eyes closed. He'd passed Osborne House a hundred times, the former residence of Queen Victoria. He'd visited the National Trust property with his teenage son many years ago. Back then, Osborne House had been maintained in all its Victorian splendour and open to the public. It was a bygone relic of the opulence and prosperity of the British Empire preserved in aspic for future generations. Jack remembered the place well from his previous visit. The stately home encapsulated all the glory and decadence of the British Empire at its height in the nineteenth century. Back then the Empire had covered a quarter of the entire globe. He remembered the tour guide telling them proudly that in Victorian times "the sun never set on the British Empire". The whole place spoke volumes about the unbridled patriotism that prevailed at the time. Right now, he snorted, the British could barely manage a cup of tea, let alone rule the world.

Until the breakdown, Osborne House had been a popular

visitor attraction with beautiful landscaped gardens, manicured lawns and ornamental ponds. Planted orchards ran down to a beach that looked back across the Solent towards the mainland. Sam and Jack had moored off that beach for a swim so many times, sunbathing on the foredeck of the *Nipper* on their way back from fishing trips or visits to No Man's Land Fort.

Jack had no idea what had become of Osborne House itself. He imagined it was likely home to a group of some description. The Isle of Wight and its islanders had suffered terrible hardship and total collapse of law and order, same as everywhere else. They had been hit hard by the virus, but their isolation had somewhat insulated them from the resulting chaos and violence that followed. The sense of unity and community afforded by its island status, together with its physical separation from the mainland, meant that rival groups were a little more willing to work together. There were fewer raids and less pressure from a starving population, less competition for resources.

On his travels, Jack had met several different groups on the island. There were dozens of them, scattered along the coastline and inland. The Isle of Wight was rich in farmland, with hundreds of greenhouses growing tomatoes, cucumbers, and other vegetables and fruit. It had its own vineyards, breweries and dairy farms, meaning there was an abundance of food in the early days, with groups gathered around farm buildings and smaller villages. Yet, over time the crop yield had collapsed. Most of those greenhouses had fallen into disrepair, growing wild and untended, with hundreds of hectares of vegetables rotting in the ground. Ripened tomatoes died on the vine, with no one left to harvest them.

Jack had heard whispers of a rising power, a man they called Briggs. Like so many on the mainland, opportunists with a thirst for power, Briggs had formed a colony of former inmates from Parkhurst Prison, near Newport at the centre of the island.

He had begun to expand his sphere of influence, forming alliances where possible. He gave short shrift to those who stood against him. Would Briggs be present at this gathering of leaders? It seemed plausible. Jack wondered which of his friends would make the trip to Osborne and which would stay away, suspicious of change, of outsiders, of the Americans, preferring to keep things as they were.

Terra joined him in the wheelhouse and put an arm around his waist. She put her head on his shoulder and gave him a little peck on the cheek. Terra loved their infrequent trips away from Hurst where they could be relaxed in each other's company, free from the prying eyes and expectations of others. At the stern, Sam stood coiling the mooring lines and stowing the food and supplies they had loaded in the lockers. He watched them with some small degree of affection. He had once confided in Jack that Terra reminded him of his mother. A proud, fiercely Catholic woman, resettled on the south coast of England from Wexford in southern Ireland. Jack knew Sam's father had died when he was very young, yet his mother was stoic in her grief. She simply got on with it, holding down three cleaning jobs and looking after four children under the age of fifteen without complaint. Terra had that same indefatigability and quiet resilience he knew Sam admired.

Sam poked his head round the doorway to the wheelhouse and tapped Jack on the shoulder. "I've been wondering about those Americans. Why do you think they're really here?"

Jack shrugged his shoulders, trying to bat away the question. He wasn't in the mood for a long drawn-out discussion. Sam tapped him on the shoulder again. "What was so special about the Isle of Wight that they would organise a meeting at Osborne House?"

Jack shook his head, claiming ignorance, but he had been thinking the same thing himself. He looked over his shoulder at

Sam. "Best thing we can do is not get our hopes up and get on with it."

Sam nodded and stooped to pick up a long thread of seaweed, throwing it over the side, before wiping the slime on his trousers. Behind them Hurst grew smaller by the minute until, when he looked back again, it was just a black line on the horizon. A castle surrounded by the tidal waters of the Solent, and the tide was just beginning to turn.

Chapter 31

S am engaged the windlass, and the anchor chain rattled out of the forward locker, splashing into the sheltered waters of Osborne Bay. At the stern, Jack was breathing heavily as he used a foot pump to inflate a six-person grey inflatable Avon dinghy. He squeezed the sides, gave another few pumps and secured the nozzle with a twist as he detached the mouth of the pump hose.

Between them they manhandled the inflatable over the side. Holding the painter loosely, the dinghy flopped on to the surface of the water, skating a few metres before jerking back. Jack lowered the stainless steel ladder and supported Terra as she clambered down, handing her the rucksack and holdall.

Sam passed Jack the wooden oars which he inserted one at a time into the hard rubber rowlocks. Jack anchored his feet against the sides of the inflatable, took a quick look over his shoulder to get his bearings and started pulling for shore.

"Keep your eyes peeled, Sam. We'll signal if we need you. First sign of trouble, cast off and head for deeper water. Wish us luck."

"You'll be fine. Terra will keep you on the straight and narrow. See you tomorrow."

The blades of the oars dived gently beneath the surface and drove them forward. It was no more than fifty metres to row and, sheltered from the south-westerly, they surfed the shallow waves, gliding gracefully inwards. When they were three metres out, he stowed the oars and they coasted the rest of the way in, bumping gently on to the sandy beach. Jack stepped ashore in his dark blue, leather-lined boots, standing ankle-deep to help Terra before reaching to grab their bags.

They dragged the dinghy above the tide line, littered with seaweed, flotsam and jetsam, frayed rope and plastic bottles. He tied the painter to a large iron ring secured to a concrete post. The lower branches of an ancient oak caressed the surface of the water as each wave came to a gentle end, swirling amongst its foliage.

They started the climb up to the main building, passing an old-fashioned bathing carriage where Queen Victoria and her ladies were said to have changed to enter the water, their modesty preserved, unseen by other bathers. A "Punch and Judy" booth was overturned by the winter storms, paint peeling from its red and yellow stripes. Its bright red wooden roof was holed in several places, revealing where an entertainer would have operated multiple hand puppets for the delight of small children and grown-ups alike. They climbed the dusty path past thickly wooded slopes, arboretums and meadows filled with wild flowers, fields of poppies and daisies.

They caught their first glimpse of the grand Italian-style palazzo house with its twin towers and sweeping steps leading up to the terraces, courtyard and entrance above them. The Victorian gardens were once the pride of the island, boasting flowers from all over Europe, surrounded by shrubs beautifully clipped and shaped. Today the flower beds were overgrown with weeds, the shrubs yellow and bushy. The ornamental ponds and fountains were dry or clogged with algae and weed. A koi carp lay belly up, twitching on the surface, bloated and rigid. Jack wondered why no bird had helped itself to a ready meal and then noticed how silent it was here. There were no birds.

They walked past magnificent statues, many of which were bullet-ridden; handy targets for bored guards with nothing better to do. Some statues were missing arms or legs, others were more or less destroyed. Terra looked nervously at Jack but he patted her on the back reassuringly as if to say "It's going to be fine."

On the top lawn, a rusted old Sikorsky helicopter perched proudly, its rotor blades drooping languidly towards the grass. It barely looked airworthy, and Jack doubted whether it had made it very far. Its pilot was leaning lazily against the cockpit door watching them both climb the steps towards him.

A guard at the side entrance waved them over and patted them down for weapons or anything else secreted about their person. He was thorough, thrusting his gloved hand deep into the furthest recesses of the rucksack. When he was satisfied, he thanked them both and pointed towards another guard by the doorway to a stone-paved corridor that echoed with their footsteps. The walls were lined with empty picture hooks and outlines of the framed portraits and artwork that had once hung there. Jack wondered whether they had been looted or simply removed for storage.

A magnificent reception room took Terra's breath away. It was like walking into an Indian palace, complete with ivory carvings, shields and swords mounted on the wall. Many were engraved silver and ornate copper works. Several of these trophies were missing, leaving dusty outlines. Terra stood and stared at the ceiling, beautifully sculpted in white plaster. She had never seen anything like it.

Jack tugged at Terra's sleeve and guided her towards the assembled group at the far end of the room. The local men were well dressed, beards trimmed and hair combed or brushed back. They were talking animatedly, cut-glass champagne flutes in their hands. At the centre of the group holding court was Lieutenant Peterson, wearing full dinner dress. His military whites and medals were resplendent, his cap tucked under his left arm.

Peterson broke off his conversation to welcome them both. "Gentlemen, I'd like to introduce you to Jack and Terra from Hurst Castle. Jack, I suspect you already know most of these guys. This is our host, John Simpson."

Jack nodded and shook hands, a little awkward with all this formality. Peterson handed Terra and Jack glasses of champagne from a silver tray and led them round the rest of the group.

"I told you I should have put on a frock," whispered Terra, self-conscious in her tired woollen jumper and blue jeans.

"You look beautiful," he replied, squeezing her hand.

"Why didn't you tell me we were coming to a party?"

She wore no make-up other than the lipstick she had the foresight to apply before leaving the *Nipper*. As the only woman here, Jack had no doubt she would light up the room. Terra had spent most of her life surrounded by men. She thrived in a man's world. She always got what she wanted. There was something self-contained about her, a bold confidence. She knew just when to turn on the charm, to have powerful men hang on her every word, but also when to stand firm. Jack had never met anyone quite like her before. He watched as she flirted conspicuously with their host, touching his arm and laughing at his laboured attempts at humour.

More people were arriving all the time and the room reverberated with conversation and the sound of popping champagne corks. Jack stood by the window, observing the group. He had to pinch himself to believe what he was seeing. People were acting like the outbreak had never happened, getting swept up in the moment. The champagne was going straight to his head. The bubbles, the fizz, the whole thing made him feel nauseous.

Terra spotted him standing alone and made her excuses, breaking off from conversation to join Jack. "What's up, Jack? You don't look like you're enjoying yourself."

His eyes darted around the room, checking to see if anyone else felt this whole evening was a little surreal. "This all feels contrived, Terra. The champagne, the cheer. It's like none of them know what's going on in the real world, over there on the mainland."

Terra smiled, but recognised Jack's discomfort. "Oh, they know all right. They've had it just as bad as us. They're just putting on a little show for our VIP American friend. A taste of British razzmatazz. That's all. Why not enjoy yourself, let your hair down? Drink their fine wine, enjoy their canapés, hear what they have to say. Come on, where's the old Jack I've heard so much about? The one who could drink the pub dry and still ride a bicycle home to bed? Come on."

She playfully nudged him in the ribs and reluctantly he responded to her encouragement. They rejoined the others, recharged their glasses and forgot themselves, at least for a little while.

There was a small commotion in the corridor as a late arrival protested loudly about being searched. With a loud greeting that silenced the whole room, Captain Anders Bjørklund from the *Maersk Charlotte* strode in, his arms raised high, First Officer Victor by his side. Anders walked straight up to Jack and slapped him on the back before hugging his friend. He ignored the trickle of champagne that dribbled down his back from Jack's glass. Victor's greeting was a little cooler. He appeared bored and aloof.

Last to arrive was Captain Armstrong, accompanied by two other Royal naval officers. They were formally attired in navy mess dress, dark blue dinner jackets, bow ties, all brass buttons and gold braid. The captain stiffly saluted Lieutenant Peterson and then warmly shook hands with the assembled guests, introducing himself and his officers. Jack watched this incongruous exchange over Anders' shoulder and despite the obvious charade, he couldn't help but feel a renewed sense of hope. He wondered whether the combination of these two military organisations would be sufficient to restore some semblance of order to this blighted region. His eyes narrowed as he studied their body language that oozed bravado and confidence. He'd been around the block enough to know that appearances were deceptive. Most military men he knew couldn't organise a piss-up in a brewery.

One of the officers did a double take when he spotted Terra, excused himself from his group and tapped her on the shoulder. She turned around and looked surprised. He seemed delighted to see her. "Good heavens. I'm sure we know each other? You're a friend of Allan's, aren't you?"

Terra looked back at him blankly, regaining her composure. "I'm sorry, you've got me there. I'm not sure..."

"Yes, I know," he continued confidently. "We met at a party a few years back. Deborah, no, Debbie, isn't it?" he said, searching, trying to make the connection.

Terra blushed and glanced towards Jack. "I think you have me confused with someone else. Excuse me." She drained her glass with a shaking hand before rejoining Jack. She feigned a smile, but looked decidedly uncomfortable. "Silly fool. Thought I was someone else. Could you get me another champagne, please?"

"Sure, coming right up," said Jack, patting her on the wrist. On his way to the bar, he noticed the officer still staring in Terra's direction. He seemed positively bemused by her failure to recognise him.

Chapter 32

The dinner had been delicious. Grilled trout followed by spit-roasted chicken, complete with all the trimmings. Each course was washed down with a succession of fine wines, the like of which Jack had never tasted before, each requiring a different glass. Even the cutlery had been overwhelming. Three separate forks, knives and spoons, all of different shapes and sizes in polished silver, fit for a royal banquet. He had watched his partner carefully to ensure he chose correctly. He quickly figured out that if he started from the outside and worked his way in, he wouldn't go too far wrong.

When the plates had been cleared, their host, John Simpson, stood and formally welcomed everyone before inviting Lieutenant Peterson to say a few words.

The American officer wiped the sides of his mouth with a napkin, touched John on the shoulder and shook his hand before slowly rising. He looked around the room at the forty-plus guests, making eye contact with several of them before starting to speak.

"Ladies and gentlemen, you honour me with your hospitality this evening. It is some time since I have enjoyed an

evening quite this much, in surroundings anything like as grand
as the former residence of a King and Queen of England. For
those of you who don't know me, my name is Lieutenant Peterson. I am the commanding officer of the United States
warship, the *Chester*, an Arleigh-Burke class guided missile
destroyer currently at anchor just off Portland Bill. I've spent the
best part of the last twenty years serving my country, sailing the
seven seas. My daddy was a navy man. You could say I have salt
water in my veins. During that time, I've seen action no less than
seven times in Iraq, Afghanistan and Syria. I had the honour of
serving alongside Her Majesty's Royal Navy on countless
missions and exercises, including a six-month secondment to
the destroyer *HMS Daring*. I have visited the White House, met
the president, visited some of the finest embassies in the world. I
guess I never thought I'd see anything like that again, so this
evening has been nothing short of spectacular, and for that I
thank each and every one of you, but particularly our host, John
Simpson."

Peterson invited the rest of the room to join him in another
round of applause. He checked the scribbled notes he had in
front of him on a small jotter pad and flipped to the next page.

"But let's get down to business. We didn't come here for a
party. I invited you here to discuss the future. I know a lot of you
have a million questions, and I thank you for your patience and
for coming here today."

He took another sip of water and then drained the glass, his
hand shaking almost imperceptibly. He proceeded to recount
their story since the *USS Chester* left her homeport of San Diego
for the last time nearly three years ago. Their tour of duty took
them to the Middle East, patrolling the shores of Yemen and
Ethiopia, protecting commercial shipping against pirates. They
had made stops in Egypt, Sudan, Qatar and Kuwait. When the
first outbreak occurred, the *Chester* was ordered to head with all

available speed to Karachi in Pakistan to provide humanitarian aid and to airlift US service personnel from trouble zones.

"When the evacuation order came, it came too late for my crew. Many had already been in contact with the locals in the performance of their mandated duties. Much of the local population was already infected. By the time the scale of the outbreak became clear, it was too late. Despite our best efforts to enforce quarantine and instigate security protocols, the virus wreaked havoc on board the *Chester* and there were one hundred and fifty-two fatalities, including our commanding officer, XO and chief engineer. The rest of the crew barely made it out of Karachi alive."

He bowed his head and paused to gather himself before proceeding.

"I know we've all had it bad. We've all suffered. We've all lost friends and family. I have a wife and two kids back in California. I haven't heard from them in more than two years since the US went dark and all civilian communication ceased."

There were a few whispers at this disclosure. Many amongst them still clung to the belief that the global outbreak had been contained and the US had been better prepared and able to immunise and stop the spread, at least better than in the UK. Peterson appealed for quiet.

"The reason we are here, as I told each of you personally when I visited you in your camps and homes, is to make a stand against the virus, right here on the Isle of Wight. This island is one of the biggest in the UK and was, until recently, the second most populous. It means the island is uniquely qualified for our purposes."

He paused to let his audience digest his words. "Camp Wight, as it will now be known, will be the first of many such bases we will need to build, but first we'll need to create a virus-free safe zone here on the island as a launch pad for a wider clean-up of the UK mainland. None of us should be under any illusion of the scale of that challenge. It will take months, maybe years, but if we work together we will succeed.

"Our first job is to secure the Isle of Wight. Then we can set up quarantine zones to process newcomers. That means building accommodation, providing humanitarian aid, ensuring security and safety, health and hygiene. Camp Wight will be a fresh start for the UK and one we'll look to replicate throughout Europe. Gibraltar, Cyprus, Majorca, Iceland, Sicily. To be successful, we will need to train civilians to perform the roles needed to get the generators back online, to secure running water, to restart food production, to plant crops, to nurture live-stock, to build towards self-sufficiency on the island."

A dissenting voice from the back shouted out, "What if we don't want the island to change? Why give up everything we've worked so hard for? Why share it with thousands of others from the mainland?"

Peterson could not quite make out the person's face but listened and nodded. "I can understand your concern. And you're right. What I'm asking you to give up is substantial. But the opportunity it presents is also significant. Whatever your private and personal reasons, this is a huge chance to be part of a fresh start for your country. You would each play leading roles in the reconstruction. I'm sure I don't have to spell it out to you all. Ladies and gentlemen, together we can relight the fires, kick-start the engine and broadcast an invitation on every radio signal to come and join us here on the island. This is our chance to build a new world."

There were several nods and murmurs of approval, one old-timer mumbling, "Hear hear."

"You don't need me to tell you that this country has been sent back to the dark ages. We have no functioning government, no police, no infrastructure, no cell phones, no computers, no electricity. Your whole country lies in ruin. Waiting for a catalyst. I'm here to tell you that that catalyst is you. It's up to all of us to lean in and help get this island and this country back online, to learn new skills and to train others to do what's needed. That effort starts right here tonight."

Anders stood and cheered, raising his half empty glass of vodka to the lieutenant, inviting others around him to join in the toast. His fellow table guests remained seated, frowning at his drunken interruption.

"My good friend Captain Bjørklund has agreed to provide whatever support he can offer. Through God's grace, the *Maersk Charlotte* is anchored not five miles from here, fully loaded with humanitarian aid that was en route to Sierra Leone. I'm told the ship's manifest lists temporary shelters, tents, medical supplies, rice, dried food, bottled water, vehicles and more. Of course, we still need to find a way to unload the containers."

The lieutenant led a round of applause for Anders, who acknowledged their appreciation with a wobbly bow and his best attempt at a salute. Peterson turned his attention to Captain Armstrong. "In addition to the *Charlotte* we are working hand in hand with our friends in the Royal Navy. Captain Armstrong, over to you."

The British officer rose slowly and adjusted his starched collar and straightened his bow tie. "Ladies and gentlemen, I know we'd all like to express our appreciation to Lieutenant Peterson. I am confident that the arrival of the US Navy will tip the balance back in our favour. At Portsmouth naval base, we have no shortage of hardware but we have very few trained personnel. With your help we can make use of the vast resources that lie mothballed in our dockyards and stores."

A small movement to Jack's right caught his eye. A shadow passing an open doorway, a face darting from view. Jack thought nothing of it and turned his attention back to Captain Armstrong.

"Our first priority is to establish Camp Wight as a refugee centre capable of accommodating many thousands, if not tens of thousands, of survivors."

He walked over to a detailed map of the Isle of Wight which had been crudely pinned next to a portrait of a nineteenth-century nobleman on horseback. He grabbed a billiards cue that was leaning next to the wall and pointed towards the eastern end of the island.

"Here at Ryde, the British will be responsible for ferrying survivors from Portsmouth and Gosport to our Processing Centre Charlie, which will be capable of processing up to five hundred people at a time in quarantine zones here and here," he said, tapping the map firmly with the cue.

He turned and gestured towards Peterson. "In the middle of the island at Cowes, the Americans will take over the route from Southampton to Processing Centre Bravo. And last but not least, the islanders themselves will handle Camp Alpha at Yarmouth. We intend to set up HQ at St Mary's Hospital with a clean zone to the immediate south, with accommodation for up to five thousand people. New arrivals will be assessed based on their experience and skills then assigned to special units tasked with reconstruction, logistics, food production and security, to name but a few. The whole operation will remain under military control until a functioning civilian government can be formed."

With a nod towards his British counterpart, Lieutenant Peterson took over. "None of us should be under any illusions that this will be easy. We'll need to defend Camp Wight, day and night, to ensure no craft approaches the island without authorisation. Our friends at Hurst will set up a blockade to prevent unauthorised vessels from entering the protected zone, while the eastern approaches will be patrolled by the Royal Navy.

"And should any other group take an unwanted interest in Camp Wight, we are well able to defend ourselves."

Their host sitting at the head of the table led another round of applause as the guests nodded and murmured their approval of the outline plans.

Captain Armstrong continued, "Ladies and gentlemen, we start work in the morning, meaning tonight is for celebration. So please charge your glasses. I give you Camp Wight."

As chairs scraped back and everyone stood, the dinner guests repeated in unison, "Camp Wight" before finishing their drinks.

Terra caught Jack's eye, mouthing "Wow". Jack smiled and raised his empty glass in a silent toast.

Peterson introduced a scientist with wiry grey hair from the University of Southampton's Centre for Biological Science. Professor Nichols pushed his glasses higher up the bridge of his nose and addressed the room in a faltering voice.

"From what I have observed, the Millennial Virus shares many similarities with the Spanish flu pandemic at the end of the First World War. Spanish flu infected close to one billion people and was responsible for somewhere between fifty million to one hundred million deaths."

He paused while his audience nodded and waited for him to continue.

"This latest strain of the flu virus is an even more effective killer. It passes quickly from person to person. Different strains make prevention and immunisation programmes difficult. The virus is capable of adapting and bypassing the body's immune system and, so far, has proven resistant to all known treatments. Without the facilities or staff to undertake a proper medical study, our best chance is to avoid all contact with the virus and to maintain strict quarantine for new arrivals. I've volunteered to lead a newly formed research team at St Mary's Hospital just up the road in Cowes. Providing the military can provide us with the necessary resources there is no reason why we can't commence trials for a vaccine. Although I would caution that this could take several years."

Suddenly, there was a scuffle at the back of the room. Raised voices heard above the dinner table chatter. A muffled cry from one of the guards as he was unceremoniously dumped on the floor. He clutched at his throat, spluttering for breath, blood pouring from between his fingers. A figure wearing a balaclava stepped from the shadows and took up position by the entrance, a knife glinting in his right hand.

Jack stood and shouted at the guards by the other doorway but it was already too late. They were wrestled to the ground and dragged from sight.

Chapter 33

A tall heavy-set figure in a grey T-shirt advanced menacingly towards Peterson and Armstrong. Two henchmen kept pace just behind, brandishing shotguns to deter any wannabe heroes. The two navy officers were unarmed and stood perfectly still.

"Everybody shut up and sit down. Jamie, you're on crowd control."

The British officer seemed undaunted, studying his adversary as he waved a matt black pistol lazily between their heads. The man's arms and neck were richly tattooed with intricate patterns, passages of text and colourful scenes of snakes, swords and full-breasted women.

"I don't remember seeing your name on the guest list. Who are you?" challenged Armstrong.

"Never you mind, navy boy." He looked around the room at a sea of frightened faces, Jack's included. A few of the guests recognised the heavily tattooed man, whispering his name under their breath as if his reputation preceded him. Briggs nodded, pointing the gun towards the whispers, wagging a finger in disapproval.

"No one thought to invite Briggs, eh?" He tutted. "Shame on you."

"So you're Briggs," interrupted Peterson quietly, puffing out his chest.

Jack found the American's expression hard to read. Peterson had clearly met his fair share of bullies.

"Career criminal, barrow boy turned gangster. Your file said you were serving eighteen years for armed robbery before some well-meaning genius cut you loose, together with all the other inmates of Park Hurst prison who survived," said Peterson without blinking.

"Call it time off for good behaviour. So you're the septic."

Peterson looked puzzled, pretending to be unfamiliar with this provocation.

"I forgot you're not from around here. Septic tank? Rhymes with Yank," he sneered. "Bit far from home, aren't you? This ain't your turf, mate. You've got no place ordering people around. Haven't you heard? I run things round here. You want something, then you talk to me."

There was a murmur from the guests that he silenced with a raised finger. "Shut it. I've had enough of you lot."

"Then may I suggest you go back to whatever hole you just crawled from?" interrupted the captain, attempting to reassert his authority. "This whole island is under military control. You have no right to be here."

Briggs laughed, turning away and shaking his head before looking back with a deadpan expression. "Who put you jokers in charge, eh? I couldn't give a toss what you think. Nothing's going to happen on this island without my say-so."

Briggs wandered between the tables, eyeballing the other dinner guests in their dusty mothballed finery. He stopped behind one of the island leaders, a portly man with a red face, and reached for a half-eaten roast potato, mopping the gravy from the plate. He chewed noisily with his mouth open, licking his fingers. He placed a hand on each of the man's shoulders and began kneading the back of his neck. The islander was perspiring heavily, beads of sweat forming on his forehead. He glanced from side to side at his fellow guests, appealing for their support.

Briggs grabbed a fork and in one fluid movement jammed it down into the man's hand, embedding it in the plump flesh. Briggs ignored the man's high-pitched wail and snaked a thick tattooed arm around his neck, dragging him backwards off his chair. The man kicked helplessly, ruffling an ornate rug with his neatly polished brogues. Briggs dumped him on the ground and raised his pistol.

"Want to know what happens to people who double-cross me? You lied, Bairstow. You think because we're convicts, we're all stupid, do you?"

The fat man on the ground was shaking his head, his hands raised in defence.

"When you do a deal with Briggs, you pay up, or bad stuff tends to happen. Well, you're going to get what's coming to you."

He fired a single shot and the man bent double, clutching at his abdomen. A sad, almost disappointed expression settled in his eyes as a red stain formed around his midriff and his body went limp. There were gasps of disbelief from the dinner guests, who recoiled in horror, pushing their chairs away from the blood that began to pool around his body.

Captain Armstrong stepped forward, spitting with indignation, pointing angrily at Briggs. "That's brave. Shooting an unarmed man. You coward."

Briggs parried his intrusion, pistol-whipping the naval officer across the face, leaving a bloody streak across his cheek. Armstrong fished a white handkerchief from his trouser pocket and pressed it to his face to staunch the flow of blood.

"You and who's army? All your men are dead, captain." He laughed in his face. "You really think a bunch of sailor boys can match my army of street fighters and career criminals? I don't think so. I'd take one of my boys for ten of yours. I've spent eight long years on this bloody island."

Peterson placed himself between Briggs and Captain Armstrong. "You should know that I've dealt with Somali warlords, drug barons in Columbia, guerrilla fighters in Syria, Afghanistan, and Iraq. You're a bunch of convicts with shotguns, nothing more. I have a Navy Seal team expert in weapons, tactics, counter-terrorism and explosives I can summon at a moment's notice." He clicked his fingers. "I have drones that can hunt you down when you least expect it. Precision weapons that can take out a vehicle travelling at 50mph. Trust me, mate," he said the word "mate" in as good a cockney accent as he could manage, "you don't have a hope in hell."

"I'll take my chances. You really want a war you can't win? My lot sabotaging your relief effort at every opportunity? Smuggling sick people from the mainland and letting them loose in your precious Camp Wight? Do you?"

"Listen, Briggs, this virus is bigger than any local feud. It's too important for petty squabbles to interfere. We're facing an extinction event for humanity. Total annihilation. Please, lay down your weapons and join us. You can't win, you know that. And there will be plenty of other battles to fight. I'm sure we can find suitable jobs for your men that would keep them, how shall we say, entertained."

Briggs came and stood with his nose almost touching the American's, a snarl on his lips. "You really think we want anything to do with your lot? Don't waste your breath. Why doesn't everyone sit down and make themselves comfortable, shall we? We're going to work out a different kind of deal."

Out of sight, within Lieutenant Peterson's trouser pocket, a micro-transmitter was flashing red, broadcasting a distress signal. Every sixty seconds it buzzed lightly against his trouser leg to confirm its activation. Even now a rescue team on a high state of readiness would be scrambling, ready to be on site in less than ten minutes.

Chapter 34

Sam's curiosity had got the better of him and he'd ignored Jack's instruction to stay with the boat. He was crouched behind a hydrangea bush, peering through the grand window of the stateroom where they were holding Jack and the others. There was nothing he could do but watch.

He caught some of the conversation whenever the tattooed man in the T-shirt approached the window or when the wind dropped and the trees grew still. He noticed a guard bound and gagged by the main entrance with a swarthy-looking guy standing over him, keeping an eye out for any late arrivals to the Osborne gathering.

Sam racked his brains. What could he do? Light a fire? Cause a distraction? Set off the fire alarm and then try and steal into the room unseen? He gripped the old service revolver Jack had entrusted him with. It was a useful deterrent if nothing else. It deserved to be in a museum, which ironically was exactly where they had found the weapon, along with muskets, suits of armour, swords and instruments of torture salvaged from nearly five hundred years of history.

In the distance Sam heard a faint mechanical sound but it

was gone again before he could locate its source. It sounded close and far away, all at the same time. It was nearly dark outside and, with his back to the bush, he was fairly sure he couldn't be seen. He had no idea what was going on in the state-room, but from the looks on people's faces, they were scared. The man with the tattoos paced around the room, jabbing his finger in people's faces, lecturing someone.

Sam kept watch for some time, pondering his next move. He was straining to hear what was being said when footsteps behind him made him freeze. Without disturbing the flower heads, all he could make out from his cramped position, were dark shadows advancing deliberately towards him, their faces obscured by helmets and goggles. They moved fluidly as one connected organism, taking up position with their backs against the brick wall of the building. Sam was only a few feet away holding his breath, hoping he was invisible in the half-light.

One of the men walked straight up to the bush where Sam was crouched within and put his finger to his lips. He removed his headset and gestured for Sam to come out from his hiding place. Sam dropped the gun and came out, holding his hands up. The soldier grabbed him, spun him round and roughly pushed him down on to his knees.

He drew Sam's arms behind his back and secured both hands together with what felt like a cable tie, doing the same with his legs. The soldier stuffed a piece of cloth in Sam's mouth and whispered in his ear. "Stay down and you'll be fine. Don't move, okay?" Sam nodded, reassured by the American accent that they were friendly.

Sam saw them move off towards the main entrance. A few seconds later he heard the soft pop of a silenced weapon as the guard went down. One of the team caught the guard's body and weapon before it could clatter on the ground.

The team moved out of sight, heading inside. Sam whis-

pered a silent prayer as he lay prone on the ground, incapaci-
tated. The grass was already damp with evening dew. A loud
explosion made the windows rattle but not shatter. An American voice shouted, "Lay down your weapons and surrender." A
volley of small arms fire answered their demands. Sam craned
his neck towards the window, desperate to see what was
happening. He could see smoke and bright flashes, then all the
lights went out.

In the half-light, Briggs's men didn't stand a chance against
highly trained soldiers with night-vision goggles. The window
nearest Sam shattered into a thousand pieces as a grenade
exploded nearby. He was stunned for a few seconds, his ears
ringing.

The fire fight seemed to move to a different part of the
building and then grew louder outside beyond view, heading
into the woods, away from where the hostages were being held.
Perhaps a few of the terrorists, if that's what they were, had
gotten away, thought Sam. There were several further shotgun
blasts from inside, a heart-rending scream and then silence.

After what seemed like an eternity, the soldiers re-emerged,
escorting Peterson and two others to safety, lowering them down
next to the wall by the front entrance. Sam couldn't see their
faces.

The soldier who had bound Sam jogged over and flashed a
torch in his face before removing the gag from his mouth. "Talk
fast. Who are you?"

"My name's Sam," he replied, his voice cracking. "I'm one of
the good guys, came here with Jack and Terra from Hurst Castle.
They're my friends."

The soldier dumped him back on the floor and double-
timed it over to the main group, where a medic was checking the
hostages and treating their injuries. He spoke in a low voice with
his sergeant and Lieutenant Peterson who nodded in Sam's

direction. The soldier relaxed a little and wandered back, flicking open a knife to cut the ties securing Sam's hands and legs, hauling him back to his feet.

"Nothing personal, just doing my job."

Sam nodded. The blood was rushing back to his extremities and he felt a little faint but unharmed.

"There's someone over here wants to talk to you, will you come with me, sir?"

Sam followed the soldier, his legs stiff and leaden. He spotted Jack propped up against another hostage and bent down to comfort him. Jack looked a bit bashed up, with a blackened face, split lip, and blood soaked down his right side.

Peterson interrupted their reunion. "Gentlemen, I suggest you come with us. We can't vouch for your safety here. Briggs's men were easily scared off but they're likely to come back in greater numbers."

Jack looked up with fire in his eyes. "Wait, what about Terra?" he said, seizing hold of Peterson's arm, to the protestation of the medic trying to dress a cut on Jack's forehead.

Peterson looked confused.

Jack continued, "Terra? The woman I came here with? What happened to her? We need to go back and look for her."

"Jack, there's no time. Listen..." He took a deep breath, choosing his words carefully. "I saw her. Briggs took her, along with some of the others. We couldn't get to her. I'm sorry."

Jack looked exhausted and distressed. "Will she be okay? I couldn't take it if they did something to her."

"I can't promise you that," said Peterson, shaking his head. "But if they've got any sense they'll look after her and make a trade. We've captured a couple of theirs. She's a smart lady, Jack. She'll do what it takes to stay alive."

Peterson turned towards the special forces team leader. "Sergeant Jones, your team stay behind to secure the area and help with the clean-up. I'll take Jack back to the ship to get patched up. Sam, you want to tag along and keep the old man company?"

Sam nodded enthusiastically and they both followed Peterson and his men through the wood behind the house, across a golf course and down a slope towards a hidden valley where the helicopter had landed to maintain the advantage of surprise and stealth.

Sam put his arm around Jack's shoulders, supporting his weight. "I'm sure she'll be fine. Have faith."

Jack shook his head. "You didn't see this guy, Sam. He's delusional, thinks the island belongs to him."

"She's a survivor," reassured Sam.

Jack's chest was wracked by another coughing fit. The medic said it was smoke inhalation. They limped a few feet behind the others to find their ride back to the ship.

Chapter 35

Zed was dreaming. It was a fitful, restless sort of sleep he'd been trying to wake from. It was as if he was trying to climb out of a giant Petri dish with smooth slippery sides. Every time he nearly reached the top, he'd lose his grip and slide back down again. The pit was an inferno, sweat dripped from the tip of his nose. Drip, drip, drip. It wouldn't stop. His skin was prickling, pulsating with sores that appeared and disappeared on his hands and forearms. He steeled himself one more time and clambered up the contour-less surface. His palms were damp with perspiration. There was a tingling sensation in his fingertips. Just as he felt himself begin to slide back down, he thrust his hand into the air, stretching every sinew. A woman's hand grabbed his and pulled him clear.

Zed opened his eyes and found Riley sitting patiently by his bedside. She looked so peaceful. Her eyes were closed. He gingerly flexed his fingers and a wave of pain shot up to his shoulder, making him wince. The bandages were clean and blood-free. The pain felt strangely reassuring. A reminder he was still alive.

Riley placed Zed's hand back down on the bed sheet and

went to find the nurse. His throat was parched, his lips cracked and blistered. There was a glass of water on the bedside table which he drained in one gulp.

The nurse bustled back into the room. She fumbled in her top pocket and inserted a digital thermometer into his right ear, waiting for the electronic beep. "It's 99.4 degrees," said the nurse, showing the read-out to Riley. "His fever has come right down. We'll keep you in one more night. You'll be back on your feet in the morning, dear."

Riley thanked the nurse who seemed distracted, staring blankly over her shoulder before turning brusquely to leave. Riley poured another glass of water and handed it to Zed, waiting for him to drain it again.

"You gave us quite a scare collapsing like that. Looks like you're not quite as indestructible as we thought. Human after all then?" joked Riley.

"I don't remember much after we got here. How long was I out?" asked Zed.

She checked her watch, a black plastic-looking Casio she never took off. "You've been asleep for about eighteen hours straight."

He raised a single eyebrow quizzically. The dividing lines between dream and reality had become blurred. With the drugs, he was no longer sure what was real and what was imagined. It was all rather disconcerting. "The fever gave me the worst dreams. I'm sincerely hoping that the three witches who have been tormenting me in my sleep are not real."

"Oh, the sisters are all too real, I'm afraid. You don't know the half of it. Everyone's terrified of them. They're trying to force Stella to stay. They say she's part of some weird cult breeding programme, that she's pregnant. Oh, and then they've got Joe locked up because he can't be trusted around all these sex-starved women."

"He'll be loving all the attention. He's never had much luck with the ladies." He tried to sit up straight but the strain on his face was palpable.

"Hey, hey, easy, fella. You need to rest up. Avoid tiring yourself out. I brought some reading material for you."

She dumped the small pile of well-thumbed magazines on the bedside table. Zed picked up the top one. Its cover was ringed with stains from half a dozen coffee cups. He flicked through grainy images of half-remembered celebrities in swimwear photos, shot through telephoto lenses by the paparazzi. Page after page of smug fake-tan couples posing in front of replica Greek columns outside their country houses, dripping in gold jewellery. Precocious young children dressed in Ralph Lauren. The upper classes playing polo on horseback watched by minor royalty. He turned on his side, shaking his head in disgust.

"Hey, it's better than nothing," said Riley. "The only other thing I could find were copies of the Bible and I didn't think you'd want that." She went through the stack and found what she was looking for, a vintage *Top Gear* magazine. "This is probably more your thing. Nuns on bikes, special on the Stig and an interview with Richard Hammond himself."

Zed's face was pale, his skin drawn and paper-thin. He looked much older with grey circles under his clear blue eyes and two days' worth of stubble, giving him a lived-in look that Riley said she found pleasing.

He flicked through the pages of Ferraris and Lamborghinis, reasonably priced cars and beautiful landscapes, burned rubber, winding roads, tarmac stretching into the distance. The colour seemed to flood back into his cheeks as memories came rushing back like soothing waves of sound. The corner of his mouth turned upwards. "I used to love that show. Seems like a long time ago, doesn't it?" He leaned back and sighed. "To think people back then were so obsessed with material possessions like cars, houses, clothes and gadgets. Remember the shopping channels on TV? Full of chintz. How could normal sane people spend hours gossiping about celebrities, who's dating who, who's wearing what? It was all so trivial, just tittle tattle for the masses."

He rolled on his back and turned towards Riley, suddenly aware of how heavy his head felt, leaning back against the pillow. He gazed deep into her grey-green eyes, a serious world-weary look on his face. It was like the accumulated strain of the last few months had caught up with him and he had given in to his exhaustion.

"It was everything I detested, Riley. It was all so superficial. Don't you look back now and wonder what it was all about? None of it mattered. It was just stuff. It felt like some people's lives were a shallow veneer, a topcoat that masked something rotten just below the surface. Scratch your fingernail across the paint and the truth revealed itself. You realised that your whole existence was skin-deep. Beyond the routine of work and life, there was just a hollow emptiness."

Riley had never heard him talk like this. They had spent a lot of time together on the road or back at camp. Zed was not normally one for soul-searching or philosophising.

"Everyone needs someone or something," agreed Riley. "If you don't have that, then sure, life can feel quite empty at times."

She encouraged him to go on. After a short pause, lost in his thoughts, he continued staring up at a stain on the ceiling where water had discoloured the paintwork.

"Back then I had a wife and family, you know. Living in Croydon. It was my own fault." He paused, swallowing hard. "I made some poor choices, took them for granted, put my work first. I came home one day and they were gone. No note, no forwarding address. I had no idea she was even unhappy. Should have realised. Then all this happened with the virus. Times like this, I find myself thinking about them, where they ended up, wondering what I would do differently. Whether they'd still be alive if we'd all stayed together. But it's too painful. Knowing I wasn't there when it mattered..." His voice faded away.

"Hey, we've all lost people, yeah? It's best not to think about it. Anyway, you've got a new family now at Hurst. A new start."

He nodded weakly, still lost in his memories. "You think everything's fine, until it's not." He took another sip of water, swallowing painfully. "Do you remember the London riots back in 2011 just before the Olympics?" he asked, pausing before continuing. "People I knew thought that was the start of the revolution, that the working classes were ready to rise up and tear it all down. Take back the streets for the people. Fight back against the ruling classes. Reject a life of poverty, mediocrity, subservience. Did I ever tell you I was there, Riley? A riot in Croydon, for God's sake. I saw it on my doorstep, and, suddenly, it was all just so tangible. The social fabric stretched to breaking point, there within touching distance."

Riley nodded.

It had been some time since he had thought about that time in his life. The world had been different back then. Life had meaning. Between family and his work as a contractor for the Ministry of Defence, he had real purpose.

"I was living in America then," said Riley, "but I remember seeing the summer riots on the news and thinking 'How did that happen?' No one saw that coming."

"It was terrifying and exciting all at the same time. Bit like 9/11 and the attack on the Twin Towers. A slow-motion car crash. You couldn't look away. Like witnessing a fold in history, live and televised. The earth's rotation knocked off its axis, albeit for a second. It was the same with the riots, a moment in time. When it's gone, it's hard to explain. But in the end that passion and fervour melted away. The crowds went home and the status quo resumed, more or less. It was all just forgotten. Everything changed and yet everything stayed the same. No, I'm wrong, something did change. CCTV saw to it that all those hooded figures who helped themselves to the latest sportswear, all those ringleaders throwing stones at the police, all those looters smashing down shop windows and helping themselves to flat-screen TVs, were rounded up and prosecuted. It was an unprecedented triumph for Big Brother and the state."

"Is that what you did before all this then? Worked for the government?" She waited for him to respond, but he ignored the question. "You're deluded if you think revolution was ever going to happen in this country. Dream on, comrade."

"No, that's where you're wrong, Riley. This country may have the longest history of democracy of any nation, but one thing that made it robust was a pressure valve of strike action, rioting and civic protest. In my book, those are the hallmarks of a high functioning democracy. But that discontent and civil disobedience always fell short of revolution because boring old British reserve got in the way. Things never reached their necessary conclusion: a change in the status quo. The closest this country ever came to revolution was tearing down the railings outside parliament in the nineteenth century." He shook his head with an ironic smile. "Funny to think that the virus did more to change the world than a lifetime of campaigning by socialists. It tore down the social fabric and replaced it with mob rule. Who knows what comes next? The virus pressed reset on the world order."

Riley bent forward and straightened his pillow as he obligingly leaned forward. "Hey, big man, less of the doom and gloom. All you need to do is focus on the here and now. That other stuff will drive you mad. Concentrate on getting better. Let someone else worry about that other stuff."

"I'm done working for those people. They chewed me up and spat me out. I was just meat for the grinder. After all this time, I've come to realise that it's man's prerogative to crave power and to exploit the weak."

"You think?"

"For sure. Have you never wondered where the virus came from? Someone, somewhere must know."

"You mean the government?"

"There's a whole military and civilian infrastructure that tracks outbreaks like these. Ever heard of Porton Down? Up near Salisbury. It's not far from here. Hundreds of scientists. Bit like the CDC in Atlanta or the World Health Organization. What they don't know isn't worth knowing."

"Anyway, who's to say that the future will be the same as the past? The slate's been wiped clean," suggested Riley, trying to lighten the mood.

"True, but you can bet that the same operating system reboots and the status quo is restored. Everything changes, but everything stays the same. What hope is there for people like us?"

"You, my friend, need to get some rest. We've all been through rough patches. I remember this one time when I was a teenager, I got followed home after school. This guy came up behind me and tried to throttle me, drag me off somewhere, but I fought back. I stamped on his foot, kneed him in the groin and then ran and ran until I got home. For weeks I didn't leave the house. But in the end I figured that it was up to me. I never wanted to feel afraid again, so I did self-defence classes. I kept fit and strong. Made sure I could look after myself. No one else is going to do that for you. I've never looked back. That day changed me. It was an awakening. Maybe this is yours. Trust me, the world will look a whole lot better after a good night's sleep."

He forced a smile and yawned, leaning his head back on the

freshly plumped pillow. "Maybe you're right. This is my wake-up call. Makes you realise what's important and what's not. Thanks, Riley. For everything. I owe you." He patted her hand and turned on his side, closing his eyes again.

"Get some sleep and shake off this neg-head bullshit. We need you. I need you," she whispered, but he was already fast asleep.

Riley closed the door quietly behind her. She'd never seen him like this. He had been running on empty and letting things get on top of him. It was like the last few days had drained all that remained of his hope. She'd seen it before during her time as a physiotherapist working with combat veterans. Physical injury sometimes impacted a person's outlook on the world. She reassured herself that the condition was normally temporary. Normally. The sooner they got out of this place, the better.

It was dinnertime downstairs and one of the sisters was ringing an old-fashioned brass handbell, summoning all the residents to the hall where they had laid out a buffet dinner. Two enormous stainless steel receptacles sat steaming, fresh from the kitchen. The smell was sensational. Fresh vegetable soup and a rich beef chilli served with fluffy white basmati rice. Any hot dinner was one to be savoured.

Two scrawny-looking women, with mean faces and skin wrinkled like old leather, were slopping generous portions onto bowls held out in turn by the next person in line. They reminded Riley of the school dinner ladies at her secondary school, with grey checked aprons and unfashionable hairnets. One of the younger girls was in charge of rationing one piece of bread and one slice of Victoria sponge cake for dessert. Apparently the cake was a rare treat, it being one of the women's birthday today. Adele ran up and joined Riley from where she'd been sitting with two other young girls about her own age.

"Hey, kiddo. What ya been doing? Staying clear of the God squad?" asked Riley.

Adele looked puzzled. "I suppose. When are we getting out of this dump? It's so, so boring here. No one lets you do anything. It's all 'do this, do that, don't do this, don't do that'. Work, work, work. My fingers are red raw from peeling potatoes."

"You poor thing. Sounds terrible. Have you eaten already?"

"Yeah, although the food's disgusting," she said too loudly, to the scorn of the one of the dinner ladies. Adele stared back defiantly but then turned away, her cheeks flushed. Riley carried her tray to the far end of a long table where a group of women was deep in conversation, ignoring their presence until they sat down anyway.

"I saw Zed. He's feeling a lot better. Reckon he'll be fit enough to move first thing in the morning. Have you seen the others?"

"Stella was at evening prayers. I saw Mila outside helping in the garden."

Out of the corner of her eye, she noticed the Mother Superior heading in their general direction. Her habit was so long she appeared to glide between the tables, pausing to make small talk, doing her bit for community relations. She paused at Riley and Adele's table, aware of eyes watching furtively from all the surrounding groups.

"I do hope you're settling in well. In time, I'm sure you will come to appreciate how we run things round here."

"We're not staying. As soon as Zed's better, we're leaving."

"We were rather hoping that you'd decide to stay for a little bit longer."

"Not unless you've softened your views on men in the last twenty-four hours?"

"Actually, quite the opposite. Their presence has provided a useful reminder of why we established this commune in the first place: to provide sanctuary from oppression. Nothing has changed for any of us, nor will it any time soon, if that's what you're hoping. It was only your kindness towards Stella that made us bend our rules. As soon as your friend is well enough, the men must leave. As I'm sure you can understand..."

"I don't understand," Riley interrupted, infuriated by the high-handedness of the sister. "I'll never understand." Those around them fell silent, turning their attention to their conversation.

"Well, in that case, perhaps it's better that you are leaving. We have tried to open your eyes, but if you choose not to see, then I cannot help you. My dear, turning a blind eye to evil doesn't make evil disappear. By ignoring something you sustain it. Until you take a stand, men's brutality will only get worse. The only person you are fooling is yourself." She turned and with a swish of her starched habit, she brushed past them and was gone.

Riley clenched her fists, ready to explode, aware of others watching her. When she had regained control of her emotions she glanced across the table at Adele who was pulling a face at her, eyes-crossed and tongue lolling on her bottom lip, trying to make Riley laugh. It worked. Riley shook her head and leaned in to whisper "Silly woman. Who does she think she is?"

After dinner, they stacked their plates, put their trays back in the rack and wandered outside, engrossed in conversation. Riley was telling Adele all about life at Hurst, their routines, the people she would meet, the views over the sea and surrounding coastline. It was a beautiful clear evening, their shoes crunching on the gravel as they walked together, side by side, Adele's hand finding Riley's and falling into step with her.

They headed through the courtyard past several parked vehicles looking for Joe who was said to be in one of the outbuildings, locked up with the other men. The guard from earlier was sat outside the stable block, reading a paperback novel with embossed lettering on the front, some trashy romance. She raised a single finger to acknowledge their presence as she finished her page. Without saying a word, she got slowly to her feet, beckoning them to follow.

At the back of the building block, along a crumbling old brick wall were some gabled doors. She wrestled with the padlock before unhooking the latch and swinging the door open just wide enough for the two visitors to squeeze through. As she closed and locked it again, she called out in a gruff voice that they were to knock when they were done and she'd come back and let them out again.

Inside it was surprisingly dark. A single window was covered with cobwebs and years of accumulated grime. It took a couple of seconds for their eyes to adjust before locating Joe in the darkness. He was lying on a low camp bed with his arms behind his head daydreaming.

"How you doing, trouble?" asked Riley. She sat on the side of the bed, leaning back against the bare brickwork. A shiver rippled through her back and shoulders. She hugged her knees tightly. Adele kept her distance, seemingly unsure of herself in Joe's company.

"Can't complain," said Joe with a sigh, pulling his sweater down over his bulging stomach.

"For someone who's been locked up in a dingy stable you sound surprisingly cheery."

He smiled and rolled on his side. There was an unexpected

glow about him. "Well, can't say I've ever been anywhere like this before. Not sure I want to leave so soon."

"What are you talking about? We can't wait to get out of this dump."

"The women here are not like any I've met before, just...to die for." He sounded dreamy, as if he'd just woken up.

"Have you gone soft in the head? What are you talking about?"

"Oh, they've kept me pretty busy. I've barely had a moment to myself. I'm now a fully signed-up member of their breeding programme."

Riley laughed in shock. "Please tell me you're kidding?"

"Nope, not a bit of it. Two visitors today already. All wanting the same thing." He put his arms behind his head, looking very pleased with himself. "No complaints from me. I've been more than happy to oblige."

"Gross," said Adele. "That's disgusting."

"Not to me," said Joe defiantly. "Best thing that's ever happened. I feel like a gigolo. Never had such fun. Never want to leave."

"You look like you've died and gone to heaven, you dirty dog," said Riley, laughing. "It's grim, Joe. Don't you find it demeaning? It's borderline inhumane keeping you and the others locked up like this and being forced to mate." He was smiling, enjoying her superciliousness, listening intently to her protestations of injustice and morality. "But hey, I can see it's pointless arguing with you. You're like a cat that's got the cream."

"Too right. Beyond my wildest dreams."

She laughed, in spite of her feelings. Riley told him about Zed and the others. "As soon as Zed is fit enough to walk, we're out of here. With or without you. If you want to stay here and live like this, fair play. But we need to get back to Hurst."

Joe nodded. It felt like days since they'd left Hurst, but in reality it was less than forty-eight hours.

Riley became pensive, thinking about their friends back at the castle, suddenly worried at how long they had been gone. "They'll be wondering what's happened to us by now. Those guys from the hospital are sure to come looking for us, whether they follow the trail here or go straight to Hurst. If this place gets attacked, we're all too vulnerable. It's a miracle they've lasted this long, unless someone is protecting them."

"Can't we stay a few more days? I'm just beginning to like it here," pleaded Joe.

"You can't live like this. You've got a job to do. Back in the real world. Hurst needs you."

He didn't respond, but he knew she was right. "Okay, okay. Just come and get me in the morning when you're ready to leave. If I'm not too busy, I suppose I could come with you, tear myself away from all this hard labour."

"That's the spirit. Enjoy it while it lasts."

Riley patted Joe on the calf and sauntered over to the door. She lingered for a second, taking in the squalor of Joe's confinement, light streaming through a large hole from a knot in the wood. She rapped her knuckles loudly on the stable door and waited for the guard to let them out.

"See you tomorrow, stud."

Chapter 36

At ten o'clock sharp, the bell for curfew rang and Riley, Mila and Adele were escorted back to the drawing room that served as their dormitory. Every resident was expected to be in her own room, with lights out by ten thirty. It reminded Riley of the summer activity camps her parents had sent her on, but without any of the fun.

It had been an enjoyable evening with Riley and Mila as guests of honour for a whole programme of entertainment organised by the Chewton Glen social committee. A general knowledge quiz was followed by an open-microphone style session, rounded off with a reading from Charles Dickens's *Great Expectations* by a young girl with an accomplished theatrical voice.

Adele fell asleep on a sofa waiting for the grown-ups to finish their conversations. Riley struggled to lift her limp body. Her skin was the colour of milk, almost translucent in the dim light of the candle Stella carried, leading them back to the drawing room where they were sleeping. She made sure they still had blankets and pillows and then stood aside as one of the guards locked them in for the night.

Riley covered Adele with a blanket and settled down into the armchair, adjusting the cushions behind her head. She stared at the empty leather sofa where Zed had slept the previous night. She had checked in on him again after dinner but he was still spark out. A plasma drip was attached to his arm, replenishing lost fluids. His complexion was regaining some of its usual colour as the medicine worked its magic.

Riley closed her eyes and was just drifting off when someone started ringing the dinner bell with an unmistakeable degree of urgency.

"What's going on?" asked a startled Mila, sitting bolt upright.

Riley raced over to the door and started banging on it, rattling the handle and shouting at the top of her voice, but there was no answer. They were in a remote part of the hotel, way down a long corridor, far from the main living quarters. Mila joined her, peering through the keyhole but all she could see was the far wall and a doorway to another room. Riley pushed her out the way to see for herself. If it wasn't her imagination, there was a thin veil of smoke beginning to form, drifting along the corridor, just under the ceiling. She banged harder on the door. In the room above, they heard footsteps and something heavy falling over.

Mila unfastened the latch on the sash window and tried to heave it open but noticed security bolts held it locked in place. Their only option was to smash the glass. Meanwhile, Adele beat out a rhythm at the door. She said the smoke in the hallway was hanging heavier from the ceiling, slowly filling all skylights, apertures and recesses moving towards them down the corridor. The smell of burning wood and plastic reached them for the first time. Someone was ringing the bell again, more insistent, this time more distant. Had the rest of the hotel residents forgotten all about them?

Riley picked up a plastic chair and tested its weight. "Stand back, I'm going to break the glass." She had a practice swing and then threw the chair with all her might towards the window.

One of the chair legs folded inwards, coming off second best in the collision against the frame of the original sash window. It bounced back harmlessly without making any impact on the glass itself. She tried again, this time with Mila's help. Instead of throwing it, they used the chair leg as a battering ram. With the first attempt, the glass cracked diagonally, but did not break. Their second effort shattered the glass into a dozen pieces and the lower half of the pane broke on to the thick pile of the carpet and flowerbed outside. They knocked out the remaining pieces and laid a blanket over the frame to cover the remaining shards. They lifted Adele through the empty window, still groggy from sleep, passing her with some difficulty to Riley standing on the other side. With the extra weight of her load Riley's feet sank deep into the earth, as the pointed thorns of a rose bush scratched at her arms.

In the cool night air, it was strangely quiet on this far side of the building. The light was eerily bright and strangely incongruous. An orange glow lit up the sky that reminded Riley of the fifth of November, fireworks night. She half expected to find a towering bonfire, explosions in a million colours and shimmering sparkles raining down above their heads.

She grabbed Adele's hand and together they raced round to the other side of the building to find a hive of activity. Smoke was pouring from two of the upper windows on the second floor, curling into the night sky. Fire had broken through the roof in one section further down. Twenty women passed bucketload after bucketload of water hand over hand down a human chain. Each bucket was sent slopping towards the French doors that led towards the lobby area and staircase to the upper floors.

With a shudder, Riley remembered Zed. He was likely still in the infirmary on the second floor. In his weakened state, he couldn't possibly get out on his own. As she hurried inside heading towards the staircase, Sister Georgina held her hand up to stop her. "It's too dangerous. No one's allowed up there."

The sister was right. From Riley's brief stint as the volunteer fire marshal at the physiotherapy centre for veterans, rule one was to get everyone out safely and wait for the fire brigade. The only problem was no one was coming to help. Either she went in herself or Zed would die. She made up her mind. She had to reach him. It was up to Riley.

"Try and stop me," she said, pushing past. The sister lunged for Riley's sleeve but it was too late. Riley took the stairs two at a time. She passed a gaggle of women coming back down, their buckets empty, ready to be refilled from the ornamental ponds.

On the first-floor landing, the line of women bent right towards the crackle and roar of the fire. She could hear raised voices shouting instructions, a note of panic as they fought to regain control. Riley shielded her face against the stifling heat. She could see flames not twenty metres away down the corridor in one of the bedrooms on the first floor. The infirmary was on the next floor up. The stairs were deserted and dark. She knew she had to be quick. The flames had already broken through between floors.

She was halfway up the next staircase when she stopped dead, overcome by a powerful sense of déjà vu. Instinct told her what she needed to do. Diving into one of the bathrooms she grabbed a bath towel, soaked it in a bowl of grey water left out for washing hands. Wrapping the towel around her head and shoulders, she poured the rest of the bowl over her, soaking her clothes to give her some protection against the heat.

Slowing her pace, she tested her weight on each of the steps, unsure of what lay ahead. There was a heavy fire door that gave access towards the infirmary. Inside, it was suspiciously quiet. There was no sign of flames, but thick smoke hung heavy from the ceiling all the way down to waist height. There was an impenetrable wall of heat and cloying fumes. She could feel the smoke catch in her throat, as she struggled to breathe. The cool towel wrapped around her head was already steaming. She hesitated, painfully aware of the danger if she continued.

Riley remembered her fire marshal training and got down on her hands and knees, staying low, just underneath the layer of smoke where the heat was less intense. She crawled along the carpet, clutching the damp towel to her mouth. The air was acrid and burned her throat. She started coughing, gulping air greedily and feeling the panic begin to rise in her throat. She felt nauseous and retched on the carpet.

Focus, Riley, she told herself, you have to do this. She continued onwards, feeling for the doorways to her left. The first door was locked, the second was the nurse's station but the room was empty. Perhaps the nurse had taken Zed with her. She had to be sure.

Putting her weight against what she assumed was Zed's door she levered it open with some difficulty. It felt as if she was fighting against an invisible force, pressure sealed against the smoke and heat. Zed was beginning to stir, oblivious to the drama that was unfolding all around him. As the door began to close behind her, it felt like all the air was being sucked from the room, as if a vacuum had been broken. She noticed the top window was ajar. The fire sucked greedily at this fresh source of oxygen. In the corridor, she heard a funnelling of air as the flames leapt, rejuvenated. She didn't have much time.

She shook Zed by the shoulders, whispering his name softly. His eyes flickered open, groggy and disoriented, then closed again. She tried again, shouting this time, an edge of panic creeping into her voice, "Zed, wake up, wake up."

He stirred, his eyes wide, blinking at her, still vacant and far away. The nurse must have given him something for the pain.

She slapped him hard across the face, shaking him by the shoulders. She raised her hand to strike him again but his free hand grabbed her wrist before she made contact.

"Okay, Riley. I'm awake."

"There's no time to explain. We need to go right now."

He got gingerly to his feet, his legs weak and unbalanced. She supported his large frame, manoeuvring him towards the closed door. At first the door appeared locked, vacuum sealed by the difference in air pressure, but she hauled it open with all her might. As she did so the roar of flames grew suddenly louder and from the far end of the corridor came a surge of heat.

Riley pushed Zed down to the ground and collapsed on top of him. An explosion of heat and flame enveloped them and swept past them into the infirmary, blasting the door half off its hinges. Riley could taste soot and burning hair in her mouth and nose.

She pulled Zed on to his hands and knees and they started crawling side by side towards the stairwell. The smoke was cloying and darker now, only a few inches from the carpet. It was hopeless. She couldn't see anything, tears rolling down her cheeks. The heat behind them was intense. Zed's whole body convulsed with coughing but she encouraged him onwards, grabbing his good arm and half hauling him a few more inches towards safety.

The fire door stood resolute at the end of the corridor. A small rectangle of light just visible through the smoke. The whole space was now completely dark. It was only by feeling her way along the wall and counting the doorways that she realised they must be within touching distance.

Her breathing was coming in short rasps. Zed had collapsed beside her, unable to go further. It seemed to be growing hotter by the second. The carpet fibres were sticky to the touch from the heat below. The whole corridor had become a furnace. Unless they got moving again, it would soon become their tomb.

She thrust her hand out one last time and touched the flat painted surface of the fire door, its paint felt like it was beginning to blister. Her fingers found the edge of the door and she managed to prise it open, forcing it outwards. The rush of cooler air was delicious and intoxicating.

Riley stood and fell outwards on to the landing, reaching back to pull Zed through. They both lay there for a few seconds with their chests heaving, panting hard, trying to get their breath back before a darkness enveloped Riley.

She was dimly aware of voices on the stairs. Hands helping them back up. She was barely conscious as they supported her down the stairs. Her head rolled against a supporting shoulder as they half dragged her down towards ground-floor level. She was carried through a conservatory filled with pot plants and acres of glass and finally outside to be lowered gently on to the grass. It felt deliriously cool and moist on the back of her bare arms, soothing the burning sensation on exposed flesh at her wrists and knees through ripped jeans.

One of the last things Riley remembered was Adele hugging her tightly around her neck. She lay there staring up into the night sky, watching clouds drifting lazily over their heads. She was a spent force, every last ounce of strength gone. The flames from two upper windows bathed the trees and grass all around her in light, casting a warming orange glow.

As she drifted in and out of consciousness, the upstairs windows began to resemble demonic eyes flaring wildly. The flames licked the outside of the building, making the iron gutters and fixings glow and spark. Alongside her, Zed's body lay motionless, as one of the women pumped his chest with the palm of her hand, trying to resuscitate him. Riley grasped his hand, squeezing it hard and then passed out.

Chapter 37

As dawn broke at the Chewton Glen hotel, the fire had burned itself out. The southern end of the main building was a scarred, smoking wreck, blackened timbers exposed to the pale light of the new day. Laid out on the lawn were a dozen bodies covered in blankets and sheets or whatever they could find to hide their faces. Most of the victims had been overcome by smoke, as they waited to be rescued, trapped in upstairs rooms by the rampaging flames.

Riley sat consoling Stella, her face blackened, hair singed in places. Judging by people's reaction to Riley's appearance, she concluded she must look as awful as she felt. Stella had her head in her hands, sobbing. So many of her friends were gone, their lives extinguished. It seemed so wrong that they should have survived the virus, only to be killed by something innocuous like a candle left to burn. Sister Imelda said the candle might have fallen over, out of its saucer and on to a carpet or against a drape. In a few minutes, the whole bedroom would have been ablaze and then from there, a fire uncontained would have spread rapidly to the other rooms.

Stella looked up, tears streaming down her face. Mila sat

cross-legged on the picnic blanket, hugging Stella tightly. There was nothing that anyone could say to make it better, so she said nothing. The three of them stared back at the hotel, as it smouldered quietly, the fire's energy spent.

Sister Theodora was busying herself organising others, handing round cups of tea, cut-up fruit and blankets for those who had fought so hard throughout the night to save the hotel and rescue the trapped women. Mila stroked Adele's hair one last time and kissed her gently on the forehead. She rose to go find the others.

The nurse had set up a temporary surgery in one of the outbuildings that had once been a soft-play gym for toddlers. Its padded floors were bright blues and reds that made for comfortable mattresses to treat the walking wounded and those more seriously injured by the fire. In the corner, on the far side, Riley found Zed wrapped in a blanket, clutching a steaming mug of milky tea. Someone had cleaned his face, but around his eyes and ears there were streaks of dirt and singed hair that reminded Riley of the 7/7 bombing victims on the London Underground all those years ago. There was a look of terror etched on his face, staring blankly with unseeing eyes. He was alive, but had needed CPR to get him breathing again, overcome by fumes. He nodded wearily at Riley and blinked his eyes rapidly as she approached.

"Looking good, Zed. You just can't stay out of trouble."

He tried to sit up but the strain was too much and he slumped back. Mila helped him upright. She leaned him back against the bright red cushions that smelled of a nursery. The disinfectant did a poor job of masking a heady blend of nappies and rancid milk.

"How are the others?" asked Zed.

"Stella got out early. She was lucky. Some of them didn't make it out at all. Six died in their sleep. They just never woke up. There wasn't a mark on them." Riley shook her head, still trying to dispel the mental image of those women lying dead in their beds. "If I was going to die, that's how I'd like to go. In my bed, dreaming of being on a beach somewhere hot." Her voice trailed off.

"We need to get out of this place," said Zed, his voice croaky. He reached for a glass of water, clearing his throat before continuing. " We need to get back to Hurst, to our own people. We've been gone too long already. They'll be worried about us. What if they sent a rescue party or followed our trail into town? They'd go straight to the hospital. We've got to get back."

"Not till you're well enough to move. Remember what the nurse said," said Riley.

"We don't have time enough to wait around here," said Zed.

"And we can't just leave these people in their hour of need. Look around." She extended her arm towards the twenty or so people stretched out around them. Some were fighting for breath from smoke inhalation, others were in agony from burns. The nurse was bustling between them, bathing limbs and foreheads with wet towels. "They need us. We can't just ship out after all they've done for us."

"There's nothing we can do for them. They brought this on themselves."

"What? You can't seriously be suggesting that none of this would have happened if men had been around to save the day?"

"Don't twist my words, Riley. I'm just saying that what comes around goes around. Let's not forget that Joe is still locked up in the stables."

"Please tell me you're joking."

"I've seen it before. Cosmic forces. Karma. Call it what you like." He glanced up and raised his eyebrows. "What would the sisters say: 'The Lord moves in mysterious ways.' I'm just saying that natural forces are at work here, rebalancing. *Honi soit qui mal y pense* and all that."

"What does that even mean?" asked Mila, puzzled.

"You know, the Order of the Garter. Evil comes to those who think evil. You must have heard that before, right? Jack's forever banging on about it."

"Nope. I swear you make this stuff up."

"It just means that life has a funny sort of way of getting its own back."

"Whatever the sisters think or believe, no one deserves to die. Just because they have strong views about men, doesn't mean they deserved this."

"I'm not saying that at all. Don't re-imagine what the sisters have done here. This isn't the fulfilment of some weird feminist crusade for female empowerment."

"People are entitled to create a new community based on different values."

"Whatever happened to sexual equality being the goal? Whoever said that to be happy and prosperous required that someone else, an entire sex, had to be subjugated?"

"If people don't like what they've done here, then they should leave."

"You mean, if men don't like it, they should leave? Careful, Riley. You're beginning to sound like them."

"Don't get me wrong. I don't want to stay any more than you do. But you can't say it's not refreshing to see the boot on the other foot for a change."

"It just goes to prove that, given half a chance, women can be just as abusive and prejudiced as men."

Riley looked back mockingly. "Prejudiced maybe, but I wouldn't say evil, would you? It's not like we're depriving you of basic human rights, forcing you to stay indoors and never show your face in public. We're not saying you can't drive a car, vote, have a job, or any of the other stuff that women were routinely denied in some countries. Women will always have more of a bias towards nurturing than men. Call it oestrogen trumping testosterone any day of the week. You don't see women slaughtering each other for bragging rights."

"And I wouldn't say locking a man up in a stable as part of some cult breeding programme is very progressive either. Would you?"

"I don't see Joe complaining. He's like a pig in mud," added Riley.

"But surely you can't defend what they're doing here? This nightmarish version of feminism is abhorrent. It's like a social experiment gone wrong. It deserves to fail."

Adele popped her head around the doorway and spotted the three of them in the corner. She skipped over and sank down on top of Riley, wrapping herself in the blanket and snuggling down in its folds. Adele's arrival defused the escalating hostility between them. Mila shrugged her shoulders watching the pair of them go at it. They could fight for hours, going back and forth like this, evenly matched, exploring idea and counter-idea. Mila couldn't see the point; both of them were so stubborn, they were never going to change.

Seeing Adele, Riley's whole face seemed to relax into a smile. "How're you doing, kiddo? Making yourself useful?"

"Yeah, Sister Mel made me make like a hundred flatbreads." She wriggled round to face Riley, her eyes wide, her expression mischievous. "Hey, guess what I just heard? Joe and the other men have escaped."

Riley sat bolt upright, her fatigue suddenly evaporated. It was like an electric shock had passed through her body. "Escaped where?" She grabbed Adele's shoulders. "This is important, Adele. You need to tell me exactly what you heard."

Adele looked puzzled but realised this was not just another

game. She sighed and told her what she knew. "Just that when the guard went to check on them after the fire, the stables were empty, the doors were wide open."

Riley and Zed looked at each other in confusion.

"Why would Joe escape when they promised to release him tomorrow? It doesn't make any sense. The finger of suspicion is going to point squarely at us," said Zed.

"They can't have gone very far. All the cars are still parked outside," added Mila.

"Well, if it wasn't one of us who let them out, then who the hell was it?" wondered Zed out loud.

Chapter 38

As the sun burst through the trees on the far side of the wood, Joe and the others were already two miles away, putting as much distance between them and the hotel as they could before the alarm was raised. They were fairly certain that the sisters wouldn't send their guards after them.

Joe had wanted to stay behind, to wait for his friends. It seemed pointless to escape. He only had another day before Zed was well enough and the Hurst team could go home. Seamus had insisted he came with them. He told Joe that he would get the blame. Perhaps Seamus simply didn't trust Joe to keep quiet. In the end he felt he had no choice but to go with them. He would bide his time and wait for an opportunity to slip away.

The small group stayed as far as they could from roads, crossing fields and following footpaths through turnstiles, along fences and hedgerows that grew wild and impassable in places. The dawn chorus of crows and rooks masked any noise they made as they hurried away. Speed was more important than stealth right now. Besides, they reckoned there was no one around to hear them.

They had Jean to thank for their escape. She was a mousey little thing, small for her age, Joe reckoned no more than sixteen. She had the responsibility of bringing the men food and water twice a day. Joe had warmed to her almost immediately. She was naive and impressionable, sympathetic to their plight. She had agreed to help them should the opportunity arise. All they had needed was a diversion.

It had been Seamus who had talked her into helping. He was always going on about the injustice of their captivity and how the right thing to do was to release them and help them escape. He had nurtured this idea almost daily for the last four months, or so he said, twisting the conversation, moulding her to his purpose.

Lying on his bed in the evenings, Joe had listened to Seamus whispering kindnesses to Jean, engaging her in conversation, trying to build her trust, gain her confidence, then bad-mouthing her as soon as she had left, his guile and artifice laid bare. Joe didn't like Seamus's methods but figured the end justified the means.

"Did I ever tell you what I was doing before all this?" asked Seamus. Joe realised he was fond of the sound of his own voice, as if he was afraid of silence. "I was labouring on this farm just north of New Milton with these Polish lads. I only ever intended to stay in England for the summer months till harvest time. I was trying to earn enough money to travel. Me and a couple of mates planned to spend the winter in Athens, doing bar work and sleeping above a fast-food restaurant we knew, near the Acropolis. But I never made it out of England."

"What happened?" Joe prompted, keen to keep him talking.

"Sure, I remember like it was yesterday. I woke at first light with the mother of all hangovers. They took the money and my car, but they wouldn't have got far. That car was only held together with fibreglass. I rewelded that chassis so many times it was a death trap. The rest of the farm buildings were deserted. The family must have left in the night. I stuck around for a couple of days but when it was clear that no one was coming back I broke in to the farmhouse and lived there on my own until the food ran out. After that I suppose I began a nomadic existence, living on my wits, until the day those bitches from the Chewton Glen captured us."

Jean glared back at Seamus but her words of reproach froze on her lips, just like every other time he criticised the sisters. Joe watched their silent exchange. He hated the way Seamus manipulated her. How he would feign interest in her teenage life, commenting on the clothes she wore, how she wore her hair, ingratiating himself slowly but surely into her favours. Joe had to admit Seamus was a good listener. Jean would hang around late into the night at least until the guard told her to leave.

In the end Seamus had convinced Jean to make the leap from sympathiser to collaborator. When the commotion of the fire distracted the guards and drew them from their posts, she crept back to the stable block. She stole the keys from a hook, released the men from their captivity. Together they ran down the drive towards open fields and freedom beyond. Jean had remembered to bring what little food she could conceal over the last few days. In Tupperware containers, she kept biscuits and leftover rice, already desiccated and stale. In her rucksack she had a metal flask for water, a torch and a pocketknife.

Joe wasn't sure, but he was beginning to think that the fire was no accident. Perhaps Seamus had put her up to that too. He had to admit, it was fortuitous for their purposes, to say the least. Judging by the smoke that rose high into the dawn behind them, the fire had been devastating. He felt terrible leaving Zed and the rest of them behind. His best option was to wait for an opportunity to slip away. He felt a responsibility to Jean, despite what she may or may not have done. Without him there, he feared for her safety. He determined to take her back with him to Hurst.

When they were several miles from the hotel, Seamus held up his hand and they gathered round a lonely bench on a country lane where the landscape opened out. Views stretched across fields of rapeseed, swaying bright yellow in the sunshine. The four men took it in turns to drink from the flask of water Jean had brought. They shared a joke, hands on hips, wiping sweat from their brows, before finally allowing Jean and Joe to share the last drops.

"Where are we heading?" asked Joe, interrupting a private conversation between Seamus and one of the others.

"Not much further now. Maybe another mile. There's a house not far from here, very secluded. Big place with an orchard and greenhouses, full of vegetables. We used to deliver animal feed there. Seems like a lifetime ago."

"How do you know there won't still be someone there?" challenged Joe.

Seamus spat something on the ground and kicked the earth with his boot. He looked up with a smile, squinting in to the sun. "I don't, but I've a feeling that the farmer's daughter will remember me. Either that, or they'll be long gone by now. It was a couple of years ago. If you've got a better idea, I'm all ears."

There was an edge to his voice that made Joe pause. It wasn't worth an argument. After all, he had no intention of staying with the group. His instinct was screaming that prime sites like these were normally occupied. If they still had stores and food, then they would not welcome the arrival of strangers.

As they approached the farm, they stopped at the boundary fence, watching the house and outbuildings for any movement or other signs of recent occupation. Seamus told the others to stay hidden while he scouted ahead. After twenty minutes, lying on a grassy bank under a sycamore tree, basking in the mid-morning sunshine, they heard footsteps approaching down the lane and readied themselves. Joe grabbed a small log, holding it high above his head, ready to strike. The others shifted uneasily from one foot to the other, waiting to grab whoever emerged from around the corner. They all breathed a collective sigh of relief as Seamus whistled a prearranged greeting.

Walking up the rough track that led to the farm, there were no signs of vehicles. A tree had fallen right across the track, blocking the road. They passed a sign for a local construction firm and immediately understood why. The whole place was mid-renovation. Scaffolding framed the far end of the farm-house, where the original red brick building was being extended. A large modern kitchen with a conservatory, patio area and stone steps led down to a landscaped slope thinly covered with what looked like newly sewn grass, stretching towards a stream that ran through the back of the property.

They took a minute to refill the flask in the lazy flow of the cool water, before cautiously approaching the front porch. There was a beaten-up old estate car parked outside with three flat tyres.

Seamus tried the handle, but found the oak panelled door locked. Its white paint had peeled away, revealing knotted wood and sturdy iron hinges. He kicked at the door a couple of times, grunting as he came off worse for wear. The others watched him, arms crossed, faintly amused by his bravado. The hinges and lock refused to budge. Seamus directed the group to split up and head in opposite directions.

Joe and Jean set off together, testing each of the shutters and windows on the ground-floor windows but found them each

securely fastened. Jean froze, hearing footsteps coming around
the house towards them. They pressed themselves against the
wall and crouched down only to see Seamus and the others
rounding the corner, completing their search. The extension
and conservatory proved more rewarding. They found an empty
window frame with no glass. Seamus punched one of the other
men on the shoulder, laughing at their good fortune.

Inside was a half-finished kitchen stacked with pallets of
floor tiles and flat-packed furniture, including various tools left
out at the end of a shift. Seamus smashed a small pane of semi-
opaque glass with his elbow and reached through, groping for
the catch. He found the key still in the lock. Seamus paused as
he and Joe had the same thought. If the house was all locked up
from the inside, did that mean someone was still living here?
Seamus raised his finger to his lips and made sure everyone had
understood his instruction before continuing their search.

The door squeaked in protest as he wrenched it open, stepping into the cool darkness beyond. The main reception room
looked untouched, dust layered grey on every surface. There
were no signs of disturbance. A vase in the middle of a long
mahogany table held what remained of wilted flowers, the water
brown and mouldy in its base. There was a musty smell about
the place. Disturbed dust drifted in shafts of sunlight that pene-
trated through gaps in the shutters. It was like stepping into a
tomb, frozen in time, untouched by human hand for months,
maybe years.

Next door, there was a snug-room with whitewashed walls
and a large fireplace, its grate covered in grey ash, from a fire
long since cold. Either side there were bookshelves set deep into
the wall. Behind the door, Joe could see a high-sided armchair
facing an old-fashioned television set. Joe had not seen a TV like
this since his childhood staying at his grandparents' house up
near Scarborough, in north Yorkshire. Televisions with cathode-

ray tubes predated plasma and flat-screen technologies by some twenty years.

A sixth sense made the hairs on Joe's neck prickle. Was his mind playing tricks or was there someone sitting in the chair? He signalled to the others behind him and leaned his head further around the door. His instincts proved right. He could see a pair of shoes resting on a footstool. He readied himself, gulping air. He picked up a glass paperweight from the side table and advanced further into the room.

Slumped in the armchair was an emaciated old man. His eyes were open, staring lifelessly at the TV, his mouth wide, with prune-like skin drawn tight across his jaw, discoloured and ravaged by time.

Joe had gotten used to seeing death at close quarters. It no longer bothered him. In fact he had developed a whole vocabulary around death that helped to dehumanise the victims. Jack had once told him it was a coping strategy and that no one ever got used to seeing dead people. They just found a way of dealing with it so it no longer held the power to shock.

Joe leaned in closer, inspecting the corpse. There was no sign of illness, no flecking in the eyes, no dried blood around the nose or ears. This man had died from old age, plain and simple. He had simply sat there and waited to die, an empty mug perched on a nested table beside him. Perhaps the old man had nowhere else to go, watching the news broadcasts until they went off air, replaced by the pre-recorded public service announcements that told everyone to stay indoors, avoid contact with others and wait for further instructions. He had died alone, on his own terms.

It seemed to Joe a better way to go than the panic and disorder in the cities, the chaos at the hospitals and treatment centres overrun with the sick. In the end the hospitals had simply locked their doors and turned new arrivals away. Fearful of further contamination, poorly resourced to deal with the flood of humanity, they were unable to do anything but reserve them floor space to curl up and die.

He was jolted back to the present by a scream. Jean hid her face against his shoulder, shielding her eyes with her hands. She looked through clenched fingers, a morbid fascination beginning to replace the initial horror. "That's disgusting," she said, unable to look away.

"No evidence of infection. This one died of old age."

Seamus gave the body a cursory look before turning his back. "The rest of the place is deserted."

Joe was still staring at the old man's face, studying his features. There was something about him that looked familiar. He clicked his fingers, pleased with himself as the penny finally dropped. "David Jason."

Jean looked up at him confused.

"You know. Don't you think he looks a bit like David Jason?" Jean was none the wiser. "You remember? The actor? Played Del Boy off that BBC sitcom *Only Fools and Horses*?"

Jean looked again but shook her head. She had never heard of *Only Fools and Horses* though she liked the name.

"Suppose you never had just the four broadcast channels to choose from. Your generation was all reality TV and box sets, YouTube and watching stuff on your phone." Joe sighed, nostalgic for a forgotten time when families would watch live broadcasts together on a Saturday evening. *Doctor Who, X Factor, Strictly.*

"You talk funny." Jean frowned, pushing past him.

Seamus's voice from the wood-panelled corridor outside interrupted their exchange. "Jean, go make yourself useful and get a fire lit. There's a whole larder full of cans and pasta in there. We've hit gold," he said, clapping his hands together in delight.

With a sigh, Jean mumbled something under her breath and dutifully headed off to grab logs from the stack of chopped wood in the garage, together with the firelighters and matches Joe had found above the fireplace in the snug.

Together the men carried the old man's body outside and dumped his frail desiccated corpse head first in a large green recycling bin. Joe rushed out to remonstrate with the men, berating them for their lack of respect, insisting they bury him properly. The other men looked at each other and walked off, laughing at Joe's protestations. "If that's what you want, then you do it," said the larger of the two.

Joe rummaged in the shed amongst an assortment of gardening tools before he found what he was looking for. He grabbed a shovel and started digging a shallow grave under an olive tree. Considering they were taking the old man's house and eating his food, it was a small sign of respect, but an important one. Joe hoped that others would do the same for him when the time came.

It was hard work and within minutes his clothes were soaked in sweat. The resulting hole was only a few inches, but deep enough for its purpose. When he stood back, leaning on the shovel, a half-smile formed on his lips. He felt a glow of respectability.

They sat in silence over dinner, sharing cans of baked beans and chicken curry that Jean had heated up for them over a fire. They washed it down with a full bottle of sherry, the first proper drink the men had had in many months. By way of dessert, they passed round a half-full bottle of Baileys, listening to more of Seamus's stories of growing up in Ireland and tall tales of personal triumph and good fortune. Joe was sick of hearing them.

Seamus yawned and stretched: "Think I'll turn in. I'll take

the master bedroom, the rest of you can fight over the rest. I found this place, didn't I?"

No one argued. He grabbed Jean's wrist and hauled her up forcefully. She looked confused and tried to snatch back her arm, but he held tight. "Come on, let's go."

She pulled away from him, her hand slipping from his moist palms. "What are you doing?" said Jean.

For a moment, she looked like a defenceless animal, caught in the headlights, painfully unaware of the danger right in front of her, but paralysed and unable to move. She looked at the others imploring for their help, but they seemed complicit in whatever was happening here.

Seamus smiled a lascivious smile, his movements were slow and imprecise from the booze. Hunched over in the semi-darkness, the man on the crate grinned back, enjoying the drama. His teeth were a dull yellow, several were missing. He took another long swig from the bottle, never taking his eyes off the girl. Seamus turned back to face Jean. His smile was gone. "Let's go, I said."

His tone towards her was different, more insistent somehow. Gone was the charming, affable Seamus who looked out for Jean, cared for her, the man she probably had a secret crush on. The person standing in front of her wanted one thing only. Wide-eyed, she suddenly saw him properly for the first time and was very afraid. How could she have been so blind, thought Joe? He looked like a predator circling his prey.

She backed towards the door, her eyes darting between Joe and Seamus, panic building. She still had time to run if she was quick. She tried to stall. "I'm not tired."

"Neither am I." Seamus shook his head, emboldened by the others.

Joe started to intervene: "Listen, Seamus, I don't think..."

Seamus whipped his head round and silenced him before he

could finish. "I don't give a monkey's what you think. Stay out of this, fat boy."

Jean suddenly grasped what was happening and started to cry. "Please, I don't...I don't want to. Joe, please, don't let him."

Joe rose quickly and stood between them, blocking his path. He raised his hands in front of him to try to defuse the situation, appealing for Seamus to be sensible.

Seamus shook his head. "Don't be a mug. We all know what's going to happen here. Don't try and get in my way. I'm warning you."

"This has gone far enough. If you do anything to that girl you'll have me to answer for," cautioned Joe.

"I thought you were one of us." Seamus looked around the others, making eye contact with each of them. "Such a disappointment."

"I'm nothing like you, Seamus."

"Locking us up in that place, for all that time, they treated us like animals. Sure, you were only there a few days, but us, we were there for weeks on end. Someone has to pay."

"Doesn't mean we have to behave like animals. We're better than that, aren't we?"

"You may be, Joe, but I'm not. Treat me like an animal and sooner or later that's what I become. I've been waiting for this day for a long time."

Jean's chest was heaving as her terror mounted, adrenaline pumping through her veins, her fists clenched. She made a break for the open doorway, but one of the men grabbed her wrist and pushed her back into the middle of the room.

Seamus nodded at his former cellmate. Joe never heard or saw it coming, and was only vaguely conscious of movement behind him and a severe blow to the back of his head. He collapsed on to the floor and the world went dark. He was dimly aware of voices and snatched fragments of conversations.

A strangled scream, hurried footsteps going up the stairs, then nothing.

When he woke, it was dark with only the flickering light of a candle in a saucer. His hands and feet were tied with what felt like bungee cord, lying on a cold limestone floor. Jean and the others were nowhere to be seen.

Chapter 39

Joe squinted up into the beam of sunlight that struck the paving stone next to his head. A dirty J-cloth had been stuffed in his mouth to stop him shouting out, which made breathing difficult. There was a metallic taste to the cloth as if it had once been used to clean paint brushes.

He'd been down here for two days now in a state of squalor that made him gag each time he woke. His underwear was heavily soiled and despite his best efforts to wriggle clear of the wet patch on the floor, he had been unable to get any real sleep for the last few hours. He was dangerously dehydrated and exhausted. Conserving his remaining energy, he listened helplessly to the shouting and intermittent screams from above. In part as a subconscious defence mechanism, his thoughts were miles away. He had been filling the interminable hours reflecting on a happier time before the outbreak, escaping from the hopelessness of his current predicament. The smell of paint and the unpleasant taste in his mouth somehow reminded him of his old neighbour Howard and his part-time work for a decorating business run by a friend. Paint brushes left to soak in white spirit on his windowsill overnight. How he wished his best mate was here with him right now. He could have done with the company.

Before coming to Hurst, Joe had spent several months holed up in a tower block in Shirley, on the outskirts of Southampton. The two friends shared a passion for bad sci-fi, Southampton football club, Britpop and video games – the more gore and violence the better. They took it in turns to car share into town to the same multi-story car park down near the docks. Howard was a crane operator, responsible for unloading large shipping containers on tight schedules and rewarded for hitting daily targets. It was dull work, but paid well and it meant he got to spend the day listening to music or daydreaming, with a window on the commercial world overlooking the port. By comparison, Joe's days were more mundane, working in the kiosk at the local cinema in Ocean Village. After work, they would sneak in and catch the latest releases, enjoying unlimited refills of Coke and popcorn till their bellies were full, belching on the front row in the darkness, laughing together.

When the first news reports of isolated outbreaks of the virus began in earnest, people left the cities in their droves, carrying what they could. Those that remained took full advantage of unprotected stores and shopping centres. When the numbers of rioters swelled, sweeping away the thin blue line of law and order, large segments of the urban population formed ant-trails to electronics and clothing stores for the latest gear. They had staggered home happy with wide-screen televisions and DVD players, unaware that the days of widely available electricity were soon coming to an end. Blackouts swiftly ensued, leaving displays lifeless and obsolete.

Joe had the foresight to borrow a Transit van from his downstairs neighbour, and drove to the local cash and carry a few blocks away. They had avoided the supermarkets. By then larger stores were surrounded by private security guards equipped with riot shields and batons to deter the hungry crowds. With Howard's help, Joe loaded up on multipacks of fruit juice and mineral water, boxes of biscuits, nuts and crisps, dried fruit and Biltong, sacks of rice and pasta, and anything else that would last without refrigeration. By the time they were done, they had ferried seventeen brim-full shopping trolleys to the van parked in a side alley. It took them the best part of a day to manhandle box after box up the eleven flights of stairs to their bedsits, the lift broken for the third time that month. It was a small block and they shared the floor with two larger flats, both of whose occupants were away on holiday or business, they weren't sure which.

He remembered the day a convoy of army trucks arrived to reinforce the police. Hundreds of soldiers did their best to wrestle back control with tear gas and rubber bullets, before they were overwhelmed and forced to retreat, leaving gangs of youths to slaughter each other in a mad scramble for what little food and water remained.

Joe and Howard, along with a family from downstairs, watched with increasing alarm. They decided to take matters into their own hands, barricading shut the ground-floor stair-well door with two sofas and a kitchen table hurled from the floor above. They reinforced the metal doors with two heavy-looking curtain rods, top and bottom. It would keep the more curious scavengers away but they both knew it was unlikely to stop any concerted effort. If the gangs thought there was anything of value inside, they would find a way. It was just a matter of time.

The family downstairs got sick first. There was nothing Joe or Howard could do for them. Through the air vents, they heard the children coughing through the night. The next day when they went to check on them, there was no response. Everything was silent.

With a smile, Joe remembered spending their days reading fiction, sometimes aloud. Howard thought it was important to stay fit, so they took it in turns to do press-ups and sit-ups, running relays up and down the stairs. Hours passed slowly, lost in conversation, arguing about the most pointless stuff, like you did when you no longer had TV, work or social media to occupy your every waking thought. Who was the best James Bond villain? Whether there really was extra-terrestrial life? Who was the best English striker of all time? Which members of the latest boy-band sensation could actually carry a tune without the help of a mixing deck?

Joe still treasured the handwritten diary he kept to record what they saw from their eleventh-storey panoramic view of the city. He tracked the movement of police vehicles. Counted the helicopters ferrying personnel in and out. The day the army arrived and started knocking on doors to evacuate whoever remained. He remembered the day they first noticed that passenger jets had stopped taking off from Southampton airport a few miles away. The unrelenting silence, broken only by car alarms set off by the last of the looters. Each event noted with times and approximate locations.

They had debated whether to leave the city, afraid of contracting the sickness. Howard talked of other dangers. Cholera and worse. Too many bodies left unburied, he said. Rats would spread disease. It was only a question of time before things deteriorated further. In the bedsit, they had been safe, rationing their food and water for as long as possible. In a few weeks, they hoped the virus would die out, along with most of those infected, giving them safe passage out of the city. They planned to head south-west towards Lymington where his aunt lived and try to find a fishing boat or a yacht to take them to France.

The nights had been long and spent in total darkness. They

conserved their candles and torch batteries for when they were preparing meals. When it got dark, there was nothing to do but sleep. They watched the stars from their balcony window, telling stories, reminiscing about school days.

After fifty-five days the food ran out. They searched the other flats for tinned goods, or anything that was still edible, exhausting all that remained. Hungry and thirsty, they waited as long as they dared before setting out for Aunt Harriet's town house in Lymington. He hadn't been sure whether she would still be there, but it was as good a place as any to head for. He could still picture the views over the estuary and glimpses of the Solent.

Joe remembered the day they left the tower block for the last time, lowering their kit down a rope from a second-floor window before clambering after it. They loaded the Transit van in silence with what remained of their supplies and set out along back streets and alleyways, choked with abandoned vehicles. After several miles of slow progress heading out of the city, they had swung south towards Hythe, hugging the coastline, avoiding the main roads through the New Forest. Rounding two vehicles locked together in a head-on collision, they got the van stuck in a deep ditch, its front wheels spinning uselessly in muddy water. Without a winch and a truck, there had been no way of getting it out again, so they continued the rest of their journey on foot.

It was further than they realised. They had no map and only a pocket compass with a mind of its own, but figured that if they stayed close to the coast, they would get there eventually. It took them the best part of two days. Keeping to footpaths that sometimes ran deep into the forest, crossing fields left to grow wild, sleeping in deserted farmhouses. When they finally reached Lymington River, they found themselves opposite the ferry port and single-track railway station. Walking into town, they caught sight of other survivors and kept their distance. Their large backpacks caught the attention of those they passed who chased them into nearby fields.

Lying on the cold stone floor, Joe's memory jumped forward to the fateful night of the attack. Raised voices in the street, someone banging relentlessly on the door. Somehow they had found a way in, smashing through a ground-floor window, even though it was shuttered and padlocked.

He had replayed the following minutes again and again in his head. Stupid and careless. They had fallen asleep with the candle burning. Somehow the light must have been visible from the street below through closed curtains. They didn't stand a chance, there were too many of them, torches flashed in faces. Howard fought back and was stabbed in the stomach, Joe was badly beaten. They took their rucksacks and left them for dead. Joe held Howard's hand as the colour drained from his face. His pulse grew fainter until the touch of his skin grew cold and his body stiffened. After that, Joe must have passed out.

It was Zed who found Joe with broken ribs and a fractured jaw. They pulled him out, cleaned him up, carried him to the Land Rover. Riley tended to his wounds, whispering soothing words to keep him conscious. He could still picture Riley's face, her long brown hair, her even smile, her green eyes. In the permanent half-light of the cellar, he felt he could reach out and touch her, but her image was temporary. The rest of his group was most likely back at the castle by now, wondering where he was. He shuddered, remembering that no one knew what had become of him. He was on his own. This time there would be no chance of rescue.

He looked deep within himself, wondering whether he had the courage and strength to carry on. His second incarceration in a week. Out of the frying pan and into the fire. Was this his punishment for finally giving in to carnal pleasure at the hotel?

His first time, after so much anticipation, had been purely functional. No talking. Watched by the guard. Then his first was quickly followed by several more. Each partner different and exciting, yet devoid of emotional connection. An exchange of services. Few words. The guard had called him a breeder. An underclass to the women who used him. To them he was no better than an animal. He wondered what real love would feel like and whether he would live long enough to experience it. Mila. He thought of his beautiful Mila, a smile forming on his lips.

He twisted his body, rolling over on his back as his thoughts turned to Jean, the young girl he had come here with. The girl he had put his life on the line to try and protect. Look where that had got him. An idea began to form in his mind, building slowly like a ray of light barely visible, half imagined. Jean and he were partners now, they both shared a common enemy. Seamus would get what was coming to him. He would teach that bastard a lesson. He was suddenly filled with hope. Jean would find a way. She was young but also resourceful. Somehow he had to believe she would get him out of here. He just needed to hold on and stay strong, whatever happened. Right now, hope and faith were all he had left. He had come so far to get to this point. He owed it to Howard.

From the kitchen above came the sound of raucous laughter and a chair scraping on the stone floor. The door at the top of the stairs swung open on its hinges and he heard the heavy clump of boots coming down the narrow steps towards the cellar. Joe looked back up into the light from the small window shrouded in foliage and whispered a silent prayer, repeating over and over: "Forgive us our trespasses – deliver us from evil".

He rolled over and managed to get himself up into a kneeling position. If only he could get to his feet, he could try something. His legs were numb and unresponsive. The renewed blood flow caused agonising shooting pains.

Footsteps stopped outside the door as he heard the rattle of keys. With a grimace he levered himself into a crouch, using the chair to support his weight. He rocked back uncomfortably on to the tips of his toes and as the door opened he launched himself forward with all his might, catching his abuser completely by surprise, barging him backwards. The man smashed his head back against the brick wall. Joe was on him quickly before he could recover. Pressing his elbow into the man's throat, throttling him until he lay still. Joe wasn't sure if he was dead or just unconscious. It didn't matter to him.

There was a call from the kitchen above. A question left unanswered. The voice was slurred and uncertain.

Joe checked the man's pockets and found a small kitchen knife. He stopped for a second, listening carefully for any further movement on the floor above. There was silence.

After several attempts, dropping the knife on the floor, he held the blade between his knees and moved his wrists backwards and forwards against the serrated edge as the bungee cord began to fray. He freed his legs and stood painfully, braced against the wall. He looked up the stairwell to the kitchen, trying to remember the layout. With the knife in his right hand, he climbed the stairs looking for Jean and Seamus.

Chapter 40

It had been a frustrating night for Copper and his men. Ahead of their attack on Hurst Castle later that evening the weather had deteriorated rapidly. A local man, they called Trevor, stood at the doorway, sniffing at the wind, making faces at the darkening sky, where grey clouds were gathering over the Ship Inn on Lymington quay.

Trevor reckoned it was blowing a force six, but gusting seven or eight, with a big sea swell to go with it. It was also a south-westerly wind, far from ideal for their intended beach landing on the exposed spit facing the Needles rocks.

Will watched from the shadows as the two leaders conferred for several minutes in heated debate. The man in black finally gave in to common sense, postponing the attack until the following night, providing the weather improved in the meantime. Copper seemed impatient, perhaps realising his men were psyched and ready to go. Will knew from bitter experience that delays weakened resolve and would dull the men's edge as a fighting force. They had all been cooped up in the pub for most of the day. They were restless and baying for blood.

Copper strode back into the bar with confirmation of the

bad news. "Attack's off, boys." There was a chorus of disapproval and disappointment. "No, listen, he's right, it's too dangerous for a beach assault tonight. We wouldn't be able to land where we need to. And with the swell, someone's going to drown, and I'd rather it wasn't one of you lot."

Will's wrists were still cuffed behind his back. The plastic ties were biting and chafing but if he sat very still, leaning forward, he found the pain lessened and he could get the blood flowing all the way to his fingers if he wiggled them slowly. He was racking his brains to figure out a way to get a message to his friends at Hurst to warn them of the impending attack. He had been trying to make eye contact with the landlord and his daughter, but they had not looked his way. Will was watching them carefully, observing their interactions with Copper and the others, trying to determine whether their loyalty to Copper was feigned or real.

The landlord's daughter collected the empty bowls from the dinner they had served the hungry men. It wasn't much, just some soup made from boiled vegetables, followed by a few chunks of "Fruit and Nut" chocolate they had liberated from a vending machine. They took it in turns to swig from a bottle of Cointreau the landlord had found behind a catering fridge. He was saving it for a special occasion.

When the girl was within earshot, Will whispered the words "Help me" as loudly as he dared. She looked at him and very deliberately shook her head. "Please," he implored. As she approached his table, he noticed she walked with a slight limp in her left leg. She reached across and started wiping the table nearest him with a cloth, even though it looked spotless. She leaned close, looking past his shoulder. Her long brown hair brushed against his right arm.

"They'll kill me if I help you."

"And they'll kill me if you don't." He smiled wanly.

Before he could say anything else she moved on to the next table, but glanced back at him from behind the bar counter. He wasn't sure if he could trust her, but right now, she was his best and only option.

With the attack off for the night, Copper took some of the men on a scavenging mission, more to pass the time than for any real purpose. They already had with them everything they needed. But as Copper had said, it didn't pay to have the men stuck in close quarters for hours on end. Like dogs and small children, his men needed daily exercise. They had all seen too many arguments boil over into fistfights and worse.

Will watched the way Copper interacted with the others. There was no question: his men respected, even liked him. Perhaps there was more to Copper than met the eye. He seemed full of contradictions that kept Will guessing. With his men, he was affable, humorous, even charming. The former policeman seemed to defy categorisation. He had come to know him as cruel and dispassionate, adept at extracting information through torture. Copper could be a vicious and vindictive bastard who thought nothing of beating or even killing a man.

When it came to Copper's interactions with his boss, Will was under no illusions that the passive-aggressive behaviour betrayed a growing sense of frustration with his leader. Beyond the adopted mask of ruthlessness was the man in black simply a weak bully playing a part, living up to his men's expectations?

Will turned his attention to the rest of Copper's squad. Their stab-proof vests exaggerated their size and bulk, but underneath they were fit and lean. In their adjusted roles, he smiled inwardly, there were undoubtedly fewer opportunities for sitting on their backsides eating donuts. His second in command, the man they called Sarge, like Copper had served in the local constabulary so he was familiar with police tactics and had some basic training with handling weapons. They were barely recognisable as enforcers of the law. All police insignia had been removed. The laws they followed were mostly of their own making. They seemed to live by a code, a mutual respect of each other, of hard work, discipline and determination. That didn't mean that they had suddenly become bad men, but their frame of reference was somewhat altered. Their filters had been removed and the justice they dispensed was a little more direct and violent. Their loyalty was now to Copper, pure and simple.

Will managed to get some rest, finding a comfortable position on his right side, lying on one of the padded bench seats under the blacked-out window of the pub. He woke after a couple of hours with his right arm numb and tingling. He stood and stretched his legs, walking around the slumbering figures laid out on the floor. The dim light from a lone candle cast flickering shadows round the room. Voices from the other room suggested several of the men were still awake, keeping watch.

Behind the bar Will spotted the landlord's daughter. She made as if to leave but he stretched out and grabbed her wrist before she could turn away. She didn't cry out but made it very clear that she didn't want anything to do with him or what he had to say to her. He released her hand, and she remained standing there, rubbing her wrist. She made no attempt to leave.

"If anyone sees us talking, I'm dead. You've got two minutes."

Will nodded and started explaining how in a few hours' time these men would launch an all-out attack on Hurst Castle. He begged her to help get a message to his friends. Their lives were in danger. He had to warn them some way, somehow, so that they could prepare themselves or get as far away as possible.

She heard him out, listening dispassionately to his story. Her face was hard to read. She seemed empathetic but eager not to take sides in someone else's fight.

"Listen. You seem like a nice person. But they will kill me and my father if they find out I helped you. I don't have a choice. It's too much to ask. If there was another way, then maybe, but short of me going there myself, it can't be done."

Will knew she was right, but that didn't stop him from trying, for the sake of his friends. "Then cut me loose."

She looked uncertain, playing it out in her head, trying to figure out whether she could help him without compromising everything her father had worked so hard for.

Will persisted. "There must be another way out of here, please."

She checked no one was listening. Logic and reason were probably screaming at her not to get involved. She struck him as impulsive, someone who liked to trust her instincts. Doing nothing would make her complicit in a crime. If she could find a way to help him and have plausible deniability when questioned, then it became a win-win.

One of Copper's men stirred on the floor, fidgeting in his sleeping bag, then turned over and went back to sleep. She waited until his snoring resumed and turned back to Will, her mind made up. She leaned her head towards him across the bar, their faces nearly touching. Will became powerfully aware of an intoxicating mix of perfume and lavender soap.

She spoke quickly, pausing only to check no one was watching. When she had finished, he leaned forward and kissed her full on the lips, lingering for a second, enjoying the orange-scented sweetness of the Cointreau fumes. She kissed him back hungrily and mouthed the words: "Good luck."

Chapter 41

The following morning the wind direction veered to the south, and its intensity abated sufficiently for Trevor to consider sanctioning the boats' departure. It remained a risky venture, but an acceptable, calculated one. There would still be a strong sea swell to contend with, but all things considered, the attack should proceed with all urgency. The attack on Hurst was back on.

Storm clouds hurried across the horizon. The bad weather was more distant now, giving way to a milder spring evening in Lymington, overcast and dry. In a couple of hours it would be sunset. The sun was sinking rapidly behind the mainly Georgian houses and cottages that lined the high street and surrounding roads leading down to the cobbled alleys and quayside of the harbour. It would be dark by seven thirty. A half-moon meant there would be just enough light, giving the attackers a further advantage.

High tide was set for around midnight. Their plan was to cast off in the failing light and head down the river estuary. Trevor had sailed these waters all his life. He was well aware of the shallower waters and treacherous mudflats weaving their way down river towards the main channel, heading west towards Hurst. Their arrival was timed to coincide with when they expected most of Hurst's occupants to be fast asleep in their beds. A nominal force would be protecting what amounted to a very large site with walls stretching over five hundred metres. They knew from the intelligence they had extracted from Will that Hurst's leaders mistakenly believed that the site's remoteness and relative inaccessibility, with ten-metre-high walls, made their base virtually impregnable to an attacking force. Their pride and arrogance, said the man in black, would be their downfall.

Yet history was on their side. Will knew from Scottie's incessant stories that Hurst's walls had never been breached in all its near five hundred years. Whatever the man in black had learned from the interrogation, Will hoped beyond hope that he hadn't revealed Hurst's security protocols, guard patrols or defensive frailties. In the end, he knew everyone broke; it was only a matter of time. There had been no need for their more experimental interrogation techniques improvised from what they knew of waterboarding. In Will's case they had simply injected him with a cocktail of drugs and viciously beaten him. It was crude but effective. There was no Geneva Convention to protect the many captives the hospital handled on a weekly basis. They had grown pretty good at extracting information. Which all meant that Copper and the man in black now knew everything Will knew, and that gave them the upper hand.

～

Copper was meticulous about their preparation. He meant to leave nothing to chance. His team spent the day checking and rechecking equipment. Several of them made a trip back to the hospital to get more food and supplies. By mid-afternoon, the weather was still holding fair, with scattered clouds and more moderate winds. They stowed their gear on board the boats, cleaned their weapons, loaded magazines, laid out the rope and grappling hook on the quay and then packed it away. The man in black congratulated Copper and his team. Walking amongst them with his hands on hips, he proudly inspected his foot soldiers. They were as ready as they would ever be. Providing the weather held, it was now or never.

Will blamed his poor luck and bitterly regretted his failure to escape when the previous guard had been on duty. For now, his opportunity was gone. He would need to bide his time and hope a fresh chance for diversion presented itself.

After Will's midnight rendezvous with the landlord's daughter, the guard shift at the Ship Inn changed and one of Copper's most trusted men had been charged with keeping watch over their prisoner. Will pretended to sleep, running through the execution of his plan, step by step, waiting for his guard to lose interest or drop off. Copper's men were professional and stuck to their task, unlike some of the others from the hospital without military or police training. He had learned through bitter experience, they were mostly nihilists or thugs with a chip on the shoulder. Definitely worth avoiding eye contact. They tended to have a short fuse and a thirst for violence.

By seven, with the light fading and the moon rising behind distant clouds, they started loading up the boats on the quay. Copper would take the lead in the first R.I.B with four of his best men, forming the tip of the spear of the attack. In the larger pleasure craft, a ferryboat with covered main cabin, Sarge would lead the main force of some ten men, including Will and the man in black. The ferryboat had spent a lifetime shuttling tourists to the Needles rocks and back, so was shallow draft but seaworthy, ideal for their purposes. Last but not least was a back-up team of four men in a second fast inflatable. They would be held in reserve until the drawbridge was down and the main force was inside.

Will was running out of time. With the attack certain to go ahead tonight, he somehow had to find a way to escape. Hurst's future hung in the balance. Everything depended on Will now. He could not let his friends down. He figured it would take at least two and a half hours to walk back to the castle. He could picture the coastal footpath that ran along the estuary and marshlands towards Keyhaven. If he jogged most of the way then he could probably shave an hour off that, but the thought of running in the tired old working boots he was wearing, having not run for months, filled him with dread. Years of unhealthy living, Cornish pasty lunches and a fondness for Ringwood ale, had left him soft around the middle. The last couple of years living from hand to mouth had done remarkably little to shift that flab. He had at least lost some weight, he was sure of that, just not in the places he tended to pay attention to. The chances of finding a bicycle or a boat were slim, but he might get lucky. Lady Luck had a funny way of smiling on him when he least expected it.

With the rest of the men ferrying equipment to the waiting boats, for a few moments, Will and his minder were the only people left in the pub. Will was pretending to sleep, his eyes closed. The guard was distracted, no longer paying attention to Will. The landlord's daughter was polishing glasses behind the bar. She had changed into figure-hugging jeans and was adjusting her hair in a mirror, applying some lipstick. She dropped her cloth and stretched down to retrieve it. Was she doing it on purpose? She was certainly drawing attention to herself, whether deliberate or not. The guard now had his back to Will. He seized his chance, taking him completely by surprise.

His body low like a rugby tackle but with his wrists still tied, he charged at the man, making contact with his shoulder, barging him with all his might. The guard slammed his head hard into the wall, knocking over one of the tables. He lay still, stunned for a few moments. Will glanced back towards the landlord's daughter. She waved him urgently towards the back door.

He wiggled under the hatchway on his hands and knees and got awkwardly back to his feet behind the bar. He needed to keep moving fast and stay unseen. Keeping low, he ducked through a doorway that led to a corridor stacked with boxes. Empty beer kegs lined the far wall. A notice board fluttered with staff notices, and fliers for visiting bands. Stairs to the right led up to where he imagined the landlord and his daughter lived above the pub. She had been good to her word. A brick blocked the fire door from closing.

Outside it was pitch black. Will blinked into the darkness. He could just make out a rusting iron gate that led to the car park. Over his shoulder he heard a woman's scream, raised voices and a glass smashing on the ground. He only had a few moments to get away.

As quietly as he could manage in all the excitement, he put his weight against the heavy iron gate. He half expected a loud screech of rusted metal, but the mechanism operated silently on well-oiled hinges. Beyond was a small staff car park at the rear of the pub, leading to a cobbled alleyway.

Taking the most direct route was a big risk, but he simply didn't have time to backtrack through side streets. With a final look over his shoulder he raced up the cobbled hill to the bottom of the high street, his hands still tied behind his back. He darted left and jogged along the narrow lane lined with rows of whitewashed cottages and town houses running down towards the waterfront marinas. Turning the corner, a forest of masts and rigging lay ahead. To his left, a boatyard full of yachts and vessels lay in various states of disrepair, waiting their turn for the huge crane to cradle them back into the slow running waters of the Lymington river. Beyond the boatyard and yacht clubs lay open fields and country lanes. Will craved the darkness and solitude of the asphalt footpath that led back towards Hurst.

Chapter 42

Tommy and the others left guarding Hurst Castle had still not received word from the scavenging team. It was not the first time that their distance from the castle had required an overnight stay, but when they still hadn't returned by dusk on the second day, the members of the council met in emergency session. Protocol dictated that a search party be mounted but with Jack, Terra and Sam also not returned, they could ill afford to further weaken their defences, when in all likelihood they could all be back at any moment. Unknowingly, the castle was at its most vulnerable in some time, and its occupants were dangerously unaware of the imminent threat to their security.

In the courtyard, Tommy tossed another log into the firepit. The red-hot ash spat sparks at his bare ankles. He kicked at a few wood ends with the toe of his boot where the logs had burned through, sending smoke and embers curling up into the night sky. Long shadows danced on the steep walls of the castle that towered over the small group as they sat round in a semi-circle, telling stories and enjoying each other's company.

Tommy stared unblinking into the heart of the fire. With a sigh, he reached behind and grabbed another log from the pile of wood they had unloaded earlier from the trailer. He resumed his seat next to Liz. She handed him her half-empty can of lager, toasting the assembled company: "Here's to our new American friends. May they bring us better food: hamburgers, pizzas and hot dogs."

"And save us from Liz's cooking," added Tommy.

Scottie and Greta raised their cans while Liz delivered a two-fingered response, adding, "Very funny."

Scottie's lilting voice from the other side of the fire added to their toasts. "To Hurst. May Jack and Terra bring us good fortune, and, aye, better food."

"Remind me what we're really celebrating?" asked Greta, toasting her toes against the blazing fire.

"Oh, don't be such a grouch," joked Tommy. "Do we really need a reason? We're alive. Isn't that enough?"

"I suppose. When the cat's away, the mice will play," added Scottie, lounging back against Greta's bare legs. She stroked the back of his head affectionately.

Tommy scowled at their quiet intimacy. It bothered him that Scottie, of all people, had scored the best-looking girl at the castle. A slightly effeminate Scotsman at that. There was no justice. Greta had her eyes closed, her head turned towards Liz. It looked almost like she was seeking her friend's approval.

"Come on, Liz. What do you miss most about the way things were?" asked Scottie.

"The Internet, for one. The world seems so much smaller now. We're so cut off from the rest of the world. I kind of like that," answered Liz.

"Are you not a wee bit curious to know what's going on out there?" added Scottie. "Don't you miss that feeling of being connected? Being part of something bigger. I don't know, the scope and scale of the way things were."

"I miss the people, that's for sure," said Liz. "My family, my friends. I miss stupid stuff like Sunday newspapers, taking the day to read all the supplements. I miss sitting in a pub next to a roaring fire, drinking Ringwood ale pumped by hand. I miss the Colemanballs column in *Private Eye*. So many things we just took for granted. What about you?"

"I miss going to the Rose Bowl to see Test match cricket. I appreciate that's a wee bit odd for a Scotsman but I loved it. What's not to like? Beer snakes, Mexican waves and the barmy army. Anyone remember stewards wading into the crowd to grab ten-feet-high stacks of empty plastic glasses? What a sight. Ridiculous."

They all laughed, lost in memories. Tommy was silent staring into the fire, as shapes and figures danced in the flames. He let out a deep sigh and lamented, "I miss summer holidays to Spain with Laura." The others shouted catcalls in his direction, mocking his sentimentality.

"More like holiday with your mum," derided Liz.

Tommy spun round and scowled in her direction before continuing undeterred, unable to suppress a smile. "No, seriously, we went this one time to Palma, Majorca. Sandy beaches, sunburned Brits, beer bellies and cheap cocktails. It was brilliant."

"Remember just going on a plane to somewhere far away? Airports? Duty-free? Needing a passport?" said Greta.

Scottie went next. "I miss live music, going to see a rock band at Wembley Stadium. Seeing Rod Stewart, U2, or Bruce Springsteen. Thousands of fans packed together, dancing, cheering, laughing. Those were the days."

The group fell silent, overwhelmed by a hundred memories, each lost in their own private reverie. Greta's voice broke the silence, sounding fragile, perhaps fearful of the answer. "Do you think things will ever get back to the way they were?"

"Of course," responded Scottie, without hesitation. "We gotta believe that. It may take time, but it'll happen. Maybe, things won't be exactly the same, but come on, humans are a resilient bunch. We've faced similar threats to our way of life. Just think. The bubonic plague, Spanish flu, acts of God like earthquakes, meteor strikes, typhoons. Then there was the Holocaust, world wars, nuclear explosions, the list goes on, and somehow, life finds a way."

"The dinosaurs didn't fare too well," challenged Tommy, smirking mischievously.

"Yeah, but how many times has that happened in, like, a hundred billion years of history on this planet? A true global killer? Once, in like, ever?" continued Scottie. "And we're only talking about an extinction event for humans, not all the other animals and insects and life on this planet. Life goes on regardless."

"Who knows? Maybe humans are the next lemming, or dodo, driven to extinction by forces beyond their control?" added Liz.

"I doubt it," reassured Scottie. "Humankind has a good record of overcoming all odds, triumphing in the face of adversity. It'll be like that again. Somewhere, somehow it stands to reason that someone is doing better than us. We can't be the only ones to have survived. Maybe whole populations, whole countries even, have immunity. There might be some gene that protects them from getting it. Or the warmer climate prevented a flu-like virus from taking hold in the first place? There might be a vaccine already, a cure for the virus. You never know, right?"

"I wonder how Jack and Terra are getting on," said Tommy, changing the subject. "They wouldn't say much about their trip or why they were going."

"It's got to be something to do with the Americans," reckoned Liz. "Nathan said it was all top secret and he couldn't breathe a word about it. All sounded very mysterious." She winked at Scottie. There was playful mischief between them.

Tommy leaned forward, animated and energised by something. "What if there was a whole convoy of ships heading our way right this very moment? Some massive rescue mission. Maybe they're evacuating Britain and they need our help. Typical Americans, always have to save the world."

"Right, trust the Americans to turn up two years late."

"I wouldn't go getting people's hopes," cautioned Scottie. "There's not going to be any relief convoy. I seriously doubt there's anyone left to rescue us. The rest of the world is probably in just as much of a mess as we are."

"No one knows that for sure," said Tommy, shaking his head. "The Americans always save the day."

"You've been watching too many disaster movies. No way Will Smith is going to save us this time."

"When the Americans come, they'll do it in style. It's normally, like now, when Britain's on its knees, they show up and turn the tide. Two world wars proved that." Tommy paused, troubled by something he remembered. It was just a feeling, a hunch really, that had been nagging him. "There was something that felt wrong when they refused to tell us anything. Makes you wonder whose side they're on."

"Oh, we're on the same side all right," reassured Scottie. The man with a thousand voices and accents affected an Alabama drawl straight from the deep south, reprising the role of Atticus Finch from *To Kill a Mocking Bird*. He continued in character: "Right now, there's a whole task force en route from the US of A. Ships filled with corned beef and ketchup. Frozen steaks as big as Frisbees. Cheerleaders with pompoms. Jet fighters streaming red white and blue vapour trails. Ticker tape parades on the docks as they unload crate after crate of good ol' lite beer, flowing from every porthole."

Tommy didn't look so sure. "Yeah, and pigs might fly. If you ask me, I reckon they're up to no good. It's a land grab or they're here to steal all our supplies before moving on, like locusts. Don't worry, Liz, I'm sure they'll leave your stash well alone."

Liz belted Tommy with the back of her hand and he fell backwards off his seat, clutching the side of his face. "Hey, there's no need for violence, woman."

"That'll learn you, big mouth," said one of the others.

Tommy glared back at Liz, dusting himself down. Greta stretched her thin arms high above her head, sweater pulled tight across her chest, yawning loudly and very deliberately. She fluttered her eyelashes in Scottie's general direction. "Right, think I'll turn in. You coming?"

Tommy made to join her but she wagged her finger. "Not you, Tommy. Scottie?"

"Can't. Not tonight. I'm on watch, with this reprobate. I'll come and tuck you in when I'm done."

"Go on then," said Liz, getting to her feet a little slowly, clutching her back from a hard day in the kitchen. "Early start tomorrow. Best turn in and leave you boys to it."

"Night, Liz, night, Greta. See you ladies in the morning," said Scottie.

The two women wandered off into the darkness towards the old castle keep, leaving the remaining group following them with their eyes. A door slammed and Nathan appeared out of the gloom, jangling a large bunch of keys. Tommy smuggled his can of lager behind a trouser leg. Nathan didn't approve of drinking, particularly when someone was on duty.

"Everyone's accounted for. The castle is yours. Try and keep it together out there tonight, yeah? No messing about." He checked his clipboard, angling the paper towards the light to read the rota. "Roger and Simon will relieve you at 0200 hours.

Remember, perimeter walk every half hour, one of you stays at the main gate at all times. Here are the keys."

"So these are quite literally the 'keys to the castle'," joked Tommy. "I've always wanted to say that. You know we've done this a hundred times before? I could walk the walls with my eyes closed."

"That's what I'm worried about, you sleepwalking again," said Scottie.

"Like to see you try," came a voice from the group around the fire.

"How much do you want to bet?" boasted Tommy.

"Gentlemen, please. Just do your jobs. Just this once, try and behave like professionals," implored Nathan.

The pair of them burst out laughing. "Aw, we're only pulling your leg, Nathan. We'll do our best, don't you worry. We're a crack team, we are, ain't we, Scottie? The A team. Butch Cassidy and the Sundance Kid, Batman and Robin, Bonnie and Clyde," said Tommy.

"Bonnie was a woman, ya giant dunderhead," corrected Scottie.

"Right, I'll leave you to it," said Nathan, growing tired of their levity. "No pranks, Tommy. Keep your eyes peeled for the *Nipper* and Zed's team. They might put in a late appearance. Unlikely, but you never know."

"We won't let you down, will we, Tommy? Come on."

The two of them said their goodbyes and left the rest of the group to enjoy the remains of the fire. Scottie put his arm around Tommy, meandering unevenly towards the armoury to collect a rifle each and the flare gun, in case of emergencies. No doubt it would be another uneventful night like all the others. Still, better to be safe than sorry.

Chapter 43

The lead boat carrying Copper and his men was making steady progress up the channel. The wind had died, but there was still just enough breeze to disperse what little noise they were making. The seventy-five horse-power twin Yamaha outboard engines drove them forward against the incoming tide. Trevor said it was slackening by the minute as it neared high water.

Surprise was critical. Copper's plans depended on his five-man team getting over the wall without being seen. From there, they would make their way to the main gate on the northern side of the fortifications, knock out the guards and secure the entrance for the main attack group waiting for their signal.

When Copper closed his eyes he had a mental map of the castle. He'd been there once before on a date with a local girl years ago. It had been her suggestion, a boat trip from Keyhaven and a walking tour of the castle. It had rained the whole day and they cut their losses and made a cursory tour of the battlements. They saw the museum and displays, walked around the castle and took the early ferry home in time for fish and chips on the village green at Milford. He couldn't remember her name. Sarah or Serena, something like that. It didn't matter now, she was likely dead, along with all the rest.

He berated himself for his wandering thoughts. He needed to get his mind back on the job at hand. If what Will had told them was to be trusted, they could expect only limited resistance. Two guards, lightly armed. It would be a turkey shoot. Once they had the two girls, Adele and Stella, together with the Hurst leaders, the rest were expendable. They didn't need more mouths to feed. They had all the human specimens they needed for the experiments. Still, if there were young women amongst them, they might take a few back to keep the men entertained. After all, their nights were long and dull. Play it by ear, that's what he'd do. He was trusted to make his own decisions.

As they passed a line of yachts on river moorings, the rhythmic throbbing and gurgling from the engines grew louder, echoing momentarily across the water. There was nothing they could do about it, other than cut the engines and paddle the rest of the way, but that would take too long. The engines were a necessary evil.

Trevor was keeping to the left side of the channel, staying out of the last of the tide and keeping clear of the mudflats marked by wooden posts every fifty yards or so, leading them out towards open water at the mouth of Lymington River.

The R.I.B was built for coastguard use and maintained with the latest equipment. It had a functioning radio, proper seating for its crew of four to six, a powerful searchlight, together with oars and flares. Copper's men were relaxed but focused. None of them was particularly enjoying being out on the water. There were a few green faces amongst them as the size of the waves grew and their craft began to pitch and yaw. The men gripped the handles nearest them a little tighter as they were tossed around, bouncing off waves, buffeted by the wind which seemed to strengthen now they were beyond the shelter of the harbour and river estuary.

In the distance they could see the dark outline of the castle. It looked enormous, more like a small citadel than a castle. Beyond Hurst Spit, on the other side of the Needles channel they could see the Isle of Wight. A shapeless mass in total darkness, stretching as far as the eye could see, punctuated by the Needles rocks like giant jagged teeth, facing Christchurch Bay. The island was shielding them from the worst of the wind, blowing in from the Channel Islands, Cherbourg peninsula and France. The remnants of the earlier storm had blown itself out.

For a moment, the wind seemed to strengthen again, gusting and swirling. Every few seconds, a new torrent of water broke against the bow of the boat, soaking the men with spray. The engine note changed slightly, lost against the sound of their wash and waves. They turned their faces away from the wind, bracing themselves each time the boat pitched into a new wave. In a few minutes their clothes and equipment were soaked. The men licked salt from their lips, as water sloshed around their feet, making the floor slippery.

The castle came closer into view and they could make out the battlements and towers of the old fort. An outline of a lighthouse towered over the encampment. A dull orange glow lit up the inside of the castle walls. Copper guessed it must be a campfire. He smiled to himself. The fire would diminish the defender's ability to see anything in the dark.

Rounding the Hurst headland, their boat kept its distance from the beach, labouring against the incoming tide that flowed faster here, funnelled over rocks. Copper's men shrank lower, hidden from sight. Copper kept his eyes focused on the shoreline. His senses were alert, ever vigilant for any waves breaking against obstructions in the water, buoys, posts, or fishing nets. He was fairly sure there were no sea defences added by the

Hurst crew to protect against shore landings by an invading force. The pilot checked his bearings and pointed the bow of the R.I.B towards the beach in between two groynes, nudging Copper to make sure he was happy for them to head in. Peering over the bow of the boat, Copper had one final scan and gave a thumbs up. It was safe to proceed.

Copper was under no illusions. Despite what he knew of Hurst's defences, he told his men never to underestimate an adversary. The castle would be well defended. A significant threat that needed eliminating once and for all. One side of Copper's mouth curled upwards. He was looking forward to getting his own back. As his boss was fond of saying, revenge is a dish best served cold. The pilot killed the engines and they surfed the rest of the way in to the beach.

Chapter 44

Will was fairly sure that he was not being followed. After his headlong dash from the Ship Inn to the outskirts of Lymington, he paused, gasping for breath behind an abandoned truck near the town sailing club, or what was left of it. It was little more than a burned-out shell, ravaged by fire and the winter storms. The car park was part waterlogged, scattered with abandoned vehicles. They were of no use to Will. Most were rusting heaps, their batteries long since flat and their ignitions dead.

On the green, beside a band stand, he noticed a large mound, with black plastic sheeting flapping in the breeze. He squinted, trying to discern its shape and purpose in the darkness. With a shudder of realisation, he recognised it as man-made, like dozens of others scattered around the town. Bodies collected from the houses that lined the riverside, ready for collection and disposal by clean-up crews who never showed up. Perhaps they themselves had succumbed to the sickness. After all this time, he recognised the faint stench of decay, of bodies left to decompose above ground. A feast for rats.

He turned away, his chest still heaving, and slumped onto a

bench, keeping his eyes fixed on the road behind. He half expected footsteps, but there was no movement, no torchlight searching out their quarry. Why hadn't they followed him? Wasn't it obvious he would head this way, making for the castle? His thighs were burning from the exertion of jogging the short distance from the town quay. He had kept to side streets as much as possible. Either he had given the men from the hospital the slip, or else they had decided it no longer mattered whether he lived or died. He had served his purpose and sooner or later they would have killed him, of that he had little doubt.

Will was just getting his breath back when he spotted something unusual, tucked behind a boat trailer. Half-buried beneath nautical paraphernalia, race buoys and coiled polypropylene rope were the handlebars of a bicycle. He debated whether it was worth burning time trying to free his hands or continue on foot.

For three long minutes, half crouching, he gyrated his whole body up and down, rubbing his wrists against the rusted metal edge of the trailer. The backs of his hands were raw from the friction and incessant scraping, but eventually with a final grimace and a gasp of elation, the plastic ties broke and he pulled his hands free. He massaged his shoulders and biceps, manipulating his painful fingers to restore full circulation. He levered the trailer upright, dragged the bicycle out from its hiding place, and let the trailer crash down again. He looked around half expecting to see a dozen men racing his way. Other than the rhythmic percussion of a hundred sets of rigging tapping against masts in the marina, there was silence.

The mountain bike was in poor condition with two flat tyres, a rusting frame and missing its saddle. Someone had discarded the bike here with good reason. He swung his leg over and tested the pedals. The chain squeaked round, crying out for some lubrication. The brake pads had either perished or were missing, he couldn't tell in the darkness. Compared to running another ten kilometres, the bike was better than nothing, but only just.

He pushed off, wobbling unevenly down the tarmac surface before picking up speed and gaining some improved stability. He didn't risk going through the gears and peddled slowly on the rims at little more than walking pace. Passing the last of the boats in their cradles, beached like whales stranded by a falling tide, he left the boatyard. He manoeuvred the bike through a kissing gate, lifting the back wheel through. Beyond, the asphalt path stretched out ahead of him. Moonlight reflected off the Lymington river's undulating surface.

He picked up his speed a little and quickly lost control, veering to the right down the bank and ending up in a watery ditch. He picked himself up, relieved to be uninjured, his left side coated with what felt like mud but smelled worse. The fetid water reeked of methane and sewage. He wheeled the bike back up the bank, and noticed the chain was hanging loose.

Alone in the darkness, he shouted obscenities into the night, startling a pair of birds nesting in the gorse and bushes below. He wasted a couple of minutes trying to get the chain back on, feeling the teeth of the gear wheels with his fingers. He tried to relocate the chain manually, but each time the tension was too loose. He tried one last time, kneeling down, spinning the back wheel before the chain could come loose again. With a sigh of relief, he straddled the frame, standing high on the pedals and pushed off once more.

The footpath meandered across the mudflats, jagging left away from Hurst before looping round across a small tidal lock with a gate at each end. He caught his first sight of the castle in the distance. He was still some way away, perhaps as far as five kilometres. It looked like a slumbering dragon, belching smoke into the night. Will picked up the pace again, making sure to stick to the middle of the path, his confidence growing now he had the measure of the bike, albeit one with flat tyres.

Where the footpath eventually rejoined a narrow single-lane road at Keyhaven, he recognised the small quay, low buildings of the sailing club and car park beyond. Keeping the water on his left-hand side, he cycled down the lane nearest the salt marshes that led out towards Hurst Spit and the tidal road that flooded in spring tides. The roadway was littered with seaweed and other detritus.

The bicycle would be useless on shingle so he dumped it in a bush near the footbridge just in case he needed it again. He started running, his feet slipping on the loose pebbles, reducing his progress to a fast walk. In the distance, he could see the castle. He was so close now. In no more than a mile he would see his old friends and be able to warn them, providing he was not already too late.

Chapter 45

It was Tommy's turn to patrol the perimeter. He took a leisurely stroll around the battlements by torchlight, stopping to look from the various vantage points. At the eastern end of the fortifications he paused, looking back towards Lymington and Cowes, scanning for any lights in the darkness. The channel buoys were mostly still lit. Others without solar panels had long since gone dark, though with the wind in the right direction the bells of some of the cardinal buoys could still be heard, clanging away.

It was now almost two years since the last ship had arrived here. A coastal steamer, seen creeping in under cover of darkness through the deep-water channel towards the deserted dockyards of Southampton. Tommy wondered what had happened to them. Being on a ship, like the *Maersk Charlotte*, sounded like the best place to wait out the virus, heavily laden, as she was, with stores and food. Perhaps enough to last a lifetime. The *Charlotte* had been anchored near the Brambles bank in Southampton Water for as long as anyone could remember, waiting to unload. He could just make out her dim anchor lights in the darkness.

The Solent had once been one of the busiest waterways of the world. A playground for the rich and famous. America's Cup yachts, square-riggers, giant motor boats, gin palaces, sailing vessels of every description had graced the Solent. Ferries transporting day-trippers to the island, packed with foot passengers, bicycles and motorbikes, children's faces daubed with ice cream, cars and lorries crammed in tight. It had been a bustling, happy sort of place. Today it was deserted and forlorn, forgotten by man, no longer master of the sea, but land-locked and decimated by sickness. And yet, each day, the tide continued its meticulous cycle, rising and falling, enslaved by the moon. Every few seconds the sea crashed against the rocks, its energy dissipated amongst the pebbles and edges, indifferent to man's desperate plight.

At the far end of the complex Hurst Spit stretched out back towards the orderly shapes of houses and retirement accommodation that lined the cliff-tops of Milford in the distance. He peered in to the darkness, trying to pick out any shapes approaching in the distance. To his left, he could make out the Needles rocks, and waves crashing against their base, and lighthouse. The lighthouse no longer cast its beam over Christchurch Bay warning ships to stay clear. His eyes were playing tricks on him, seeing things that weren't there. He blamed the beer he'd been drinking, long past its sell-by date.

Walking back along the length of the southern wall, he headed over to the gateway to the central courtyard of the original Tudor fort and the imposing gun tower at its heart that looked out over the whole castle complex. This inner part of the castle was kept locked after hours. He took a minute to find the oversized key with ornate ironwork and engraving the length of its shaft. The lock was original and for a moment he imagined himself as a Tudor guard dressed rather differently in chainmail, holding a lantern, opening the same door, making the same midnight patrol in service of the king.

One half of the door swung open and he stepped inside, sliding the heavy bolt into place. Crossing the stone-paved inner courtyard he climbed the outside staircase that curved around the main building till he reached the first-floor entrance to the main living area. Inside the twelve-sided walls of the tower it was cramped and dark, packed with sleeping bodies and stores. The doorway had once been a first-floor Tudor window, but Scottie said the internal spiral staircase had been adapted during the reign of Queen Victoria to act as a conduit for light for the lower level.

As silently as possible Tommy lifted the latch back into place to avoid waking the pair nearest the entrance. Treading lightly around a row of camp beds and sleeping bags, he headed up the stairs to a flat roof. Pushing open the half-size hatchway, he crawled out on his hands and knees.

He loved it up here. The three-hundred-and-sixty-degree panoramic views of the Solent were unparalleled. Even in the darkness, the sense of space was intoxicating. He closed his eyes and breathed in deeply, savouring the salt and seaweed in the air. It was an overcast and virtually moonless night. The strong breeze ruffled his hair and made him shiver slightly. He could hear waves breaking against the groynes and rocks below, pebbles scraping and sliding in sync with the pull of each receding wave.

Was it his imagination or was there also something else? He thought he heard a voice and then a metallic sound that seemed out of place, coming from just outside the castle walls. He was convinced his mind was playing tricks on him. With so many sleeping under canvas in the castle grounds, it was likely someone sleep-talking or knocking something over. With a shake of his head, he continued on with his sweep.

Looking north towards Keyhaven, he could make out the line of moored yachts in the tidal estuary. Silhouetted shapes and masts swayed in the protected waters, their bows nodding gently towards him. All was quiet, as it should be.

He yawned and was just about to head back down when he heard a scrape of metal on stone. It sounded like an anchor dragged along the quayside. He couldn't place its source, but he thought it came from the direction of the beach facing the Needles passage. There it was again, it was like someone cutting fish heads on a stone slab. Was someone out fishing tonight? Another shiver travelled down his spine, though he was no longer cold.

He hurried over to the parapet but saw nothing out of place. He realised there was a blind spot beneath him where he suspected the noise had come from. He shrugged his shoulders, blaming an overactive imagination. He should never have drunk that last beer. He needed to get a grip and head back to the gate, before he weirded himself out.

He thought he heard the sound again, convinced he could see movement. First, a pair of hands broke the straight line of the wall's edge, followed by the head and shoulders of a figure clambering over the wall. For a moment, the figure lay prone, turning its head slowly while it got its bearings. As Tommy looked on, pinching himself in disbelief, another figure clambered over the lip of the wall and joined the first, lying flat, waiting.

Tommy froze, unsure what to do next. If he moved, they'd see him. In his rucksack slung across his back, he had a flare gun and a pistol with two loaded clips. Very slowly, he sunk down behind the parapet, hoping that they were too occupied to notice him. He rummaged through the bag and found what he was looking for. He cocked open the flare gun, checked there was a cartridge loaded, released the safety, pointed it high above his head and fired.

On the shingle beach, making slow progress towards Hurst, hands on hips, Will was spent. He had hardly eaten today, other than the apple smuggled out to him. There had been barely enough food at the pub for such a large host, and the unplanned extra night's stay at the Ship Inn had exhausted the landlord's meagre stores. Will had been last in line for scraps and hand-outs. He was also parched, his lips dry and sore. He pushed on. There would be plenty of time for food and drink when he reached the castle. In his mind, he visualised sitting in the Hurst canteen wolfing down second helpings of his favourite vegetable lasagne and a tankard of Jack's home-brewed ale. He salivated just thinking about it, licking his lips with a dry tongue.

A red light soared above Hurst and exploded in the night sky, bathing the whole of the castle and its surroundings in an orange glow. Will froze, watching the flare drift on the breeze over the estuary, pick out a large boat that was approaching the small jetty behind the castle. It looked like he was already too late. The attack on Hurst had begun.

Chapter 46

In the guardhouse by the main gate, Scottie heard the pop of
the flare. He sat bolt upright, dropped the book he was
reading and threw his glasses on to the table. He grabbed the
large handbell from its place on a bookshelf and scrambled
through the doorway, peering up at the orange glow as the small
blur of light blazed in the sky above him.

Scottie's first thought was that this had to be one of Tommy's
practical jokes. It was the kind of stunt that Tommy was notorious for, but surely even he wouldn't go this far, would he? He
dithered for a few precious seconds, suddenly unsure whether it
was a false alarm or a real emergency. He found it difficult to
imagine what could possibly be worth waking the whole camp
for in the dead of night.

Scottie was still gawping up into the night sky, wide-eyed,
adrenaline pulsing, when he heard shouting from up high.
Suddenly gripped by a very real fear, Scottie started ringing the
bell as loudly as he could.

All around Hurst, men, women and children were roused
from their slumber. Shaken awake and turfed out of their beds

by the prospect of an imminent though unknown threat. To Scottie, it sounded like a village coming to life at once, voices and noises in the darkness. He grabbed the rifle and stood alone, alert and waiting, scanning the battlements, watching the flare as it drifted over his head towards Keyhaven, casting long shadows in the eerie silence that followed. What could have spooked Tommy? He rocked backwards and forwards on his heels, looking around him, puzzled.

A rifle crack splintered the stone close to his head, and his right ear seemed to explode with a searing pain. His hand came away slick with blood. He crouched down, manoeuvring himself back behind the doorway to the guardhouse. The bell was still in his right hand and he started ringing it again as loudly as possible. He clasped a pocket handkerchief to his ear, trying to staunch the steady flow of blood. Who the hell was firing at him?

Back on the Gun Tower, Tommy was still cowering behind the parapet, watching the flare drift on the wind. He steeled himself, trying to get a grip on the surging panic threatening to get the better of him. His heart was pounding so fast he thought he might be having an asthma attack.

He poked his head over the ledge, trying to get a look at what was going on beneath him. A short burst of automatic fire made him duck down again. Bullets seemed to ricochet off the lip of the wall, showering him in stone fragments and dust. He moved to his right and tried again. This time he got a clear view of three men, edging slowly across the roof towards the courtyard and front gate. One man took up position behind a chimney, getting ready to provide covering fire. A silhouetted figure took the strain on a rope, while another abseiled the short distance to ground level.

Out in the western wing of the complex, he could see a small crowd of people pointing at the men on top of the wall. Tommy shouted at them, realising the danger. For a moment, the intruder was clearly visible by the fading light of the flare. He turned and brought his weapon to bear, aiming squarely at the group.

A heavy-set man emerged from a doorway, gesticulating at the man on the roof. A short deafening burst split the air. The first salvo downed the man before the gunman moved on to his next target. He fired indiscriminately now. Standing in the open, they were like fish in a barrel. Tommy's warnings were lost as a second gunman began firing.

Something suddenly snapped inside Tommy, an anger he had not felt since his father died. This time was different. There was a channel, an outlet for his rage. Whoever these men were, they would pay for what they had done. He shook his head and tried to blink away the last traces of alcohol still coursing through his veins. Perhaps it would give him the Dutch courage he needed.

Tommy hurried down the stairs to join Nathan and Liz who were assembling a motley group of volunteers. One man wore no shoes, another looked half-dressed. Despite their training, they all looked terrified. Everyone looked at Tommy as if the rifle lent him some authority. With Jack and Terra away, and Zed and Riley still not back, it was up to them to rally the defence of the castle. Tommy cleared his throat and stepped forward, his voice breathless and full of emotion. Inside, he was fighting to control the fear which gripped his chest like a vice.

"Listen up." His voice sounded weird in his head, like it was coming from someone else. His father's voice. "We don't have much time. I saw four men, but there could be others. We have no idea how many are already inside the castle walls and how many of them could be waiting outside."

Nathan took over from Tommy, his voice trembling. "Jamie and the rest of you with rifles, get back up on the roof and give us covering fire. We've got to stop them reaching the main gate."

Nathan handed out the few remaining guns to the volunteers, together with the knives, swords and a medieval crossbow with a single bolt.

Greta stood ready by the locked door to the courtyard. She drew back the bolt as quietly as she dared. Nathan's party of five sized each other up with gritted teeth, trying to hide their terror. None of them were fighters but they had no choice. This was tantamount to suicide. They didn't stand a chance. Tommy noticed a wet patch appear on the crotch of the man next to him. His hand was shaking uncontrollably, as a large puddle pooled next to his left boot. He patted the man on the shoulder before racing up the stairs to join Jamie on the roof.

Once Tommy was in position, he shouted to the party below. On the count of three, Greta unlocked the gate and the five of them jostled through the doorway, with two shotguns at their head. Greta slammed the door behind them and closed her eyes, saying a silent prayer. Nathan's team made a dash for the guardhouse where Scottie was waving them forward. He had taken up position with a rifle, taking pot shots at the two men on the roof as they advanced along the rooftop towards him.

As Nathan's group surged forward, a hail of bullets felled two of the Hurst men in quick succession. One man took a shot to the leg, passing clean through his calf and the other went down clutching his abdomen. The rest of the group promptly lost their nerve and turned tail, retreating to the safety of the Tudor archway. With their fists, they banged impotently for Greta to let them back inside. For a few moments, they were trapped.

Tommy and the other Hurst riflemen on the roof couldn't get an angle of fire. Without exposing themselves to a volley of return fire, no one had a clean shot. Hidden out of sight with a field of fire covering the courtyard and entrance, Copper's men had Scottie pinned down.

Tommy looked on helplessly. Two of Nathan's men writhed in agony just out of reach. Each time one of them reached forward to try to pull the others to safety, the ground between them seemed to explode with bullets. From round the corner, in the archway leading to the main entrance, Tommy could hear Scottie shouting for help. For a few seconds, each side waited for the other to make the next move.

From behind a buttress, Scottie took up a kneeling position, firing sporadically towards the men on the roof opposite. He didn't have a shot and was running low on ammunition. There was still no sign of reinforcements. Behind him came the sound of a rifle butt smashing against the raised drawbridge. He smiled for a split second, knowing it would take a battering ram.

He whipped his head round as a smoke canister landed just in front of his position, swiftly followed by a second. With a loud pop and a hiss, smoke began to fill the courtyard. In a few seconds, his whole field of vision was shrouded in billowing clouds of choking, cloying gas.

Two of Copper's men shimmied down a rope from above and emerged from cover, advancing towards Scottie wearing gas masks. Without a clear target, they fired controlled bursts at shapes and shadows. Unable to see anything, Scottie peered into the cloud. As the smoke swirled towards his position, he stifled a cough. The smoke completely enveloped the Tudor gate, rendering Tommy and the others blind.

Scottie took his chance. Unseen by the invaders, he dived across the archway. Scrambling through the open doorway to the guardhouse, he slammed and locked the door behind him. He was safe for the time being, but had just cut himself off from the rest of the Hurst group.

Meanwhile, Nathan must have seen or heard the invaders advancing towards him, hammering on the door until Greta let them back through. They collapsed inside, coughing and spluttering. Wisps of the smoke dissipated slowly around them. Tommy raced down the stairs to confer with Nathan. They were outgunned. Their nerves shredded by the speed of their demise and the ferocity of the fire they had faced. Nathan had lost half his group in a matter of seconds.

The battle for the main gate was lost. Tommy knew that now. And yet, he consoled himself with the fact that the bulk of Hurst's occupants were safe for now. Between them and their attackers were stone walls from another time. Six feet thick and built to withstand the very worst the French and Spanish navies of yesteryear could hurl their way. Tommy was fairly sure that the castle could hold out against a superior force for many days. The unlucky few trapped on the wrong side of the Tudor gate would have to fend for themselves. Unfortunately, that included Scottie.

Outside the castle complex, the man in black waited impatiently, pacing around. His plan was working perfectly, but not knowing what was going on inside was killing him. Why was it taking Copper so long?

The main force had arrived unopposed in the small harbour

area. They had silently approached the main gate, crossing what would once have been a moat surrounding the original Tudor fort. Today it was little more than a ditch. They had their backs pressed against the stone walls, looking up nervously in case there were any sharpshooters on the ramparts above them. They knew first-hand that it paid to be careful.

The drawbridge was still raised and beyond the formidable stone and wood defences they were listening to the fire fight. The man in black smiled and pressed his cheek against the cold of the stone, trying to interpret the sounds from within. He seemed to be enjoying himself and started to whistle. When he heard the pop and hiss of the smoke grenades, he clicked his fingers and gesticulated at one of the others in the darkness, recognising his plan playing out.

The interrogation of Will had been decisive. The castle was indeed vulnerable and would be taken with minimal casualties. Losing a few of Copper's men was neither here nor there. It was an acceptable price to pay for this jewel of the Solent. Hurst was to be an important strategic pillar for his new empire.

Back on the roof of the tower, the man next to Tommy took a bullet to the shoulder, sending his rifle clattering. Tommy picked it up, checked it was loaded and scanned for targets. The smoke masking the movement of the invaders as they fought their way towards the gate parted suddenly exposing a solitary figure for a second.

Tommy took careful aim, letting his breath out slowly as Zed had taught him, before squeezing the trigger. The recoil from the rifle surprised him and he lost sight of the figure below. When the smoke next cleared, he could make out a body lying prone on the ground, then the smoke obscured his view again.

He punched the air in delight to muted congratulations from the man next to him clutching his injured shoulder. How many more were there? Nathan had tasked them with stopping the men from reaching the front gate, but with the counter-attack over, almost before it had begun, the balance of power had swung violently against them.

Scottie could only listen to the fire fight, wondering helplessly what had become of his friends. The door handle close to his ear silently began to turn. He heard whispered voices. There were two men outside. Would they try to break down the door? Or would they leave him there, trapped while they tried to open the drawbridge? A second group shouted instructions from outside the gate. He could hear muffled sounds, perhaps struggling with the release mechanism for the drawbridge. Scottie smiled, remembering how stiff and awkward it was unless you knew how. The footsteps hurried away back to the courtyard and he relaxed in the brief silence that followed, beginning to feel safe behind the barricaded door, jammed shut with a heavy oak desk and metal filing cabinet stacked on top of it. He had his back to the desk, ready to push back if someone tried to force their way in.

The silence stretched. Perhaps they had given up. Where were those reinforcements? Either his friends had been beaten back or they were dead. On his own, stuck in the guardhouse, there was nothing he could do. He checked his ammunition. Twelve more rounds, then he was out.

He searched the desk, looking for anything he could use, but the drawers were mostly full of paperwork, ticket stubs, pencils and pens. The shelves each side of the window were stacked with guidebooks of the castle and maps of the local area, together with assorted merchandise from when the guardhouse served as the ticket office and gift shop. The second room towards the back proved more rewarding. He found biscuits and bottled water, together with a walkie-talkie with working batteries. He turned the volume dial and got a burst of static. He left it on low in case someone else in the castle was trying to contact him.

Two explosions a couple of milliseconds apart sent dust showering down on top of him. The deafening noise echoed round the confined space. He staggered against the wall, dazed and disoriented. The ringing in his ears drowned out all other sounds, including his own cries of anguish.

The blast from the two charges had torn one side of the drawbridge from its hinges and its wood was broken and splintered. Copper waited for the dust to settle. A draft of wind through the new opening slowly dispersed the smoke from the explosion. Scorch marks discoloured the walls and ceiling. Through the blast hole clambered Copper's boss, quickly followed by the rest of his men.

The two men embraced but their moment of self-congratulation quickly passed as a bullet ricocheted on the stone floor. Out of sight, in the shadows, the defenders on the roof of the Gun Tower were exchanging fire with the intruders below. A sniper had taken up position behind a chimneystack on the roof of one of the gun batteries. In the gathering darkness, he was all but invisible, picking off the Hurst men whenever they revealed themselves above the parapet.

Copper's team rounded the corner, staying close to the wall. He attached the last remaining set of charges to the inner gate leading to the old Tudor castle and the eastern wing beyond, where the bulk of Hurst's occupants were now cowering.

Inside the Tudor fortress, Tommy and the others were barricading doorways and fortifying firing positions with anything they could get their hands on. Overturned beds and mattresses were dragged against windows overlooking the courtyard. Tommy was confident that if the invaders did get through the gate, they would be walking into a kill zone. Anything and anyone that came through would be cut to shreds. It would be a turkey shoot.

When the last of the charges exploded, the blast reverberated in the enclosed space. The deafening sound rumbled throughout the Tudor complex and network of dark tunnels and chambers beneath their feet. For a few long seconds following the explosion, nothing happened. No one dared come through the doorway. Tommy and the others stood ready, guns trained on the gap, where light now streamed through from a high-powered torch or lantern.

Something metallic came skidding through the doorway, followed by the now familiar pop and hiss of a smoke canister as it came to rest in the middle of the courtyard. One of the defenders emerged from the shadows to try and kick the grenade back where it came from. A hail of fire threw him back against the wall where he slid down, clutching a wound to the chest. He disappeared from view, shrouded in an impenetrable cloud of orange gas that began to fill the courtyard. The cloud rose inexorably towards Jamie and the men on the roof of the Gun Tower. They could now see nothing at all below them and scanned for any shapes or movement. They could hear footsteps and one man fired on instinct towards the source of the noise. Standing to see if he'd hit anything, there was a loud crack and the man to Jamie's right went down. The others dropped lower behind the parapet and waited. The attackers were inside the Tudor castle. There was nothing now between them and taking control of the whole complex. Only the Gun Tower now remained secure.

Chapter 47

The fire fight was over. For a few minutes, there was an eerie silence, bar the cries for help from the wounded on both sides. Tommy peered out the window into the courtyard from behind a curtain in the Gun Tower.

From beyond the damaged gate, he heard a measured hand clap. One of the men below spoke in a slow deliberate voice, imbued with a calm authority that reminded Tommy of a high-court judge delivering his sentence to a condemned man. "Bravo, bravo. You have fought well. History will remember your bravery. But enough is enough. There is no need for any more of you to die unnecessarily. Lay down your weapons and come out from your hiding places with your arms raised. This is not a battle you can win."

The voice paused, its words echoing around the battlements. Tommy looked on, his face hidden, aware of faces pressed together behind him, trying to get a look at the silhouetted figure behind the disembodied voice in the darkness. He looked over his shoulder and studied their faces. They looked defeated, the fight gone from them.

Outside, a figure dressed in black emerged from the archway, marching two prisoners ahead of him, using one as a shield, a pistol held to the side of his head. Tommy recognised the human shield immediately. It was Jackson, one of the recent arrivals. Jackson stared straight back at the window where Tommy was hiding as if he could see him as clear as day, despite the near darkness. It chilled Tommy to the bone, knowing that they would have to choose between surrender and watching his friend be executed.

"If you surrender now, I give you my word that no one else from Hurst will die tonight." The speaker's sense of theatre was not lost on others. He seemed to be relishing this moment of drama, milking the tension on both sides, knowing eyes were watching his every move, wondering what he would do next.

There was silence. Tommy stayed completely still, his mind racing. What would his father have done in this situation? A thought occurred to him and he smiled in spite of the circum-stances.

"Of course, if you do not surrender, I can assure you, you will all die," continued the voice from below. "Of that be absolutely certain. Starting with these two right here." He jabbed the gun in Jackson's neck and kicked out his legs from behind so that he fell forward onto his hands and knees, gasping with pain.

"I will give you five minutes to consider my offer. Surrender and live. Or fight and die."

Tommy let the curtain fall back into place and crouched down below the window to confer with Nathan, their backs pressed against the wall. There seemed no way they could win this fight. Surrender now and they could avoid further bloodshed, but could they trust this man to keep his word? What did they want anyway? To seize control of Hurst? To steal their food and supplies? Or was there some other motive?

They had put up a good fight, Tommy was sure of that. Including the two he had killed or wounded, he estimated at least ten of them had been injured, but guessed there were at least as many attackers again. All told, the Hurst defenders far outnumbered them, but were poorly armed. In their favour, however, they held the high ground and could pick off anyone who entered the inner courtyard. With a bit of luck, they might be able to hold out here for days, even weeks with the food and water they already had. If they could just get word to their allies, then perhaps they could survive the siege or fight their way out. It was a risky move. If only Jack was here, he would know what to do.

Tommy surveyed the faces of those around him and made up his mind. They should play for time. Try and reason with this man holding Hurst to ransom and find out what he wanted.

With the window pushed open a few inches, Tommy called out, "We appreciate the offer and everything." He shook his head, hearing his own words. That just sounded weird. Nathan patted him encouragingly on the shoulder. Tommy swallowed hard before continuing. "But before we give you our response, we have some questions for you."

The man below laughed. "Very well. I will allow you three questions. Use them wisely."

Tommy closed his eyes, trying to organise his thoughts. His first question tripped out before he could think it through. "Why are you here?" He flinched, cursing himself. It was a dumb question.

"Why are we here?" he repeated in a mocking voice, mimicking Tommy's nasal twang. "Isn't it obvious? You have something we need. A mutual friend told us everything. Need I say more?"

"Perhaps if you could be a bit more specific, we could come to some kind of arrangement?" offered Tommy tentatively, beginning to relax a little.

"You misunderstand," he replied, shaking his head. "You are in no position to negotiate. Hurst has a debt to pay."

.   .   .

Tommy exchanged puzzled glances with Nathan, who was mouthing the word "debt". What debt was he talking about and who was this mutual friend? Perhaps they had captured Jack or Terra or even Zed. He opted to play for more time, trying to gather more pieces of the puzzle.

"If we surrender, what guarantees can you give us that we will be allowed to leave here in peace?"

"My word is my bond." He clapped his right hand to his heart sanctimoniously.

"You mentioned a debt. What debt?"

"Your men attacked us, killed my men. You took something that does not belong to you."

"We know nothing about an attack. I'm telling you, it wasn't us."

The man wagged his finger. "You've had your three questions. I need your decision. Do I have your surrender?"

Tommy paused, remembering the many nights they had played poker. "Play the man opposite you," Jack would say. It didn't matter if you held a pair of twos. Tommy took a deep breath and gambled.

.   .   .

"I suggest you look around you. You're outnumbered. Whoever your mutual friend is, they did not tell you the whole truth. Your men have walked into a trap. Below your feet is a network of tunnels. Right now, a small army is readying itself to fight. You caught us cold once, but it won't happen again. Last chance. Leave now. What debt could possibly be worth this?"

"If you knew what was taken…" He paused. "You're bluffing."

"I wouldn't count on it. Why don't you tell us what you want and maybe we can come to an arrangement."

The man in black laughed. "I'm growing tired of your childish games. Either you're playing a very dangerous game, or you really have no idea what your men did." He looked at his feet and the hostage on his knees, a gun still pressed to the side of his head. "Very well. Your group broke into the hospital and took two patients, Adele and Stella. We need them back. They're sick and need treatment. There, I've told you more than enough. Return them to us immediately and we will spare the rest of you."

Tommy looked around the group and saw only blank expressions.

"We have no one by those names here."

. . .

"In that case, you have nothing left to bargain with. If you refuse to surrender, then you will face the consequences."

In the silence that followed, Tommy and Nathan conferred quietly and passed a message up the stairs to Jamie on the rooftop. They had a surprise or two up their sleeve.

Two rifle shots shattered the silence. Jackson was hit in the shoulder and the other prisoner in the leg. Both men collapsed and lay gasping on the ground. The man in black stepped back, suddenly exposed, his cheek splattered with blood. Calmly, he took a handkerchief from a breast pocket, shook it open and wiped the spots away, inspecting the stains.

"I take it that's a no then. On your head be it." Shaking his head in disappointment, he slowly walked backwards out of the gate, lingering for a second to stare up at Tommy before disappearing out of sight.

In the outer courtyard, near the main gate, Copper had rounded up half a dozen prisoners, faces pressed against the brick wall. They were shoeless, unarmed, defenceless, at the mercy of their captors. Several of the women were sobbing, pleading for their lives. Copper looked away, avoiding eye contact, forcing their heads back, knowing what was coming next.

. . .

His boss walked down the line, studying their faces without a flicker of empathy. "Kill them all," he commanded.

Copper heard the order but delayed a few seconds, remaining rooted to the spot. He processed the words but a shadow of his former self seemed to reject them as nonsensical. Since when had he grown a conscience? The moment of doubt passed. Copper nodded and relayed the order to his men, his face calm and emotionless. They raised their weapons and fired until their magazines were empty and no one was left standing, bodies jerking and twitching on the ground. Copper turned his head towards the man in black.

"What about the rest of them? What are your orders, sir?" asked Copper, an unusual edge to his deference.

"Burn it down. Smoke them out, those little piglets in their house of stone."

"Yes, sir." Copper gathered up a work party and set off to the campfire still smouldering in the distance. They grabbed firewood and piled it high inside the canteen, storerooms and living quarters that lined the castle walls and set them alight. In a few minutes the whole place went up like a tinderbox.

Chapter 48

Sam supported Jack the last few yards from Osborne House through the long grass to the helicopter as its engines went into their start-up cycle and the rotors began to turn. The airmen hauled the wounded man through, laid him flat and strapped his legs and torso down tight, before taking a pair of surgical scissors and cutting the material of his blue woollen jumper, exposing the injury to his shoulder. He made Jack comfortable for the journey, setting up a drip and stabilising the wound before take-off.

The painkillers were numbing his senses but he noticed Sam was in some distress. He guessed he was still thinking about Terra and what could have happened to her. She was like a mother to Sam. The American had said they would take her back to a convict camp near Newport, but how did they really know?

Sam was shown to a jump seat just behind the pilot, facing backwards. When Peterson and the two other navy personnel were safely inside, the airman gave the nod and the two Seal team members who had been covering the aircraft left their kneeling positions and double-timed it to the aircraft, clipped into the safety harnesses and sat on the floor sill, their feet dangling free, weapons poised and ready. Peterson handed Jack what looked like a large pair of headphones with a microphone attached. He weighed the headset, turning it over in his hands before putting it on. The cabin was suddenly silent, the noise of the engine almost eliminated and he could hear Peterson talking to the pilot, relaying a message to the *Chester* with an update on their status and due warning that they would be on deck in less than fifteen minutes.

The helicopter, a MH-60R Seahawk, achieved full power and with a gentle tug on the stick lifted off into the night sky. Its navigation lights remained off as it banked round a few metres above the tree tops, staying low, following the river valley that led straight downhill back to the open water of the Solent. Peterson spoke rapidly into the radio, though the military jargon was hard to follow. Outside it was pitch black. Jack craned his neck to peer out of the right side of the aircraft. The pilot's night-vision goggles allowed him to see in complete darkness. Jack could just make out treetops and the sweep of fields and farmland as they headed back out to sea.

Flying low, they banked left when they were over water. In the distance towards the mainland, they could just make out the oil refinery at Fawley bathed in orange light from billowing flames that leapt unchecked into the night sky. Further to the west, two tower blocks in the city of Southampton smouldered. The inferno that had engulfed them had moved on, spreading slowly across housing estates and residential areas, fanned by the night's breeze.

Below them, in the lee of the land, the sea state was relatively calm, but further out Jack could make out white horses as the waves rose and fell, their crests foaming and breaking in the wind. The helicopter hugged the coastline of the island, accelerating as it turned west towards Yarmouth and Hurst Castle, before heading south-west into Christchurch Bay where the *USS Chester* was cruising towards them at impulse power. As they flew towards the western end of the island, Peterson's voice came over the headset.

"Jack, you better take a look at this."

Jack unclipped his safety harness and levered himself up to look out of the cockpit window, clinging on tight as the aircraft lurched violently. Out in front of them, he saw suddenly what Peterson was worried about. In the distance, they could make out the sweep of the shingle spit that joined Hurst to the mainland, with the castle at its eastern tip. Part of the castle was ablaze, flames leaping up above the walls and parapet. Jack couldn't believe what he was seeing.

He pleaded with Peterson to slow down and circle the castle to see what was going on. The instruction given, the pilot pulled the nose up to slow their airspeed as the helicopter came into a hover around two hundred feet above the eastern wall, circling slowly around the gun tower, its searchlight picked out several figures on the roof. Peterson pointed towards the fire and the helicopter proceeded along the southern wall, trying to make out what was going on beneath them.

As they neared the centre of the complex, a hail of gunfire pinged off the underbelly of the aircraft as the pilot began an evasive manoeuvre. One of the soldiers had been hit and was hanging by his harness, clinging on to the doorway, while the other team member returned fire towards the origin of the muzzle flashes. As soon as they were back over the water, Sergeant Jones reached a gloved hand down and hauled his squad member back up, slamming the sliding door shut.

Peterson was shouting over the intercom for the pilot to gain height and get the hell out of there. They had seen enough action for one night and now had another casualty to bring home.

Jack stared out of the window, his eyes wide in disbelief. One of the crewmen put a hand on his shoulder as his whole body seemed to sag. Head in hands, he started to sob, tears streaming down his face, his imagination running wild. The castle and the flames slipped from view as the helicopter skimmed the waves past the Needles, flying fast and low back out to sea. The *Chester* was cruising north-east five nautical miles south of Portland Bill, rapidly closing the gap to meet them.

Chapter 49

In the bowels of the castle, deep within an alcove of one of
the dark, dank cellars that had once been a dungeon for
prisoners held at Hurst, Tommy and the others sat shivering
under blankets. They were listening to the faint sounds of the
battle above them, with the dim flickering light of a candle for
company.

"We're going to be fine, Toby," said Simon, sat to his right.
"There's really nothing to worry about. We're all perfectly safe
down here."

Toby pulled the blanket tighter around his shoulders,
clasping the two corners in his clenched fists. The boy nodded,
but said nothing. From the first explosion he had been terrified,
cowering behind his father as they shielded their ears and
watched the dust rain down upon them. They were not alone;
there were as many as twenty others hiding down here, on the
instructions of Liz. This was the safest place in the castle.

The only way in was defended by a dozen armed men, not to
mention countless feet of thick stone and concrete. It was a
bunker complex that would probably withstand any number of
direct hits from heavy weapons and certainly impenetrable to

small arms fire. And yet, knowing all that did little to reassure the younger members of the Hurst group. Many of them still carried the very real and psychological scars of the breakdown. They had each seen more than their fair share of death and destruction. They had witnessed sane people driven to madness. In the race for survival, it had been every man for himself. They had seen neighbours fighting, riots in supermarkets, men shot in cold blood before their very eyes. Hearing the explosions and fire fight above them brought those memories flooding back in technicolour.

Tommy knew from their stories that little Toby had seen his mother die. She had been wrenched from his hands, not by the virus, like so many others, but knocked down and killed by a motorbike, stolen and out of control. The driver had been hell-bent on getting out of town. Dodging stationary traffic he had mounted the pavement and clipped a bench, lost control and careered into two children holding hands, before striking his mother. She had died instantly, her eyes fixed with a look of surprise that was seared into Toby's memory and nightmares forever.

Footsteps in the stairwell shook Tommy from his melancholy. Nathan stuck his head around the corner, putting on a brave face. His cheer was paper-thin. His eyes betrayed him.

"How are we all doing down here?" He stuck his thumbs up, trying to make eye contact with Toby and some of the other children, who looked at their feet, nodding their heads. "Good, good. Simon, Tommy, Shannon, we need you up top. Rest of you, stay put, we'll bring you down something to eat as soon as we're done, but for now, this is the safest place in the castle. Okay?"

Simon and the others got gingerly to their feet, exchanging sheepish glances. Toby started moaning, clawing at his father's leg, pleading with him not to leave.

Simon smiled back at him. "I'll be back as soon as I can." He ruffled his son's hair and steeled himself for the task at hand.

At the top of the stairs, there was a palpable tension in the air, with half-seen faces hurrying through dimly lit passageways, torchlight dancing on walls. Nathan handed Tommy a revolver and deposited a box-full of bullets in his outstretched hand.

He handed out an antique sword and a machete to the other two and motioned them to huddle in close. "I need you three to guard the Drake doorway on the ground floor. Barricade it with whatever you can find. And if anyone or anything tries to come through, shoot them. This is our last line. We have to defend this bit of the castle, at all costs. All our lives depend on it."

Tommy led the trio down to their station, checked the door was locked and bolted top and bottom and started piling up chairs and boxes, with an old carpet dumped on top to hold everything in place. They stood back and admired their handi-work. It would hold. Tommy was sure of that. No one was going to push their way through that lot, especially with him taking potshots at them. He loaded the revolver with six bullets and emptied the rest of the box into his waist pocket, discarding the empty carton.

Tommy froze. From just outside the door, they could hear muffled voices and scuffed footsteps on the stone floor. The three of them unconsciously stepped backwards, awkwardly clutching their weapons. There was a series of dull thuds against the door, although it didn't sound like they were trying to force entry. Another louder thump and then the sound of liquid, like someone relieving themselves against the door. They smelled the fuel before they saw it as a rivulet snaked under the door, pooling directly below the stack of chairs and boxes, soaking into the cardboard. They heard the strike of a match and then a whoosh as the fuel vapour ignited.

Tommy reacted first. He ran down the corridor back towards

the basement where Toby and the other children were cowering. In the corner of the room was a bucket that the children had been using as a toilet. It was half-full, stinking and slopping as Tommy ran back towards the doorway. When he reached the passageway, the smoke on the inside was already spreading rapidly throughout the complex, blown by drafts and air currents that made the castle freezing in the winter. He got as close to the door as he could and threw the bucketload of slops across the floor, trying to sluice the petrol away. It did little more than disperse the fuel more widely around the doorway.

The other three had raced off to try and find the buckets of sand placed around the castle complex, leaving Tommy alone watching the fire take hold. He kicked at the furniture stack, trying to dislodge the nearest item. Their hard work to secure the door had turned out to be misplaced effort. The chairs and boxes were wedged solid and he was forced back by the heat and choking fumes. He tried one last time, grabbing hold of the carpet balanced precariously on top. Gravity did the rest and the whole stack collapsed against the opposite wall, blocking the passage. The initial flash from the petrol began to die down as flames licked harmlessly at the stone walls.

Tommy shielded his face from the heat, retreating back down the passageway. He stayed low until the smoke was less dense. From all directions men and women were shouting, panicked by cloying fumes that made their chests heave.

Nathan raced down the stairs, appealing to Tommy and the others to get back to their posts. "For God's sake, put those fires out. Smother them in blankets, or whatever you can find. They're trying to smoke us out," he shouted over his shoulder, racing to the next post.

In the shadow of the castle's western wall, Will was making slow but steady progress, creeping towards the main gate, making as little sound as possible. He was keeping his eyes on the vessel that had moored up a few minutes ago, hoping he was invisible in the darkness. He counted eleven men as one by one they dashed across the roadway to wait by the drawbridge, pressed against the stone.

Will crouched behind a gorse bush, waiting for them to make their move. When he heard the explosions, he was paralysed for a few minutes. Without a weapon, he stood little chance against Copper's heavily armed paramilitaries. His best chance was to disarm a lone guard and attack from the rear where they would least expect it. He thought he glimpsed Copper giving orders, but he couldn't be sure from this distance.

He lost sight of the group when Copper's men headed inside. There was now only a single figure left guarding the entrance. This was the best chance he was going to get. Will crept closer and was now no more than thirty metres away. He recognised the guard from his time at the hospital: a spotty youth, seventeen at most. Will fancied his chances and readied himself to pounce. He was a dozen footsteps away when his boot slipped on a rock.

It was as if the next few milliseconds were in slow motion. The kid whipped his head around, surprised to see Will so close. He glanced down to flick the safety off his semi-automatic rifle before bringing it to bear. Will threw himself the last few metres, lunging at the weapon, trying to knock it from the kid's grasp. The boy fumbled for the safety and was a fraction of a second too slow. The gun fired just as Will's lead hand knocked it sideways, the bullet passing harmlessly through the fabric of his shirt. Will wrestled the gun from the boy's hands and brought the butt down against the side of his head, knocking the youth out cold.

Will searched the boy's pockets and found a torch and two more clips, before climbing through what remained of the gate and drawbridge. Standing in the covered entrance were two more of Copper's men, facing away from him, oblivious to his approach. At the last moment, one of the men turned his head. It was one of the guards from the hospital, responsible for many of the beatings and blows Will had suffered. The other man he had seen at the pub.

Will's lip curled into a snarl, as he squeezed off a short burst from the hip at close range, propelling the man forward against the wall. His next victim suffered a similar fate, slumping to the ground, clutching at the wound in his lower back. Will stepped over their bodies, pausing to meet the look of pained surprise from eyes that were already closing.

He stood with his back against the wall to the guardhouse, catching his breath, considering his next move. Will crouched down suddenly as a face appeared at the window before darting out of sight again. Will smiled, struggling to contain a laugh. A blur of red hair remained just visible. It had to be Scottie. There couldn't be more than a thousand people left alive with hair like that. He put his face close to the glass and whispered quietly. "Hey, Scottie. It's me."

Scottie must have recognised the friendly voice instantly, but remained hidden, not quite believing his ears. "Will, is that really you?"

"Who else would it be, you giant sporran? Get this door open will you and get out here."

There were a few seconds of loud scraping and thumps as Scottie moved the desk and cabinet out of the way. The key turned in the lock and the heavy door swung open. Scottie's beaming smile greeted Will and they hugged each other.

"Right, laddie. Time to get our own back."

Chapter 50

The helicopter carrying Sam and Jack lined up astern of the American destroyer making final course and speed corrections to compensate for the fourteen-knot crosswind. The *Chester*'s landing area was fully floodlit. The rest of the ship was still shrouded in darkness, its slow turning radar just visible. A forest of radio masts and antennas were silhouetted against a grey skyline, growing brighter in the distance. On the deck below them, an air marshal was standing in the shelter of the aft superstructure, holding high two illuminated hand beacons to guide the pilot. A light sea swell required precision timing to adjust for the rise and fall of the ship. To Sam's relief, they touched down safely just off centre of the "H" in the landing area at the stern of the destroyer.

The pilot powered down the engines as the ground crew hurried out to slide open the side door, ready to transfer the injured on to two trolleys that were brought out to meet the aircraft. Sam wiped tears from his eyes, still haunted by what he had seen as they'd flown over the castle. He unclipped his harness, and helped the airmen lift the first gurney holding the wounded soldier on to the deck of the ship. On a count of three, they levered Jack's barely conscious body up and over the trolley's metal rail, which was promptly raised and clamped into position. Two crewmembers from the *Chester* took over the care of the injured and wheeled them inside, towards the dim red light of the ship's hatch.

Sam followed silently behind Jack's trolley, his mind still trying to make sense of the confused scenes he had witnessed on their return, in particular the inferno burning in the canteen and stores. What could have happened? He could only assume the castle was under attack, but by whom and why?

Peterson caught up with them: "Wait up." Sam paused in the cramped confines of a passageway, just wide enough for two men to pass, with pipes and overhead cabling stretching as far as he could see. Peterson put an arm around Sam's shoulder. "I'll ask the master of the watch to set you up with somewhere to sleep. You hungry?"

"If it's okay with you, I'd like to stay with Jack," said Sam.

"He'll be well looked after. The medic will patch him up. If I were you, I'd get some rest. As soon as it's light, we'll take a squad back to Hurst to find out what happened. Petty Officer Flannigan will take care of you. Just tell him what you need and he'll fix you up."

Flannigan was standing ready, his hands behind his back. He wore a blue T-shirt with the ship's insignia on it. He acknowledged the order and invited Sam to follow him down to the medical centre.

The surgeon attended to Jack, dressed in green overalls and a surgical mask that obscured half his face. He looked up at Sam with smiling eyes, noting his melancholy. "You must be Sam. People call me Doc. I'm the senior medical officer on this ship.

Looks like your friend Jack here has been in the wars. Don't worry. We'll have him back on his feet in no time."

Sam thanked the surgeon and lingered shell-shocked as a female nurse swabbed the nasty-looking wound to a shoulder that would need several stitches. Flannigan escorted him back to a waiting room along the corridor. As soon as Sam sat down on the plastic chair, he was overwhelmed with tiredness. By the time Flannigan reappeared with a mess tray complete with a mug of coffee, a carton of milk, some pasta with tomato sauce, together with canned fruit in syrup, Sam had his head back against the whitewashed wall, already fast asleep.

Flannigan left him to sleep, shaking him awake a few hours later, the tray still beside his chair, untouched. Sam looked up, his eyes red and swollen, to see the welcome sight of Jack standing there, braced against the doorway. Jack wore a US navy grey sweatshirt, his face still pale, his arm in a sling, but with a purposeful look about him.

"They told me what happened, Sam. About Terra. About Hurst." His voice was croaky when he spoke. He swallowed hard, before continuing in a low voice, through gritted teeth. "We've got to get back there. We should never have left our people."

The surgeon appeared behind him, eavesdropping on their conversation. "Now hold up, Jack. When my men found you, you were in shock, in no state to do anything. What you need, my friend, is a couple of days' bed rest." He paused, noticing the wild look in Jack's eyes. "But I can see from the half-crazed look in your eyes that that's not going to happen. Best thing I can suggest is that I take you straight to the bridge and you talk to the commanding officer, Lieutenant Peterson. I think y'all have met."

"I appreciate your concern, doctor, but I need to get off this ship and find out what happened. My place is with my people."

"Very well. Flannigan, can you take these gentlemen to the bridge and find the CO?"

It was a long walk through countless corridors, upstairs and along a maze of passageways that twisted and turned past rooms full of sleeping men, of loud machinery, panels with flashing lights, knobs and dials, mess halls and store rooms, looking left and right. It was a busy hive of activity. All the crewmen they passed were polite and stepped out of their way into recesses or doorways, staring after them. Jack could sense they were being watched.

It was possible they were the first civilians they had seen in quite some time, being insulated and cut off from the outside world. The look on their faces masked a thousand questions, but at the same time, they were wary of the newcomers. They stepped back; some of them shielded their faces or even held their breath. Jack imagined that they had seen the virus at close quarters on board and remained cautious of outsiders, giving them a wide berth.

They approached a grey security door with the letters "Bridge" stencilled across its centre. An armed guard stepped into their path and asked them their names. Jack noticed a sidearm in his holster. He eyed the two civilians suspiciously, glancing from one to the other and back at Flannigan, before pressing the intercom to announce their arrival. The door was buzzed open and the group stepped inside.

The bridge reminded Jack of stepping into the cockpit of an airliner, just much bigger. Every wall and panel was a sea of lights, computer monitors and flashing buttons. Uniformed men with binoculars scanned the horizon for other vessels. Looking out over the ship's bow cresting through the waves, Jack realised it was just before dawn. The sky was brighter in the east towards the island, just visible in the distance. To their north-west, towards Bournemouth and Christchurch, a patch of black clouds hurried through, rainsqualls falling beneath. Sunrise was around twenty minutes away, but it was growing brighter by the minute. Once the rain cleared it looked set to be a clear, crisp morning. Peterson was speaking into what looked like an old-fashioned grey-green telephone, relaying commands, talking animatedly but with calm authority. He looked up and saw Sam and Jack waiting patiently and hung up.

"How are you feeling, Jack?" He inclined his head with some concern. "Doc tells me you'll need time to recover your strength. Recommended you stay put for a couple of days until you're better." Jack's eyebrows narrowed and he was just on the point of saying something he might regret, when Peterson raised his hand. "Please, Jack, let me finish. I told him in no uncertain terms that while I respect his medical opinion, if it was me, I would probably jump over board and swim the rest of the way to be with my team."

Jack smiled. He admired Peterson. He had an easy manner around other people, a sense of irony uncommon in the few Americans he'd met, and a very "British", or at least transatlantic, outlook. Altogether it made him a good leader in the circumstances. He was capable of uniting all the disparate groups. Peterson maintained eye contact with Jack, watching his expressions change, studying him carefully before continuing. Jack was normally so good at reading people, so why did he find Peterson so intriguing, so full of small contradictions? He suspected there was more to him than met the eye.

"So here's what I'm going to do," continued Peterson. "We have a UAV prepped for launch once there's enough daylight to see anything. What do you say we make a sweep over Hurst? Find out what's going on there and then push on to Osborne and see if we can't track down Briggs. Sound like a plan?"

Jack looked from Peterson to Sam and back again, wondering what the hell he was talking about.

Peterson noticed Jack's confusion and apologised. "Sorry, navy jargon, Jack. Unmanned Aerial Vehicle. I'm sure you're familiar with the Predator or Reaper drones used by the Air Force for hunting down terrorists."

Jack nodded. He knew exactly what Peterson was talking about now. He remembered the grainy footage from Syria, Iraq and Afghanistan live-streamed for TV news audiences of vehicles exploding, remote piloted from a darkened room thousands of miles away. He had no idea they had drones on ships too.

"Of course, the drones we use are a little bit different. Shorter range, smaller payloads, but very effective at getting eyes on a target for missile strikes. We use them for reconnaissance before we put boots on the ground. We like to know what we're up against. If it's okay with you, why don't we grab a cup of coffee and go watch on the big monitors in the stateroom? We'll be more comfortable there. Acting XO, you have the conn. Jansen, can you pipe the feed through? Follow me, gentlemen."

Sam and Jack followed Peterson through the ship to a stateroom that was luxuriously appointed, beyond their expectations. Leather chairs, Lavazza coffee machine, highly polished mahogany table, walls lined with trophies. There were colour photos of the ship and its crew, of the president, of their home port in San Diego, of their former captain and XO, buried at sea with full military honours. He invited them to take a seat, served them hot drinks and waited for the screen to power up. In the corner, a technician busied himself at a control panel. Checking connections and settings, he looked up expectantly before the screen sprung into life.

It took a few seconds for the feed from the drone to stabilise. They could make out markings and numbers along the bottom of the screen, giving flight data back to the operator. Peterson put on a headset and, when he spoke, his voice was broadcast to the room so they could all hear the exchange. The feed now showed the drone flying at around one hundred metres above sea level, heading north-east towards Hurst. After a few minutes of flight time, they could see the Needles rocks in the distance looming large before the nose of the drone seemed to come up as its speed slowed and the welcome sight of the castle came into view.

Jack leaned forward, trying to make out the detail. Two separate plumes of smoke were rising hundreds of feet into the air; one from around the centre of the flank wall facing the Needles and the other seemed to originate from the Tudor castle itself. The drone came into a hover descending slowly above the southern wall, panning around to left and right. The original gun battery was now beneath them, where cannon would have faced outward guarding the entrance to the Solent. To Jack's and Sam's surprise, a figure they both recognised stood on the ramparts, waving a weapon above his head, beckoning towards the drone, his lips moving. He seemed to be shouting something.

Jack turned excitedly to Peterson: "Do we have audio?"

"I'm afraid not. Not on this UAV model. Do you know this guy?"

"Know him? You could say that." He slapped Sam on the back, relieved to see Will returned safe. "Looks like he made it back just in the nick of time."

Chapter 51

Will and Scottie had fought their way on to the western ramparts of the castle complex and were exchanging fire with two of Copper's men. They took turns to provide covering fire. Copper's men were looking nervously over their shoulders, perhaps worried about being cut off in case of a retreat. The main attacking force was still locked in skirmishes with Tommy and the rest of the riflemen on the roof of the gun tower who, by all accounts, were putting up a robust defence.

The fire in the canteen was dying down. There was nothing left to burn. The cardboard boxes and flammable contents of the storeroom had burned themselves out. The heat of the inferno had been considerable. Most likely fuelled by the industrial-size drum of cooking oil that Will assumed must have exploded, sending a massive smoke cloud billowing into the pre-dawn sky. The canteen was now a shell. The kitchen and serving counter were barely recognisable in the charred and blackened wreck.

On Scottie's belt, the walkie-talkie crackled with static on its clip. He fumbled with the volume dial, straining to hear over the exchange of gunfire. It was Nathan again, checking on their progress.

"We're making our way to your position," responded Scottie breathlessly. "ETA five minutes, if we can just get past these two guys firing on us. Any chance you can help?"

Nathan regretfully informed him that they had their own battle to fight. There was nothing for it. Will and Scottie were on their own.

Copper's men finally made their move. Firing wildly over Will's position, they scrambled towards the rest of their group sheltering just outside the Tudor gate. Will saw them leave cover and took careful aim, squeezing off a short burst that scythed down the two figures. They landed in a tangle of limbs on the grass. One clawed his way to safety behind a pillar, his weapon abandoned a few yards behind in the open. Scottie patted Will on the back and covered him as he moved up to the next doorway, scanning for targets. Their rapid advance attacking Copper's exposed flank induced panic as several faces pointing apprehensively in their direction. A strange humming noise to their right made Will reach out and haul Scottie back. It sounded like a large insect trapped inside a greenhouse on a summer's day. He craned his head round, scanning the skies trying to place what had to be man-made. Its pitch altered as the drone changed position, moving closer towards them. Keeping close to the wall, staying out of sight, Will backtracked to the stairs and climbed back up on to the ramparts.

Standing on the top with a panoramic view of the Needles passage, he was shielded from view by an old concrete machine gun nest, dating from the Second World War. To his surprise, he came face to face with what looked like a child's toy on steroids. Six rotors supported the drone's weight, like a large bumblebee. Will guessed it was military, and sincerely hoped it was friendly. It seemed to be paying particular attention to him, so he started waving and shouting in case they could hear his voice. Perhaps they were trying to communicate.

Copper was already wary of being cut off from his prearranged exit route towards the waiting ferry. If things did not go to plan, he wanted to avoid having to go back the way they came. Going over the wall on to the beach and the waiting R.I.B. was too exposed, too dangerous. There was no sign of the kid they'd left to guard the main gate. Chances were he was already back on the boat. He knew it was a mistake to bring a boy. It had been the boss's idea to "blood" a teenager.

Where had these other two come from? How did his men fail to find them during their sweep of the outbuildings, when they were rounding up prisoners in the western wing? Perhaps there were more of them hiding out of sight. He could not be sure there was not a network of tunnels running beneath their feet, the length and breadth of the castle, like the man had suggested. Copper was already getting cold feet. This whole attack had been a grand folly. The girls were probably never brought here. He had already lost too much tonight. He counted seven dead and five or six wounded. They could now barely muster an effective fighting force.

He looked around him at the contours of the grey walls and up into the brightening sky. Dawn was only a few minutes away. Their plan had depended on darkness, the advantage of surprise, not to mention superior weaponry and tactics. They were running out of time. The boss's plan to smoke the defenders out had failed. It was an old building, made of stone, and none of the fires they had lit had really taken hold, bar one. What's more, it had begun to rain, a fine drizzle falling, dampening down what few flames they had managed.

His boss seemed increasingly frustrated by Copper's inability to make any headway against the Hurst defenders. The man in black cared little for their losses.

"There will always be plenty more like them. Men wanting to bear arms and vent their fury on the world," his boss had once said. It was like a game to him. He seemed strangely amused by how even the most rational, sane, law-abiding person could be corrupted by power. Acting without consequences was intoxicating, for anyone. He called it a licence of impunity. It was a grand experiment to see who could be influenced. His boss took a perverse delight in manipulating others, pulling their strings, like some puppet master. Copper allowed him his small victories. He understood the game and played by its rules, for now. His boss even boasted once that winning over Copper and his squad of former policemen was one of his finest achievements.

According to his boss, no one was immune to the lure of power. Copper had seen it so many times, even before the breakdown. In this new world without boundaries, formerly respectable figures of society, judges, teachers, and particularly policemen, had been driven to extreme behaviours, in the secure knowledge that the justice system had failed. There would be no knock on the door, no repercussions. Killing was like a drug, and his boss saw himself as the pusher. He believed that every red-blooded human had the right to quench their base thirst for violence and destruction.

Copper leaned in close to his boss and spoke quietly: "It's time we were leaving. Daybreak is less than an hour away."

The man in black cocked his head and stared back at Copper, refusing to lower his voice. "What exactly are you afraid of? We haven't come this far to give up now." He seemed unconcerned by who might hear their conversation.

"If we stay here much longer, we'll be vulnerable to a counter-attack," counselled Copper, appealing to his common sense. "We can't risk getting cut off. If we leave now, we live to fight another day."

His boss sneered at Copper. "We're not leaving without those girls. Unless we find them, all this will be a wasted effort."

"We have it on good authority that the girls were never here. Staying to fight is folly." Despite his attempt to remain calm, he was growing increasingly frustrated with his commander's refusal to listen.

"You shouldn't believe everything you're told," he mocked.

Copper noticed the rest of his men had stopped talking and were listening to their exchange. He knew what they were thinking. Their boss had lost it. This was pure rage. He wasn't thinking straight. The men's loyalty was to Copper and it was up to him to put an end to this. He needed to take control.

Sarge waved Copper over and whispered conspiratorially for a few minutes, standing a few yards away from the rest. Copper nodded back to the sergeant but didn't look totally convinced. On reflection, it seemed like the only option. It was in the best interests of the group. Their commander could no longer be trusted, Copper had to take charge before anyone else got killed.

His boss was oblivious to their discussions, keeping his eyes fixed on the gate, listening to the movement and voices beyond. Copper walked up behind him, raised the butt of his rifle and brought it crashing down against his skull, knocking him out cold. His body collapsed limply on to the grass. One man took his arms, another his feet and they carried the unconscious man back through the courtyard towards the main gate, hugging the cover of the wall.

A hail of bullets tore up the ground in front of them. The gunfire was coming from the west, leaving them totally exposed. As one man tried to continue forward, the other pulled away and between them they dropped their boss's inert body on the ground. They both raced into the covered main entrance, throwing their backs against the wall.

Copper shouted after them. They couldn't leave him behind. Mutiny was one thing, but leaving him to be captured was far worse. The remainder of Copper's group didn't look back and walked on. They supported the walking wounded out with them. Squeezing through the blast hole in the drawbridge, they trudged dejected from the castle towards the waiting ferry boat whose tired-sounding engines were spluttering noisily, ready to cast off as soon as the last of the group was back on board.

Copper paused at the drawbridge, one foot through the blast hole, as he looked back towards the courtyard with a heavy heart. This was not what he'd planned. This time there would be consequences, of that he had no doubt. Regardless of how he felt, he couldn't reach his leader now without risking his own life, running the gauntlet under fire. He shook his head, turned towards the jetty and jogged after the others. There would be hell to pay for this treachery.

The UAV controller chewed gum in a swivel chair in the semi-darkness of the Chester's control room, bathed in a red glow from several night lights. Various screens and flashing buttons cast a ghostly grey monochrome over the operator's furrowed brow and wire-framed glasses. He was squinting at the screen trying to lip-read what the man on the rampart was saying. He'd zoomed the camera in close, but the resolution wasn't great and the drone was as close as he dared to the castle walls without endangering its rotors.

"CO, are you getting this? Looks like he's mouthing something, trying to send us a message?"

"Copy that. Any idea what he's saying?"

"The boys reckon he's saying: 'Send help, many casualties'.

But honestly, sir, without audio, for all we know, he could be ordering pizza."

"Okay, let's take a look around, please. Get the XO on the line, and get a medical team prepped to go help those guys. Let the team know that they have multiple casualties. Urgent medical attention required. Make sure they have an armed escort. We won't know what's going on there."

The drone rose high over Will's head and panned around the rest of the castle. The on-screen image showed the dying embers of a campfire, passing over the courtyard, pausing to take photos of the damaged canteen. Along one wall, there were several bodies, slumped against the wall. From the groupings of bullet marks in the stone, it looked to Jack like a scene of execution. Jack and Sam leaned closer, trying to make out any distinguishable features or clothing. Sam let out a pained cry as he recognised two of his mates. Jack said nothing, clenching his fists repeatedly, grinding his teeth.

The drone moved away, hovering over the gate to the inner courtyard. It picked out more bodies. Injured men and women were being tended to and made comfortable. There were no signs of flames in the main building, just smoke and blackened doorways, some burned-out debris lying nearby. The eastern wing of the castle appeared untouched. They could see figures emerging from their hiding places, pointing up at the drone as it rose higher over the castle.

"Okay, we've seen enough here. Don't worry, Jack, the helicopter is refuelled and ready. Our medical team will be on station in ten minutes. We'll take care of them. Jenkins, take me on to Osborne House and let's see what we can find. Are we in contact with the away team?"

"Yes, sir. I can patch you through now? Give me a minute."

There was a delay of a few seconds as the drone continued

on, passing the Lymington river entrance, heading across the Solent towards Cowes.

"Go ahead, sir. I have Sergeant Jones on the line now."

"Good morning, sergeant. I trust you have things under control at Osborne House."

"Yes, sir. Quiet night. No sign of Briggs. Looks like he high-tailed it out of here. The good news, sir? The tracker is active. We have a strong signal and show Briggs's convoy on the main road heading north back towards us now. They're about three clicks away from our position."

"How're our new friends from the Royal Navy doing?"

"We're having quite a tea party. Looks like the rest of the men are enjoying what they call a 'Full English'. Real eggs and bacon, sir, fried tomatoes, toast and mushrooms. Beats powdered egg and beans any day, sir."

"You're making me hungry, sergeant, and not a little jealous," smiled Peterson. "Listen up. We can divert the UAV to locate that convoy. We're sending a helicopter to Hurst to tend to their wounded and then we'll head on to pick you up. They had quite a night of it, but looks like the good guys came through."

"Yes, sir. We'll await further instructions and hitch a ride back to the ship when you're good and ready."

"Very good, sergeant. *Chester* out."

Back on the screen, the UAV had crossed a beach and was heading inland over the Isle of Wight. To the right of the UAV feed appeared a digital map with the location of the convoy as a white dot moving slowly north. The tracker signal was pinging loud and clear from a transmitter, allegedly hidden underneath Briggs's motorcade.

Jack's eyes flicked from the video feed to the map and back again as the distance between the two closed rapidly on a conversion course. There it was. In the extreme distance on the

viewfinder, they could just make out the motorcade. There were
four, no, five vehicles bumping along the road from Newport
heading back towards Cowes. At the head of a convoy was a baby
Humvee, likely stolen and adapted for Briggs's own purposes, with
a large cattle grill on the front, a bank of spotlights on the cabin roof
and what looked like metal plates welded to the front and sides.

"Chances are they're heading back towards Osborne with
reinforcements, sir. Finish what they started. What are your
orders?"

"We may not get a better chance at this, sergeant. Let's take
them out here and now. CO to fire team. Prep a Tomahawk for
us, can you, please?

"Fire team, aye. Programming coordinates now, sir. Coordinates locked and ready. At your command."

"Fire when ready."

A forward missile hatch on the *Chester* slowly levered its bay
doors vertical, its hydraulic pistons whirring in the morning
peace on deck. On the big screen in the stateroom, the image
switched to a camera showing the missile hatch now fully open.
The ship's bow crested through the waves, sending spray twenty
feet either side. There was a pause before the rockets fired. Out
of an eruption of smoke, the missile accelerated vertically into
the grey morning sky, leaving a vapour trail behind it. The
column of smoke drifted to their starboard in the breeze.

Jack jolted, his whole body shaking, as if he'd been woken
from a dream. "Wait, wait..."

Peterson and Sam glanced sideways at him, as if he'd lost his
marbles.

"Call off the attack, lieutenant. How do we know Terra's not
with Briggs? She could be sat right next to him in that convoy."

Peterson's eyes flicked from Jack back to the screen. He was
considering this new information, weighing his options before
seeming to nod, his mind made up. "I can't do that, Jack. This

may be the only chance we get to take out Briggs. He's the biggest risk to Camp Wight we have right now. Lives at Osborne are at stake. We need to take this."

"There must be another way? Please. I'm begging you."

"I'm sorry. There's no way to stop the missile. There's nothing I can do now." He clasped his hands together, to impress upon Jack the finality of his words.

The missile had only five miles left to run and stayed relatively low. It tracked north-east, speeding south of the Needles. Accelerating towards its maximum velocity, it arced over the island and just as suddenly started its descent. The screen in the stateroom alternated between the view from the missile back to the drone, keeping pace with the convoy at about five hundred feet. The missile raced towards its target, dipping down as it reached terminal velocity, zeroing in on the heat signature of the lead vehicle carrying the tracker. Jack found he was holding his breath, fearing what was to follow. The screen went completely white, followed by static as the missile detonated.

The operator switched views back to the drone. It showed a massive explosion and a mushroom cloud of smoke. It took a couple of minutes for the smoke to clear sufficiently for them to make out the scene of destruction. A huge crater emerged in the roadway. One vehicle was a tangled mess. Bodies lay motionless nearby. Two other vehicles were on their sides. The last car, further behind, had its four doors open. Figures stood gawping down the road.

"Can we zoom in at all, Jenkins? Would be good to get a look at those guys."

The drone dropped altitude and zoomed right in. The four figures hove into view. Peterson squinted and blinked, not quite believing his eyes. "Isn't that...?"

"It couldn't be, could it?" added Jack, leaning closer.

"It most definitely is," Peterson said, shaking his head. He lifted the grey-green handset to his lips and said, "Jenkins, let the XO know that we have a miss. Repeat, we have a miss. Briggs is still alive, and it looks like he's got a new friend."

"I didn't even know those two knew each other. Perhaps they've been in league all this time?" said Jack.

The camera zoomed in further and sure enough, standing next to Briggs was Victor, the first officer from the *Maersk Charlotte*.

"The double-crossing rat," spat Jack. "I wonder if Anders knew about this."

Chapter 52

Terra woke after a restless night and immediately felt a shooting pain down her side from sleeping on a hard bed in the cold, damp room. It took a few moments to get her bearings as memories from the last few days came slowly back into focus. The trip to Osborne House, the dinner, Peterson and Armstrong's speech, the sense of renewed hope for the future. Then Briggs had taken that all away. Kidnapped, imprisoned, forsaken. Alone again. She was a survivor though, wasn't she? She'd survived worse than this.

Her surroundings were relatively spartan, bare stone walls cold to the touch. A simple chair and table nestled under a bare timber-framed window, which looked down over the ruins of an unfamiliar castle. In the foreground were a small chapel and courtyard, ornamental gardens and high stone walls covered in moss and lichen.

She had been brought here under cover of darkness, hooded for most of the journey. Disoriented, she was unsure where exactly she was on the island. Her best guess was that this was Carisbrooke Castle as she could think of no other site of this scale or grandeur. It also fitted the bill, based on what she knew of Briggs and his men. They had been incarcerated in Parkhurst Prison, no more than a couple of miles away.

She stretched out her arms, ran through a few warm-up stretches and yoga positions to stimulate her circulation and stop the shivering. It took a few painful minutes to eliminate the stiffness she felt in her lower back and arms. Staring out the window, a light drizzle flecked the windows from rain clouds blowing in from the sea.

She heard footsteps in the corridor and the rattle of keys as the door swung inwards and one of Briggs's most trusted men stood waiting to take her downstairs for another audience with the man himself. Her escort was a curious-looking individual. The facial tattoos that decorated one side of his head reminded her of a Maori warrior. His beard and sideburns were in need of a good trim, with only a small tuft of hair at the scalp. The rest of his head was shaved smooth. Nevertheless, despite his radical appearance, he seemed cordial enough.

Terra had been pleasantly surprised by Briggs's behaviour towards her so far. He had been kind and attentive, asking her repeatedly what she needed to make her stay comfortable. His men had returned several hours later after an exhaustive search of Newport. They brought clothes that were several sizes too big, together with expensive toiletries, the likes of which she had not seen in years. He had insisted she wear a particular dress, the yellow one, knee-length, classic style with the floral pattern. The autumnal yellow of the dress set off her red hair in the sunlight. Apparently, the dress reminded him of a special someone he had known long ago, and this seemed to put him in a good mood.

Her escort knocked but didn't wait to be invited in. Briggs was in the middle of an angry exchange with another prisoner whose hands were bound behind his back. She recognised the man from Osborne House but didn't know his name. He was in his mid to late fifties with a full head of white blonde hair. A large cut had been patched up above his left eye, a purple bruise darkening underneath. She exchanged a pained look of sympathy before he was led away. He tried to say something to her, straining against the rope binding his wrist but was quickly pulled away. As the door slammed shut behind him, she heard him shout "Don't tell them anything."

Briggs's expression softened as soon as he spotted Terra. He threw his arms wide, beaming. "Good morning, Terra. How fares our Queen of Hurst this rainy day?"

"Well, thank you," responded Terra awkwardly, maintaining her distance. The great hall made her think of Hurst, though the castle was clearly much older judging by the roof and brick-work. It reminded her in so many ways of the historic places she had visited as a child. The Tower of London, Hampton Court, Windsor Castle. The musty smell, the damp and cold, but also the sense of awe and wonder at standing somewhere so rich in history. It was almost as if she could sense the ghosts of kings, queens and noblemen who had graced these royal surround-ings. There was a very real aura of history and drama that impregnated every stone, every brick. One could not help but feel a little bit inadequate and unworthy standing there amongst these magnificent surroundings. The incongruity of Briggs and his men's occupation of the castle was not lost on Terra.

"Come and sit and have some breakfast with me." He studied Terra, trying to anticipate what would make her happy. "Hatch, bring us some coffee, and I think cereal and fruit today, am I right?"

"Thank you," responded Terra, modestly taking her seat opposite Briggs, aware of his attentions. He couldn't seem to take his eyes off her, like a kid with a new toy, enjoying the shape of the dress and the way its cut accentuated her curves. He watched, absorbed by her every move as she helped herself to an apple, which she cut carefully into slices and ate one by one. When she had finished, he asked for the plates to be cleared before restarting his inquisition. There was no artifice, no subterfuge, no threat, albeit implied, to his questions, and she willingly complied, answering his every request with a direct-ness that he found refreshing.

"Now, why don't we go back to where we left off last night? You were telling me all about Jack and Zed. Where are my notes?" He rummaged through a pile of papers in front of him and pulled out a sheet of lined paper. The handwriting looked childlike, accompanied by doodles and scribbles in the margins.

"So, I've got here that your friend Zed likes to carry around a double-headed axe. Who does he think he is? Spartacus? Bit cumbersome, isn't it?" He turned towards his henchmen standing nearby and laughed bawdily. Turning back to Terra, without a hint of irony, he went on, "I prefer a butcher's knife myself. More up close and personal." He crudely gestured a slice across his neck to demonstrate how he liked to use it, prompting another laugh from his men. "I look forward to meeting him. Sounds like my kind of guy. I might put his head on a spike outside my castle as a reminder to any other jumped-up wide boy who thinks they can mess with me."

"But, Briggs..." She paused, a little embarrassed. "Can I call you Briggs?" He nodded and encouraged her to continue. "As I assured you yesterday, the people of Hurst had nothing to do with the attack on your convoy. They're mostly pacifists. They spend their time fishing and growing vegetables, not fighting. They're not looking for trouble."

"Bullshit. Anyone who's in league with the Americans is no pacifist. The missile or bomb that killed my men may have been American, but you can be sure that someone from Hurst helped pull the trigger."

She leaned forward, her eyebrow raised playfully. She felt

composed in Briggs's company, demure, playing along. She knew from last night that Briggs had a weakness for her. She suspected he was more than a little bit susceptible to her charms. She intended to use every advantage that gave her, without crossing the line. The bruise on her left cheek ached when she moved her jaw, a reminder that you could push him only so far.

Briggs had expressed his regret immediately and the man who struck her had not been seen again. She remained unintimidated by the threat of further violence, though not oblivious to the danger. She was deliberately provocative, working hard to retain his attention. She wasn't sure how much Briggs had heard of the plan for Camp Wight, but it wouldn't hurt to test the extent of his knowledge and spread a little disinformation at the same time to downplay Hurst and create a degree of separation.

"I can assure you the Americans want little to do with Hurst. It's an outpost, nothing more. They have no appreciation of history. No real understanding of local politics. Like a bull in a china shop, they're, well, just doing what Americans do best. Throwing their weight around, sticking their noses in to other people's business. Trying to do the right thing, but in the process, treading on a lot of toes."

"Okay, Terra. If you're so bleeding clever, what would your counsel be?" asked Briggs, in a moment of indulgence.

She smiled and Briggs looked at her suspiciously, his head tilted to the side as if he was torn between wanting to believe her and beating her to a pulp. She was under no illusion that the moment she ceased to please and beguile him, her life would be expendable. Careful, Terra, she told herself. Be very careful.

She leaned forward and fixed him with her most winning smile. "If the Americans want to set up camp here, let them." She shrugged and looked over his shoulder. "Wait until they've ferried over their supplies and stores, got everything set up. Bide your time. What harm can it do? If you risk an all-out war with them, you'll lose. Remember the war on terror? Remember what happened to every army that invaded Afghanistan or Iraq or Syria and tried to fight the Taliban, ISIS or Al Qaeda in a conventional way? They all failed. You could do worse than learn from their experience. Your men need to become invisible, like shadows in the night. Go underground, become fifth columnists, fill every position of power. Bide your time, like sleepers waiting for the right moment to strike, when the allies are at their most vulnerable." She leaned back again, her smile gone. "Anyway, that's what I would do."

"Interesting. You and I think alike. Terra, you might just make a name for yourself around here. I need a good adviser, someone I can trust. I'm just not sure I can trust you, Terra. For a start, you're a woman. Never trust a woman. That's what my mum used to say, God bless her. Every woman I've ever known has lied or cheated on me."

He stood up and leaned across the table, over the fruit bowl that had been placed between them. He picked up a ripe peach, biting down to the stone and tearing away its flesh, allowing the juice to dribble down his chin. He wiped the liquid away with his sleeve and grinned lasciviously at Terra.

"Of course, if you could prove to me that I could trust you, that would be different. But right now, my head is full of questions about you, Terra. Questions, questions. You're going to have to earn my trust. Do we understand each other?"

Terra swallowed involuntarily, her mouth and throat suddenly dry. She knew exactly what he meant. She was beginning to ask herself what she was going to have to do to keep Hurst safe and her enemies close. She had started down a very dangerous path and it was already too late to turn back without consequences. The only way was forward, deeper and deeper into the maze, and one wrong turn could prove terminal.

Chapter 53

Riley reversed the Land Rover Defender up to the main entrance to the Chewton Glen hotel and opened the boot for Mila to load the rest of their gear. Other than minor burns and watery blisters on her fingers and forearm, Riley had nothing more to show for her suicidal dash through a burning building than some singed hair and scorch marks on her trousers.

She hurried back into the lobby area and helped Zed to his feet, levering him up from a large leather sofa where he had been playing cards with Adele. One of the guards kept watch on the Hurst group as they manhandled Zed across the gravel driveway to the Defender's front passenger seat. He swung his legs up over the sill and slumped back against the headrest, beads of sweat already forming on his brow. He was slowly getting his strength back, but the strain was clear for all to see. He masked his pain well, but Riley knew him better than to be fooled so easily. It would be a while yet before he was back to his normal world-weary laconic self.

With Joe gone and Zed on the road to recovery, there was nothing left for them here. Riley was desperate now to get back to Hurst. Despite the efforts of the whole group to persuade her otherwise, Stella was adamant that she was staying put at the hotel.

Riley gave Stella a long farewell hug before stepping back to look into her eyes. They were already welling with tears. She held her shoulders at arm's length.

"Are you sure this is what you want, Stella? I know these are your friends. I get that. But living here in this convent..." Her voice trailed off. "You know you don't have to live like this, right?"

The sun appeared from behind a cloud, blinding the group with brilliant sunshine. Stella squinted back, irradiated by the light. To Riley, she looked almost angelic, her flawless skin seemed to shimmer. Through her tears, Stella's passion and conviction was clear.

"I can't explain it. I just feel like I belong here. You have to see beyond the Sisterhood with all their rules and religion. The way of life they are espousing is pure. It's what I want, Riley. I think all of us secretly crave that simplicity, don't we? A life with purpose and structure."

"Sometimes, it's not that simple. But listen, if you tell me that this is what you really want, then I won't try and dissuade you."

"I do, Riley. I really do." She paused, looking at her shoes and then back at the hotel and the trees beyond, composing her thoughts, choosing her words carefully. "I know you think that this whole place is false, that it's not sustainable. That we're all burying our heads in the sand and ignoring what's going on in the real world out there, but I've made my choice. Please respect that. I don't want to go back out there. I'm safe here now. I don't have to wake up and worry about where my next meal is coming from. I'm tired of living in fear, of watching my back all the time. Life here is pure and simple, free of violence and struggle. I like that."

"But is survival enough? It's up to us all to help rebuild what's out there," she said, pointing beyond the wall. "Don't you want to be part of that, to play your part?"

"Honestly...?" Stella scrunched up her face. "No. I'd prefer to live out my life right here." She patted her belly, which was just beginning to show signs of swelling. Though anyone who didn't know she was pregnant would have a hard time spotting it. "I've got another life to think about now. I need a safe environment to bring up my baby, and the sisters can give me that. It's not much, maybe, but it's enough for me."

Riley smiled and hugged her again. "I'm happy for you, really I am. I'll come back and see you as soon as I can. We all will."

As they were talking, the nurse appeared in the doorway holding Adele's hand. The little girl let go of the nurse's hand and ran towards them, a small rucksack bouncing on her back. She attached herself to Stella and Riley, hugging them both, before heading towards the Land Rover with a dismissive wave over her shoulder. She slammed the car door and pressed her face to the window, looking back at Stella, her hot little breaths misting up the glass.

There were voices behind them, footsteps crunching on the gravel. A small posse of women rounded the corner of the building, walking swiftly and purposefully towards them. Sister Theodora was at the head of the group, flanked by the two other sisters.

"You there! Yes, you." She jabbed her finger accusingly at Riley, her voice shrill and contorted. She reminded Riley of the Wicked Witch of the West in *The Wizard of Oz*, all dressed in black. All she was missing was a green face, pointy hat and long nose. Right now, Riley wished she had a good bucket of water to throw at her.

The Mother Superior came to a halt right in front of Riley,

breathing heavily. She pointed directly at Riley and bellowed, "Seize them and take her into custody."

One of the guards grabbed Riley from behind, forcing her arm behind her back before she had time to react. Mila raced round to wrestle with the woman, ripping her hand from Riley's arm, releasing the pressure momentarily. "Get your hands off her!" The guard pushed Mila out the way and twisted Riley's arm back into a lock.

"It's all right, Mila," said Riley through clenched teeth. She stared back at the sisters defiantly, ignoring the pain for a second. "Perhaps you'd be so good as to tell me what I'm being accused of?"

"We have reason to believe that the fire was no accident." She enunciated each syllable of the word "accident" slowly and with particular emphasis.

Riley's mind was racing. Why would anyone have started the fire deliberately? For what possible reason? She suddenly thought of Joe and their escape. Could the two events be connected? But how? From the way the sisters were behaving, they clearly had evidence that supported this conclusion. Although she had no idea why she was implicated in all this.

"Considering you had all of us locked up when the fire broke out, I find it highly unlikely that you could think we had anything to do with it," said Riley.

"So it was purely coincidence that your friend escapes on the same night a fire breaks out?" mocked the sister. "Rather convenient, wouldn't you say? We only have your word that you were where you say you were when the alarm was raised. Did anyone see you? Can anyone corroborate your version of events?" She shook her head, not waiting for an answer. "I thought not."

Riley tried to wriggle her arm free of the guard's grasp. She had terrible pins and needles, but the guard only twisted her arm tighter to stop her fidgeting.

The sister seemed to enjoy her discomfort and continued. "There were no witnesses. You could have smashed the garden window any time that night."

"Hold on a minute, you left us in there. Your guard locked the door. What else were we meant to do? Stay there and die of asphyxiation? Zed would have died too had we not acted when we did. Anyway, why would anyone deliberately start a fire and be responsible for the murder of so many?"

"Why indeed?" Sister Theodora let the question air for a few seconds. "Unless they were trying to help their friend. We hold you and your party fully responsible. Those deaths are squarely on Hurst's shoulders."

"That's preposterous. So you're saying that you have no other suspects? Are all the other residents accounted for?"

Sister Theodora whipped her head round at the other sisters. It seemed a reasonable question, but in her mind, there was only one plausible explanation. "You held the roll call this morning, Sister Imelda. Are all the residents accounted for?"

Sister Mel hesitated. Suddenly she looked uncomfortable, a seed of doubt germinating rapidly in her mind. "All residents were accounted for, sister. Except one."

Sister Theodora looked irritated by this disclosure, disappointed that no one had thought to mention this detail earlier. "And you waited until now to inform me of this? Well, go on, sister. Who was it?"

"It's one of the girls, sister. Jean Farley. She's been taking food to the prisoners every day. It's possible..." She looked down at the ground, afraid of the consequences of what she was about to say. "It's possible that she could have helped the men escape."

"Nonsense. Why would she do such a thing? No, I refuse to believe that one of our own could..." Her voice trailed off. "I have every confidence that it was the group from Hurst who are responsible for this outrage, not one of our own girls."

Riley shook her head. "You believe what you like, but I'm telling you, my group had nothing to do with this."

"I propose we take them all into custody until the truth can be determined." She gestured for the two guards to tie their hands behind their backs, but Riley wriggled free. In one fluid movement, she pulled a concealed blade from under her belt buckle and held it out in front of her. There was no way they were going quietly.

Stella stepped forward and tried to intercede on behalf of the Hurst group, placing her hand lightly on the guard's shoulder. Sensing Stella's approach, the guard swung round wildly with her elbow, striking Stella hard across the face. The blow left a red welt that took Stella's breath away. She gasped in pain, as the guard stuttered an apology. Sister Mel rushed to her side to comfort her.

A sharp wolf whistle from the Land Rover silenced the group and they turned as one to find Zed, index finger and thumb to his lips. In the other hand, he clutched a shotgun resting the barrel on his hip, pointing squarely at the nearest guard.

"Let's everyone settle down, shall we."

Zed had watched the arrival of the Sisterhood from inside the vehicle with a weary shake of the head and guessed what would happen next. He had retrieved the shotgun from its hiding place strapped under the front passenger seat where he liked to keep it, in case of trouble.

Using the tailgate to support himself he kept both guards in his field of view. He was feeling a little shaky, sweat beading on his upper lip, despite the cool ambient temperature. He was trying his damnedest to look like he meant business. Riley and

Mila distanced themselves from the two guards, acutely aware that he might lose his grip on the tailgate and topple sideways at any moment.

"You two. Lay down your weapons and back away. No one needs to get hurt here," said Zed, his voice thin but authoritative.

Sister Theodora stared back at Zed, motionless. With a heavy sigh, she conceded defeat, signalling for the guards to lay their rifles on the ground and take two steps back.

"You have our word that none of us had anything to do with the fire," continued Zed. "Anyone who believes otherwise is even crazier than I thought."

He adjusted his grip on the tailgate and nearly fell before recovering. Mila hurried over and slid a supporting shoulder under his arm, taking the gun from his shaking hand. She tilted her head and peered down the barrel, training the sights on the two sisters, who shifted uneasily, their hands half-raised in alarm.

"What's going to happen next," confirmed Zed confidently, "is that we are all going to get in our car, drive right out of here and you're not going to try to do anything to stop us. Are we clear?"

There was silence.

Zed repeated, inclining his head, "Are we clear?"

"We are clear," echoed Sister Theodora. "May God have mercy on you for what you what you have done. All of you have blood on your hands. All of you."

"You can believe what you like. It doesn't make it true," said Riley defiantly.

Riley climbed into the driver's seat and inserted the key in the ignition, looking back at Zed and Mila in the rear-view mirror, just standing there, showing no signs of moving. Mila let out a deep sigh, like she had been holding her breath all this time and lowered the shotgun towards the ground. Mila motioned towards Stella. "You staying or coming with us?"

Stella was still nursing her cheek, where the guard had struck her, tears streaming down her face. She studied Adele's and Riley's imploring looks from inside the vehicle, forcing a smile. "Thanks, but this is my home now."

Sister Mel put an arm around Stella's shoulders, squeezing her tighter in a show of solidarity. Mila clambered into the vehicle and slammed the rear passenger door, resting the shotgun on the open window, pointing over the heads of the group. Riley started the Land Rover's engine, which coughed into life, its exhaust rattling, wheezing a little before finding its rhythm.

"Perhaps one of you would be good enough to get that truck out of my way," shouted Riley over the noise of the engine.

The guard hurried inside to find the keys to the truck hanging on a hook behind the front desk. As she walked down the gravel driveway, the Land Rover kept pace, rolling a few yards behind her, back towards the front gate, its two pillars with ornamental lions mounted either side.

The guard reached up for the handle and heaved herself up into the cab. With a plume of diesel smoke from its roof mounted exhaust, the truck roared into life. Inside they could see the driver fighting with the gear stick to get the lumbering beast into reverse, before lurching slowly backwards. She revved the engine impatiently, allowing just enough space for them to drive out and on to the main road beyond, before rolling back into place.

Just before the gap closed behind them, Zed glimpsed Stella's lone arm raised in farewell in the rear-view mirror, and then she was gone. He had a bad feeling it wasn't the last time they would tangle with the Sisterhood.

Chapter 54

It was less than five miles back to Hurst from the hotel, but the roads were virtually impassable, clogged with abandoned cars. The traffic backed up all the way from the roundabout on the edge of town along the coastal road they were attempting to navigate. They had no choice but to detour around obstacles, onto pavements, grass verges, through people's front gardens, even smash through a garden fence. In doing so, they managed to hook a children's climbing frame, wrapping the ladder around their front grill. They had to stop to prevent it from jamming in the front wheel arch. They used any means they could to pass the blockages that littered the roadway.

In a couple of places, they had to nudge other vehicles out of the way, or get out and push them by hand. Riley had grown desensitised to the sight of death. It was all around them. She thought nothing of pulling corpses from vehicles, of wrenching victim's hands that still gripped steering wheels, or heads resting against dashboards. She no longer felt squeamish, or was it just fatigue? Cumulative tiredness played tricks on the mind. She reached over a body to release the hand brake and steer a two-seater sports car out of their way, as Mila pushed from behind.

After a couple of hours, they caught their first glimpse of the sea. Milford beach stretched out to the east of them with the Needles rocks and island beyond. Riley was still troubled by what Stella's friend had told her. She had been very clear. She had seen smoke rising from Hurst Castle. However unlikely, that's what she said. Why would she lie?

Visible from that distance, it had to be more than just a campfire or burning rubbish. It sounded like a proper fire that had got completely out of control. She imagined the widespread panic, the plans and preparations they had made for exactly this eventuality. They had stored fire hoses in the lighthouse for pumping water from the dock back into the castle and placed buckets of sand near doorways and access points around the camp. They were as prepared as they could be, so she was still wondering how a fire could have taken hold. Just thinking about fires brought back memories of the previous night when she put her life on the line to save Zed. The pain in her hand was a living link. She cradled her left wrist, still bandaged, pinching the dressing to relieve the pressure on the watery blisters that were painful to the touch.

They drove on through Milford village, each of them fearing the worst. Riley leaned forward in her seat, anticipation growing as they drew closer to home, her imagination running riot, giving voice to her fears. As they reached the end of the road and the last of the buildings at the far edge of town, they screeched to a halt.

Ahead of them was a dirt track that hugged the start of the raised man-made sea defences and shingle spit. To their left was what remained of a caravan park, half flooded and storm damaged. Ploughed fields lay beyond. In the corner of the field, sitting next to a broken wooden fence, a yellow tractor stood idle and abandoned beneath a cluster of trees. Riley engaged first gear and they continued the last leg of their journey along the dirt track towards the castle.

There it was in the distance, across the estuary and tidal waters. There was little sign of smoke now, in fact, nothing that suggested anything untoward. Riley picked up the pace, pumping the accelerator and bumping over the many potholes, deep groves and dips, where the dirt track was waterlogged.

They reached the end of the track and ascended the steep incline in low gear, slipping and sliding until they crested the top of the shingle bank and the vehicle levelled out again. The view over Christchurch Bay was spectacular, the island glinting in the morning sun.

Riley braked hard, scattering stones in front of the car. She could barely believe her eyes. She reached across Zed, fumbling in the glove compartment for the binoculars. It took a couple of seconds for her eyes to adjust and find what she was looking for. Far out to sea was a ship. It was definitely military, a navy frigate or destroyer, she couldn't tell from this distance.

"A ship?" asked Zed, peering into the distance, following the line of her binoculars at the indistinct grey shape on the horizon.

"Definitely not a steamer or container ship. Could be a warship," suggested Riley.

"Is it one of ours?"

"Hard to tell but it's definitely heading this way."

Riley handed the binoculars to Zed and shifted the Land Rover back into gear. She accelerated hard, showering the underside of the car with pebbles and loose shingle. There was now an added urgency to get to where they were going. Zed panned the binoculars towards Hurst and pointed out that there was no lookout on the castle walls. That was unusual. Riley made a mental note to have strong words with whoever was on guard duty that morning.

Where was everyone? The whole place looked deserted. The closer they got, the more worried they became that something terrible had happened in their absence. Riley cursed herself for being away too long.

Rounding the western edge of the fortifications, they headed down the short slope going too fast. Riley jammed on the brakes and the car slid to a halt outside the main entrance to the castle. All four doors flew open as the group emerged, alert and ready. In front of them was the blast hole in the drawbridge. They could see wisps of smoke caressing the leading edge of the stone walls, before dissipating on the morning breeze. To the right of the entrance, high up on the old grey stone walls, mottled with black lichen, someone had spray-painted a tag in blood-red graffiti. Stylised letters a metre high spelt the word: "Hurts".

Mila held her hand over her mouth, slowly taking in the scorch marks from the explosion at the front entrance and trying to make sense of the graffiti. "Who would have done this?"

Adele spelt out the letters aloud, one by one. "What does it mean, Zed?"

"It means someone has a sick sense of humour."

Riley opened the tailgate and unloaded their weapons. She slid a pistol into her belt and rammed two shells into each barrel of the cocked shotgun. "You don't think that the guys from the hospital had anything to do with this?"

"It's possible they came looking for us." Zed stood scratching his beard, angling his head to the side. "Don't take any chances." He sniffed. "They could still be here. Mila and Riley, you two head inside and see what you can find out. Be careful, yeah? Adele, you stay here with me."

Riley clambered through the blast hole and tiptoed through

the covered entrance, staying close to the wall, making no sound. It was eerily quiet inside. She closed her eyes and took a couple of deep breaths. Mila was right behind her. Very slowly, they both peered around the corner to take a look at what lay beyond. Inside, bodies littered the courtyard. Mila gasped, her eyes flicking from one body to the next, before recognising one of the faces furthest from her: "Oh no, please."

Riley heard voices close by and froze, gesturing Mila back against the wall, weapons raised trembling in front of them. She listened carefully, straining to hear, before recognising Tommy's voice. She called out to him, warning the defenders not to shoot. Nathan and Liz hurried out to meet them.

"My God, where have you all been? We thought you were dead," said Nathan, wide-eyed in disbelief.

"It's a long story. What the hell happened here?" asked Riley.

"We were attacked by the group from the hospital," said Nathan.

"My God," she gasped, realising the chain of events they had set in motion several days before. "But how did they get in? What about the guards?" Riley had a dozen questions crowding each other out.

"They came in the dead of night. Used climbing gear to get over the walls at the back. Once they were inside they blew open the front gates. There was another group waiting outside. There were too many of them. We mounted a last stand at the Gun Tower. It was bad, Riley. It was a bloodbath for the guys in the west wing."

Liz took over and explained in detail what had happened. They helped Zed through to the guardhouse to sit down. He was still a little unsteady on his feet.

Tommy bent down on one knee and shook Adele's hand, welcoming her to the castle. She looked back at him a little bashfully and cringed as he ruffled her hair. She shot a grumpy glance towards Riley as if to say, "Who is this guy? I'm not a kid, you know."

Inside the main building, Riley waved at Scottie who nodded back, wrapping a bandage round the scalp of one of the injured, whose dark Barbour jacket was slick with sticky blood. Only his eyes and the lower half of the man's face were visible. Liz had him propped against the wall with a hot cup of tea to hold. He seemed to be suffering from concussion. He was non-responsive, almost dejected. There was an air of melancholy about him. In truth, no one was quite sure how he'd got there at all. He was unarmed and had nothing identifiable in his pockets. And yet, there was something familiar about him, but Scottie couldn't quite place it. Something about his voice when he had asked for something to drink.

Tommy helped the injured man through to the makeshift triage area where more than a dozen wounded were laid out on mattresses on the floor. One of Copper's men was tied to a bed, a bullet still lodged in his abdomen, oozing blood when he breathed. They didn't hold much hope for him but Liz had insisted that whatever he had or hadn't done, it didn't make any difference. The people of Hurst were not barbarians. They would administer what medical care they could offer and make the wounded comfortable.

The man tied to the bed seemed to perk up at the sight of Tommy and his charge. He tried to mouth something, but no words came out. Unnoticed, he extended a single finger towards the man with the bandaged head, his eyes flickering as his head slumped back against the pillow. Tommy lowered the wounded man back onto an empty bed, unlacing his boots. The man's pupils were dilated, his vision cloudy. He was struggling to maintain focus as Tommy moved a finger back and forth in front of his eyes.

"What's your name?" he asked softly. There was no response, so he tried again. "Can you tell me your name?"

The man blinked back at Tommy and whispered, "Damian. My name's Damian King." His voice sounded familiar to Riley. Clipped, northern, hard to place.

"How did you get here?" Tommy continued, suddenly intrigued.

There was another pause as the wounded man tried to make sense of the question. "I'm not sure. I don't remember. Where am I?"

"You're at Hurst Castle," said Tommy. "Liz says you'll be fine, but you've had a nasty blow to the head."

Riley spotted Nathan doing what he did best, bustling around, making lists of names and their symptoms. There were some casualties with more serious injuries, gunshot wounds and the like, who would need urgent treatment. They didn't hold too much hope for a couple of them. Zed spotted the man Tommy had supported through and did a double take.

Riley noticed his puzzled look, following his stare towards the man with the bandaged head. There was a flicker of intelligence in his eyes, something Riley recognised.

"Do you know him?" asked Riley.

"Don't you? This is the piece of work who executed Bob and tortured Will at the hospital. What's he doing here?"

"You're joking? This scumbag," said Scottie, all traces of empathy towards the wounded man gone.

The more she looked, the more Riley thought she knew the man. How could everyone have been so slow on the uptake? Of course, they had likely never seen his face in daylight, only glimpses in torchlight and shadows. It seemed implausible, but impossible to deny.

"Why would they leave their leader behind?"

"I don't know. Perhaps they thought he was dead."

"What do you want us to do with him," asked Scottie.

"We'll deal with him later," spat Nathan, gritting his teeth. "Take him to the dungeon. Jack will decide when he's back."

As Tommy and Scottie led the prisoner from the room, Will appeared in the doorway, blocking their path. He grabbed the wounded man by the scruff of the neck and lifted him off his feet, smashing him back against the wall. "I told you we'd meet again. I'm going to enjoy wiping that grin off your face," spat Will.

Damian King's face was a picture of puzzlement. Unfazed by Will's anger, he stared back with cold lifeless eyes.

Nathan prised the two men apart, inserting himself between them. "Back off, Will. Look at his eyes, he's all messed up, he doesn't even know where he is."

"Well he's going to wish he never came here," snarled Will, incredulous. "The two of us have unfinished business." Will grabbed the prisoner by the hair and hauled him in close. He hawked up some saliva and spat in his face, before dumping him back down on the ground. "I'm going to make you regret what you did to me. What you did to all of us." He slapped King across the cheek and watched as Tommy frogmarched the prisoner away to the dungeon.

Chapter 55

The *USS Chester* passed the Needles rocks and iconic red and white lighthouse on its northerly tip. Staying within the main shipping channel, the warship towered over the castle at Hurst and the corresponding fortifications on the island side, Fort Albert and Fort Victoria. The *Chester's* progress slowed momentarily as she entered the tidal race flowing westwards.

On the bridge, Lieutenant Peterson had ordered the crew to battle stations. Jack watched enthralled as the deck-mounted heavy machine guns swung around and trained their sights on the battlements of Hurst. Spotters on the ship's superstructure scanned the shoreline on both sides with high-powered binoculars, in constant communication with sniper teams posted on the upper decks. They were still trying to establish contact with the Royal Navy at Portsmouth, getting no response. The radio operator couldn't explain why they weren't answering. The panel of lights and screens in his communication centre were all green. Weather conditions were moderate. They should have easily been in range. Peterson requested one last system check.

Sergeant Jones's team had reported in a few minutes earlier. They had managed to commandeer a vehicle to inspect the missile crater and tangled wreckage within the blast area. Briggs was not one of the five bodies they had recovered, nor for that matter was Terra. They said the Humvee was barely recognisable, upside down on its roof. They had videoed everything, collecting what physical evidence they could before heading back to Osborne to meet the Seahawk.

Jack waited on deck as the crew lowered one of the *Chester*'s fast R.I.Bs to speed them back to Hurst. As soon as they were through the tidal race and into calmer waters, they were ready to launch. Sam was watching a crewmember prep the machine gun mounted at the front of the R.I.B, loading ammunition and checking the firing mechanism. Tommy would be so jealous. Sam said he couldn't wait to tell everyone about the ship and the ride in a helicopter. Two crewmembers helped Jack over to sit on a large grey container loaded with medical equipment. He was unable to stand for long, but had insisted on coming ashore to inspect the damage to the castle.

When the bags and boxes were safely stowed and the rest of the team assembled, the command was given and a hydraulic winch whirred into life. It slowly lowered the R.I.B and its crew until it splashed down in the ship's wash. The pilot started the outboard engines and steered away from the destroyer's towering hull towards Keyhaven estuary and the sheltered dock behind the castle.

Even after a lifetime at sea, Jack still found it exhilarating being in a high-speed launch. After the ocean-going *Nipper*, the R.I.B felt like a seagull, skimming the surface, barely feeling each wave as they sped towards their destination. They passed the end of the Hurst battery, its familiar dark grey rectangles where heavy artillery would have faced the Needles channel, the white lighthouse and outbuildings that Jack called home.

Stretching ahead of them were the narrow-gauge railway tracks that led to the castle gate from the original docks where munitions and stores would have been unloaded. Jack noticed his Land Rover with its doors still wide open, as if it had been abandoned. Rounding the eastern tip of the spit, they headed into the small dock, avoiding a half-submerged yacht. Only its mast and foredeck were visible above the surface at high tide, seawater swilled over its guardrail, tangled with seaweed and grey foam. A large gull hopped across the rail as they approached, before rising gracefully on the breeze, gliding a few metres away on to the crosstrees of another yacht, nodding at anchor.

Jack could see Tommy racing down to meet them at the dock. The gunner swung his bow-mounted weapon round to bear on Tommy's chest. Jack tapped the man on the shoulder and explained that he was friendly, much to Tommy's relief.

As soon as the R.I.B. nudged against the pontoon, the four marines jumped ashore and fanned out left and right, scanning for targets. Sam seemed relieved to see his old friend Tommy again, punching his shoulder as they fell into step, sharing a smile and a joke, no doubt eager to swap stories.

Jack interrupted their excitement, impatient for every detail, anxious to hear news about any casualties. When Tommy mentioned that they had captured the man who led the attack, Jack straightened up, setting aside his pain and discomfort, emboldened by this unexpected consolation. He rolled the name Damian King around his mouth, as if trying it for size, searching his memory for any mention of the man. He was certain he wasn't local. And yet, he was intrigued by the revelation that Will seemed to know the man from before. Where could he have met him?

Back within the protected confines of the austere stone of the Tudor castle, Jack seemed to relax a little, his painkillers kicking in. Arm in sling, he stopped to shake hands with several on their route. They descended the steep stairs that led to the cellar. It was damp and musty down here. The whole place still reeked of smoke, with noticeable fire damage and scoring in several places along their route. In the very corner of the main block, in the bowels of the castle, they arrived at a small dry storeroom where they would have kept munitions and explosives in centuries past. In the half-light thrown from the flame of a lantern hanging on a hook by the door, the guard leaning against the wall looked exhausted, waiting to be relieved. He roused himself as they approached, a flicker of recognition as he noticed Jack. They waited for the youth to retrieve the key from a pocket of his green Parka coat. The heavy oak door swung open to reveal total darkness within, a small rectangle of light from the doorway at their feet. Nathan powered up a small penlight and they stepped inside.

It was not immediately obvious that there was anything or anyone in the shadows until the torch beam located the soles of a pair of boots. A recumbent figure with a bandaged head was slumped against the brick wall, shielding his eyes from the light. The room was inhospitable, to say the least. It was freezing cold so close to the waterline. A silver rivulet of seawater ran past the prisoner's boot towards a drain in the floor. Cobwebs hung from the low ceiling and oak beams that forced the standing men to bend double as they advanced further into the cramped confines of the cell. Mould had found a home in every brick and every stone here. Jack could taste it on every breath.

For a few seconds, they all stood in silence as the others shuffled in behind. The guard handed them a hurricane lantern to throw some more light on the pitiful conditions of the prisoner's captivity. The room stank of sweat and urine from the blue plastic bucket in the corner. The latch clicked shut behind them. The captive assiduously studied each of them, taking in every detail, his arms folded, staring back with no shortage of contempt. At least he appeared to have recovered his wits since his capture.

Nearly an hour later, the three men shuffled out, shoulders slumped, their body language dejected. The youth relocked the door and resumed his lethargy outside the cell. Jack and Nathan walked a discrete distance away from both the cell and the guard before discussing what they had learned. Jack felt exhausted as if being in the same room, in the presence of this man, this monster, had drained him of every ounce of energy.

"How do we know he's not lying? He could have invented this whole story," suggested Nathan.

"No, I'd say he's telling the truth all right." Jack nodded. "The question is why he's telling us in the first place?" he added, stroking his chin with his free hand. "Zed and Riley saw at first hand that they were experimenting on people up at the hospital. It stands to reason that a small percentage of the population would have natural immunity to the virus. Who knows, perhaps with sufficient time and resources, they could find a way to enhance those natural defences or even inoculate against the virus. Maybe Adele *is* one of those lucky few, but why would he tell us that? What could he hope to gain by telling us the truth?"

Tommy shook his head, frustrated by Jack's response. "You don't know him like we know him. You weren't here. Didn't you hear what he did?" He leaned forward, imploring Jack to listen. "He deserves to die for what he did here. He executed our people. Innocent, unarmed men and women. He ordered his thugs to shoot them in cold blood. Don't be taken in by his lies. He'd say and do anything to get himself out of here and that's why we can't trust him. He's telling us what we want to hear. Don't you see that?"

Jack stroked his wiry beard, flecked with grey hairs that caught the light. He closed his eyes, collecting his thoughts. Was he being naive in taking the prisoner's words at face value? He thought he detected conflict, almost as if the man wanted them to know the truth.

"Listen," added Tommy. "Let's agree that he's trying to manipulate us. To what end, we don't yet know."

Jack patted Tommy on the back to reassure him. "Don't worry, the truth will reveal itself in the fullness of time. It always does."

Tommy and Scottie nodded silently, still puzzling over their earlier interrogation of the prisoner. Jack was replaying the conversation in his head. Something didn't stack up, but he couldn't put his finger on it. Somewhere within that stream of disinformation were hidden truths, he was sure of it. King must have known they would share what they learned with the Americans. He would figure it out in the end. He normally did. Tommy was a hot head, but he would learn. Patience, it had to be said, was not one of Tommy's strong points.

"Nathan, you go talk to the girl and see what you can find out about these tests they were running. Ask her about this other girl he talked about, Stella. Even if there's a chance they have immunity, we need to get the girls to a secure location. This could accelerate the search for a cure. The allies are setting up a centre for research on the island, near Newport, led by Professor Nichols. This could be a breakthrough."

"You need to tell me more about the Americans and their plans. Right now, I have fragments only. I need to know the full picture," implored Nathan.

"First, I want a one-on-one chat with this Damian King. If it's just the two of us he might let his guard down, open up a bit more."

"Be careful, Jack. Don't underestimate him. He'll be plying

you for information, just as much as you he, trying to influence you," warned Scottie.

"He'll find I'm more than a match for him," laughed Jack. "Although, why doesn't Tommy wait outside, just in case," he conceded.

Chapter 56

Jack retraced his steps to the improvised cell, waiting for the guard to unlock the door. Once inside, he crouched down on his knees opposite the prisoner, setting the lantern between them on the floor. The prisoner seemed to ignore him, staring up into the darkness, his eyes locked on a spider in the corner, quietly spinning a silvery web that glistened in the half-light.

After a prolonged silence, King finally turned his head towards Jack as if noticing him for the first time. His eyes were devoid of life, like dead pools. His face was expressionless, an impenetrable mask. Jack's eyes narrowed, steeling himself to the task at hand, trying hard to maintain a calm exterior and air of authority, as he pondered his next move. He imagined himself as a chess-master facing his greatest adversary, exploring cause and effect, waiting for his opponent to make a mistake.

"Something you forgot to ask, Jack? I think I've told you everything I want to tell you, for now."

"Why don't we cut the crap and start again, leader to leader, so to speak? But I warn you, no more games. Until you start telling us what we want to hear, well, as far as I'm concerned, we can leave you in here until you're ready to talk, however long that takes. No one's going to come and bust you out." Jack paused, waiting for his adversary to take stock and reflect on who held the balance of power. "Why don't you start by telling me why you really attacked the castle? And why your men saw fit to leave you behind? Everyone seem to think you're some kind of Trojan horse, but it sounds more like you got careless. You'd served your purpose and they discarded you like a broken pencil."

The man in black smiled, shifting his body weight and adopting the same kneeling position as Jack, mirroring his body language. Leaning forward, the lantern lit his face from below. His features seemed suddenly contorted in the pale light, his eye sockets empty, almost ghoulish, his smile demonic.

"Oh, I don't know," he opened brightly. "I always saw myself living in a castle one day. An Englishman's home is his castle, isn't that what people used to say? But after seeing this old dump, I've changed my mind." He paused, staring unblinking at Jack. "If you really need me to spell it out. There's no big secret. That Bok of yours, Will, told me all about this place and I figured, why not? Eliminate a rival on our doorstep, claim the castle for myself, live happily ever after. Perhaps you haven't noticed, Jack, but it's dog-eat-dog out there."

"Whatever goes on out there is none of our business. We're peace-loving folk here; we're not looking for a fight."

"Nevertheless, sooner or later someone was going to come along and take this place away from you. It was just a matter of time."

"We're hardly defenceless, as I think you found out for yourself last night."

"You can't live in your little bubble forever."

"Bubble? Live and let live, I say. We're doing what we can to get by. Providing we catch enough fish and grow enough vegetables to feed the hungry, then we're happy to stay clear of the madness. It may not seem like much to a power-hungry megalo-maniac like yourself, but to us this is home. The life and security people craved. This is survival."

"It's all a bit 'Kum-ba-yah', isn't it, Jack? Sitting round a campfire, singing songs, saying prayers, slowly dying a little bit every day. Then what? Out there people are doing more than just surviving. They're getting organised, reconnecting with other groups, rebuilding. What are you doing? You have your heads in the sand. Sooner or later you're going to have to choose a side. Alliances are forming and you can't stay neutral forever. You're not a colony; you're a castle. A pile of bricks and stone, nothing more," goaded the prisoner, trying to rile Jack.

Jack parried with a dismissive wave, trying his best to remain calm, adopting his best poker face but marshalling his rising sense of anger. "What makes you think we haven't chosen sides already? You think we're isolated and alone here? We're not. When you attack Hurst, you attack a whole network of Solent forts and small communities pulling together. We don't stand alone, we're an interconnected alliance growing and expanding. Just because we've chosen a life of neutrality and non-aggres-sion doesn't mean that we won't stand up for our way of life when challenged."

"You don't have the balls," he snorted.

"I wouldn't be so sure. We'll hunt down the men who did this like the vermin they are. Wherever they're hiding, we'll find them. We have powerful friends who protect us and watch over us. There's a new order coming to sweep away people like you."

"Oh, I know all about the Americans and Camp Wight. Don't tell me that's your big secret? You really think you were the only ones invited to the meeting at Osborne House? Some of us chose not to go. Ever considered that?"

Jack was blinking furiously, trying to keep his emotions

under control, while his mind raced to play catch-up. He took a moment to compose himself, genuinely lost for words. "Whatever you think you know, you only know the half of it. Things are moving quickly," he said, before pausing abruptly. "Oh, but forgive me, perhaps you don't know, all cooped up in here, cut off from everything that's happened over the last few hours."

"Capturing me changes nothing."

"I wouldn't be so sure. You'd do well to realise that you and I are but pawns in a much larger game. There's nothing you can do to stop our plans. The wheels are already in motion. Unless, that is, you have a whole army at your command?"

"Oh, I have something much better than an army, or a navy for that matter. I have a virus. A pandemic virus. Left unchecked, it's capable of wiping out human life on this planet as we know it. Phase one of that process is already complete. Whoever controls the cure pulls the strings, holds the fate of all those who remain alive. Just think of the power bestowed upon whoever can be first to manufacture and distribute a vaccine? Wealth and influence beyond anyone's wildest dreams."

"And yet, despite all that *power*, you risked your own life to get the girls back." Jack laughed scornfully. "You're bluffing. Without the girls, you have nothing."

The prisoner sneered back at him, mocking Jack's attempts to provoke him. "Losing the girls was an inconvenience, a trifle, nothing more. A minor setback to our plans. The girls are of little importance. And you should know that without their daily injections, they'll die like all the rest and then you will have nothing. But I will still have months' worth of research. We already know so much about the virus. We have samples of their blood, more than enough to continue our experiments. The girls mean nothing now. You can have them. They're yours."

Jack was beginning to panic. He was running out of moves. He'd played his cards, and found his adversary always seemed to hold the upper hand, or at least was better at bluffing than him. He was taunting Jack that he knew everything he knew and more, but how? He had to be in league with someone else who had been at the Osborne House dinner. In his mind, he replayed the mental image of the drone footage, of Briggs standing next to Victor from the *Maersk Charlotte*. An idea began to form. A conspiracy. Was it possible they were all working together? A powerful alliance that would stop at nothing to see the plans for Camp Wight fail and chaos continue in the region. But why? To what end?

"Poor Jack," King continued. "You really don't understand, do you? You really think that the Americans can just waltz in here and everyone will roll over and welcome them with open arms, share all our food and resources with a foreign power? Don't be so naive."

"Au contraire," gambled Jack. "You're the one who's being naive. Perhaps you haven't heard? Oh, how silly of me, I forgot. You've been stuck in here. Out of the loop."

"Very well, Jack," he said with a sigh. "What have I not heard? Surprise me."

"The Parkhurst crew. Dead. Destroyed."

King pursed his lips and grimaced: "Parkhurst Prison? What are you talking about?"

"Your friend Briggs is dead. The axis of evil is finished, before it ever had a chance to get going."

King laughed again, throwing his hands up in mock despair but showing no flicker of recognition that he knew what Jack was talking about. Jack's gambit had failed. His lie about Briggs fell on deaf ears and he did a poor job at concealing his frustration.

"Axis of evil? If that's what you really think then you're even more deluded than I thought. Please don't kid yourself that the world is somehow a safer place now you've captured one evil genius hell-bent on your destruction. The new world is full of people like me. I'm just like you, Jack. Fighting for what I believe in, looking after my own. Trying to make a better life. You want to know the difference between us? You see the world through rose-tinted glasses. You think everyone is inherently good. I don't. I'm a realist. Life is a game and people are merely pieces on a chessboard. You just have to figure out how to use them to win." King shook his head with a pained expression, enjoying the moment. "You still don't get it, do you? You think because you live in a castle you're better than the rest of us? You're pathetic. You see the world in absolutes. Good versus evil. Life is never that black and white. Don't judge a book by its cover. Next, you'll be telling me that living in a lighthouse makes you a shining beacon to others, you self-righteous arse."

Jack was shaking with rage, his left eye flickering involuntarily. "No, King, you're wrong. Our actions define us as people. Not our clothes, or what we say. You see the world in shades of grey. I don't. I draw the line at killing innocent people."

"Innocent? Guilty? The search for a cure is what matters. Our very survival depends on it. The end justifies the means. If that means a few thousand extra people need to die while we test a vaccine, isn't that a price worth paying? That's progress, no?"

"I'm not talking about all those hundreds of people you killed in the name of science. I'm talking about the women and children you murdered in cold blood, right here. My people. They were unarmed. They didn't stand a chance."

"You think the death of your people makes the slightest bit of difference? Don't be so sentimental. Thousands of people are dying every day." He clicked his fingers repeatedly to emphasise the point, then paused and smiled, remembering something. "Curious to think that your people were put out of their misery by former policemen. Interesting, no?" He put his finger to his lip, tilting his head before continuing in a mocking voice laced with irony. "How quickly people change. It didn't take much to persuade men who dedicated their lives to upholding the law that killing others is right and necessary. The rules of the game have changed. Wake up and smell the coffee, Jack. The world has changed and it is you who haven't kept up. You bury your heads in the sand here like ostriches. You're no better than me or anyone else. You just think you are. If you're not careful, you're going to find yourselves isolated and alone here. Perhaps you've forgotten that Camp Wight will be on the wrong side of the Solent."

"We fought you off before. We'll do it again."

"Really? How can a bunch of fishermen like you hope to protect this castle against a whole army of trained paramilitaries? My men won't give up until this place is razed to the ground. Next time, you won't stand a chance, even with your new friends."

"You really think they'll come back and risk their lives to save you? They'll leave you here to rot."

"My men won't come back here for me. So long as they have breath in their lungs and bullets in their guns, they'll keep coming until your pathetic group is wiped out. It's just what they do. Your people came to Hurst to die. They just don't know it yet."

Jack had taken all he could take for one day, but King wasn't finished yet. He had one last poisonous thought to share.

"Perhaps it hasn't occurred to you that I could be a carrier, slowly spreading the virus. Immune myself, but infecting you and your people even now. Bet you didn't think of that. Careless, Jack, sitting so close, breathing the same air as me."

Listening to the man in black's hollow laugh, Jack shuddered. It had occurred to him that the girls may not be the only ones immune to the virus, but the chances of any of the rest of the hospital group being immune were a hundred-to-one. He shook his head, refusing to rise to the bait.

"I have better things to do than listen to the delusions of a man who's never going to see the light of day again. I'll leave you to your twisted thoughts. We'll talk again when I'm good and ready. Enjoy your silence and solitude. That's all you'll get from us."

Jack had had enough of this goading. For the last few minutes, he'd been clenching his fists, tighter and tighter. He could feel the veins on the side of his neck throbbing. He swore that if he spent one more minute with this man, this monster, he'd tear him limb from limb. He stood up too quickly, clumsily kicking over the lantern that stood between them. The glass smashed and the flame was extinguished in the dust on the ground, its wick and mounting tumbling clear.

The whole room was suddenly plunged into darkness. Jack scrambled towards the doorway, feeling with his hands in front of him. He started hammering and shouting Tommy's name, trying to keep a lid on his mounting fear. The man in black's disembodied voice in the darkness seemed to come from multiple directions, echoing off the walls of the dry storage room.

"Poor Jack," he repeated, followed by that same hollow laugh.

Jack banged louder before the key turned and Tommy's friendly face appeared in the doorway, peering in to see what was happening. Jack wrenched the door open wider and barged Tommy out of the way, desperate to get as far away from the prisoner as he could. Tommy stood for a second, staring after Jack as he hurried away. Behind him, Tommy looked back into the darkness, wondering what had spooked Jack, searching out the face of the man inside. All he could see were his legs and the smashed lantern on the ground. He stooped to pick up the lamp and the larger shards of glass and slammed the door shut.

On the stairs, he found Jack limping heavily, perspiration on his forehead. Tommy supported him through the narrow doorway to the roof of the Gun Tower. Jack fell on his hands and knees and dry retched, breathing hard. When he had recovered his wits, he hobbled over and found Nathan looking out over the battlements, surveying the USS Chester's progress east towards Cowes and Southampton Water. Jack snatched the walkie-talkie from Nathan's belt and depressed the talk button.

"Peterson, it's Jack here."

There was a few seconds delay before a voice he recognised well came back loud and clear. "Go ahead, Jack."

"We've got a major problem. I don't know how, but they know. King knows all about Camp Wight." There was no response from Peterson so Jack continued, the stress obvious in his voice. "And it sounds like the story about the girls is bona fide. They do have immunity to the virus."

There was a long silence, while Jack checked the volume on the radio to make sure it was still transmitting and the battery hadn't failed, before he heard the American's response. "Copy that. Let's continue this conversation face to face. Be careful what you say, Jack, this is an unsecure line. Let's get those girls to a safe location."

"Okay, one of them is safe. And we think we know where to find the other one. We're going to need some transport though."

There was another silence. "We've got our hands a little full right now, but we'll send the chopper as soon as it can be spared. Hang in there, Jack."

Jack signed off and looked back towards the island. Dark clouds were blowing in from the south-west. He could see light rain falling underneath. The dull ache in his shoulder intensified as the painkillers began to wear off. His heart sank and his eyes closed as he remembered the loss of Terra. It was as if he'd locked that memory away and stumbled across it again unexpectedly. Sam was right. She was a resourceful woman. She would do whatever it took to stay alive. He had to believe that and trust to luck.

Chapter 57

I t was late on the second day after the attack on Hurst when the helicopter was released from its more pressing duties ferrying military personnel. Osborne House had been set up as a temporary command centre for the newly formed Camp Wight, under the protection of a detachment of US marines led by Sergeant Jones.

Peterson had re-established communication with the Royal Navy and now had a permanent liaison officer based in Portsmouth to foster improved relations between the two allies. As a gesture towards reciprocity, Captain Armstrong had installed one of his trusted deputies on board the *USS Chester* to act as local guide and pilot to orient the Americans around the Solent waters.

Peterson and the helicopter crew collected Riley from the grassy area next to the lighthouse, where she had been waiting for some time, scanning the skies. Once she was safely on board and the crewmen had helped secure the straps of the jump seat next to the sliding door, they took off towards the Chewton Glen hotel in search of Stella.

The helicopter flew low over the trees and houses of Milford, hugging the water's edge towards Christchurch. Riley braced herself by the open door, thrilled by the sensation of speed, wind blowing in her hair, straining against her seatbelt to see below the aircraft. Her long brown hair flicked in her eyes and face and she held back a handful of fringe with her free hand. With her other hand, she gripped the handle nearest her. They passed over a golf course, where grass grew long and verdant on deserted fairways and greens. Turning inland over Barton-on-sea, they traversed roads and roundabouts clogged with stationary traffic.

She gestured to Peterson to slow down and the nose pitched upwards as they lost speed, coming into a hover above the main road and front gate to the hotel fifty metres below them. Riley leaned out as far as the seatbelt straps would allow. The truck blocking the front entrance was gone. Something was wrong.

She pointed towards the main block and cluster of buildings a few hundred metres away and Peterson relayed the message to the pilot. They continued onwards, following the path of the driveway that curved left and then right past trees and the first of several planted fields and vegetable patches. The fire damage to the roof of the hotel was worse than she had first imagined. It seemed to extend along half the length of one of the buildings. They lost height and gently touched down on the side lawn. A swimming pool visible just beyond some bushes looked like it had been drained and used for storage.

Riley was fully expecting a crowd to rush out to welcome them, Stella and Sister Mel at its head, waving towards them. No one came. The place seemed deserted. Where was everyone?

They waited for the twin engines to power down. Two marines set up defensive positions covering the front and rear of the aircraft, before the airmen allowed Riley and Peterson to climb out on to the soft grass. The first marine ran to the corner of the building and took up a kneeling position, scanning to their right. Once he signalled all-clear, the rest of the group ran towards the main entrance, staying low.

They were a dozen paces from the entrance when Peterson held out his arm to block Riley from going any further. She looked up at him puzzled, following the line of his outstretched finger. It took her a couple of seconds to see what he was pointing out. Riley clasped her hand to her mouth to stop herself screaming. To the right of the doorway, someone had spray-painted a large red skull and cross bones, warning others not to enter. Riley gripped Peterson's arm, trying to keep a lid on a mounting sense of panic.

"Peterson. It's not possible. We were here not two days ago. There was no sickness. There must be some mistake. Everything was fine."

"No one goes inside without a biohazard suit, am I clear? Pavlowski, break out the suits and breathing gear."

Riley had never worn an airtight suit before. They were standard-issue in green PVC material with an oversize clear Perspex front panel that restricted the wearer's field of vision to the sides. The suit she was handed was several sizes too big for her and went over all of her clothes, zipping up and sealing tight from behind. The head section and breathing gear took a while to get used to. The suits were claustrophobic and she found the Perspex viewing panel had a minor magnifying effect, like reading glasses, distorting the world outside. Corporal Pavlowski helped tape her sleeves closed and turned her air on before attending to his own.

When the group of four was ready and had checked each other's equipment and seals, Peterson split them into two-man teams and they proceeded inside. Riley could hear her own breathing as she moved and stayed tight behind Pavlowski. In his gloved right hand he carried a pistol just in case they met any resistance. She tapped him on the shoulder and pointed down the corridor towards the main living area. In the lobby there were suitcases, plastic sacks and equipment stacked near the door, rubbish strewn across the carpet as if people had left in a hurry. There was no sign of Stella, or anyone else for that matter.

Peterson took his team up the main stairs as Riley searched the ground floor of the building. Riley knew the layout of the hotel directing Pavlowski as they went from room to room, through the kitchen, canteen and living room. Everywhere they went told the same story. The place looked like it had been ransacked; contents of desks rifled and drawers left hanging, books missing from shelves, papers strewn across surfaces. Had they been attacked, she wondered? There were no obvious signs of a fire fight, no bullet holes, no bodies. What had happened here?

They heard a loud banging on the ceiling from the floor above and Pavlowski grabbed Riley and gestured for her to follow. The suits were bulky and cumbersome. She found it difficult to run any faster than a slow shuffle without the head section bouncing awkwardly and the seams securing them to the main body threatening to tear open.

When they reached the top of the stairs they found Peterson and the other crewman. His body was braced against the closed fire door, as if something was trying to break out from the inside. The suit muffled Peterson's voice. "We've found something."

Riley's eyes darted left and right, waiting impatiently for him to continue. "What is it? What did you find?" she implored.

"We're going to need to limit our time inside. I'm sorry but there are many casualties. Find out what you can, but don't hang around. The suits are airtight, but we're not taking any chances. We're looking for the girl. We're not here to help the injured. Are we clear?" The three others nodded and Peterson released the fire door, and the two groups stepped inside.

The corridor stretched ahead of them with doors either side. Riley was not familiar with this part of the hotel but recognised the style and layout from the rooms she had already seen. She stood outside, waiting for Pavlowski to give her the nod that he was ready, gun poised in case someone tried to rush them.

Inside the first room, there were a total of seven bodies. The two shapes in the bed were already dead, or as good as, non-responsive and barely breathing. Two more were in armchairs positioned to look out of the large sash window at the garden and flowerbeds beyond. It was as if someone had wanted their last conscious moments to be contented ones, contemplating the beauty of the trees and the lines of carrots and potatoes growing in turned earth nearby. The heads of the two figures in the armchairs rotated towards the strange pair standing in the middle of the room. One of the women weakly held out a hand towards Riley, her hair matted with dried perspiration, greasy and lank. She recognised the woman's face from the canteen, one of the kitchen staff. Riley inclined her head sympathetically as tears started to stream down her face. She couldn't wipe them away.

Pavlowski heard her sob and was behind her in an instant. "You okay, Riley? Keep it together, yeah? If our girl ain't here, we keep moving. We finish our sweep and get out of here."

Riley nodded and reluctantly moved to the next room. Room number twenty-eight. They tried the handle and found it was locked so proceeded on to the next. Inside room thirty, they found the nurse all alone, keeping a silent vigil over the sick. She seemed to be sleeping and did not respond to their voices or touch. Pavlowski shook her hard and lightly slapped her face. She jolted upright in the chair as if an electric shock had been passed through her. Her eyes were wild, frightened by the two figures standing in front of her like astronauts from another planet. Riley spoke to her, but she didn't seem to recognise her at first or understand what she was saying.

"Nurse, it's Riley. You looked after my friend Zed. Do you remember me?" She leaned in close, slowing her words, annunciating clearly. "The man who hurt his arm. We were here a couple of days ago." Riley grabbed her shoulders and shook her again.

The nurse shook her head, looking through her, clasping her hands together in her lap, stroking a rough patch of skin on the back of her wrist where she had rubbed it raw with worry. She was rocking backwards and forwards, terrified and confused. Riley tried again.

"What happened here? Where is everyone?"

The nurse seemed to come to her senses momentarily. "It's just us now. They left me all alone with the sick."

"Gone where?" Riley shook her again by the shoulders but the nurse grabbed her wrist to make her stop, staring angrily into her eyes through the plastic, resenting this intrusion into her private despair.

"The sisters took the rest of them to a safe place. They left me in charge. There's nothing I can do, except make them comfortable."

"I don't understand. There was no sickness here when I left."

"Mother Superior said the men brought the sickness. She blamed your friend."

"But that's impossible. None of our group are sick," replied Riley incredulously.

"Not now. They may not know they are sick. Carriers, unaware that their every breath is deadly to others. This is how the virus spreads so fast. People carry on until they have infected everyone around them."

Riley was unconvinced. She knew the virus well through observing the new arrivals at Hurst and their forty-eight hours of quarantine. Symptoms presented themselves quickly, coughing, sneezing, fever. It simply wasn't possible that the members of the Hurst team could have spread the virus, unless they were immune themselves. None of that seemed to make any sense. She addressed the nurse again.

"Who fell ill first? That might give us a clue."

"Let me think. It all happened so fast. I think it was the two girls. They were brought to see me first, complaining of feeling run-down and feverish. Of course, I knew right away what it was, or what I feared it might be. But by then it was already too late. They had been in contact with half a dozen others, and they in turn had been in contact with half a dozen more."

"What were their names?" asked Riley urgently, grabbing her shoulders forcefully.

"It was Lexie and her friend Gina. They were the first, I'm sure of it."

Riley remembered them well. They had been the two teenagers who told her about the boys they used to meet from outside the hotel grounds, drinking cider and smoking together behind the shed. The snatched kiss. Riley was convinced. In all probability, the girls were the most likely source of the outbreak. She didn't for a moment believe that the team from Hurst had brought the virus with them. There had been no other reported cases at Hurst for months. They were clean, but it was pointless trying to convince the nurse otherwise. She at least knew the truth.

"Where are the rest of them? Do you know where they were making for?"

"I know they were headed east towards Christchurch. They'll most likely find another hotel or large building, an abandoned school or trailer park to camp out there until the outbreak has died out. They'll send a messenger every two days to check on us and wait until it's safe to return." The nurse turned her head and looked out of the window, lost in her thoughts. Without turning back, she continued in a low voice, barely above a whisper. "She knew you would come back."

"Sorry. Who knew? Do you mean the sisters?"

"Sister Theodora said you would come looking for Stella and I was to give you this note when I saw you." She reached into the folds of her apron. Deep inside a front pocket was a folded note that she held out to Riley with a shaking hand. Riley was intrigued and took the single side of hotel stationery with its distinctive masthead in her gloved fingers. She opened it slowly to reveal sculpted words, loops and letters written in the sister's handwriting. It reminded her of the calligraphy pen she had been given on her eleventh birthday by a doting aunt and the hours she had spent perfecting her strokes and shapes. The note was addressed to her personally, but the bulk of the text was made up of two extracts from the Bible that she didn't recognise immediately, but both sounded familiar.

There will be no more night. They will not need the light of a lamp or the light of the sun, for the Lord God will give them light. And they will reign forever and ever.

Revelation 22:5

He that is unjust, let him be unjust still: and he which is filthy, let him be filthy still: and he that is righteous, let him be righteous still: and he that is holy, let him be holy still. And, behold, I come quickly; and my reward is with me, to give every man according as his work shall be. I am Alpha and Omega, the beginning and the end, the first and the last.

Revelation 22:11-22:13

Dear Riley,

Every day we say a prayer for you and your people. We forgive you for all the hurt and pain you have inflicted upon our flock.

The Lord in his almighty wisdom sent you here to show us the error of our ways. The fire and the outbreak of the sickness here were God's will, of that I am certain. The Lord moves in mysterious ways.

Do not look for us, you will not find us. Do not return here. Only sorrow remains.

Sister Theodora

Riley refolded the letter and handed it to Pavlowski who scanned the handwritten text and shook his head. "Don't take it personally, Riley."

She feigned a smile and answered, "I won't."

Chapter 58

After a leisurely breakfast and friendly inquisition, Terra and Briggs adjourned to a well-appointed drawing room in one of the oldest parts of Carisbrooke Castle. He held the door open and waited for her to enter. Following close behind was the enormous bulk of one of his most trusted deputies. Earlier, Terra had witnessed Briggs speaking with the man with the extravagant tattoos on his face with what appeared to be genuine tenderness, his arm around his shoulder like a brother, sharing a joke. The man's name was Hatch or Hutch. Anyway, something that made her think of rabbits.

A fire, recently lit, crackled and spat sparks in the enormous hearth stacked with logs and kindling that was just beginning to catch. She could see scrunched-up paper still burning at its core. To the right of the fire was a large pile of newspapers. She angled her head, trying to make out the masthead, cover picture and headline on the topmost copy. It was dated more than two years ago at the very start of the outbreak. She scanned the copy. Rumours of a terrorist attack, photos of a royal baby, political crisis. It had been several months since she'd read a magazine or paper. At Hurst, Scottie had made a habit of collecting hundreds of broadsheets, local papers, trade journals, science papers and fashion magazines, chronicling the chaos of the outbreak. The first early warning signs had been ignored. Dismissed as localised winter flu spikes, of little concern to the developed world. As the scale of the outbreak became clear, wild theories proliferated. The final issues of *The Times* and *The Telegraph* had been single-sheet publications as printing works and newspaper offices closed in short order.

Terra reflected on the fact that the world had become an altogether smaller place. So little was known of what was happening elsewhere beyond their immediate environment. Nowadays people tended to view the world with blinkers on, busying themselves with what was in front of their noses. There seemed little point worrying about what lay beyond. She was reminded of Jack's mantra that one of the keys to happiness was to never worry about things outside your control. Concentrate on the here and now, or at least that's what Jack had always told her.

There was a chill in the air that the fire had not quite dispelled. Terra stood barefoot, her back to the flames. She scrunched her toes in the deep pile of a large red rug, marked by small burn holes where coals had fallen from an unattended grate. The room was impressive, with portraits of distinguished noblemen that graced the walls. A framed watercolour had been left propped against a bookshelf, jostling for space with statues and trophies collecting dust against the walls, presumably stolen from the surrounding area by Briggs's men. In the corner, in pride of place, stood a suit of armour in richly polished metal, a mace in one hand together with a ball and chain in the other.

Briggs closed the oak-framed door and slumped into his favourite armchair set nearest the fire. He watched Terra as she moved around the room, noting where she lingered, what she picked up, and what she ignored in his growing collection of looted artworks.

She felt his eyes following her and accentuated the sway of her hips as she walked, planting her bare feet carefully to avoid pieces of glass on the wooden floor. She made sure he was watching closely and retained his attention by flicking her head coquettishly to the left, making eye contact over her shoulder. She was enjoying this fleeting sense of power and sway she held over him. She thought she sensed conflict, as if he was fighting his instinct to trust her. She smiled inwardly, encouraged by his uncertainty.

He waited for her to finish her turn around the room, enjoying the contours of the dress and the way it hugged her figure, before patting his lap, inviting her to join him. She blushed and tried to laugh off his request, but quickly realised from the humourless expression that, on this occasion, he would not take no for an answer.

She approached the armchair but hesitated, looking awkwardly at him. It reminded her of unwanted attentions from an affectionate relative when she was young. She remembered Uncle Sebastian at Christmas time, insisting that she still sit on his lap, despite being a pubescent teenager. She shuddered, even after all these years, thinking of his arm snaking around her waist, his coarse hands massaging her shoulders.

Briggs patted his knee again. "Come on. I'm not going to bite."

She modestly perched on his knee, but he grabbed her waist and quickly manhandled her across his lap. She was powerfully aware of the smell of the man. He was in need of a good bath. She did her best to remain calm as he studied his prize up close, drinking her in, angling her chin to left and right, studying the contours of her face.

In the folds of her cardigan sleeve she adjusted a small blade she had smuggled from the breakfast table. It was a wooden-handled kitchen knife with a serrated edge. Hutch had been careless leaving a blade this sharp within reach and not realising its absence on clearing.

She might never get this close to Briggs again. His neck was thickly muscled above a black sweater, his bulging vein close enough to bite. She summoned the courage to do the deed, to get it over with, to rid the world of this tyrant. The neck was her best option. An unsurvivable wound. A clean kill. A quick stab with the knife and it would all be over in seconds. And yet, she found reasons to defer. Could she really kill someone in cold blood?

He smiled at her, enjoying her discomfort, but growing impatient at her reluctance, her body stiff and tense, unresponsive to his touch. The smile faded on his lips and turned into a snarl as he bared his teeth and whispered, "You need to learn, woman. Learn to appreciate me." He pulled her closer. His mouth was right next to her cheek, his breath sour and hot. His lips caressed her ear lobe, sucking at the stud earring she wore, nibbling it gently between his teeth. She fought to maintain control, her heart racing. He mistook her shortness of breath for excitement and continued.

The wooden hilt of the knife slipped against her wrist and the blade caught in the flesh of her index finger. With the weight of his body against her arm, the knife threatened to break the skin and draw blood. Her moment had come, if she could free her hand. Strike now or lose the chance forever. It would be over in a moment.

There was a knock at the door and without waiting for an answer, one of Briggs's henchmen strode in, followed by Victor, the first officer from the *Maersk Charlotte*. Briggs looked affronted by this interruption, his head buried in Terra's neck. He loosened his grip slightly and Terra took advantage of the distraction, springing to her feet before he could grab her wrist again.

There was a smirk on Victor's lips as his eyes flicked from Terra back to Briggs, conscious he was interrupting this moment of intimacy, enjoying her discomfort as she stood awkwardly, hands fidgeting like a frightened child.

"What do you want, Victor? Don't you have somewhere else to be?" said Briggs.

"Sorry. I can see you're busy. I won't keep you long. I've just finished interrogating the others. They know nothing. Next time, we need to get an American."

His voice was heavily accented, East European, certainly. Terra couldn't place it. Baltic states, former Soviet Union. Latvian or Estonian, she guessed, waiting for Victor to continue, wondering how many other hostages they had taken from Osborne.

"I thought you should know the *Maersk Charlotte* is on the move," he added. "She weighed anchor this morning and is heading into Southampton docks to begin unloading. The Royal Navy has rigged up power to one of the giant cranes. They will begin unloading the humanitarian supplies, unless that is, we choose to stop them. Construction of the first of the refugee centres is expected on the island within the week."

"Good, good. Just like we planned. And our men? Are they in position?" asked Briggs.

"They are, as you instructed. We have made contact with the hospital. Copper is now in charge. It would seem that his boss met with an untimely accident during their failed attack on Hurst."

"How careless. And this new man, Copper, is he someone we can do business with? Can he be trusted?"

"Oh yes, he is a policeman. None more trustworthy, no? He and I go way back. He should prove a useful ally. He tells me their doctors are working on a prototype vaccine. They have already synthesised a strain of the virus, portable and deadly. They are conducting clinical trials to perfect them. He can start sending us samples as soon as we're ready."

Victor was about to divulge further details when he paused, his mouth half-open. His eyes darted across to Terra who was listening to the exchange, betrayed by a look of concern she failed to hide on learning about the attack on Hurst, her thoughts turning to Jack and the rest of the team.

"What about her? Are we to trust her? Surely, her loyalties lie with Hurst and the Americans. You should not be fooled by her kisses."

Terra made as if to speak, to defend herself at Victor's accusations, throwing her arms wide in a gesture of innocence. Victor nodded to the henchman who grabbed Terra by the wrist, bending her arm back until she winced. He patted her down for concealed weapons and wrestled the small kitchen knife from her sleeve and held it up for Briggs to see.

"This one you must watch like a hawk. She is not to be trusted. One of my men saw her take this earlier, but failed to mention it till just now. You were lucky I got here when I did."

Victor presented the handle of the knife to Briggs who took it and weighed it for size, patting it while he nodded, fixing Terra with a look of reproach. He made a low tutting sound and got wearily to his feet, seemingly disappointed by this small act of treachery.

"It's lucky you were here, Victor. Your instincts serve you well, unlike you two, you useless bastards," he said, gesturing towards his bodyguards who were doing their best to blame each other. "It's stuffy in here. Let's take some air. I can't think in this room. Victor, Terra, Hatch, follow me. There's something I want to show you."

He opened the door and waited for the three others to head

out into the front lobby area and courtyard beyond. Outside it had stopped drizzling. Rainwater was dripping from roofs and gutters, collecting in large barrels positioned underneath drain pipes. Their shoes crunched across the wet gravel. Terra was still shoeless and tiptoed in bare feet, pushed from behind when her pace slowed.

They climbed the steep steps covered with moss through a large archway on to the ramparts of the old keep and the walls that ran along the top. The view up here was magnificent, stretching across the island. The city of Portsmouth was visible in the distance to their right across the Solent. To the south and west were sweeping fields and countryside, the houses and streets of Newport set out below. Briggs stopped at the highest point, leaning against the railing, out of breath, waiting for the others to join him.

The thin wooden rail was all that stood between them and a vertical drop some hundred feet or so down to the ruins of buildings nestled against the castle walls below, shrouded in bushes and trees. He put his arm around Terra's shoulders, pulling her towards him. His fingers kneaded the muscles at the base of her neck. She flinched, trembling slightly but made no attempt to move away.

"What do you see, Terra?" He extended his arm over the sweeping landscape stretching into the distance. She stayed silent, terrified. "What do you see when you look at this beautiful island? I'll tell you. Opportunity." He smiled, grasping the air with his hand. He squeezed her around the waist before pushing her away roughly. "But you disappoint me, Terra." He let his words hang for a couple of seconds before continuing. "I don't like disappointment. I have no time for liars. Without loyalty, without trust, there is nothing. Do you understand?"

Terra nodded, feeling the wooden rail give a little as she leaned against it. Suddenly she felt very afraid, staring down into the abyss beneath her bare feet. She gripped the edge of the stones with her toes and swallowed hard. She fully expected this to be her last breath before tumbling over to meet her maker, consoling herself that at least it would be a quick end. A short fall and then nothing. The pain would be momentary.

"You and I could have been something. We could have ruled this island like King and Queen. Don't you see that? But how can I ever trust you again?" He shook his head, staring out over the countryside beyond. She started to apologise but he raised a finger to silence her. "Hatch, get over here." He gestured towards the gentle giant of a man, who wandered closer. "How long have we known each other? Five, no, six years. You, my friend, have one job. You know what it is? To ensure my safety. To stop people like her trying to do me harm."

"Yes, boss, it was like this..."

"No explanation needed, Hatch. You did your best. I get that. I can't ask for more. And yet your best is not good enough. Not by a long stretch of the imagination. You let this, this feeble woman, smuggle a knife in close without anyone even noticing."

"Sorry, boss, it won't happen again." He was all of six feet four inches and yet he looked like a scolded schoolboy.

"That's right, Hatch, it won't happen again."

Briggs stepped back and braced himself against the raised outer wall of the castle and kicked hard into the small of Hatch's back. Despite his size, he was off balance and the railing did little to arrest his forward momentum. He crashed through the barrier and plummeted some hundred feet down on to the rocks below.

Terra and Victor followed his flailing arms and brief fall, hearing his skull crack against the stone foundations of a storage shed. Terra could just make out the slow trickle of blood from a head wound dripping onto the white stone and start pooling beneath his body.

Briggs turned to face Victor. "Victor. Looks like a position in my organisation has just opened up. Do you want in?"

Victor was staring down at the man's body below, the left foot still twitching. He looked up into Briggs's expressionless eyes and nodded. Briggs turned his back on them and started walking away.

"You can start by clearing up that mess. Get that railing fixed, will you? It was an accident waiting to happen."

Victor nodded and mumbled his assent, hurrying after his new boss. He stopped and turned to find Terra still staring at the crumpled body below, its shape twisted awkwardly, broken against the rock.

"Come on. That's enough excitement for one day. Let's get you inside and back in your cell."

Terra looked up with tears in her eyes as she shivered in the morning breeze. She took a step towards the edge, backing away from him. "Don't come any closer or I'll jump."

Victor stared at her motionless. "We both know that's not going to happen," he said, mocking her.

"I'll do it. Don't think I'm not capable," said Terra shaking her head, her whole body trembling with fear and adrenaline.

"Oh, I know you're capable, Terra. But I also know that you won't jump."

"Don't be so sure. You don't know what I've done to survive."

"You're like me. An opportunist. You've survived because you evolve and adapt, stay close to those in power. Bide your time, make the most of a good thing.

"You know nothing about me. Don't underestimate me, Victor."

"You're wrong. I hold you in the highest regard." She looked confused and relaxed a fraction, puzzling over his words. "Things are about to get interesting. If I was you, I'd stick around. Don't give up now, just when you've landed yourself a position of influence. Those others he took. The hostages. They were worthless, except to trade or use as human shields perhaps. Whereas you, Terra. You're the key to all this. The Queen of Hurst, he calls you. You could help unite these disparate groups. He needs you. Stay close to Briggs and you'll be at the heart of this growing rebellion. Just imagine, riches and power beyond your wildest dreams. If we work together we can rule this new world. It's ours for the taking."

She put her hand back against the railing post behind her, blinking back at him, digesting his offer of partnership. Victor seized his chance and reached out to grab her sleeve before she could react.

"Don't touch me. You're wrong. You're as bad as the rest of them. You all deserve to die."

He slapped her hard across the face and hauled her away from the edge, dragging her back towards the stairs to the main building. Terra took one last look across the countryside to the north and west. She couldn't see Hurst but she imagined Jack and Zed standing on top of the Gun Tower in the distance. If only she could get a message to them, tell them where she was. She had to believe they would come for her. In the meantime, she must bide her time, do what she could to stay alive and regain Briggs's trust, whatever it took. The future of the island, even the whole region, depended on her. Fail and nothing would stand between Briggs and his plan for chaos and disorder.

It was an impossible choice. Bend to Briggs's will, betray everything she had worked so hard for. And for what, wealth and power? What did they really count for versus the new life she had built for herself at Hurst? And yet part of her was silently screaming that it was a price worth paying, wasn't it?

With a loud sigh, she swallowed her pride and succumbed to logic. She gave in and allowed herself to be hauled back to her cell. There would be no shortage of hours to ponder her next move. It was time for metamorphosis, for the real Terra to emerge and spread her wings.

Was it her imagination or could she hear the sound of breaking waves, carried on the wind? Perhaps it was the remnants of the late spring storm that had battered the island over the past week, rollers surging in from the English Channel. The sound was distant yet somehow familiar and soothing. It reminded her of home.

Chapter 59

R iley sat down next to Adele, supportively holding her hand, while the little girl buried her face into her shoulder. The medical officer from the *Chester* swabbed the inside of Adele's arm with a cotton ball soaked in alcohol. He tapped two fingers against her inner arm and inserted the needle into a raised vein.

"It'll all be over in a minute." The doctor smiled as the syringe slowly filled with the little girl's blood they hoped would help them understand more about the virus. He withdrew the needle, keeping the pressure on the puncture mark with his gloved finger, and stuck a plaster over the expanding pinprick of blood, handing the syringe to his assistant.

Riley's thoughts were elsewhere. She couldn't stop thinking about Stella and what she had seen at the hotel. After the fire, an outbreak of the virus was a cruel blow. She had to believe that Stella was indeed immune, as was being suggested.

The ride home in the helicopter had been in silence. There was nothing Peterson could say that could possibly make things better, so he gave up and left Riley to her dark thoughts.

"We'll need to get this blood sample to Professor Nichols's

team at St. Mary's as soon as possible. Can you make the arrangements, please?" the doctor asked his assistant.

He turned back to face Adele who was rubbing her throbbing arm, keeping it elevated. He leaned in closer and lowered his voice. He was used to treating burly marines and tattooed engineers, so was doing his best to adjust his bedside manner. His breath was stale and stank of coffee. It was making the little girl screw up her face in disgust. Riley nudged her in the ribs and told her to behave.

"You've been very brave, young lady. You know you're a very special girl, Adele. There's a good chance that your blood can teach us how to stop people getting sick. What do you think of that?"

"That's what the other doctors told me back at the hospital, right before they hurt me. Are you going to hurt me too?"

The doctor exchanged puzzled glances with Riley and the nurse before reassuring Adele. "No, child, no one's going to hurt you. We're going to look after you and make sure no bad men hurt you ever again. You're safe here. Okay?" The doctor noticed the rabbit's foot key ring the girl was clutching in her right hand. "That's a nice key ring. Did someone give it to you? Your mummy or daddy maybe?" he asked with interest, turning it over in his hand. It felt surprisingly real to the touch.

"No one gave it to me. I made it myself," she responded in a flat voice. "I couldn't look after him any more and knew he would die, so we ate him and I kept his foot as a memento. It brings me luck."

The doctor dropped the key ring into her palm, puzzled by her detachment, wondering at how desensitised she had become. He shrugged his shoulders and patted her on the shoulder with a wry smile. "Well, I sure hope he brings you a lot of luck."

Riley thanked the doctor and led Adele down the corridor

and outside to the castle courtyard where some of the other children were playing a noisy game of baseball with bored-looking grown-ups. Riley and Adele stopped to watch as Toby whacked the ball high into the air, threw down his bat and set off to first base. The ball came rolling to a stop to their right as two boys raced to retrieve it. All eyes turned in their direction. Adele looked up at Riley for permission before hurrying after the ball and athletically throwing it back over the head of a small boy with foppish blonde hair.

"Nice throw," he muttered begrudgingly before running back to join the game.

Above them on the roof of the Gun Tower, Zed had clambered through the narrow opening from the floor below. He found Jack scanning the horizon with an old pair of binoculars, his mop of greying hair flattened by the wind. Jack was lingering over the superstructure of the *Chester* anchored a couple of miles away in the main channel. In characteristic pose, he had his glasses pushed high on his forehead. When Zed closed his eyes, this was his residual mental image of the man. Jack sensed Zed's presence to his right and flicked his eyes in his direction.

"How's the arm? Feeling better? Or are you planning on staying the rest of the week in bed?" said Jack tersely.

Zed's eyes narrowed. He was on the verge of venting about everything he had done for Hurst, before remembering that Jack was just winding him up, as usual. He took a deep breath, joined him at the rail, looking out to sea. "I've slept enough, thanks. Liz says I'm as good as new." He nudged Jack in the ribs. "How's the shoulder, old man?"

"Sore. Stitches will come out in a few weeks. Hey, Zed," said Jack, changing the subject, "I need someone to take Adele to the hospital at St Mary's. There's a professor there who wants to run some more tests. He's got a lab set up and a team ready to start work. You up for a trip?"

"Sure, no problem. Sounds right up my street. I'd like to meet the professor. Ask him some questions," he said to a puzzled Jack. Zed swallowed and recovered. "You know me. I can't stand being cooped up. Getting cabin fever already. Would be good to get back out there. Can you spare Riley as well?"

"I don't see why not. Take the *Nipper*. Sam will go with you to helm the boat. That is, if you don't mind listening to the Bee Gees all the way."

There was a moment of silence between them as both stared out east, lost in their separate thoughts. Dark clouds had gathered in the distance to the south heading towards the island, but it looked as if they would escape the worst of the weather at Hurst.

Beyond the *Chester* lay the *Maersk Charlotte*, just visible towards Southampton, her bulk unmistakeable against the shoreline and the inlet to the Beaulieu River. Zed wondered how Anders had taken Victor's treachery. Jack said he never trusted that guy. His eyes were just a little bit too close together. Suspicious eyebrows that met in the middle, Zed knew the type too well. A gun for hire, loyalty for sale to the highest bidder.

He spotted something in the distance and asked Jack to pass him the binoculars. It took a moment to find it again, but there it was, a grey patrol vessel powering towards them, hammering into the waves and eastward-flowing tide. He passed the binoculars back to Jack who identified the ship as an Archer class patrol vessel, though it was relatively uncommon in these waters. On the flying bridge, he picked out two figures bracing themselves as spray shot high into the air as they ploughed into the crest of a new wave. At the back of the ship was a white ensign. It was Royal Navy.

There was some static and the crackle of a voice hailing them over the radio. Jack unclipped the walkie-talkie from his belt and turned up the volume.

"Hurst Castle, Hurst Castle, this is Royal Navy patrol vessel *HMS Marker*, come in, over?"

"*HMS Marker*, this is Hurst Castle. Go ahead."

"Good morning, Hurst, this is Captain Armstrong. Do we have permission to come ashore?"

"Absolutely. I'll get the kitchen to put the kettle on."

"Copy that. ETA ten minutes at current course and speed. We have Captain Anders with us too. He tells me he's rather partial to Highland shortbread if you have any."

Jack grinned at Zed, who was shaking his head. "We'll take a look. No promises, mind. Hurst, out." He tucked the radio back on his belt clip. "Bloody navy types. Always inviting themselves over for tea and biscuits."

"Shouldn't they be protecting the island or something?" said Zed sarcastically.

"No need, I expect. With the *USS Chester* moored up off the island, no one's going to be stupid enough to attack. They have enough firepower to keep us safe, for now."

"How do you figure that out? What use is a destroyer against a virus and a bunch of terrorists hell-bent on disrupting relief operations?" scoffed Zed.

"I wouldn't be so sure. The Americans have already made a difference, maybe even turned the tide. Think back even a few days and we were just a bunch of dysfunctional survivor groups, struggling to get by. Now, there's a very real sense of hope. With their leadership, they'll rally others to the cause. Camp Wight is a fresh start. A chance to rebuild."

Zed didn't respond, lost in his thoughts and fears, refusing to believe that salvation was at hand, just because the Americans had showed up. Typical of Jack. His over optimism was his weakness, always seeing the best in a situation. His refusal to accept that the world had changed, that people had changed troubled Zed. He leaned over the parapet and watched the game of baseball going on below.

Everything seemed normal again, children playing and laughing. It was like the last few months had been forgotten. With the navy patrolling the seas, keeping them safe, Zed had every right to feel secure. And yet, he felt anything but safe. What Jack had told him about King, about his plans to use the virus as a weapon and a vaccine as leverage, made him fear for the future. He knew only too well the power that would command. The occupants of Hurst Castle could not allow themselves to relax any time soon, to let down their guard. They did that once and got attacked. Many people died for that mistake. Jack's pride and naivety had been exposed. It made Zed question Jack's leadership. It was up to Zed to stay sharp, to keep others on their toes, to stay alert. Keep Jack focused and grounded. That was how they would survive all this.

Jack's voice interrupted Zed's internal monologue. "Make yourself useful, will you?"

"Sure, Jack. What do you need?"

"Why don't you dust off that old flag Greta found and put on a bit of a show for our navy friends?"

Zed chuckled at the thought. He wasn't the slightest bit patriotic but it seemed right in the circumstances. They had found a dusty old Union Jack in a locked cupboard that had waited for just such an occasion. He retrieved the flag from the shelf downstairs and unfurled it, making sure it was the right way up. He crossed the courtyard, climbed the stairs and untied the halyard, securing the flag top and bottom before hoisting it high over the castle battlements.

Zed stepped back, admiring his handiwork, the Union Jack fluttering proudly in the strengthening wind. Jack watched the flag's ascent, ignoring its faded colours and torn leading edge, momentarily overcome by a sense of pride and patriotism, of everything they had achieved thus far. It felt appropriate to honour the moment and Jack saluted the flag, as he had been taught so many years ago.

"Sentimental old sod," muttered Zed under his breath, spotting Jack with his arm raised in salute.

Riley joined Zed on the upper walkway as he finished lashing the flag halyard in place on to the small cleat on the shaft of the flagpole. She looked him up and down. He'd lost weight, she thought. His trousers seemed to bunch at the hip, his belt a couple of notches tighter than before. She wandered over and they both stood perfectly still, studying the flag, heads tilted to one side, neither of them quite sure what to make of it all. Seeing the flag flying over Hurst seemed both incongruous and fitting all at the same time. The sense of history, shared purpose, and unity the flag symbolised felt like a relic from another age, familiar and alien to this new generation living here, five centuries after the first. Zed shrugged his shoulders and made as if to leave, taking a final deep breath of sea air before heading inside.

The breath seemed to catch in his throat and he was suddenly wracked by a fit of coughing. Riley's head whipped round and watched with increasing concern as he seemed to fight for breath, bent double, hacking away. The words of Sister Theodora in her letter were still fresh in her mind as she puzzled over what she had said about Zed being the carrier and source of the outbreak. She took a couple of steps away from him, as if somehow suddenly disconnected, their bonds fractured, watching his coughing with a strange sense of detachment.

With a final heave, gasping for breath, he gesticulated at Riley who ran up behind him and slapped him forcefully between the shoulder blades. Zed spat something on the ground and straightened up, red in the face. She slapped him again for good measure as he wiped spittle from his lips.

"How long have you had that cough?" she enquired suspiciously, backing away slowly.

"What, that little thing? I swallowed a fly, that's all," he said, his voice raspy and brittle. "Bit jumpy, aren't we? Scared of a little cough? Teach me to breathe with my mouth open." She stared open-mouthed at him, caught somewhere between mirth and anger, not sure whether he was joking or not. "Seriously, Riley. I'm fine. Trust me."

Riley remembered that he always said that when he was lying, a smile beginning to form on her lips, despite her not being completely certain.

Jack looked on from a distance, trying to read Riley's expression as she remonstrated with him, straining to hear the exchange that followed, but her words were lost on a gust of wind. A rain-squall heading towards them from the island deposited its first drops on his bare head. Not liking what he saw, he hurried back inside to the comfort and warmth of the castle keep. The storm would be here soon enough.

"What are you thinking?" asked Zed when he'd got his breath back, watching Riley leaning over the battlements, surveying the island across the waterway.

"I was thinking about Stella again," she said, looking down at her feet. "She's in good hands. Those nuns will look after her. They have enough hot towels and volunteer midwives to get the baby out safely. Don't you think?"

Zed nodded then laughed, struck by a question that had been niggling him but never articulated before. "What if it's a baby boy?" He grinned at Riley, like someone laughing at their own joke. Riley smiled back at him, a mischievous look on her face.

"Now that would put the cat amongst the pigeons, eh? Love to see the look on that old bat's face when she finds out."

"Hey, did you hear about Terra being taken hostage?" asked Zed.

"Yeah, good riddance, I say. She and I never saw eye to eye. And let me tell you, she isn't your biggest fan either."

"Terra's all right. Come on, what's she ever done to you anyway?"

"She's such a fake. Says what people want to hear. She's always working an angle. Lies through her teeth most of the time. Trust me, it takes one to know one. Watch your back when she's around. Seriously." Zed didn't look too convinced and tried to change the subject.

There was a shout from the far end of the complex, followed by the ringing of the handbell. Zed and Riley raced towards the western wall that looked back along the shingle spit towards the village of Milford.

Tommy was there first, along with several others, taking it in turns to look through the binoculars. By the time they got there, one of the younger guys had got the rifle out and was looking down the telescopic sight, trying to make out the shapes in the distance. Behind them they could hear Jack hobbling slowly across the courtyard shouting at the assembled crowd on the ramparts, looking for answers, but being ignored. Zed took the stairs two at a time, Riley right behind him. He grabbed the binoculars and took a moment to locate the approaching figures.

"I can take them as soon as they're in range," said the kid with the rifle. "Which one first? The guy or the girl?"

"Don't shoot, you idiot. That's one of ours. The girl I don't recognise."

"Can I shoot her then?" asked the boy mischievously.

"No. Give me that rifle before you injure yourself," said Zed, snatching the gun and cuffing the lad on the back of his head.

Zed and Riley ran around to the front entrance and out onto the shingle, meeting the two new arrivals as they reached the castle complex. The heavy-set man wore a hoodie whose front was stained with dried blood, his face covered. His jeans were filthy and shredded in places. There was something familiar about his gait, supported by a young girl who Riley seemed to half remember. She nodded in Riley's direction, a sheepish smile spreading across her gentle face.

"Top of the morning to you, Zed. Riley, how are you?" said the man, in a croaky voice, parched and hoarse. His face was badly bruised, his nose broken.

"Joe? I thought it might be you." Zed grinned. "Not looking your best, buddy. Where the hell have you been? We thought you were dead."

"I think I was, briefly. They had me locked up in a cellar for a few days. Nasty bunch. I took care of one of them and managed to get Jean here out. I rescued her, or rather, she rescued me and then I rescued her right back."

"So how did you get away?" said Riley, puzzled.

"They underestimated the fat man, what can I say?" He shrugged.

"Big mistake. Big mistake." Zed laughed, slapping him on the shoulder and welcoming him home. "Let's get you inside and cleaned up."

"Thanks for the welcome committee. And for not letting those kids up there shoot at us," he said, waving at one of the kids above them with his arms crossed. "Glad to be home."

Joe grabbed Jean's hand. She was waiting patiently to be properly introduced. "Jean? This here's Riley. She's a friend of Stella's. She'll look after you, get you a bed for the night."

Riley warmly shook her hand and looked her up and down. "Any friend of Stella's is a friend of mine. Come on, you're going to like it here. There's a few more men than you're used to, but you'll get used to that eventually."

Jean glanced at Zed as if uncomfortable in his presence until Joe put his arm around her shoulder, escorting her the last few yards to the main entrance.

"Welcome home. Welcome to Hurst," said Riley with a wry smile. "You'll be safe here."

Zed watched them leave, taking a moment to shelter from the wind in the shadow of the castle wall that towered above him. He peered up into the darkening skies, pondering Riley's choice of words, wondering whether they would ever be safe again.

The fortress's thirty-feet-high walls would never stop people like Briggs, but it was as good a place as anywhere to make their stand. Perhaps King was right. The island was their best hope now. They were isolated and vulnerable at Hurst, but at least they had each other. They were stronger together, he was sure of that now. Zed shrugged and hurried after the others as the first drops of rain began to fall all around them. It would soon be dark again.

An extract from book two of
The Hurst Chronicles

Sentinel
by Robin Crumby

"For when I bring them into the land flowing with milk and honey, which I swore to their fathers, and they have eaten and are satisfied and become prosperous, then they will turn to other gods and serve them, and spurn Me and break My covenant."

Deuteronomy 31:20

Chapter One

The early winter storms had been raging for days. The noise was deafening. It wasn't just the howling wind; it was also the giant rollers sweeping in from the English Channel from the South West. Surging past the Needles and the western tip of the island, the waves were sent crashing against the weathered groynes and battered sea defences at the base of the castle walls. Spray flew high into the air before being carried away by powerful gusts.

Hurst Castle had seen storms worse than this. Every winter for nearly five hundred years, Mother Nature threw her worst at the man-made structure. The castle squatted resolutely on this most remote and desolate location, at the far end of a shingle spit that connected the fortress to the mainland and, like an unwanted guest, nature made her resentment known on a regular basis. Little by little the raised causeway that ran along the top of the shingle defences was being slowly washed away. It was only a matter of time before the castle would be completely cut off from the mainland, reachable by boat across narrow tidal channels that ran between the salt marshes around Keyhaven.

Jack slammed shut the wooden door to the lighthouse that he had made his home over the long months since arriving here. It needed another lick of paint, its surface blistered and peeling. Buffeted by another gust, he wrapped his coat tighter around his trunk, shielding his face against the sheeting rain. He hurried towards the shelter of the castle wall, relaxing a little as the wind dropped and he could hear himself think again. The drawbridge was already down and the two guards who were taking shelter in the covered entrance straightened a little upon seeing Hurst's leader striding towards them.

"Morning, lads. Anything to report?"

"Not really," said Tommy, rubbing his cheek, trying to remember anything of note from his shift. He glanced jealously at Scottie who had just appeared, cupping a hot brew. "Other than a couple of false alarms around midnight, we've mostly been chasing shadows as usual."

"Did you manage to get some sleep, Jack?" asked Scottie, blowing the steam off his coffee. "Stormy night, eh?"

"Me? Oh, I slept like a log, thank you." Jack laughed. "But I'm used to it. Remember, I spent half of my life at sea. Bit of wind and rain never hurt anyone. Did the patrols find anything?"

"Oh, nothing out of the ordinary." Scottie shrugged. "We got the call from the *Chester* that there were a couple of radar blips heading out of Lymington harbour, but by the time we got a team out there, they were either turned round or had vanished into the night."

"Sergeant Flynn said they were probably in a dinghy or rowing boat. Virtually impossible to pick up on radar," added Tommy.

"Same pattern we've seen for weeks. People trying to make the crossing to the island in the dead of night. Not much we can do about it," lamented Scottie.

Jack nodded, scratching his beard. It needed a trim. He normally relied on Terra for haircuts, but she still hadn't returned from the island. He hadn't given up hope she was still alive. It was common knowledge that she was being held captive by the former inmates of Parkhurst Prison and their leader,

Briggs. He thought back fondly to the times she had grabbed hold of his head and started chopping away at his locks with a blunt pair of scissors, despite his protestations. Like shearing a sheep, she had said. He smiled at the memory.

"Makes you wonder how many are getting through the net," reflected Tommy.

Jack sniffed at the wind. There was something foul in the air this morning. He turned his back against a forceful gust as the three of them moved back within the shelter of the entrance.

The Solent was now under the watchful protection of the allies. For the first time since the outbreak of the Millennial Virus, order was slowly returning to this coastal region. Its many waterways, creeks and harbours were scrutinised day and night by a radar operator sat in near permanent darkness, staring at a screen on board the *USS Chester*. Anchored in the Solent, the American missile destroyer worked hand in hand with the Royal Navy's growing fleet of patrol boats and fast launches, co-ordinating the defence of the island. Hurst Castle was again a critical outpost defending the western approaches. Built by Henry VIII as part of a chain of forts and castles along England's southern coast to guard against attacks by the French and Spanish navies, today Hurst had resumed its military role. Like a passive sentinel, Hurst remained alert, day and night, ready to do its duty.

Thus far, there had been little to do. Chasing shadows in the night, seeing ghosts and echoes. Urgent radio calls from command would request they check out an unauthorised vessel attempting to make the crossing under cover of darkness. They had a powerful searchlight set up on top of the lighthouse, but with limited fuel for the generator, they rarely had it running. They relied on handheld lanterns and high-powered Maglites to scan the darkness from the shoreline or from a R.I.B scrambled to intercept.

"We need more men," said Scottie. "It's a huge stretch of coast to monitor with such a small force. We need more boats on patrol, 24/7. It's like trying to find a needle in a haystack. As things stand, we've got no chance."

"Well, it's not like we're the only line of defence," corrected Jack. "Even if they run the gauntlet and make it to the island, all the beaches are defended with barbed wire, obstacles and armed guards."

"They're turning that place into a fortress. Next thing they'll build a wall. Then what?" asked Tommy.

"If that's what it takes to keep the island virus-free and control the population flow through the quarantine zones, then so be it."

The attacks had started several weeks ago. Most came in the dead of night. At first, they were disorganised, sporadic incursions, initially dismissed as desperate people trying to reach the sanctuary offered by the newly formed Camp Wight on the island. More recent attempts suggested a systematic probing of the allies' defences. To what end, Jack had no idea. Forces unknown were orchestrating events, keeping the defenders chasing shadows, scrambling interceptors only to find the small vessels they were sent to find had disappeared or were returning to safe harbour.

There came the sound of footsteps echoing around the battlements as someone raced across the courtyard towards the guardhouse. The three men turned to see Sam trying to catch his breath, one hand on the stone wall nearest him.

"What's up, Sam?"

"It's the *Chester* on the radio, Jack. Command wants us to take the *Nipper* and check something out."

"Surely not in this weather?"

"Probably another false alarm," suggested Tommy.

"They wouldn't ask unless it was urgent, Jack. Apparently

there's a ship about five and a half miles south-east of Portland Bill heading this way. Command said that, from the size of it, it's probably a coastal steamer or small tanker. They need us to intercept, make contact and find out their intentions. We're to take Sergeant Flynn and a squad of marines, just in case."

"Can't they send the helicopter?" asked Tommy. "It would be much quicker."

"Not in this." Sam gestured skywards. "The winds are gusting storm force."

Jack looked back outside and squinted at the rain clouds. The storm was strengthening. It would be lunacy to take the *Nipper* out. She was a thirty-five-foot coastal fishing boat, broad in the beam and more than capable of operating in all conditions. Nevertheless, Jack was experienced enough to know that a good skipper never underestimated a storm.

"I'm assuming they don't have any other patrols in the area that could check this out?"

"Apparently everything is returned to port on account of the weather. We're the nearest."

"Okay, Sam. Can you let Sergeant Flynn know, grab the oilskins and safety gear and get her ready? We'll call the *Chester* for an update when we're on the way. I don't want to go out in this unless we have to."

Jack grabbed two sets of oilskins from the coat rack in the guardhouse and hurried down to the lighthouse to find his rucksack. He hastily repacked the bag with binoculars and a revolver before joining Sam at the jetty a few minutes later, where the *Nipper* was sheltering from the storm. The engines were already spluttering noisily and the mooring lines were being held on a slip. As soon as Flynn and the three other men and their packs and weapons were on board, they cast off.

It was approaching high tide and together with a storm surge, they had plenty of water to get out through the mudflats and shallows to reach the main channel. As they rounded the spit and turned west into the teeth of the gale, they met the full force of the wind and waves sweeping towards them. The Needles channel was narrow where water funnelled over rocks creating an overfall. Coupled with an eastwards flowing tide and a westerly wind, it made the half-mile out to the deeper water of Christchurch Bay bumpier than usual. In front of them, further out to sea, lay a maelstrom of wild, heaving water.

Sam came back inside the small cabin and braced himself against the next set of rollers surging towards them. The waves were building in size and power, towering over the small fishing boat. The four marines were below decks looking decidedly green around the gills. One man was retching into a bucket he was clinging on to, both arms wrapped around it like his life depended on it. Up the steps to the wheelhouse, the wiper blades on the windscreen were fighting a losing battle to clear the spray as it swept in on the wind. Looking behind them towards Hurst Castle, the sea had become a roiling mass of white horses.

Jack kept both hands on the wheel, working hard to keep the *Nipper*'s bow in to the wind and waves. Their engine was straining to make headway and he estimated their forward progress no better than two or three knots. He picked up the radio again and tried to contact the *Chester*. The first attempt had proven unsuccessful, their transmission lost between waves more than twenty feet high.

They had been told to steam south-west and meet what was likely to be a steamer or small tanker making for the Solent, now some three miles beyond Portland Bill. The vessel was unresponsive to all attempts to contact it and moving very slowly. Jack reckoned that they should be no more than a mile or two away from it. Right now, visibility was so poor they could pass within one hundred yards and not see anything.

The radio crackled into life and they heard an American voice, faint but intelligible. Jack snatched the receiver from its cradle.

"*Nipper* here, *Chester*. Receiving you loud and clear. We're entering the sector. No contact to report. Can you confirm bearing to intercept?"

"You're right on top of it. Should be dead ahead of you now. Less than a mile. Just off your port bow," said the radar operator.

"Copy that," said Jack. "Right, stay alert, keep your eyes peeled."

Sam grabbed the binoculars and started scanning the horizon, adjusting his stance to compensate for the yaw and pitch of the boat. Each time the bow of the *Nipper* collided with a wave, the forward momentum seemed to slow as the propeller fought hard to drive them forward again. Jack was worried the engine would overheat and they would be left without power to drift onto the rocks. He'd seen it happen before. A powerboat washed up on the shingle beach at Milford, holed and broken. He sincerely hoped that this wasn't another wild goose chase.

Sam nudged him in the ribs and pointed to an enormous shape that had appeared from nowhere off the port bow. It took Jack a few seconds to make sense of what he was looking at.

The ship was a tanker in some distress. It sat broadside to the waves, heavy in the bow and listing a little to starboard. It had taken on a lot of water and seemed to be without power, drifting along the coast towards the island.

Jack circled to the ship's stern and scanned the bridge, walkways and railings trying to spot any crewmembers, any signs of life. Across the ship's stern was written *Santana* and its registered home port of Panama underneath. Sergeant Flynn joined them in the wheelhouse. As they nudged closer, Jack handed over his binoculars for Flynn to take a closer look. A huge wave swept over the bow of the *Santana* and the whole ship seemed to lurch towards them. Jack rammed the engines in reverse and withdrew another fifty yards, suddenly concerned that the whole ship could roll on its side if it was hit again with similar force.

"Better call it in," said Flynn. "Let's find out what they want us to do."

ALSO BY ROBIN CRUMBY

Hurst

Sentinel

Wildfire

Harbinger

ACKNOWLEDGMENTS

Writing a book is a lot like starting and running a business. It takes a whole village! Thank you to the small army of people who supported me and generously gave up their time to read successive drafts of Hurst. You all know who you are. I won't attempt to mention all of you. No Gwyneth Paltrow Oscar acceptance speech here. But as anyone who's been involved in writing will know, it's a long and iterative process. It takes hard work, dedication and an unfaltering belief that it's all going to be worthwhile in the end. So a big thank you to all the friends and family who helped: Tor, Jake, Bea, Rose, Tom, Bobbie, Ems, Katy, CC, Pete, Dan, Jess, Bertie, Ed, Janet, Andrew, Serena, H, Sarah, Mark, Tina, Adrienne, Chris, Shona, Jim, Jane, Darren, Cameron, Derek, Raoul, Howie, Linda and Marlene.

Disclaimer

Hurst is a work of fiction. Names, characters, businesses, places, events and incidents are either the products of the author's imagination or used in a fictitious manner. Any resemblance to actual persons, living or dead, or actual events is purely coincidental.

Stay in touch

Join the Hurst Chronicles Readers' Group and be the first to hear about upcoming books in the series, news and offers.

Website: HurstChronicles.com
Twitter: @HurstChronicles
Facebook: Facebook.com/robincrumbyauthor

© Robin Crumby 2016

ABOUT THE AUTHOR

Robin Crumby is the British author of *The Hurst Chronicles*, a post-apocalyptic series set on the south coast of England in the aftermath of a deadly flu pandemic. Since reading John Wyndham's *Day of the Triffids* as a child, Robin became fascinated by end of the world dystopian literature and was inspired to start writing by Cormac McCarthy's *The Road* and Emily St. John Mandel's *Station Eleven*. Why? Because post-apocalyptic fiction fires the imagination like nothing else. Pondering what comes next, who would survive, what would life look like? His Eureka moment came wandering the shingle beach at Milford-on-Sea, inspired by the beauty and rich history of the Solent. Where better to survive the end of the world than a medieval castle surrounded by water? Robin spent much of his childhood messing about in boats, exploring the many waterways, harbours and military forts of the Isle of Wight, where *The Hurst Chronicles* series is set.